Also by Chris Bohjalian

"A cautionary bio-horror tale à la *The Andromeda Strain* and *The Hot Zone*." —Bookreporter.com

"You'll keep flipping pages, discover new complex characters, see the mysterious situation from different points of view—and you'll be surprised at each well-plotted turn." —Katie Yee, Literary Hub

"A globe-spanning adventure, one that combines international intrigue with the high-adrenaline, high-pressure realm of the big city emergency room. It's a book that sets the healers against those who would do harm, the selfless against the selfish." —Allen Adams, *The Maine Edge*

"With his usual strong plotting and well-conceived characters, Bohjalian's story unfolds slowly and with terrific pacing." —Alan Rosenberg, *The Providence Journal*

"A must-read global thriller. . . . Hits Bohjalian's trademark notes of intricate plot, in-depth research, high tension, and unexpected turns—with a very timely dose of pathogens and biological weapons—in a twisting story of love and deceit." —*Mystery Tribune*

"[An] intricately plotted thriller. . . . A diabolical plot. . . . Each character, including secondary players, is carefully drawn, and Bohjalian keeps the tension high all the way to the surprising finale." —*Publishers Weekly*

"Tantalizing. . . . Bohjalian manages to keep us guessing and turning pages until the very end." —*Kirkus Reviews*

"In this tightly drawn, steadily hair-raising thriller, Bohjalian once again demonstrates his keen affinity for strong, capable female protagonists." —Carol Haggas, *Booklist*

Chris Bohjalian

THE RED LOTUS

Chris Bohjalian is the #1 *New York Times* bestselling author of twenty-two books, including *Midwives* and *The Flight Attendant*, which is now an HBO Max limited series starring Kaley Cuoco. His other books include *The Guest Room*; *Close Your Eyes, Hold Hands*; *The Sandcastle Girls*; *Skeletons at the Feast*; and *The Double Bind*. His novels *Secrets of Eden, Midwives*, and *Past the Bleachers* were made into movies, and his work has been translated into more than thirty-five languages. He is also a playwright (*Wingspan* and *Midwives*). He lives in Vermont and can be found at www.chrisbohjalian.com or on Facebook, Instagram, Twitter, Litsy, and Goodreads.

THE RED LOTUS

THE RED LOTUS

A NOVEL

Chris Bohjalian

Vintage Contemporaries
Vintage Books
A Division of Penguin Random House LLC
New York

FIRST VINTAGE CONTEMPORARIES EDITION, JANUARY 2021

The Library of Congress has cataloged the Doubleday edition as follows:
Names: Bohjalian, Chris, 1962– author.
Title: The red lotus : a novel / by Chris Bohjalian.
Description: First edition. | New York : Doubleday, 2020.
Identifiers: LCCN 2019013892 (print) | LCCN 2019014449 (ebook)
Subjects: GSAFD: Suspense fiction.
Classification: LCC PS3552.O495 (ebook) | LCC PS3552.O495 R43 2020 (print)
| DDC 813/.54—dc23
LC record available at https://lccn.loc.gov/2019013892

Vintage Contemporaries Trade Paperback ISBN: 978-0-525-56596-3
eBook ISBN: 978-0-385-54481-8

Book design by Maria Carella

www.vintagebooks.com

Printed in the United States of America
10 9 8 7 6 5 4 3 2 1

For
Todd Doughty and Jennifer Marshall,
years of planes, trains, and automobiles—
and patience that can only be called heroic

And once more for
Adam Turteltaub,
a great friend,
who has read drafts of my work on five continents

Redemption? Sure. But in the end, he's just another dead rat in a garbage pail behind a Chinese restaurant.

—WES ANDERSON AND NOAH BAUMBACH, *MR. FANTASTIC FOX*

There can be no lotus flower without the mud.

—THÍCH NHẤT HẠHN

PROLOGUE

The opposite of a hospice? Not a maternity ward or a NICU. It's a trick question.

The correct answer? An emergency room. In a hospice, you do everything you can to allow people to die. In the ER? You do all that you can to keep them alive.

It was why she loved the ER, especially the night shift in the city. The relentlessness. The frenetic drive to keep a heart beating or to get someone breathing. Oh, sometimes you lost. You called it. You declared the suicide or the stroke victim or the accidental overdose dead. But far more often you won. Or, at least, you won long enough to get the patient into the OR or into a room upstairs, you won long enough that whatever happened to the man or woman or child or toddler or (dear God) baby was someone else's problem. And so she became a different person in the ER. She had, in fact, become a different person there. She was a tectonic re-creation that was unrecognizable even to her own mother, an evolution wrought in months rather than millennia—sixty-six months, if she was going to be precise—that had begun in her first rotation and culminated during her first July night as an attending physician. It was in the midst of the ER madness—the light and the sound (and there were just so many sounds, the human and the mechanical, the dying and the wounded and the supportive and the scared)—that she morphed into an adrenaline junkie. She was no longer a shy soul that balked at attention, a girl as wary of kindness as shelter cats with torn ears that even after adopted would shrink into the dark of the closet. She was something bigger, inexorable and unyielding.

There was just so much pain and so much fear and so much

incredulity in the ER. So many tales Alexis heard that began, "It's a long story" or "It happened so fast" or "You won't believe it when I tell you"—and so much urgency that she could forget who she once was. In the ER, there was no chance that she might slip back into the anxiety or the despair or the self-loathing that as a teenager had her using an old-fashioned razor blade or X-Acto knife to cut deep into her thighs. To feel something other than depression or doubt, to be the captain of her own pain. She felt no need to tend to herself when she was tending to people who, at least that moment, were dramatically worse off than she was. Than she ever was (at least on the outside). She was just too busy.

And so it was perhaps fitting that it was in the ER that she met him. Just as fitting was how she met him.

Though he was probably in no danger of dying.

It was a bullet wound, but nothing like the horrors she'd seen bullets inflict in her years in trauma bays and cubicles. The worst (and worst was a high bar when it came to guns and emergency rooms) were the three teenage girls who were shot after school at field hockey practice by a boy (of course) for reasons that would remain forever unfathomable because then he'd gone home and shot himself. He'd used an AR-15 semiautomatic rifle, and the girls had holes in their abdomens and chests and legs. One of the three was still awake, and just before she was intubated, she begged Alexis to tell her that she wasn't going to die, her voice so strong that when Alexis murmured, *No, no, shhhhh,* she believed it. She really did. One of the others had a heart that stopped beating twice as they worked, and so they gave her the paddles, and the child (and she was a child, she was fifteen, for fuck's sake) had lived long enough to die in the OR instead of the ER. Only one of that trio had lived, and when the last of the girls was gone from the room, Alexis had looked at the ER and how everything—everything—was awash in blood. The gloves and the gauze, the bone saw and retractors, the tubes and the tape and the trash cans. The sweatshirts and skirts the girls had been wearing. The white socks. Their cleats. The floor was streaked and splattered, and the team that had striven to save them had left footprints, the soles of their surgical booties sometimes traversing the red veins left on the tile by the wheels of the gurneys.

This was different.

Austin's bullet wound was different.

He appeared on a Saturday night—Sunday morning technically—and Alexis was very, very good with a needle, a toothed forceps, and a pair of suturing scissors. With the trauma scissors, when she began by cutting away his sleeve. She was also very good with a scalpel (and probably would have been well before medical school), which mattered because the bullet was lodged near the largest bone in his right arm, three inches below the greater tuberosity of the humerus. It was a low-velocity wound and had chipped off a piece of the bone, but it hadn't shattered it. It hadn't, thank God, ripped a hole in the brachial artery, which might have caused him to bleed out in the bar, and it hadn't shredded his rotator cuff, which might have crippled him for life. He was in pain, but not so much that he couldn't laugh at the fact that he had only been in a dive bar in the East Village because he'd left a party and his Uber app had said the nearest vehicle was twenty minutes away. So, on a lark, he'd gone into the bar to watch a couple of guys throwing darts. His smile was ironic and crooked, but far more boyish than rakish. He'd been drinking, and that certainly ameliorated the pain, too, his eyes a little more narrow than she would come to know them, but still open enough that she could see instantly the intangible spark and the tangible green. The muscles in his jaw would tense and untense as she worked, his breath beery, as he grimaced like the men at the gym who would lie on a bench and press three hundred pounds up off their chests. He had what she would eventually come to learn was a biker's body: slender but a strong, solid core, and legs that were unexpectedly muscled. His hair was black-coffee dark. He and another dart player had taken a cab the twenty blocks north on First Avenue to the hospital—where, of all things, it would turn out, he worked, too. The two of them hadn't waited for an ambulance, and they hadn't waited for the cops. The guy who'd fired the shot? Some crazy junkie, homeless they presumed, who had run from the bar like a madman—no, he *was* a madman—when he realized that he'd actually discharged his crappy little handgun. Some ridiculous Remington pocket pistol.

"What do you do here?" she asked as she treated him. "At the hospital?"

And he told her. He told her that he worked directly for the hospital's chief development officer. He raised money. He worked with the folks who managed the hospital's money. They laughed about meeting here rather than, say, in the hospital cafeteria or on the promenade along the East River as she removed the bullet and stitched him up, and then as they sat in the ER cubicle behind the thick blue drapes and waited for the police to arrive so he could tell them what happened. He guessed that they were probably still at the bar interviewing the bartenders and anyone willing to stick around after someone had nearly killed some yuppie dart player at one in the morning. She asked him about the Band-Aids on the fingers on his left hand. He admitted—sheepishly—that he'd been bitten by a cat the day before. It had been in some woman's lap in the bakery where he was getting a scone and a cup of coffee, and he startled it when he went to pet it as he was leaving.

"Flirting with the woman?" she'd asked him, which was, in truth, flirting itself.

"Nope. Just surprised to see a cat. The animal was sitting up in one of those cat carriers."

She insisted on removing the three bandages, none very big, and was startled by how deep and ugly the cuts were. She disinfected them and they talked about rabies, and he was clear and he was adamant: the cat was fine. (And clearly the cat was fine, because it had been nearly seven months ago now that he had taken a cab that night to the hospital. If that cat had had rabies, he would have been long dead.) Still, she'd cleaned the wounds herself, applied an antibiotic ointment, and added a prescription for Augmentin. Meanwhile, his new friend (acquaintance, really) had sat outside in the bright lights of the ER waiting room, stewing, and seemed far more annoyed than scared that there was a guy in a cubicle with a bullet in his biceps.

She had tended to other patients as they waited for the police, pulling on and off the latex gloves, including a little boy with a fever whose mother was terrified (needlessly, it would turn out, when they looked at the blood work) and a deli man who'd snipped off a sizable chunk of his finger with a meat slicer—he was turning tongue into cold cuts—but hadn't nicked bone and needed only stitches and antibiotics. Nothing very hard and nothing very stressful. No X-rays and no CT scan. For a Saturday night, there weren't all that many to-be-seen clipboards hanging on pegs on the wall, there weren't scads of bodies, some stoic and some whimpering, waiting on stretchers like supplicants before royalty.

Looking back on their first moments together, it wasn't exactly a "meet cute," but they knew if their relationship lasted until old age, it would be one hell of a good story for their grandchildren.

ELEVEN DAYS

THURSDAY

1

The swallows skipped like flat stones across the surface of the infinity pool, their wings spread, and a lone woman in a gauzy beach coverup—what she might have called a kaftan if that word didn't sound so matronly—watched them. The tunic didn't merely protect her pale skin from the sun, which already was sinking into the trees to the west, it hid from the world the scars on her thighs at the edge of her bathing suit. The birds, their feathers a deeper blue and a more pristine white than their cousins in North America, looked playful and frivolous, and she was beginning to resent their happiness because her disquiet was morphing moment by moment into dread. She lowered her sunglasses to gaze beyond the pool, down the long, flat stretch of driveway she could see from here, and the lines of statuesque dipterocarp trees that bordered the pavement like sentinels and were at least seventy or eighty years old. They'd been planted by some French overlord and they'd survived the wars. She was hoping to see him on his bike, hurtling through the open wrought-iron gates, past the guardhouse (manned this afternoon by a sweet and slight teenage boy in a uniform that looked like it belonged on a bell-man from a grande dame hotel from a distant era) and down the straight stretch of asphalt, but she saw nothing. No bicyclist. No cars. No delivery trucks. The idea crossed her mind that he had stopped at one of the massive beach hotels to dive into the ocean on his way back; he'd expressed his disappointment that the bike tour hadn't booked them at a property on the water, the way they had the last time he was here. No one would presume that a tall American wasn't a guest if he raced in, leaned his bike against a palm tree, and cooled off in his bike shorts in the waves.

Still, she tried to will him to appear, she tried to fashion an image of his black-and-red bike helmet from the heat that hovered, even this late in the day, like mist atop hot, fresh pavement.

She swatted a mosquito on her knee and sat up on the chaise, her bare feet on the bluestone tile, and dropped her magazine. Her hands were moist with sweat and sunblock, and she wiped them on her coverup. An animal, a tiny rodent of some sort, skittered beneath the chaise and into the nearby brush. A salamander froze. She reached for her phone and sent him yet another text asking him if he was okay. She'd sent him five now, each one a little more urgent and anxious than the one that had preceded it. He was an hour and a half late. If he'd had a flat tire, he would have texted. The sag wag—their slang for the support wagon, a van technically—would have left to rescue him. There was pretty good cell coverage in this corner of Vietnam, though apparently it was spotty in some of the inland stretches and up over the pass that would comprise a part of his ride. If he'd stopped for a cup of iced coffee—or even hot coffee; he was obsessed with the way the waitstaff at so many places here would bring a French press to the table—he would have let her know. If he were lost, he would have sent her what she imagined would have been a comical Mayday. She'd heard nothing from him since they'd parted midmorning.

The sun wouldn't set for a few hours, but it troubled her that his bike didn't have a light.

For an hour now, her thoughts had grown steadily darker, a step-by-step ascent into the thin air of trepidation: He'd been hit by a car that had left him hurt by the side of the road. He'd been hit by a truck that had sent him careening over a guardrail, and his broken body was bleeding out amidst the rice paddies or in some thick copse of bamboo. He had a head injury, and he needed her right now to do a SCAT 2—a sport concussion assessment—on him. How many had she done in the ER on others in the last year? Thirty-five? Forty? Probably more. Maybe one a week, whether it was a pedestrian hit by a cab or a teen in a pickup basketball game or a college kid who had just done something stupid. How was it you could give yourself a concussion playing beer pong or quarters? She'd treated university freshmen who'd managed the seeming impossibility playing both.

Once again, she made a list in her mind of all the innocuous possibilities for Austin's absence. There were the villages along the route, and there were the little places on the flats on the north side of the mountain where the fishermen would get their provisions and the small snack shacks on the southern slope where tourists would stop to gaze out from their plastic chairs at the sea. Maybe he'd pulled over for noodles or steamed rice cakes or even a can of the Tiger beer that he loved, and he'd forgotten his phone on a little round wooden picnic table at the restaurant. Or his phone had run out of power. Or the cell coverage on the switchbacks was worse than they knew. Or he'd thought he'd sent her a text and forgotten to press Send. Certainly, she'd done that in her life, finding the text in its bubble, unsent, hours later or even the next morning. In this scenario, his phone was sitting in the left kidney pocket of his cycling jersey, and he had accidentally put the device on mute. (The scar from where the bullet had struck his arm was right around the hem of the short sleeve of most of his bike shirts.)

But no matter how many scenarios she crafted in her mind, the bottom line was that he was still late.

He spoke enough Vietnamese to ask directions on the street and order dinner in a restaurant—though the waitstaff had spoken English at every spot they had dined as a group on the bike tour—and when he'd had a tailor make him a suit in Hoi An, he had started to speak to the tailor and his two young female assistants in Vietnamese, but it was clear early on that they were being polite and indulging him. They saw so many Western tourists that they spoke a little German and French, as well as the King's

English, and soon they all stopped the charade and it was as if he were ordering a suit at a tony Manhattan department store. The same had occurred when he'd had her fitted for a black and silver cheongsam—this one cut so short it was like a chemise—the neck hole so tight it was like a dog collar. She couldn't imagine in reality that she'd ever wear it as anything but foreplay. Both outfits were going to be delivered to the hotel that night.

In any case, she presumed, he could probably ask his way here in Vietnamese in a pinch. In her mind, she saw him smiling and asking a farmer or an old woman or a waiter, "Da Nang?" "Hoi An?" and pointing in one direction or another.

She pulled off her ball cap and adjusted her ponytail. He would tease her about her anxiety when he returned; she would chastise him for making her worry.

And she would remind him that they met when she dug a bullet out of his arm, so she would always have cause for alarm when it came to him. For worry. He was who he was. One time, he'd been biking in the Adirondacks and hit fifty-five miles per hour on a long, steep downhill into Keene Valley, passing logging trucks and then UPS trucks and then a guy in a Lexus. She had heard the story from a cycling acquaintance of his that past summer, who told her that he had beaten the rest of the riders to the bottom of the hill by minutes. Literally, minutes. A year ago, the first time he had come to Vietnam on a bike tour, he'd nearly driven the tour guides mad one night by disappearing for three hours after dinner in Ho Chi Minh City. They'd actually waited up for him in the hotel bar. They'd been moments from calling the police and the American consulate when he finally returned. His excuse? Just exploring the city. He'd met three French bicyclists, and they'd compared notes on the different stages and mountains in the Tour de France, because they had all biked them for fun at some point in their cycling lives.

She had brought to the pool, along with her magazines and her iPad and phone, the map for the day with the two possible bike routes. There were eight of them on the bike tour, a smaller group than usual, apparently, and today they'd been allowed to choose rides of twenty-four and thirty-nine miles. She stared at it now, even though she knew that he would only be on the route at the very end. He wasn't doing either ride. Yesterday the group had planned to ride the Hai Van Pass over the mountain, a thirty-five-mile route along Highway One and the only real climb on the itinerary: twenty-three hundred feet of ascent. Austin had been looking forward to it immensely, in small part because of the exertion, but mostly because of the pilgrimage. The road would take him near where his father had been wounded and his uncle had died in what the Americans called the Vietnam War and the Vietnamese called the American War. Unfortunately, it had poured all day long and the tour leaders wanted no one—not even a rider as experienced as Austin—biking down the tortuous, steep slope of the mountain in the rain. The road would be too slick and the descent too dangerous. And so the whole group had taken the van from the hotel in Hue to their next stop on the outskirts of Hoi An, and gone shopping there in the City of Lanterns. It was when Austin had bought his suit and picked out her dress.

Now, today, Austin was doing the ride in reverse and doubling the ascent by riding north over the mountain to the Hue side, and then back over it and through Da Nang to their little hotel near Hoi An. It would be a ride of about seventy miles and forty-six hundred feet, which was grueling and long, but not all that grueling and long for him. He did at least a half dozen rides that distance every summer. He did at least two centuries—rides of a hundred miles. And the forecast today had been nothing but sun with the temperature in the high seventies. It was a perfect afternoon for him to stretch it out and get what he called that good wobbly feeling in his legs at the end of a lengthy, exhausting ride. It was the perfect day for him to pay his respects, the cerulean skies a sign that he was meant, finally, to visit the corner of the world that in so many ways had defined his father's life. Austin's wasn't a military family, but it was a family of privilege and responsibility where it was expected fifty years ago that you did your duty when you were asked: both of his grandfathers had served in the European theater in the Second World War, both had survived, and both had gone on to esteemed (and lucrative) careers in different facets of banking. And so when Austin's father's number came up in the lottery in 1970 and he was drafted, he went. He postponed his freshman year at Bates by, in the end, three years. His brother, four years his senior and a newly minted graduate of Syracuse, enlisted, because he couldn't imagine his younger brother in the jungles without him. It didn't seem fair. He was sent to Fort Benning and Officer Candidate School, where he would leave a lieutenant and be given command of a forty-three-person rifle platoon almost upon touching down in what was then South Vietnam.

Alexis knew Austin had not felt the same pressure or evidenced any desire to enlist thirteen years earlier, when he'd finished college. At the time, America had been trying desperately to extricate itself from Iraq and determine whether it would ever be possible to leave Afghanistan. And Austin? He once told her—and it had felt like a confession, the way he had shaken his head ruefully—that he wasn't his father and his uncle. He simply wasn't hardwired that way.

Alexis sighed when she imagined those siblings, so close that they went to a spectacularly unpopular war together.

She wished she had demanded of Austin that he let her accompany him on his ride today. But she also knew that her body probably wouldn't have forgiven her if she'd tried to ride the seventy miles and forty-six hundred feet of climb with him. And, of course, she would have slowed him down. She could barely keep up with him on even the shorter rides; he was always pulling a little ahead, realizing how far behind him she was, and doubling back. And so along with the two single women in the group and a pair of married accountants, today Alexis had done the long ride: thirty-nine miles. Only the elderly couple from North Carolina, the Coopers, had done the shorter, twenty-four-mile route, but that was more because Alan Cooper wanted to spend the afternoon at some nearby bird sanctuary than because they were incapable of riding farther. They were in their early seventies but stupendously well preserved. If she lived another forty years, she hoped she'd be half that together.

The night before they had left for Vietnam, a guy roughly Alan's age had been brought in to the ER just after dinner with an intracerebral hemorrhage. He'd collapsed at the dining room table, spilling his wine and toppling a tower of polenta and basil and sliced tomatoes, and was long unconscious by the time the EMTs arrived. She suspected instantly that's what it was, and that the poor man's brain was quite literally drowning in blood. The CT scan confirmed it. It was clear that emergency surgery was necessary and even if the fellow survived, he was likely going to be a vegetable when they were done. But she kept him alive until the family could all arrive or at least be allowed to weigh in long distance on how to proceed. They decided on the surgery, which was fine, and Alexis had learned the next morning, when she'd called the hospital before leaving for the airport, that the old man had died in the OR. The memory made her love the idea that the Coopers were on a bike trip in Vietnam. You just never knew when a stroke was going to leave you a stringless marionette on the dining floor beside the half-eaten remains of your supper.

Until Austin had suggested this trip over the Fourth of July weekend, she hadn't imagined that she'd ever ride a bike again, other than the Citi Bikes she rented every so often when she was exploring an outer borough or distant corner of Manhattan for fun. (If there was ever a pandemic in New York City, a nurse in the ER had once joked to her, it would be attributable to the great seas of germs on the handles and the seats of those bikes.) But she was young and in good shape, and the extra spinning classes that autumn had made this adventure surprisingly easy. Her legs had been a little tired the first night and her knees a little sore, but she had settled in since then and felt just fine.

Giang, the local leader of the group, had offered to ride with Austin that day, but he'd insisted on going solo since he was the only tourist interested in the route. One of the two American leaders from the bike tour, a cyclist from the company named Scott, had chimed in that he'd feel better if he tagged along. But Scott's knee looked pretty swollen and sore from a fall the day before. And Austin was clear that he could manage it physically and he was adamant—stubborn—in his desire to make this trek alone. The route would skirt both the rice paddies where Austin said that his father had been wounded and the patch of jungle where his uncle had died, and he wanted to pay his respects in solitude. It was an emotional expedition and the principal reason why they had come to Vietnam in the first place—or, to be precise, why he had come back. Last year the rains had also intervened, a storm that was relentless and violent and had lasted three days, and he had never made it to either spot. He and the tour had hung out at the resort on the beach, getting treatments at the spa and watching the winds bend the palm trees from their luxurious little villas by the sea. And so Giang and Scott had indulged Austin this year—or, at least, chosen not to fight him. Scott rode with the couple from North Carolina on the short loop, and Giang and the other American tour leader, a woman from Vermont named Colleen, joined the rest of the group on the longer ride. One support van dropped off the Coopers and Scott here at the hotel, and another babysat the rest of the tour on the remainder of the thirty-nine-mile ride.

She decided to call Austin now and, as she expected, she got his voice mail. "Hi, honey," she said. "It's me. It's nearly four thirty. I'm worried. Where the F are you?"

After hanging up, for a long moment she stared at the image of him she had added a month ago to her home screen. He had a little black scruff on his cheeks in the image, and it made him look so much more bohemian than he appeared when she would see him, always clean-shaven and in a suit, in a corridor or the cafeteria at the hospital when they would grab a quick bite together. Then she stood and slipped her feet into her sandals and started up the steps to the villa—a working farm long ago, then the magnificent estate of a French diplomat, and now an elegant little hotel—planning to find Giang or Scott or Colleen. Giang was her age, early thirties and, like her boyfriend, he was tall and lean, except for his calves and thighs, which were muscular and almost (but not quite) thick. Colleen was in her late twenties, new to this tour company, but an avid cyclist who had a degree in international relations from Bucknell. (Austin had joked that she was a spy. Traveling around the world leading bike tours? What a perfect cover!) Scott was in his midfifties, short and stocky with a body that just wasn't built for bike shorts. And yet this was what he did. Tomorrow was the last leg of the tour, the ride south toward Tam Ky. Half the group, including Alexis and Austin, were scheduled to fly home on Saturday. Others were going to continue exploring Asia on their own.

She found Scott in the living room that had been converted into a wine bar, chatting with the two unattached women from St. Louis. They were a decade older than she was, one was divorced, and the pair had been friends since childhood. Like Austin, they were beasts on their bikes. They were tall and slender and the sort of cyclists who could destroy a mere mortal's self-esteem in a spin class. They were leaning forward on a long red leather settee, their knees bent, their bare feet flat on the floor; Scott was perched against an exquisitely sculpted antique desk that probably weighed more than a car. His knee was not wrapped in ice, but she saw a blue gel pack, now thawed, sitting on the Oriental rug like a beached jellyfish. The desk was walnut and had carvings of angels and saints on the front, and the corners were as ornate as anything one might see at a cathedral in France or a duomo in Tuscany. The wood matched the bookcases along the walls, the books shelved there a combination of dog-earred paperbacks left by previous guests, mostly in English but some in French and some in Chinese, and beautiful leather binders dating back a century that chronicled the estate's fruit business from the era before the war.

"Ah, Alexis," said Scott, smiling. "I'm guessing Austin's returned."

Alexis and Austin. Austin and Alexis. People who knew the two of them seemed to like the alliteration of their two names and the fact they were usually in such intensely close proximity when they would go out in groups to restaurants or bars in Brooklyn or Manhattan, or when they would be at parties. Sometimes it surprised people that they didn't actually live together. Yet.

Because, of course, someday they would. It seemed likely. It crossed her mind; it had to have crossed his. They'd been dating nearly seven months now.

Scott was fluent in at least three languages—Italian, English, and French—because he also helped lead bike tours for the company in Europe. His Vietnamese was solidly conversational, because they had more and more riders wanting to come here, and because the company had so many repeat customers who had already ridden the roads in Normandy and Ireland and Umbria. He said he couldn't write a word of Vietnamese, but he had impressed the heck out of her when they had stopped in small villages and he would chat with the locals. He had grown up in Savannah, Georgia, and still had a trace of a southern accent, and that made the pairing of their names—Alexis and Austin, Austin and Alexis—downright mellifluous.

"No, he's not back," she corrected him.

"Oh, God, how many extra miles is he doing?" asked Talia. "Wasn't seventy going to be enough for him?" She'd showered, her tight cornrows still damp, and was in a pair of black gym shorts, and her legs, even bent at the knees, went on forever. She shook her head and then sipped her wine.

"I don't know what's happened, but something's wrong," Alexis told Scott, aware of the quaver that had crept into her voice, and she watched how instantly he stood up a little straighter. "I mean, I think something's wrong."

"Go on."

"He's not back and he thought he'd be back by three. Three thirty at the latest. That was an hour ago."

"And you haven't heard from him?"

"Nothing. Not a peep."

Reflexively the guide looked at his watch. "Yup, he's late all right. But he was climbing the Hai Van Pass—twice. Up and over and then back. There are some really steep grades, and I know he wanted to pay his respects on the other side. I told him, when we looked at the maps, that I thought that little detour on the far side was going to demand three or four miles on dirt. Or six or eight miles total. That might have slowed him, given all the rain we had yesterday. Maybe there's a little mud."

She shook her head. "You've seen him ride. You said yourself he'd be here well before three thirty. And there hasn't been any rain today, none at all. I'm sure it dried out nicely in the heat. He said he'd only get back that late in the afternoon because he'd probably stop and have a cup of coffee or a beer after visiting the sites."

"Have you texted him?"

"Of course. A bunch of times. I just left him a phone message."

Talia went to the credenza against the wall and brought an open bottle of Cabernet Sauvignon and a glass to her. "Here, have a glass of wine," she said, handing her the goblet. Alexis took it and watched as the woman gave her a hefty pour. Sheri, the other rider, rose as well and stood beside her.

"I'm guessing you're not in the habit of letting your guests bike on their own," Sheri said. She was a lawyer, and Alexis couldn't miss the disapproval in her tone. She was suggesting that this was not just an irresponsible decision on Scott and Giang's part; it might have disastrous legal ramifications for the touring company if, indeed, something had happened to Austin.

"It's not as uncommon as you'd think," he told her defensively. He, too, had heard the implications in her tone. "Especially with a rider of Austin's caliber."

She challenged him: "I don't know. It's one thing to let a person disappear on her own in Siena. It's another thing here."

"I'm sure you don't mean anything by that, but it sounds a little provincial. Don't you think? We've been bringing riders to this country for years. You've seen yourself how kind the people are."

"No foul," she said, raising her hands, palms open, to lessen the tension. "It was just an observation."

"Look, we can discuss our company's policies when he's back. I think now I'll just go retrieve him," Scott said. "I'll tell Colleen I'm going, and then I'll get Giang and one of the vans." Their leader seemed to feel the aesthetics of the van with its bulky bike racks on the roof were too coarse for the villas and the small boutique hotels where they stayed, and so the guides always parked them out of view. They were the deep yellow of a perfectly ripe banana. Here that meant parking the eyesores behind a stone outbuilding a few hundred yards distant that once had housed pigs.

Alexis took a long swallow of the wine. "I'll go with you."

"You don't need to," he said, and she could hear in his voice a small ripple of apprehension. It was as if he, too, expected the worst.

"I do need to," she said definitively. "Remember, I work in an ER."

There was the napalm, of course. That's what a lot of Americans think of first, regardless of whether they've ever set foot in Vietnam. Apocalypse Now, *right? I mean, that's what I thought of. We all hear in our heads the guttural howls of pain as it burned through flesh. The naked little girl in the photo. The images of the creosote corpses, smooth and black. The teeth—God, we've all seen those pictures, too—in the lipless, open mouths of the dead. The fingers, splayed and curled like the tines of a garden claw. (I used to garden. The claw was my favorite tool.)*

Napalm was a jelly—think marmalade, someone once told me—and when it was lit, it clung like pine pitch to plants and people and birds and rats and water buffalo and whatever else was in its path. Water boils at 212 degrees Fahrenheit; napalm burned at temperatures six to ten times hotter. The flames were two thousand degrees. Can you imagine? (I can't. I just can't.)

The stuff was made by mixing naphthenic and palmitic acids. Hence the name. Then the mixture was weaponized with gasoline. The chemists who created it worked at Harvard in the 1940s. Initially, no one saw it as a jungle weapon. The first napalm bomb, ever, fell on the city of Berlin in 1944, and it was over Tokyo in 1945—five months before Hiroshima and Nagasaki—that it created the firestorm that would kill over one hundred thousand people in a night.

Two decades later, however, it was sprayed from flame throwers in Vietnam to burn down the swaths of brush in the American soldiers' paths, eliminating the cover for guerrilla fighters. But one scared little soldier with a couple gallons of the gel in a tank on his back was far less efficient than an F-100 that could swoop in and drop exploding bombs of the goo, obliterating whole forests. A dragon taller than palm trees exhaling a tsunami of fire. That's what I think. A fairy-tale dragon.

Again, the movies gave me that. They gave us that.

Eight million tons of napalm cocktails fell from the skies on Vietnam, a decimation that was volcanic. I mean, it was revelatory. It was biblical.

And yet it was the herbicides that stayed with us and changed the world. Figuratively. Literally. That's my point. That's what interested us. I don't mean they've stayed with us in terms of visual memory, because nothing augured deep into the brain's amygdala quite like the horrors of a charred corpse or those three- and four-story rolling pinwheels of flames. (In our minds, the sky is always sapphire, right? It's like Hollywood never imagined we'd napalm a forest on a cloudy day.) It was the chemical poisons that lingered.

The name of the operation was Ranch Hand. Twenty million gallons, much of it Agent Orange, dropped on our ally, South Vietnam. We wanted to defoliate the jungles so the Viet Cong would have no place to hide and to deprive the fighters of their food. No one knew for sure then what it did to people. But on some instinctive, visceral level, someone must have suspected. The researchers. The chemists. The soldiers on the ground. The farmers in the rice paddies and the fields.

It couldn't be good.

Still, no one really pondered the question until we looked at the cancers and the birth defects in America and Vietnam—the children of the men and women who'd been sent there or lived there, the babies with their devastating deformities nursing at their devastated mothers' breasts—as the war receded into memory. The dead that we saw from napalm, each mouth a rictus of agony, and those end-of-the-world infernos that turned rain forest to ash became fading photos we could repress.

But the herbicides? We saw what they did to humans years and years later.

What we didn't see, but people smarter than me began to contemplate, was what those chemicals had done to the wildlife that somehow managed to survive the firestorms.

Or, to be precise, the way those chemicals had changed the descendants of the survivors that scurried now through the jungle and brush.

2

He saw them emerge from the elephant grass that grew high along the side of the road, and initially he was only surprised. Two men appearing ahead of him out of nowhere. Farmers? No. Clearly not. He felt the hair on the back of his neck start to rise, and he glanced behind him, over his shoulder, hoping there was a vehicle approaching. A truck or a car or even one of those scooters. Someone to witness whatever was about to unfold. There wasn't. He considered pedaling faster, falling into the handlebar drops and accelerating.

He considered turning around and pedaling in the other direction.

But wouldn't that be an overreaction?

Worst case, wasn't this only a robbery? It had to be. It couldn't possibly be more, he told himself. But, of course, it could. He knew.

All of these thoughts moved through his mind in little more than a couple of heartbeats—and he was sure his heart was beating fast now. It all happened so quickly. And then his decision had been made for him, and there was nothing at all he could do, because he was upon them.

He unclipped his right shoe and skidded to a stop because the two of them were standing smack in the middle of the road and wanted him to, and at least one had a gun—and the weapon looked, as he approached, like a Russian assault rifle. He'd been shot once before, a bullet from a very different sort of gun in a Manhattan dive bar, and it hadn't been pleasant. This one looked like it was capable of doing a hell of a lot more damage to flesh and bone.

He stood for a moment with his right foot on the ground and his left still attached to the pedal.

Instantly he offered them money—and he used the word for money because his mind was racing and he couldn't remember the Vietnamese word for wallet. He held up his hands, even though the kid with the gun (and he was a kid; he couldn't have been more than sixteen years old) wasn't pointing it at him. Then, slowly, keeping one hand in the air, he reached into the back of his cycling jersey with his other. He felt his wallet and the small packets of Psych energy gels. He grabbed the wallet and extended it out to them, palm flat, as if it were a plate with hors d'oeuvres. The other fellow, a man older than he was—midforties, Austin guessed—smiled at the kid with the gun, and it was then that the cyclist's fear began to mushroom into something considerably more visceral. Not terror. Not even panic. But the dawning realization that he was in over his head and this wasn't likely to end well. They didn't want his wallet. They shared a joke and laughed, but they had spoken so quickly that he hadn't understood most of what they were saying. But he thought, from the few words he had picked up, they were mocking the idea that he thought this was a negotiation.

"My bicycle?" he asked. "Take my bicycle, please. It's a good one I rented," he told them. He unclipped his left shoe and swung his leg over the top tube and held the bike a couple of inches off the ground. "It's worth a lot, even used."

The fellow who seemed to be running this show rolled his eyes. And it was then that he saw, rounding the bend perhaps a hundred yards distant, a van. A tourist van of some sort. It even had bike racks on the roof, though they were empty now. It was white with a cheerful logo with a waterfall in its center, but he couldn't translate the Vietnamese wording beside it. Here, he thought, was the cavalry. Here was his rescue. It was a different company from the bike tour he was on, but it was still other human beings who might, by their simple presence and mere witness, stop whatever was about to go down. He felt relief that he might survive this, after all. But then, when he looked at the guns, he began to wonder if a greater calamity was simply about to occur. A more significant slaughter. Increased collateral damage. They'd kill him and whoever happened to be driving down this road at this moment.

He saw a fellow hopping out of the passenger side of the van, and he was wearing a black blazer and a white oxford shirt.

Tour guides didn't wear blazers and dress shirts. At least not usually.

Which meant this probably wasn't a tour guide.

And then, when the newcomer got closer and pulled off his sunglasses, Austin recognized him. A tall American, a fellow perhaps a decade his senior. It was Douglas—never Doug, never Dougie. Always Douglas. (Occasionally, Austin had wondered if this was his real name. One time when they'd been tossing darts in a bar, he'd noticed that the fellow had looked up twice, reflexively, when someone at a nearby table had hollered for a guy named Karl.) His presence here in Vietnam meant one thing: He knew. He had followed him here. Come all this way. Austin considered dropping the bike and collapsing onto the ground, literally onto his knees, and begging for mercy. To plead for his life. But he wasn't sure how much time it would buy him. Still, if they wanted him to beg, he was confident he could disgorge all manner of degrading and pathetic entreaties, and he could do so with his shins in firm communion with the earth.

When the other American reached him, Austin nodded. "I'm guessing you didn't come here for the darts," he began, hoping his comment sounded innocuous enough to mask his terror.

"Alas, I did not," Douglas told him.

"Whatever you want, it couldn't wait until I got home?" he asked. "Until I was back in America?"

"It's easier here."

"For you."

"And you." He took Austin's wallet, which was still in his hands, and dropped it into his front blazer pocket. "Give me your phone."

Obediently Austin handed it to him. The other American turned it off and took a paper clip from his pocket. Carefully, as if he were doing very small piecework or repairing something fragile and small—or, perhaps, doing the exact opposite and pulling a wing from an insect—he unbent it so that it was a long, thin metal tube. Then he pushed one end into the hole on the side of Austin's phone and ejected the SIM card. He held it up to Austin as if he were a magician performing a card trick, and then put both the SIM card and the paper clip into one pocket, and the phone into the other.

"There now," Douglas said, smiling. Austin looked down and noted a thick crack in the asphalt that ran parallel to the road. It was the sort of chasm that caused bicycle flats. On a downhill, it was the kind of gouge that caused bone-shattering bicycle crashes.

"You won't need it where we're going," the fellow said.

Austin said nothing, but he felt his chest growing warm. He tried not to pant, because he didn't want to telegraph his fear. He knew Douglas had removed the SIM card from his phone so it couldn't be used to track him. He took a little comfort from the idea that the other American hadn't just walked to the side of the road and hurled the phone as far as he could into the swamp. In his head, he could imagine the small splash it would make. He could hear it. Not destroying the phone might be a good sign: it meant there was still some negotiation to be had.

Douglas took a canvas bag with a drawstring from his pocket—it had been flattened and pressed practically into the size of a handkerchief—and Austin took additional comfort in its existence. It was a hood. He almost felt exhilaration when they walked him to the vehicle, one of them lifting his bike off the ground and carrying it with him, because the hood—along with the fact that Douglas had merely extracted the SIM card from the phone—meant they weren't going to kill him.

At least not yet.

They sat him in the second row of the van, and the other American told him to take off his helmet. He did, placing it in his lap. He stared straight ahead as they took it away from him, tossing it into the row behind them, and draped the hood over his head. He pressed it against his forehead, mopping the sweat there with it as if it were a towel. He heard one of the Vietnamese hoisting his bike onto the roof and locking it into the rack.

"I trust you can breathe?" Douglas asked.

"I can," Austin answered, and he nodded vigorously, obligingly. It was strangely courteous.

He sat back in his seat as they started off and was aware of how different his cycling jersey felt without his phone and his wallet. But then he felt, in their absence, something else. The pockets were completely empty. He reached his hand back to search inside first the left pocket and then the right and then the middle. But they were gone. No doubt about it, they were gone. The lemon-yellow Psych energy gel, as well as the two chocolate-flavored packets. They must have fallen out when he had reached for his wallet. They were, in all likelihood, back there on the road. He thought he was going to be sick, and carefully brought his hands to his lap and breathed in slowly and deeply in his hood, trying to calm himself. He couldn't tell them; he didn't dare.

"You probably know this, but last year's floods in the Mekong Delta obliterated the rat population there. Decimated it," Douglas was saying.

"Yeah. I'd heard that," Austin told him, hoping the panic he was feeling was not evident in his tone.

"It was a real yin and yang sort of moment. The rats were always a plague on the rice harvest. But they were also really good eating for some of the farmers. Rat sour soup. Rat curry. Grilled rat. The rat is an excellent source of protein."

This was all so collegial, despite the bag on his head, that he allowed himself a slight disagreement, if only to take his mind off the packets he had accidentally left behind on the pavement: "I would say a common source of protein. Excellent? That might be a stretch."

"Maybe. I'm supposing you've never eaten one."

"No."

"Me neither. I'm told they taste just like chicken."

Austin nodded. "People say that about a lot of things."

"They do. They really do." Then: "You shouldn't have come here, Austin."

"Yeah. I know that, too. But it really is just a bike tour."

"Right. Of course it is."

"I'm telling you the truth."

A thought came to him as he felt the van accelerating. If Douglas had followed him here to Vietnam and knew right where he was today, that meant he knew where Alexis was, too. And if that were the case, what in holy fuck had he just done to her?

3

In their guest room, Alexis went straight to her cosmetics bag on the dresser and pushed aside her toothbrush and lipstick and found the Xanax. Once upon a time, she had popped them like M&M's, but these days she only swallowed one before flying. Not now. Not this afternoon. She unscrewed the top and took one. She washed it down with the last of the wine that Talia had given her downstairs. She didn't bother to change out of her bathing suit, which was dry except for her sweat, and simply pulled over it a pair of jeans and a T-shirt. She knew there was an emergency aid kit in the van, but she'd never bothered to look inside it. She wondered now what was there and whether she'd need it.

The bike tour's support vans always brought their luggage to the next destination, and she saw Austin's suitcase on a rack just outside the closet. She remembered his laptop and his tablet were in the front pocket, and an idea came to her. She took out his computer and booted it up. She'd use it to find his phone—and him. They were linked by the Cloud. But then she saw that she would need a password to log on to the device, and she had no idea what in the world it might be. For a long moment, she stared aimlessly at the screen. Then she shut it off and tried his tablet, and saw instantly that she would have the same problem.

She shook off her disappointment and ran back downstairs. She was moving quickly now: there it was, the adrenaline from the ER. She was doing something instead of stewing beside the swimming pool. Already Giang had pulled the van up to the roundabout at the front steps to the villa, and Talia was offering to come with them.

"No, we'll be fine," she told the woman, and Talia surprised Alexis by giving her a hug.

"You're sure?"

"I'm sure," she answered, though she certainly wasn't. She tried to walk herself in from the ledge, reminding herself that things were rarely as dire as they seemed in her mind. Even in the ER.

No, that wasn't true. Things could get gnarly fast in the ER. The construction worker who'd been impaled on three rebar spikes when he'd fallen two floors onto them? That had been pretty damn grisly. He'd been brought in after hanging atop them nearly ninety minutes while the EMTs and the firefighters figured out how to cut him down. He'd arrived with the spikes still skewering him, however, piercing his abdomen and his shoulder and his leg. He'd lived. She'd helped keep him alive long enough to get him into the OR. And then there were the two teen boys who'd had a gunfight on meth with a pair of nail guns: they had nails in their feet and forearms, and one had them in his back. There was the woman who had wedged a potato into her vagina to prevent her prolapsed uterus from spilling out onto the kitchen floor.

There were all those blue babies and cold babies and beaten babies . . .

Sometimes, the ER was a museum of the monstrous and the macabre. There were the failed suicides, there were the kids too young to drive. There were the incontinent elderly who were unaware where they were, and the mentally ill from the streets whose coughs, you knew, were harbingers of very bad news for them.

And yet there were other times when it was oddly cerebral. It wasn't all nail guns and rebar spikes, or restarting the hearts of teenage girls shot playing field hockey. It was abdominal pains

and headaches and dizziness. It was vomiting and diarrhea, peculiar skin lesions and inexplicable welts. It was pattern recognition
in the quiet of a cubicle, as you asked questions about symptoms
and history, where the patient had just been and what sorts of
illnesses and surgeries were in the past. Sometimes she created a
whiteboard in her mind, the symptoms written in black marker
and their connections in blue. You worked backwards, moving
intellectually from effect to cause. She'd been in one ER or another since her first year as a resident, and that was seven years
ago now. Her match as her fourth year neared its end had been a
hospital in Houston, where she had lived and learned—worked—
until she had finished her residency at twenty-nine. For the last
four years, she'd been in Manhattan. Kip's Bay. And though she
was thirty-three now, she was still learning. The shifts when she'd
see something unrecognizable—a pattern she'd never encoun-
tered before—were less frequent, but still she saw new things all
the time. When she'd had an ER rotation during her third year
of medical school, a physician had told her that Arthur Conan
Doyle had been a doctor. She wasn't surprised. So much of what
they did back then was detective work based largely on deductive
reasoning.

"We'll trace the roads he should be on first," Giang was saying. Scott motioned for her to take the front passenger seat, but
she shook her head and climbed into the second row, allowing
him to sit there. Altogether, the van had four rows. "You were on
some of them just a few hours ago," Giang continued.

"Yup," she said. "That magnificent city of the dead. The rice
paddies and that astonishing family temple. Gorgeous. I saw an
egret there."

"Did you? Lucky you."

"It did feel lucky," she agreed as the three of them started
down the driveway. She took solace in the fact that the two men
seemed so very calm. Still, she was an addict when she thought
consolation was at hand and so she pressed her luck: "I'll bet you
have to send out the van in search of stragglers who've disappeared

pretty often. I know this is the first time on this tour. But it happens all the time, right?"

The two men glanced at each other. Then Scott shrugged. "Absolutely," he told her, "all the time." She knew instantly that he was lying, but she nodded her head and smiled.

As Giang pulled onto the road, he had to swerve into the other lane to avoid a half dozen scooters whipping past them, one with a dead pig strapped to the back. "I love the sound of those little motors," Scott said, but the Vietnamese guide looked at him like he'd lost his mind.

"They sound like giant mosquitoes," he said. Then he turned around and asked her, "Good ride today?"

"It was. I wish there'd been a breeze. Even a headwind. It was hotter than I expected. The forecast said seventies, but it felt a lot steamier."

"Then your Austin, who's very smart, is going to be sipping coconut water or a Tiger beer when we find him. He'll be at a café or resting for a moment at the summit with a chilled bottle of water."

"I can see that," she agreed. She smiled at the idea and sat forward in her seat, her hands on the backs of the headrests ahead of her, scanning the road before them. Their plan was simply to drive north through Da Nang and then up and over the Hai Van Pass toward Hue. Giang knew the dirt road on the north side of the mountain where Austin was going to detour briefly off Highway One. This time of the day, they expected to find him either racing down the southern side of the mountain or churning his way methodically up the northern side. Or, perhaps, they really might find him resting somewhere along the flats on either side. Or, indeed, at one of the snack shacks.

Soon they were climbing up toward the summit and the concrete bunkers the French and Americans had built to control the pass and protect the seacoast to the east from the Viet Cong. In her angst, Alexis was struck by the steep, curving gradient that could send a cyclist—even one as accomplished as Austin—careening into a tree or over the side of the hill. Or, at the very least, give a person a pretty gruesome case of road rash if he fell. Or a broken bone or two. And she knew that Austin missed his bike in America. He had paid extra for the best road bike the tour group could provide, but it still wasn't the—his words, not hers—crotch rocket he was accustomed to.

She stared at the map. His uncle had spent most of his time in country between Hoi An and Hue, though he had arrived after the Tet Offensive in 1968 had destroyed so much of Hue and the ancient citadel there. His father had been wounded in roughly the same area, his platoon ambushed in the rice paddies that back then were west of the American playground known as China Beach. He'd been taken to a hospital on the coast near Tuy Hoa. His uncle had been a little farther north when he'd died, but still on the seventy-mile trek that Austin was making today. He'd tripped a Bouncing Betty, a landmine that was thrown upward a couple of feet before detonating, and been—quite literally—decapitated. Austin said he had done his homework and knew more or less where his father's platoon had been when he'd taken machine-gun fire in his thigh and his hip, and where in this area his uncle had been killed.

She looked out at the rice paddies and then the mountains in the distance, a landscape as enigmatic as it was vast, and tried to convince herself once more that she was worried for naught. They all were. This would be fine. She rested one of her hands on the inside of her thigh, and through her blue jeans reflexively ran her fingers along one of the scars that was there.

·　·　·

Quickly they were beyond the roads and sites that Alexis had seen the past two days in the van or on her bike, and there had been absolutely no sign of Austin. Nor was there any sign of him on their way to the mountain peak. There was a stretch of switchbacks along a cliff, the S a giant snake, and they stopped twice to peer over the side, calling down into the boulders and the brush, but the world looked undisturbed as far as the sea. When she wasn't studying the side of the road, she was checking and re-checking her phone, but the message square on her home screen remained disappointingly empty.

At the top of the hill there was still a crush of tour buses and entrepreneurs with their cut-open coconuts with straws, and their bottles of water and cans of beer. There were still dozens of tourists milling about the ancient brick tower from the Nguyen dynasty and the military bunker from the last century. There they stopped and found a German couple who spoke English.

Alexis showed them a series of pictures of Austin on her phone, but they hadn't seen him. There was an old man at the tower who served as an informal docent, and she gave him a hundred thousand Vietnamese dong—not quite five dollars—and showed him photos of Austin, too, and Giang asked him a variety of questions in Vietnamese. Over and over again, the old man shook his head.

"He saw a group of bicyclists about two hours ago," Giang told her. "But they were all together and all part of the same tour. He doesn't believe your Austin was among them."

"How can he be so sure?" she asked.

"Because they were all women."

She took this in and closed her eyes for a moment, gathering herself amidst the sounds of the jibbering insects and the chatter-ing birds, of the growling tour bus engines as they tried to back through the crowds and onto the road.

And so they drove down the other side, the northern slope, and at Alexis's insistence stopped at some of the bridges on the hairpin curves and peered over the sides there, too. But still there was no sign of him.

When they arrived at the bottom of the pass on the Hue side, they pulled over beside a snack shack with two rickety outdoor tables at the edge of a small outdoor market, and Alexis looked around, frustrated. She peered inside the restaurant, but she didn't see anyone but a pair of elderly fishermen. She went to them and opened her phone, showing them the photo of Austin on the home screen, but they shook their heads. Outside, in the back, she saw a young boy in a chair, tossing scraps of food from a red garbage pail to a couple of dogs. She showed him the photo, too, but got the same response.

"I wouldn't know how to begin to search for him here," she murmured when she returned to the two men, aware for the first time of how desperate her tone sounded. Soon they would lose the daylight. Then what?

Scott ran his fingers through his hair, nodded, and then looked at Giang. "She's right, you know," he said.

"Okay, let's not stop here. Let's try that dirt road," he said.

And so they did, and the red dirt was packed down hard and solid, despite yesterday's storm. There was no sign of him and there were no bike tracks in the ground.

A half hour later they were back on the other side of the mountain, the pass behind them, and on another of those long, flat stretches of road bordered on one side by elephant grass and by swamp on the other. And it was there, as Alexis stared straight ahead, that she saw some garbage on the road that usually she would have ignored, but didn't this time because it was so very yellow. You couldn't miss it; it was like a flare. She didn't want to get her hopes up, but she did, and she demanded they stop.

Scott followed her from the van, and Giang sat behind the steering wheel, waiting and watching.

The garbage was, just as she had suspected, packets of Psych energy gel, one that was lemon flavored—the yellow she'd seen like a flare—and a pair that were chocolate. They were about four inches long, reminiscent of the ketchup packets that were ubiquitous at ballparks and fast-food restaurants, but filled instead with a cake icing of amino acids, sodium, and caffeine, flavored to taste like chocolate or lemon or caramel. There were easily a dozen flavors. Austin just had his preferences. He liked chocolate; she hated it. Sometimes she'd eat the lemon flavor, but usually under duress. Out of desperation. You ripped off the top and squeezed the tablespoon or so of stuff in the package into your mouth, and five minutes later you were revived and ready to pedal. Or run. Or climb. Or whatever. The lemon label was the same ridiculous canary color as the van, she had joked with Austin their first day on bikes in Vietnam. He'd brought two dozen packets of the gel with him on the trip—maybe more—mostly lemon, but a couple of chocolates. Athletes, even weekend warriors, liked them because they were lightweight and small, and you could throw three or four into your pocket.

"He was here," she told Scott, lifting the packets off the asphalt.

The guide took the lemon one from her and examined it. "It's unopened."

"It must have fallen out. Maybe when he stopped for a breather," she said.

"Are those unopened, too?" he asked.

"They are. So, he didn't stop here to consume one," she replied, and a thought came to her: "Besides, he wouldn't have stopped in the middle of the road."

Scott handed it back to her. "Maybe they fell out when he was reaching for his phone or something," he said.

"Maybe. But wouldn't they be by the side of the road, in that case?"

"It's possible that a car blew them here from the shoulder when it passed."

She nodded, unable to decide whether a vehicle would have blown them off the road or toward the middle of the lane. "Either way, it could mean this: he could be somewhere between here and the hotel where we're staying, and somehow we missed him. That's good news, right?"

"Would he have gone to Da Nang?" Scott asked her. "Or Hoi An?"

"I doubt it. Why?"

"He's not back at the hotel."

She shook her head. Why would he have gone to either place?

"And, let's face it," Scott went on. "I hate to be a downer, but maybe he dropped them this morning—on his way out—and we didn't notice them earlier. And maybe they aren't even Austin's. I'm sure he's not the only bicyclist in Vietnam who uses Psych gels. I mean, there are other tour companies bringing other Americans here."

He was right, but she had an idea. She made a flap with her shirt and dropped the gel packets into it so she didn't need to handle them any more than she already had. She returned to the van, opened the emergency kit, and found an epi pen in a small plastic bag. Carefully she placed the energy gels in the bag and sealed it. She hoped this wouldn't turn out to be evidence or that she'd need to prove that Austin had been here with fingerprints or DNA from the packages. But she had to do this, just in case. Then she emerged once more from the van and took photos of the area in all directions. She asked Giang to mark the mileage.

When they started off once more, Giang flipped on the headlights and the anxiety she was feeling was no match for the Xanax. In the gloaming dark of the van, she felt herself sinking into the great, black maw of fear.

.   .   .

Alexis didn't know whether it was Scott or Giang who was keeping Colleen and the rest of the bike tour abreast of their search, but she presumed it was Scott since Giang was driving. But their Vietnamese guide was as comfortable as any American teen driving with one hand (or his knees) on the wheel, while texting with the other. He might have been texting Colleen or Sheri or Talia. But by the time they returned to the villa a little past nine at night, the group was assembled in the living room waiting for them, and it was like a wake. The other six riders, as well as Colleen, were quiet and somber, and they all stood when she and the other two guides entered the room. Everyone already knew that they hadn't found Austin, and Austin hadn't miraculously turned up at the little hotel. Scott reported that they'd come across no one who'd seen the American bicyclist on the roads, and no one had seen him in Da Nang—though the city was big and they certainly hadn't searched it thoroughly. They'd simply stopped at some of the more popular restaurants and bars, one of the hospitals, and driven some of the streets, now dark, near the suspension bridge. Then they'd taken the beach road to the area's massive and stately Lady Buddha. Roughly twenty-five stories tall, Scott had told Alexis.

"This is devastating, but your guy is pretty resilient. I know he's okay and there will be an explanation for all of this," said Alan Cooper, the older fellow from North Carolina who, along with his wife, had spent the afternoon at the nearby bird sanctuary. He was standing with his hands in the pockets of his khaki slacks, trying to look upbeat but appearing more like a forlorn grandfather. He was completely bald at the top of his head, and the little hair that he had around his ears and the back of his skull was white and short as a marine's. But his eyes? They were brown and soft, and Alexis imagined them growing wide with feigned wonder as he read aloud to a grandchild, the boy or the girl curled in his lap like a conch in its shell.

"Do I call the embassy?" she asked Scott. She hadn't gotten sick in the van, but she presumed that was only because she hadn't eaten. Or, just maybe, it was the Xanax. Nevertheless, she believed that she was still firmly in her ER mode; she felt an urgent need to do something.

"We should call the consulate. The embassy is all the way in Hanoi. The consulate's closer: Ho Chi Minh City. They can get someone here a little faster."

"Someone . . ."

"I don't know. Someone. Someone in consular services. Maybe an FBI attaché. Maybe someone who can work with the local police."

He took out his phone, and for a moment she thought he was

going to hand it to her. Instead he scrolled through his contacts and then started telling her the number. She asked him to stop so she could retrieve her own phone.

"Okay." He read her the number once more, slowly this time, and she called it. When somebody answered, it was a man with a youthful but extremely formal voice announcing that this was the Consulate for the United States of America and he was Brendan Sutter. She began—and the words were lost in the thrumming she heard in her head—"Hi. My name is Alexis Remnick, and I am at a hotel called the Villa Haldina. It's near . . ." She looked at Scott, astonished that she had momentarily forgotten the name of the town, and he mouthed the words *Hoi An*. "Hoi An," she continued. "I'm on a bike tour with a bunch of other Americans, and my boyfriend, Austin Harper, has disappeared."

"When did he disappear?" Sutter asked.

"He was last seen around midmorning today. He was due here in Hoi An at three or three thirty this afternoon. No later. I just returned with guides from the bike tour and we retraced his route and we didn't find him anywhere on it."

"You said he was last seen around midmorning. Was that the last time you heard from him?"

"That's correct."

"No calls or texts since then?"

"No," she told him. "Not a one."

"Okay. Let me have someone call you right back. Is this the best number?"

"It is."

"I'll ring the duty officer right now. Someone will phone you soon."

"Soon as in five minutes or soon as in an hour?"

"Somewhere in between—but that's a guess."

"Okay, I'll sit tight. Thank you," she said, and she hung up and collapsed into a wing chair at the edge of the library.

"Have you all eaten anything?" Talia asked.

Alexis shook her head.

"You must be famished."

"I'm really not," she said.

"You should eat something," Alan told her. "You all should. I know the chef is still here. He can whip something up."

"Sure," she agreed. "Fine." She thought of the energy gels in the emergency kit. When she had the strength, maybe she would go upstairs and grab another one from Austin's suitcase to hold her over. And then she would retrieve the ones that might have his DNA and fingerprints from the van.

No, she wouldn't have a Psych gel right now. She was a doctor. She was a grown-up. She would wait for some real food.

4

The person who called back was the FBI legal attaché stationed at the United States embassy in Phnom Penh. Her name was Toril Bjornstad. She spelled it all, first and last name, before Alexis even asked. Her accent, if Alexis detected one, was vaguely midwestern. She imagined the woman was originally from Minnesota or the Dakotas, but she had a feeling that she had made this assumption because as a child she had once had a doll whose backstory was that she was a Scandinavian immigrant and had lived on the American prairie in the 1850s. For all Alexis knew, Toril was from Oslo or Los Angeles or Miami, Florida. What mattered to Alexis, however, was this: she sounded efficient and she sounded implacable. Still, a part of her was confused, because the woman had begun by saying her office was in Phnom Penh.

"So, you're in Cambodia?" she asked her.

"Usually," Toril said. "We don't have an FBI presence in Vietnam. So I cover Vietnam out of Phnom Penh. But I'm actually in Ho Chi Minh City right now. I had a meeting here today and another tomorrow."

"I'd say I'm in luck, but I don't feel that way."

"No. I understand."

"Would you mind calling all the hospitals in Hue and Hoi An and Da Nang?" Alexis asked. "We went to one in Da Nang, but he wasn't there. At least not yet. But could you please see what patients they've all seen or who they have waiting in the emergency rooms?"

"We already have. We called them before calling you," she said, adding that no American bicyclist had turned up in a hospital in any of the cities. She said she had also reached out to the police in Da Nang, but there wasn't much they could do at nine thirty at night. It wasn't as if there was a crime scene to investigate. They said they would send out a couple of cars to run the roads, and Alexis was grateful, but not confident. They'd done that themselves. Alexis told her that both Austin's father and uncle had served here during the war, and the attaché took down their names. Then she asked for Austin's cell phone and passport numbers and said she would be at the little hotel in Hoi An by eight in the morning. Assuming that Austin hadn't turned up, she would join Alexis while she was interviewed by local police officers. She added that she expected she'd have questions herself.

The bike tour was supposed to check out of the hotel by eight thirty the next morning with the riders on their bikes heading south by eight forty-five. The plan was to bike toward Quang Ngai, visiting the memorial to the My Lai Massacre and the twelve-hundred-year-old citadel at Chau Sa. Then, the next day, Saturday, they'd have a short ride in the morning and a farewell brunch, and the bike tour would conclude. The accountants were going to prolong their stay in Vietnam with a few days in Ho Chi Minh City—the tour had begun with a day in Hanoi before flying to Hue to begin the cycling portion of the trip, and among the group, only Austin had ever seen Ho Chi Minh City—and the Coopers were continuing on to Hong Kong. Sheri, Talia, Austin, and Alexis were scheduled to begin the long journey back to America after that brunch.

But the six other riders agreed they weren't leaving Alexis. At least not until they had to. They'd remain in Hoi An the next day, hoping (along with her) that Austin would turn up. Alexis had come to realize that this library, now the wine bar, had become the little group's sanctum sanctorum and war room: it was where they had first gathered when the crisis had begun, and it was where they would congregate now to make their decisions.

"I'll call his parents," Alexis said now to no one in particular. "Austin's. It's late morning in the Berkshires."

"That's where they live?" Sheri asked.

"Yes. They're semiretired. They live in Lenox. Western Massachusetts."

"I'd try not to alarm them," Scott suggested.

She understood why he would say such a thing, but still she felt a ripple of anger and snapped, "I'm pretty damn alarmed, Scott. They should be, too." She knew her response had verged on the unreasonable, but she didn't care.

"How well do you know them?" Talia asked.

"I don't. We've never met. All I know about them is what Austin's told me. And they're not very close. That's clear. I think Austin was hoping this trip would rebuild the family bonds. Re-establish some of the ties that have frayed."

"Austin said something to me about that," said Colleen, the youngest of the tour guides. "His dad served here?"

"Yes. His uncle, too. And his uncle died here in 1971."

"Are they estranged?" Scott asked. "Austin and his parents?"

"Oh, it's not that bad," she told him. "I mean, I met Austin in the spring. I know he's gone to the Berkshires to see them at least once since then. He spent the Labor Day weekend biking in Massachusetts because I was working."

"Biking," Talia repeated, nodding. "Of course."

"And you've never met them?" Scott pressed.

"Nope. But, then, I haven't introduced him to my mother, either, and she lives in New Jersey and works in Manhattan."

"Why?" Talia asked, frowning ever so slightly.

"Time. Distance. Work."

"Sounds like a physics equation."

"Oh, if you knew my mother? Introducing my boyfriend to

her? Infinitely more complex than physics, in my opinion," Alexis said, her tone more sheepish than declaratory. "Our relationship is . . . fraught."

"How so? You said she works in the city."

"She's based there. But she's an investment banker, and so she travels a lot," Alexis replied evasively, an excuse to migrate her response from rapport to logistics. Discussing the afflictive and wearisome realities of her relationship with her mother was just too long a conversation to have right here and right now. Then she rose and left the library to call Austin's parents from the privacy and the dark of the terrace that looked out upon the infinity pool. It had underwater lights and looked strangely sacred at this hour, especially the way the branches and great leaves from the tropical plants around it undulated in the evening breeze. She got the number from information. The answering machine picked up after the fourth ring. She imagined Austin's father outside raking leaves and his mother putting one of their gardens to bed. She saw phantasmagorically beautiful piles of red and yellow and orange leaves, a pumpkin on the porch steps of a white clapboard colonial. For all she knew, however, his parents were at a grocery store or even still in bed, ignoring the phone because they were sleeping late or having sex. She realized that she had no idea how a couple their age spent their days when they were alone. According to Austin, his father had married late and had his one child late: he was the Coopers' age, and apparently not in nearly as good shape. He walked with a slight limp, Austin said once when he had had a lot to drink, and had endured a variety of large and small illnesses over the years, many of which he attributed to his time in country. To his time right here. His mother, who was eight years younger than her husband, was a dynamo and took spectacular care of his father as the aches and pains of old age grew more frequent and more pronounced. She had only recently retired from the middle school in Pittsfield where she'd been the principal for a decade and a half.

Alexis hung up when the answering machine kicked in. She

was about to say their son was missing, but couldn't bring herself to panic them. Not just yet. God, did they even know she existed in their son's life? They had to. But she realized that she couldn't be sure. So, she stared at her phone and wondered whether she should take a breath and call back. Leave a lengthy message introducing herself and telling them exactly what she knew and what she didn't, speaking with the authority she used when she was speaking to family members or friends who were waiting outside the ER cubicles where she had just finished sewing or intubating or resuscitating someone, or after a patient had been admitted and was either in a bed upstairs or on a gurney in a corridor awaiting a room.

Or, yes, after a patient died. That happened, too. It was an emergency room in a hospital, after all. People arrived dead and they couldn't be saved, or they arrived so close to death that there was no pulling them back from the brink.

In the end, she did call back. She said simply who she was—a friend of Austin's, she decided upon at the last moment, fearing that if she said "girlfriend" and he hadn't told them about her, their feelings would be hurt—and to please give her a call when they had a moment. When she was done, she realized they would see that it was late at night here in Vietnam, and they might wait until the morning. A lot would depend on what they heard in her tone.

She considered calling her own mother. But she wasn't prepared yet to have that conversation. Maybe if her mother were a different sort of person—the sort of mom some other girls had, a Marmie from *Little Women,* or an individual as gentle as her father—she might have called. But her mother made tiger moms look like laid-back hippies, especially after her husband died when Alexis was in the third grade. Her mother was loving without being compassionate, caring without being kind. In all fairness, she was also one of the reasons why Alexis had gone to med school. Her mother had driven her: compelled her, pushed her, pressed her. She saw her potential. Dina Remnick was a human prod, importunate and intense. A moment ago, Alexis had told Talia that her mother was an investment banker. She was, in fact, a senior partner—and a senior partner at a large bank on Maiden Lane in lower Manhattan.

Moreover, as she had just confessed (and it had felt like a confession), her mother hadn't even met Austin. They'd toyed with different dates for a dinner in New York City, and twice had actually gotten one on the calendar—no small accomplishment, given how much her mother and her boyfriend traveled, and her own schedule at the ER. And both times, Austin had had to cancel, once because he had to help entertain a hospital donor and once because he was asked to fill in at a conference in Chicago. Her mother had felt slighted and scorned because, in her opinion, neither her interest in meeting this new beau nor her own time, which was pretty damn valuable, had been taken seriously by this suitor. (And both times, Alexis herself had been frustrated and furious, but Austin had managed to dial down her anger with apologies that were sincere and with flowers that were lavish and lush.)

In any event, that phone call to her mother? It could definitely wait until the morning.

·   ·   ·

But she did call Eleanor Thomas, her closest friend since she had moved to Manhattan. She felt an acute need to talk to someone she knew and who really knew her. Eleanor—who went by Ellie—was a veterinarian a few years her senior who worked at an animal hospital on the Upper East Side and still described herself as a southern girl. She'd grown up in South Carolina. They each had a small apartment in the same rent-controlled building in the East Village, a soulless fifteen-story concrete rectangle built in the 1960s, the apartments lacking balconies or views or windows in the kitchens. Most of the world thought it was an NYU dorm when they passed it. The two of them had met in the elevator, a pair of women from different floors who, it was clear, were single and didn't wear heels at work. Since then, Ellie had met Austin a couple of times, and it was clear to Alexis (and reassuring) that Ellie liked him, too.

She phoned the animal hospital, hoping to catch her between cats and dogs, and she got lucky: the vet was finishing up with an animal and would be available in a minute or two. And so, despite the cost of waiting, Alexis did wait. She listened to the recorded admonitions to vaccinate one's pets and the ads for dog walkers and groomers, and paced amidst the small gardens surrounding the pool, eventually sitting down on a chaise near the very one where earlier that day she had hoped to hear her phone ping with a text from her boyfriend. Finally, Ellie came on the line, and Alexis could hear the trepidation in her friend's voice. She knew that no one called this late at night from Vietnam unless something had gone horribly wrong.

"You're right, I am calling with bad news," Alexis said, and then she told her the little she knew.

"This sounds pretty disturbing on the surface. But maybe just on the surface. Want some platitudes?" Ellie asked her when she was done.

"Yeah, I do," Alexis said. "I really do. Lie to me."

And so Ellie did, telling the woman whose father had died when she was a girl and who hadn't a sibling to talk to that Austin was fine and would appear momentarily with a perfectly logical explanation. She told Alexis stories that were obvious and stories that suggested a fertile imagination, tales that included incredible, unfathomable coincidences—meeting long-lost friends from college on the road and getting hammered on Bia Saigon—and hypotheses that Alexis had certainly considered but found comforting to hear voiced by her friend: Austin had been hit by a car and taken to a hospital, where he was still unconscious but was going to be fine. The FBI attaché didn't have this information because Austin hadn't been brought in on a bike and whoever she had spoken with at the hospital hadn't made the connection. Austin had been robbed of his wallet and his bike and his phone, and was now walking and hitchhiking his way back. All of the stories, whether they involved an accident or alcohol, shared one thing: a happy ending. In all of them, either Austin was going to return to the elegant little hotel in Hoi An any moment now or she was going to get a phone call from a hospital telling her that they had an American named Austin Harper and he was asking about her and he was going to be discharged in the morning.

"Thank you," Alexis said when Ellie eventually ran out of stories. Even Scheherazade had had a finite supply.

"This may still turn out okay, Lexi," Ellie told her, but it was apparent that the optimism in her tone was forced. Ellie was the only person in the world who called her Lexi. She'd started calling her that one night in a bar soon after they met, teasing her about something, and the moniker had stuck.

"I know," Alexis agreed, even though in her heart she didn't believe that. But, still, she had been buoyed, if only slightly, by Ellie's encouragement. After they hung up, she stood and felt the cool, sepulchral night winds against her face.

.   .   .

Alexis watched Scott and Giang devour the scallops and the duck the chef had prepared for them, but now she was more tired and wrung out than hungry, and so she only ate a little of the tofu and lemongrass, and she ate that mostly because she knew that she should. A bellman brought her the clothing that she and Austin had bought yesterday—his suit, her cheongsam—and then she went up to bed. She took another tranquilizer and pulled on a crimson sleep shirt. Outside her window, a smile of a moon sat in the sky, yellow and crooked and sharp.

She wondered if she would have called home if her father hadn't died almost a quarter of a century ago. In her memory, her father was the one who would have said the right things now, but she knew in her heart that she gave him attributes that may have been more imagined than real. Were it not for the photos she had of him, including the one of him someone had taken at her dance recital when she was in the second grade, she wouldn't even re-call what he looked like. His voice had long grown vaporous and faint, because it existed now only on those VHS cassette tapes that she could no longer play and neither she nor her mother had taken the time to have converted into digital files. These days, those tapes were drowning in mouse shit and dust somewhere in her mother's attic.

He'd died in a car accident. Skidded on black ice into the con-crete stanchion of a bridge on a cold night in March and passed away in the ambulance on the way to the hospital, despite the ministrations of the EMTs. She knew now the sorts of things they had probably done to keep his heart beating until they reached the ER, but from the little she had learned of the accident, it was clear that his injuries had never been survivable. Not even an open coffin at the funeral. People, including Austin, liked to suggest that his death was the real reason she had become an ER doctor, but she thought that sort of psychoanalysis was both sim-plistic and wrong. There were too many other reasons. Still, there were moments when paramedics would be telling her about the patient they were wheeling into the cubicle, barking out back-ground and vitals, when briefly she would imagine the EMTs try-ing to keep her father from bleeding out and then simply trying to keep him breathing. And, of course, she thought of him almost always when they brought a car crash into the ER. (She hated to reduce people to their accidents or ailments—*There's a stroke in cubicle eight,* or *There's that OD in three*—but she knew that she did, if only because shorthand saved time and saving time could save lives, and *car crash* was a pretty efficient two-syllable descriptor.)

Her father, before he had died, had been a literary agent. He had read to her four picture books every night before bed when she was little, and then—even when she was old enough to read to herself—for easily forty minutes a night from chapter books. He was coming home from the train station after a dinner with an author, one of those rare evenings when she was home alone with her mother, when his car had hit the black ice and spun into the buttress of a bridge.

She thought of his black marble tombstone in the cemetery in New Jersey, and tried to imagine it among the cities of the dead they had ridden past this week in Vietnam. Some families here still exhumed their dead relatives after three years in a temporary plot, sometimes a rice paddy or field, lovingly cleaned the bones, and then reinterred the remains in the great, sprawling necropolises that appeared out of nowhere in the countryside. Occasionally, they used loose stones instead of a concrete lid on the crypt so that the soul might more easily soar. According to Giang, on the chosen day they would retrieve the bones, they went well before sunrise, so the deceased would feel no pain from the sun after three years underground in the dark.

And then there were the magnificent family temples that the wealthy built for their ancestors, rich with golden pagodas, flying dragons, and rainbows of glazed tiles.

Ancestor worship. That was the term Giang had used.

She opened her eyes and wrote Austin another text:

I don't know where you are and if you'll ever see this. I don't even know if you're alive. But please come back. Please. Come. Back.

After she had pressed Send, she rolled onto her side. She had never told Austin that she loved him because he'd never said those three words to her. But she thought she did—no, she knew she did, she knew this now that he was gone—and so reached for her phone and texted him:

I love you.

Then she tossed her phone onto the mattress behind her, within reach if his parents should call back, and brought her knees to her chest and wrapped her arms as tightly as she could around her shins. He had never slept in these sheets because they'd been changed in the morning, and so there was no trace of him in the bedding. She could breathe in the aroma of the sheets and the pillowcases, but she'd never find him. She opened one eye and gazed at his black roller suitcase on the rack beside the closet door. It looked like it belonged in a Marriott or a Hilton, not this elegant bedroom in what had once upon a time been a French colonial mansion. Still, it only made her long for him even more.

What was that Vietnamese word for when you miss someone? When you long for them?

Nhớ.

It had come up while they were walking along the Perfume River in Hue. Their guide had said the water most likely had gotten its name from the fragrance of the orchid and frangipani flowers that fell into the river as it flowed past the citadel that once housed the Nguyen dynasty. But, he'd added—and here was where Alexis heard the word—the water was also where the concubines bathed and where in myth one young woman had taken her life because she would yearn so desperately for her king when he was away or with another of the courtesans.

Alexis loved the phonetics of the word. N-yo. To her, it sounded almost, but not quite, like a single syllable.

She recalled how in the summer Austin had toyed with the idea of getting a pet turtle. He'd researched painted turtles and red-eared sliders, and he'd talked about it all with ever greater earnestness until, suddenly, it dawned on him: the animal would outlive him. They lived forty or fifty years. If he cared for it properly, and he insisted he would, it would be a pet for life. Forever. And clearly that sort of commitment terrified him. One Saturday he had insisted they visit a pet store that sold turtles, and the two of them had watched the animals for an hour. He pointed at one and observed, "God, see him? The two of us would grow old together. We'd be like those retired old guys at the diners who have breakfast together every Tuesday or Wednesday, and they have all these memories that no one else has, because they're the only two who are left."

He'd never see her text, she decided. She knew it. And suddenly her eyes were starting to well up, and she thought of the cutting kit that she had created when she'd started work at the hospital in New York and refreshed periodically, but had never—not even once—used. At least not yet. Still, she was relieved it was so very many time zones away. No, if she wanted to cut, she could. She would. She'd take a needle from the sewing kit in the hotel room bathroom. She'd go downstairs to the hotel kitchen and swipe a paring knife.

But she wouldn't. At least not now. At least not tonight.

Instead she did what she did when she was younger and, with the help of the therapist her mother had found for her, had first started to fight hard against the urge to cut: she stripped off her nightshirt and went into the shower. There she turned on the hot water—hotter than she would normally tolerate—and instead of standing beneath it, curled up in that same little ball on the tile, and she sobbed and sobbed so that her body shook and her tears ran down the drain, lost in the torrents of water.

5

Two of the men walked him from the van along a slate walkway, while Douglas trailed behind: Austin was aware of the crack of the cleats on the bottom of his bike shoes against the slabs. Then he could hear the van being driven a short distance—no more than fifty yards, he guessed—and being parked there.

"There are three steps, then a front entryway, and then you'll be inside," the other American told him.

He nodded beneath his hood and carefully lifted each foot to climb the stairs. He wanted to be obedient, though he knew he was deluding himself if he thought good behavior or submission would in any way affect their decision whether to kill him. If they spared him, it would be for no other reason than because they believed he could still help them. But the urge to live? It was unrelenting and it was ferocious. He knew that most people would say almost anything or do almost anything if they thought it could buy them a little more time. He was no exception.

He guessed they'd only been driving an hour, but he had to admit that it was hard to gauge time when you had a canvas sack over your head. Douglas hadn't said a word to him once they had started off. No one had spoken.

The front door sounded heavy when they closed it, and inside he smelled bleach. A lab, he wondered? But then he heard the sound of oil spitting in a wok and smelled scallions and lemon basil as well.

"We're here," Douglas said. Then, to someone else, he added, "You can take off his hood now."

When the Vietnamese kid removed the canvas sack, it took a moment for his eyes to readjust to the sunlight. He saw they had brought him to a modern house, single story, with one great room with a kitchen separated from couches and a coffee table by a bar with a black marble countertop. A girl who couldn't have been more than fifteen or sixteen was at the stove cooking lunch, and she was dressed in blue jeans and a long-sleeve floral tunic. She may have nodded at the group when they arrived and Austin was still wearing that hood, but now she was focused entirely on the vegetables on the cutting board and the wok on the range. He saw there were three place settings at a dining room table.

"You must be hungry," Douglas told him.

"A little."

"Don't worry: Phuong isn't going to serve anyone rats." Douglas stood for a moment before one of the couches, coughed into his elbow, and waited. "Aren't you going to join me?"

So Austin went to the leather chair opposite the couch, and as soon as Douglas sat, he did, too. He saw an elegant go table and, on a wooden pedestal, an antique opium pipe that looked like a dragon and he thought had probably been carved from an elephant tusk. There were two copper basins sitting in stands with round holes on the tops to cradle them: handwashing stations from an earlier era, he guessed.

"You must be thirsty after all that biking. How far had you ridden this morning?" He crossed his legs at his knees and brushed a bit of dirt off his slacks.

Austin looked behind him and saw the young man who'd pulled off his hood was standing by the door with an assault rifle, watching them. "Not very far. I'd only been riding about ninety minutes," he answered.

"That's not very long, is it?"

"Not really."

"You didn't seem tired. You didn't seem in particular need of a lift," Douglas said.

"No."

"Good for you."

"But you did give me a lift."

"True enough."

He smelled fish sauce now and reflexively looked back at the kitchen.

"You are hungry," Douglas said.

"I guess."

"You started a little south of Hoi An, correct?"

"That's right."

"You have the cao lau last night? Local specialty. Noodles and caramelized pork."

"We went shopping."

"Ah, the tailors. No doubt you bought yourself some very fine clothes and paid practically nothing."

"I got a suit and—"

"Of course you did," Douglas said, cutting him off. Then he brushed a lock of hair off his forehead, gathering himself. It was as if he regretted snapping at him just now, and Austin found himself incapable of interpreting the other man's signals. If Douglas was allowing him to see the inside of the house and feed him, was that an additional sign that they weren't going to execute him? They'd put a bag over his head, but now they were chatting about local cuisine and what he'd bought yesterday in Hoi An. When he said nothing, one of the other Vietnamese men who'd led him inside told Douglas, "I'm having a glass of wine." He was standing beside Phuong, the young woman who was cooking. "We have a nice Bordeaux. But, Austin, the bar is fully stocked. Is there something stronger you'd prefer? Or, perhaps, less strong since it's only lunchtime?"

Austin turned around to look at him: he'd seemed so much more menacing when he'd appeared out of nowhere on the road, supervising that kid with the gun.

"Water, please," he replied simply.

"Only water? We also have fresh watermelon juice."

"Water's fine."

Douglas smiled at him, then looked over toward the other fellow. "Since you're pouring, Bao, I'll have a glass of the red, too."

"I think you'll like it."

Bao brought Austin his water and Douglas his wine. Then he went back to the kitchen and said something to the young woman at the range.

"Cheers," Douglas said, raising his glass.

"Cheers," Austin agreed halfheartedly. He recalled that some people thought it was bad luck to toast with water, and right now he needed all the luck in the world. And so, as if it might actually make a difference, he brought his glass back into his lap without taking a sip, resting it on his cycling shorts.

"Tell me, Austin: why are you here?"

"I'm guessing you won't believe me if I tell you it really is just a bike tour. That's all."

Douglas sipped his wine and pursed his lips. He shook his head. "No, you're right. I won't believe that. Not for a second. I see you were in Hanoi for a day, when you first arrived. I checked the schedule. Take a cyclo tour?"

"I did."

"Visit the mausoleum? Ho Chi Minh's?"

"Yes. And the Hanoi Hilton."

"And now you're enjoying your time on a bike?"

"I am. We were rained out yesterday, which was a shame because it was the day I was going to see where my uncle died and where my father was wounded. And so I was trying again today. It's why I wasn't with the rest of the group."

"Did you get there?"

"No. I need to go up and over the mountain."

Douglas seemed to think about this. "Your itinerary brought you nowhere near Ho Chi Minh City this time."

"That's right."

"So you didn't visit the National University?"

"I did not."

"Well, even if you had, they're dead, you know. The scientists."

Austin knew this. He waited. Remained silent.

"No, we didn't kill them. Natural causes. Their . . . research."

In his mind, he saw the swelling and the bleeding and the sores, the respiratory failure, but still he said nothing. He didn't dare.

Douglas smiled, and Austin could feel the humid draft of condescension when he continued, "You said you were a miserable biologist in college. I checked. You really were. Have you understood a damn thing you've seen in either place? Ho Chi Minh City? New York?"

"I've understood enough. I mean, you knew what you were getting with me. I've never pretended I'm something I'm not. And I'm not a scientist."

Bao sat on the couch beside Douglas. "Maybe he's gotten better."

"Maybe he has," Douglas agreed, the two of them speaking of Austin in the third person as if he weren't there. "But he only survived his science requirements in college because he cheated on midterms and he cheated on finals. Isn't that right, Austin?"

He nodded. He didn't know how they'd found out. He'd thought that scandal would be hidden forever, just like the time he'd violated the academic honor code at boarding school. His grandfather had made sizable gifts to the school and then to the university.

"I think he's here in the capacity of a salesperson," Douglas told Bao.

"He does work in development now," Bao observed.

"Ostensibly," said Douglas.

"Yes. Ostensibly."

"But I've no idea if he's any good at that—any good at all.

Development is in the same wing as the university's research labs, which is the only reason he's ever had value." Douglas pulled Austin's phone from his pocket and handed it to Bao.

"Password, please?" Bao asked, and Austin gave it to him. He watched Bao open his phone and start moving amidst the apps. He assumed the fellow was reading his emails, and so he was surprised when Bao observed, "This new girlfriend of yours: the blonde. She's very pretty. How is it having a girlfriend where you work?"

"It's a big hospital, as you know," he said, unsure whether they were about to threaten Alexis.

"Still, Austin," Douglas said, "you don't shit where you eat. No good comes from that."

"We hardly see each other there."

"Fair enough," Douglas murmured, as Bao continued to scroll through the photos.

"And I'm guessing this older couple with you at Fenway Park is your parents. True?" Bao asked.

"Yes. You're a baseball fan?"

He shrugged. "Not really. But I enjoyed the vibe at Fenway the time I was brought there by friends. I discovered I actually liked Neil Diamond when the crowd started singing 'Sweet Caroline.'" Then he hummed a few bars, smiled, and put the phone down on the couch beside him.

"So, Austin," Douglas continued. "The labs. Development— or advancement, as some of you fund-raisers like to call it. Let's talk about all of that, shall we?"

"You make it sound so easy," Austin told him, feeling the need both to defend himself and remind them of his value. "The university labs and hospital development are pretty separate. A Berlin Wall. Yes, it's a university hospital, but a guy like me doesn't just go in and out of the labs. They're not even on the same floor. You have no idea how hard it is, what I do. The protocols, the clandestine meetings. It's why you need me. You know that. Wilbur's work is so damn secret."

Douglas lifted his wineglass from the coaster on the coffee table and then turned toward Bao. The coaster really wasn't necessary, because while the table's base was black wood, the top was striated white marble; the surface reminded Austin of stracciatella gelato. "Wilbur? Should be Dr. Sinclair to you."

"Fine. Dr. Sinclair."

"I don't know if I told you this, Bao, but Austin only changed his major from premed to business because he couldn't hack organic chemistry two. Once he'd been caught cheating, his only out was a massive gift to the university from his family and a new major."

"I made it through orgo one," Austin volunteered. After he spoke, he hoped he sounded more sheepish than scared. He hoped he hadn't sounded antagonistic.

"A low bar," Douglas replied simply. "And you cheated."

"Besides," said Bao, "it's the biology that really matters in this case."

Douglas sipped his wine and returned it to the table. He folded his arms across his chest and sat back. "What the hell are your strengths, Austin? You suck at chemistry. You suck at biology. You suck at darts, for God's sake. What, really, are you good for?"

The short answer, alas, was sales, but he couldn't say that after Douglas's accusation that he was in Vietnam as a salesperson. He considered answering *negotiating,* but he feared the response would only anger Douglas further and serve as a straight line. *Negotiating? Okay, smart boy, negotiate your way out of this.* And so he replied with what he hoped was an inoffensive joke, "Biking. Maybe."

"You a blood doper, Austin?" Bao asked.

"God, no. I'm not that good."

Bao laughed. "Ah, but if you were that good, you would be?"

"Oh, he would, Bao," Douglas assured the other man. "Austin would. There is no shortcut he won't take. If there's a way to cheat, he'll find it."

"I'm honestly not sure why you'd say that," he told them. "I'm really—"

"You don't have an honest bone in your body, Austin!" Douglas snapped, cutting him off. "You don't have an honest cell, you don't have a single honest nucleus. You don't have a single honest strand of DNA. You're a liar and you're lying to me right now." He took a deep breath. He was utterly disgusted.

"I'm here on a bike tour, Douglas. That's all this is," Austin said.

Bao looked at Douglas. "What would be a good word to search in his emails? I was thinking *plague*."

"I'm going to wager that's too obvious," Douglas said.

"*Rat?*"

"Sure. Maybe you'll find it used autobiographically, as in, 'I'm a duplicitous rat.'"

"Rats are many things, Douglas, but not duplicitous. Pretty much what you see is what you get," Bao corrected him, his tone good-natured. Then he continued, his voice growing more serious, "There's also the Korean and the dude from India. They have their own labs at the complex, too."

Austin took a breath and said adamantly, "I'm telling you both the truth: I've come here on vacation. I've come to pay my respects to an uncle I never met and see where my father was wounded in the war. That's all this is: a bike tour and an attempt to connect with a part of my family. It's—"

"Horseshit! That's complete and utter horseshit, Austin! Who are you meeting? Or who have you met with already? What's that expression, 'in country'? You've been in country nearly a week. Who did you meet with and what did you give them?"

"I met with the tailors in Hoi An. I bought a suit. Other than waiters and shopkeepers and docents and the people on the bike tour? Not a soul. I swear it."

Douglas reached into the breast pocket of his blazer and pulled out a dart. "This is a Black Widow. Tungsten barrel. Steel tip. Sharp. Newly sharpened, as a matter of fact." Bao rose from the couch and sat on the arm of the chair in which Austin was sitting. He took his right wrist in both hands and yanked him forward.

"I promise you, I've seen no one, Douglas," Austin said, and now, for the first time, he heard the pleading, desperate tone in his voice. He saw where this was going.

"You're lying. You're not even good at that."

Bao pulled his wrist toward the white marble tabletop and Austin tried to resist, but the other fellow was strong—considerably stronger than he was—and he knew that what loomed was going to hurt far more than a bullet in his biceps. Bao placed his hand palm down on the slab and, for good measure, spread wide his fingers. Douglas leaned forward, the dart gripped in his fist like an awl. He raised his eyebrows and waited. He didn't have to tell Austin that this was his last chance; it was obvious.

"Okay, then," Douglas murmured, and he drew in his lips and shook his head. Then he slammed the dart down as hard as he could into the back of Austin's hand, and Austin's bellow was so loud that the barbets on the roof of the house and the Siamese firebacks in the trees by the pool all flew away at one time.

The cranes and the tigers and the water buffalo were victims of the herbicides, too, you know. Sometimes they died because their habitat was destroyed and sometimes it was because of the poisons themselves. The active ingredients in Agent Orange are unpronounceable: trichlorophenoxyacetic and dichlorophenoxyacetic acids. (You thought I was exaggerating. I wasn't.)

But there were some species that did not merely survive but, in the end, flourished. Among them? Rats and mice.

Scientific research showed that dioxin caused cancer in lab rats, and even future generations of the animals had a greater likelihood of developing all kinds of nasty diseases.

But the ones that didn't die? They thrived in the new Vietnam. They flourished. Partly this was the habitat that was created in the wake of the massive defoliation. Partly it was cellular. Darwinian.

And, of course, it wasn't just rats. It was people. The Vietnam Red Cross chronicled millions of human deaths from the defoliant and nearly half a million children born with birth defects. Half a million. Think about that. But if you managed to survive the American War, it was a bustling new cosmos and a brave new world.

Anyway, the big question was this: why were some rodents so bloody fruitful in the midst of all that chemical carnage and why were others mere evolutionary jetsam?

In upper Manhattan, researchers at Columbia studied mouse shit from eight buildings across the city, and found the usual pathogens, such as Salmonella and E. coli and Clostridium. But they also discovered nine new strains of antibiotic-resistant bacteria. That was problematic—even unnerving—if you worked at the metropolitan hospitals.

(As far as I know, the other hospitals near us—NYU Langone and Bellevue—had labs that did research with rats and mice, but I believe a lot of it was focused on rodent behavior and neuroscience. No one ever told me if they were also studying the pathogens that local rats carry.)

Some people presumed that, in the end, it would be the roach that ruled the world. But others? People like me? We put our money on the rat.

6

They wrapped a towel around Austin's hand, and Bao held it between his own hands, applying pressure to stop the bleeding. The tableau was weirdly tender, Douglas thought. The dart hadn't augured a hole through one of the bones there—Douglas hadn't created stigmata in Austin's palm or dinged that impeccable marble tabletop with its tip—but clearly it had broken something. It had, most likely, chipped off a piece or two. Douglas guessed that Austin's ER girlfriend would know the name of the bone. Douglas knew he didn't. He was pleased he could even recall doc-speak for the term when little chunks of bone splintered off in a break: *comminuted*. And Austin, if he did know the name (which Douglas rather doubted), was too busy hyperventilating from pain, his head bowed, clearly desirous of swearing but keeping his mouth closed. He'd howled when the dart had smashed into those little bones in the back of his hand, but now he was silent. And the dart? Wasn't even dented.

"Just breathe," Bao was murmuring, his voice melodious and kind. "Deep breath in, now out." Austin's skin had become the color of the paint Douglas's interior designer had picked out for the guest bedroom in his duplex: eggshell, the paint chip said. Usually Austin's skin was darker. This wasn't the first time that Douglas had turned a man pale, and the physiology of it never ceased to fascinate him. The blood literally drained from a person's face, centering around the heart and lungs for a dimly contemplated but often critical burst of energy: it was all part of that great animalistic fight-or-flight response.

"Yes, wait for the pain to recede a little bit," Douglas told him. He glanced at the tip of the dart. "I think I've made my point."

Austin looked up at him, and his eyes were hooded and small; he was thoroughly diminished and absolutely terrified. Douglas had only bothered to put a bag on his head to give him the delusion that he had a prayer in hell of getting out of here alive, and it crossed his mind that perhaps he'd skewered him too quickly.

"Would you like some more water?" Bao asked, but Austin shook his head.

Douglas noted that Phuong had resumed her work in the kitchen, but the young woman was still keeping a wary eye on the three men in the living room. He presumed that Bao had told her what was coming, and he doubted it was the first time that she'd seen a man hurt. Still, he regretted wounding the other American in front of her. They'd have to deal with the rest of it—finish it—elsewhere. Bring him someplace. He didn't want her to witness that or even be aware that the execution was occurring on the property. He rather doubted that Bao did, either. In fact, the more Douglas thought about it, the more he wanted her convinced this would still end well for the man in the sweaty bike shorts and Speed Racer cycling jersey. They'd tell her they were driving him back to the hotel. Plausible deniability. It was better for everyone.

Austin might even believe the plan—certainly he'd want to believe it—and that would make his end a little bit easier. The last moments were always less stressful, less emotionally fraught, when the dead man walking had managed to delude himself into believing that somehow he'd been spared. Douglas decided he'd tell him whatever lies would elicit the information he wanted. Really, why not if it made this easier for everyone?

And then it came to Douglas. They'd give the man back his bike. After sunset. He knew precisely how and where the man would have a lethal accident.

"Phuong," Bao asked, "perhaps you could bring our guest some painkillers. The red pills. Ibuprofen. I believe they are in the medicine cabinet in the bathroom." She nodded and turned off the burner beneath the wok and started down the hallway.

Austin closed his eyes and rolled his neck. When Douglas watched him, he thought of yoga and the woman who taught his favorite class back in New York. They looked nothing alike—that yoga instructor was gorgeous, all lean limbs in Lycra—but that neck stretch just now was similar. "Tell me why you're here, Austin. You're in your salesman mode, I get it," he said. "But this is your absolute last chance."

"I'm here—" he began, and then he stopped.

"Go on."

"Yes, there is a market, Douglas. Or I thought there might be."

"Of course there is. Who's your buyer?"

"And if I tell you?"

"We give you your bike and send you on your way."

"Assuming I can even grip the handlebars."

"That is my assumption, yes. You bike back to your hotel in Hoi An. Or not. We drop you off somewhere and you return to your little bike tour friends. Your eye candy in scrubs. You tell the folks there whatever the hell you want."

"Including the fact you broke my hand with a dart?"

"Well, perhaps you should take some license there. Leave Bao and me out of it, thank you very much. But I think you know that's in your best interest, too."

Bao released his hand, and Austin curled it on his lap, keeping it draped inside the towel. Douglas supposed he was afraid to look at it. He doubted it was still bleeding. The back of the hand didn't bleed much when punctured. Douglas knew this from experience. Austin wasn't the first person he'd spiked.

"It's clear," Bao told Austin, "you were going to meet with

or already met with someone. Someone in Hue or Hoi An or Da Nang. That's where you were going or coming from—and not because of some need to reconnect with the ghosts of your family."

"Why didn't you just follow me, if you believe that?"

"We feared a bloodbath," Douglas said. "Or, so to speak, we feared swollen lymph nodes—those horrific buboes the size of chicken eggs—fever, chills, skull-piercing headaches. And, yes, those disgusting bleeding welts. That kind of bloodbath. Not pleasant. And, as you know, antibiotic resistant. Fatal. I assumed you'd brought the toxin with you: that you had it on you. Perhaps, we were mistaken. We'd do a full-body cavity search, but, well, I can't imagine anyone—even you—would try and mule that stuff in your system or up your ass."

"No."

"There was none in that little bike tour bike bag you strapped to your bicycle."

"Of course not!"

"But it's still evident that you came all the way to Vietnam and then parted with your bike group because you're up to something, and that something has absolutely nothing to do with sentimental bullshit about your family. You don't know the meaning of ancestral worship. You wouldn't know what the fuck to do at the cities of the dead other than take a selfie. So, I want to know what you're really doing here—and with whom."

"I'm supposed to tell you that I was on my way to meet with someone—or I already met with someone—and then you'll send me home?"

"Chastened and forgiven." Douglas pointed at Austin's hand and murmured, "A little worse for the wear, maybe. But otherwise intact. Still breathing."

"And what will you do to them? Those people?" Austin asked.

Douglas smiled munificently. "Nothing—assuming you don't reach out to them ever again. I'm really not interested in a trade war." Once more he was lying, and he supposed that Austin knew this. But, like everything else he was hearing, he would convince himself it was the truth because he wanted so desperately to believe it. Then Douglas watched Austin's face as the fellow reviewed his options in his mind. He really had none. Even a man such as Austin—frat-boy bonhomie in a thirtysomething body, a man whose perspicacity stretched to the horizon when it came to bars and bicycles and what the hospital called "institutional advancement," but a mere fogbound trawler when it came to common sense and knowing the limits of an acceptable betrayal—could see that.

"And you won't hurt anyone on the bike tour?" he asked.

"Are they involved?"

"Of course not!"

Douglas shrugged. "Then why in the name of God would we? Are you worried about your doctor friend? If so, let that go. She's of no interest to me, unless you're using her for something."

"No. I'm not."

Douglas nodded to reassure him, but Austin had unintentionally planted a seed. He hadn't meant to; that was among the last things the fellow probably wanted. But he had. Douglas couldn't help but wonder now: Had Austin actually recruited the woman for something? She worked at the same hospital. She was a physician, which meant that she knew something about biology and chemistry. And Austin was an excellent salesperson. Most of the time he was convincing people to do ridiculously altruistic things with their money. "Good," he said simply, but he made a mental note to research her a little more carefully. "Then I have no bone to pick with her." He raised an eyebrow and motioned ever so slightly with his jaw at the dart on the coffee table, a gesture that was irresistible after using the words *bone* and *pick* in the same sentence.

Bao swallowed the last of his wine. "We should let you get back to your group. Tell us where you were going—or where you've been."

"The three place settings?" Austin asked, his tone more confused than anxious.

"What about them?"

"I . . . I thought . . ." he stammered.

"You thought you were joining us? No. I mean, you're welcome to. But I assumed you'd rather rejoin your friends in Hoi An."

Phuong returned with a bottle of painkillers, already open, and shook two red pills onto the table.

"Thank you," said Bao. "But give him three."

She nodded and dropped another pill onto the marble.

"Phuong is my daughter, Austin. She's the third place setting," Bao continued.

"I see. My mistake."

"Not at all," said Douglas. "Phuong, do you mind, please, adding a fourth setting? It looks like Austin is going to stay for lunch, after all. A little sustenance will do him good." Then he turned back to the bicyclist. "So: the name of your buyer."

"Middleman, really," Austin said.

"Fine. Middleman," Douglas agreed, fighting hard the urge to roll his eyes.

Carefully Austin lifted his left hand off his right and reached for the pills. "Not poison, right?" he asked, only half kidding.

"Not poison," Douglas reassured him.

Austin swallowed the pills and finished the water in his glass, and then, after taking a breath, told them where he was going and with whom he was going to meet.

FRIDAY

7

In the morning, Alexis awoke to the alarm on her phone, pressed the button to shut it off, and in her grogginess momentarily forgot that Austin wasn't there. She presumed he was beside her in that massive four-poster bed, and rolled over to drape an arm upon him. To nuzzle against his neck and bare chest. But, of course, she saw that his side of the bed was empty and instantly recalled that he was gone. That he had disappeared. She knew she'd slept only because she had taken that second Xanax.

It was a little after seven. The area's FBI attaché and the Vietnamese police were due in less than an hour. She checked her phone again, hoping for a miracle: a text or a missed call from Austin. But there wasn't either. Nor was there anything from Austin's parents. The solitude in the room felt alive, a thing that breathed beside her. She sighed and rubbed her eyes, her temples, trying to exorcise the phantom presence. Then she pushed off the sheet and stood up, inhaling deeply to pull herself together. Despite the amount of time she had spent on the floor of the shower last night, she went there first, but she resolved this time to remain on her feet.

. . .

Her mother was neither humorless nor grim: both of those words were too strong. But she was demanding and relentless, and for a long moment Alexis stared at her phone. It was 8:30 at night in New Jersey. Arguably, it wasn't a bad time to call: her mother might still be at her office or she might be commuting home. She'd pick up if either of those possibilities were the case. If she were at a dinner meeting, she probably wouldn't pick up. On the other hand, Alexis was seeing the FBI attaché in a few minutes, so she didn't have a lot of time. She shook her head: she should have called her mother yesterday, when she had tried to reach Austin's parents. If she phoned now, her mother would chastise her both for not calling right away and for calling when she really didn't have time to speak, and her mother would—with cause, for a change, with cause—have Alexis feeling so guilty that she would be angry inside. Angry on top of being frightened and angry on top of being numb with worry and (yes) grief. Because Austin was gone. Because Austin had disappeared. Because Austin, most likely, was dead. And fear and anxiety and remorse were just too toxic a combination, too poisonous a cocktail, and so she didn't phone her mother. She would wait to call until after she had met with the FBI.

. . .

She was still standing there in her room in a sundress printed with lilacs that was absurdly cheerful for her world that moment, her phone in her hand, when she heard a car in the long driveway and peered out the window. There actually were two. There was a white police car, a Toyota, with its iconic blue stripe and red, white, and blue light bar across the roof, and a black SUV with embassy plates. Together they coasted to a stop. It wasn't even seven thirty. Either Toril Bjornstad had made very good time, or the gravity of the situation had compelled her to leave early. She was the first to emerge from the cars, climbing from the front passenger seat of the SUV: she was tall, her hair the reddish brown of Tuscan terra-cotta, and she was wearing navy slacks and a white blouse. She had a blazer in her arms, and it was evident that she couldn't decide whether protocol should triumph over comfort: already the air was getting sticky, and, in the end, she tossed the coat back into the vehicle. Alexis guessed that the woman was her age. Her driver—or her bodyguard or both—was Vietnamese and wearing dress slacks and a white shirt, but no necktie. Based on the gray in his temples and the way his middle had started to grow a little heavy, she estimated he was at least a decade older than Toril. The two police officers who emerged from the cruiser were also Vietnamese and dressed in black uniforms. The pair could have been a father and son: an avuncular-looking gentleman with a thick shock of white hair and a lean young man who shared the same aquiline nose and placid smile.

She went downstairs, and Scott and Giang were already welcoming the four of them into the villa. Everyone introduced themselves, and she was struck by how firm Toril's handshake was. She tried to recall everyone's names, but by the time they had passed the dining room where the rest of the bike tour was eating breakfast, she had forgotten every name but Toril's, and every detail but the fact that the older of the two police officers was a captain. She was relieved that both of them spoke English and she would not need someone to translate. This was going to be hard enough as it was.

As they were finding seats in that beautiful library, Scott offered to get everyone coffee or tea, but Alexis alone said that she could use some coffee. He nodded and said he'd be right back.

Toril began, and she wasted no time on pleasantries. She opened a leather portfolio with a pad on one side, used her thighs as a desk, and said, "Captain Nguyen and Officer Vu are with the Canh Sat Co Dong. The CSCD is the mobile unit that focuses on terrorism, organized crime, and—I'm sorry to use this word, Alexis—kidnapping."

The word was in some ways a relief because it suggested that Austin might still be alive, and Toril's comment and demeanor struck Alexis as both eerily reminiscent of her own behavior in the ER and utterly unlike what she did. It was similar in that Toril went right to work, and it was different in that she didn't endeavor to establish any sort of relationship. The one universality of every ER patient Alexis saw was this: they hadn't planned on coming. The people she saw never woke up and noted a scheduled visit to the ER on their calendar or phone. And so it could be profoundly destabilizing for them, especially given how vulnerable—sick or mutilated, wounded or dying—these patients were. They didn't feel good, that was almost an absolute. They were, sometimes literally, in shock. Frequently they were in their pajamas. Often they were stripped fast, their clothes cut away, because of the injury. Usually their breath was bad, sleepy or boozy or sickly, or it had just been too damn long since they'd had a chance to brush their teeth. The elderly on occasion were in diapers and hadn't changed that diaper in hours. Alexis never lost sight of their need for connection when she worked, even when it was the eleventh hour of a night shift and all she wanted was to sit at the bench before her locker and peel off her scrubs and go home. Always (at least when the person was conscious and neither drug addled nor drunk) she tried to bond in some small, distinct way with whoever was on the gurney or the bed before her: remind the patients that they were, first and foremost, people.

"So, you think Austin might have been kidnapped?" she asked the agent.

"It's possible."

The captain leaned forward. "And among the possibilities to explain your boyfriend's disappearance, that is among the ones most likely to have a happy ending, Ms. Remnick."

"Yes," she agreed, "that thought crossed my mind. And the other possibilities?" The two policemen and Toril exchanged looks, and so Alexis added, "Let's not mince words. I know this is bleak."

"Well, if he wasn't kidnapped," the captain told her, "then it's possible that he's had a very bad accident: he was hit by a vehicle, perhaps, or he rode over the side of one of the switchbacks on the route. The Hai Van Pass can be a treacherous place to ride."

Toril jumped in: "Right now, Quang—Captain Nguyen—has a CSCD team running the roads he should have been on, looking for any sign of an accident."

"I assume the regular police found nothing last night."

The agent shook her head.

"And then," Quang continued, his voice grave, "there's the possibility that he was murdered."

"That's crossed my mind, too, of course," Alexis assured him. "After all, he's a rather obvious tourist. But would someone be so desperate as to kill a lone bicyclist for whatever cash or credit cards he had on him?"

"Did he have his passport with him?" the captain asked.

"No. It's upstairs in our room. He had it in his suitcase that was transferred here by the touring company."

"But someone might not know that when they attacked him," Quang said. "And then there's this: maybe he's run away."

"He wouldn't run away."

"People do. It happens. I don't personally believe that. But we can talk more about the possibility."

"I'm assuming there's been no use of his credit cards," she said.

"We don't know that, yet," Toril told her. Then she raised her eyebrows: "Alexis, what was the last thing he posted on the social networks?"

"He's not on the social networks. He's just not into them."

"None? Not even any dating apps."

"I don't think so. He thinks they're ridiculous."

"The dating apps or, I don't know, Facebook or Snapchat or Twitter?"

"He told me that he'd never used a dating app. As for the rest? He never got any satisfaction in posting party photos or kitten pictures on Instagram. It's just not his thing."

"So, he was on them once?" asked the captain.

"Yes."

"Where does he get his news if he isn't on Twitter?" the FBI agent asked.

"He has plenty of news apps on his phone. In New York, he subscribes to a paper copy of the *Times* and a bunch of magazines. And, in all fairness, I think he also left Facebook and Twitter a few years ago because he was creeped out by the way Russia uses Facebook and by the way some companies mine our data."

"I see."

"Have you tried tracking his phone?" Alexis asked.

"We have. Nothing. It's either off or disabled or out of juice."

"How did you two meet?" Quang asked her.

And so Alexis told them the story of the Saturday night when he came into the ER with a bullet wound in his biceps, and as she spoke, she could see everyone in the room growing fixated on the tale. It sounded silly and sweet—downright comic—when she shared it with other doctors or friends from college, or at a party in the East Village. But she realized quickly that what she had always viewed as a quirky, idiosyncratic first meeting sounded far more ominous now that Austin was missing.

"Look," she added, when she could see the intensity in everyone's gazes, "it's an ER. I see a lot of weirdness. You have no idea how many people I treat who've tripped over their dogs. You have no idea how many babies or toddlers I see who've gotten into something nasty under the sink. You have no idea how many stab wounds and bullet wounds come through, especially between Thursday night and the small hours of Sunday morning. An urban ER is just a madhouse. It's crazy town."

"Did the police ever catch the shooter? The person who shot Austin?" Quang asked.

"No."

"So, it was just some junkie who was holding up the bartender and accidentally fired his weapon. When he did, you're telling us, he panicked and ran."

"That's correct."

"But the bullet hit your boyfriend and not the bartender? Why was he pointing the gun at Austin? He wasn't behind the counter."

"He—the junkie—was waving the gun around. He fired it, we all assume, by accident. He just happened to hit Austin," she explained.

"This is according to Austin," observed Toril. She sounded dubious.

"This was according to the police, too," Alexis said defensively.

The captain turned to the bike tour leaders, who were leaning against one of the magnificent bookcases with the villa's old farm records. "How common is it for you to allow your guests to ride alone? Does it happen on most excursions?"

The two men looked at each other nervously, wondering who would stick his head on the chopping block and answer first. Scott shrugged and replied, "It happens on maybe a quarter of the tours. Maybe. There's a rider or a couple or maybe a parent and one of his or her teenage kids who clearly know what they're doing. It's not a big deal. So we let them carry on. And Austin was—is—a terrific rider. And this is at least his second time in Vietnam. So, I must admit, I really didn't think twice about it. Did you, Giang?"

"Not really. Besides, we felt bad that the ride over the Hai Van Pass was rained out on Wednesday. That happened to him last year, too. It would have been awful to deny him the chance to go where he wanted, especially given why he wanted to go there."

"You didn't have a support van trail him?"

"No."

"Do you usually?"

"Look," Scott said, his tone defensive, "we offered to ride with him, we offered to trail him. He seemed a little insulted by the very idea. Besides, there was all that emotional baggage about his 'journey.' His 'emotional journey.' We gave him the space that he wanted."

The captain already had what looked like a copy of the possible routes for the day, and Alexis wondered whether it was a general one from the company's website or the actual one with the specific options they had all been given the day before. "So, he wasn't riding alone simply because he was the only one in the group who wanted to climb Highway One? There was more to it than that?"

"Yes," Alexis explained, "it was sort of a pilgrimage. He wanted to see the spots—roughly—where his uncle died and where his father was wounded in the war. His father was shot in an ambush near here. He lived. But his uncle was killed when he stepped on a landmine. Austin planned to collect a few pebbles from each of the sites and bring them home."

The captain leaned forward and nodded. "Well, there was a hell of a fight in Hue."

"His family arrived after that battle."

"After that, it was all Viet Cong around here—and mostly up in the hills. Away from China Beach. My father was NVA: Army of North Vietnam. A little farther north. Khe Sanh. The Americans were never going to mistake him for one of the doubtfuls."

"Doubtfuls? That's so interesting you'd use that word. That's an ER word," Alexis told him.

"The American soldiers used it when they couldn't decide whether one of us was Viet Cong or a civilian on their side. They used it when they had no idea whether to trust someone—or, for that matter, a whole village. When in doubt? Well, you know. We're not all that far from My Lai. What does it mean in a hospital?"

She averted her eyes. She hated to admit this. "It's a triage shorthand for someone who probably isn't going to make it. You try to save them; you try as hard as you can. But you know in your heart, you—they—never had a chance."

Quang smiled cryptically. "Well, back in the war, most doubtfuls sure as hell didn't have a chance."

"No. I guess not," she admitted, and she felt a deep and unexpected pang of guilt at the American legacy here.

And almost as if he sensed it, he threw her a lifeline of sorts. "Your people were here for a decade. We fought you for ten years. But the French? A century. And before them? The Chinese. You were but a blip." And then he reminded her that most American soldiers weren't committing war crimes. "You probably don't know this, but there was an antiwar protest in Pleiku from the American soldiers and nurses there."

She waited.

"In November 1969, during that great Thanksgiving holiday of yours, all the troops at the base there refused to eat their turkey and mashed potatoes and, along with all the nurses, fasted for the day. Maybe your boyfriend's father or his uncle was there then."

"No," she said. "They both arrived after that."

"Were your boyfriend's family marines or just regular old-fashioned grunts?"

"Just soldiers, I guess," she told him. "His uncle died a lieutenant. His father was a private when he was shot."

Alexis saw Toril straighten her back: it was almost a flinch. It was quick but it was clear: something had made her uncomfortable. She couldn't imagine it was the conversation about a war that had ended generations ago. Clearly the captain hadn't been offended in the slightest. Nor was it likely that anyone cared now that some soldiers and nurses once upon a time had passed on the stuffing and gravy at an army base outside Pleiku. She considered asking Toril what she was thinking, but the woman looked down at her portfolio and then directly at her: "Austin told you that his father and his uncle were near here? And his father was wounded in an . . . an ambush?"

"Yes," she said, but the tone in Toril's voice—the incredulity—had already set off an alarm inside her. "That's right."

Toril took a deep breath and steepled her fingers in front of her face, gathering herself. Then she said, her voice firm, "When you told me last night that two family members had served here, I had their records pulled. I was curious. His uncle did die in Vietnam. That's true. But it wasn't near here. As a matter of fact, it was up in your father's part of the country, Quang. Near Khe Sanh."

The captain nodded and seemed about to add something, but stopped himself. "Go on," he said simply.

"Austin Harper's father was stationed nowhere near here. He was at Long Binh. That's where he was 'til he was sent home."

"I'm sorry, I don't know where that is," Alexis said, confused.

"It's near Ho Chi Minh City. It was army headquarters. He was a . . . a lifeguard."

Quang and the other Vietnamese officer smiled at each other. In other circumstances, they might even have laughed. Still, the captain couldn't resist telling Toril—an inside joke, it seemed— "He was U.S. Army and REMF."

"So it would seem," Toril agreed.

"And that stands for what?" Alexis asked.

The agent cleared her throat uncomfortably. "It means, basically, rearguard."

"I'm a grown-up. Tell me what REMF stands for," Alexis said, and then, fearing she had sounded too much like her mother, added, "Please."

"Fine. *Rear Echelon Mother Fucker.*"

"It was a term the guys actually fighting my father would use for the guys playing basketball and sitting around getting tan at the swimming pools," Quang explained. "You were a grunt? You might get a silver star. You were REMF? You might get a silver paper clip."

"And they actually had a swimming pool at an army base?" Alexis asked.

"Pools. Plural at Long Binh," said Toril. "I mean, I don't have the exact number, but easily ten or twelve of them. Plus the tennis courts. The softball fields. The libraries. The weight rooms. The nightclubs. The base was massive. Largest in country, by far."

"And Austin's father was a lifeguard?"

"The family has a . . . a pedigree, Alexis. Boston Brahmin. Patrician, old money. You must know that."

"I know a little. But, clearly, not a lot. I didn't know his father was a lifeguard, for God's sake."

Toril sighed. "Look, I don't have a whole lot here. But from the little I've seen, I would guess that Austin's uncle was the family rebel. He didn't play the Harper family get-out-of-jail-free card. He volunteered and served like any grunt or any nurse from the middle of Iowa or downtown Detroit. And, in all fairness, Austin's father probably could have gotten a deferment, if he'd wanted. Or he could have been one of the thousands of well-connected young men who joined the National Guard and kept Alabama safe from the Viet Cong. But he didn't. So I'd cut him some slack."

"I'm not judging him for that. I'm not judging him at all. I'm just trying to understand my boyfriend's lie. Was his father even really wounded?"

"Sort of."

"Go on. I need to know this."

Toril was looking down at the paperwork before her as if she didn't quite believe it herself. It was as if she had to read it twice. "He was injured in a go-cart accident on the base. He rolled the cart. It was kind of a race, apparently. Broke his leg and his hip."

Alexis sank deeper into the plush couch, wanting to lose herself in it. She felt humiliated and betrayed, and could just as easily have laughed as cried.

"A go-cart," she repeated.

"That's what it says."

Her voice was small, almost girlish, when she said—and she almost couldn't hear her own words because the thrumming inside her head was so marked it was like she was under water—"Is there any chance that all of the paperwork you have is incorrect? Wrong person or something? Austin told me that his father was shot."

"It's possible, but not likely. I have the service records here of both siblings."

"So, he was lying. Austin."

"Look, I don't know the specifics of what he told you," the agent said. "Perhaps it's all just a misunderstanding."

"Perhaps," she said, nodding not so much because she agreed, but because she was digesting all that she'd just heard. Trying to make sense of it. She rested her elbows on her knees and her chin in her hands, utterly bewildered. Was he ashamed of his father? Embarrassed by how he'd been injured? Or was it possible that it was his father who was self-conscious of how he'd served, and so he had lied to his son? She wanted to believe this, and brightened ever so slightly at the idea. But she had the common sense to know it was unlikely: it was far more logical that Austin had lied to her than that his father had lied to him.

Still, she offered it as a possibility—and realized as soon as she had spoken that it had been a mistake. Toril and the two CSCD officers shared a glance, and she knew the look well: she shared it with doctors and nurses weekly when a patient or a patient's parents or friends were lying to themselves.

Nevertheless, the captain indulged her and said, "At this point? Anything's possible."

And maybe it was those two words—*anything's possible*—but another revelation was beginning to appear through the mist in her mind, racing like a distant corsair on the horizon, and just as unnerving. This one, however, didn't strike her as quite so delusional. "Or," she began, speaking to all of them in the little hotel's living room, at once light-headed with anxiety at the idea and resolute as she tried to bring it into focus, "Austin did lie. But he lied because he needed an excuse to come here. To come to this part of Vietnam."

8

The term came back to her once again: pattern recognition. When it wasn't, for instance, a broken leg on a stoned college student who fell down a flight of stairs or (worse) a half dozen broken bones on a half dozen high school musicians whose van had just been rammed by a dump truck at the intersection of Twenty-Seventh and Third, it was about deciphering the clues. It was harder in the small hours of the morning and it was harder when you were exhausted and it was harder when the ER was in chaos. Those were the moments when she—when any ER doctor—was most likely to miss something and make a mistake. And right now, she was feeling far more like a patient than a doctor, and she needed to flip the tables and force herself to think clearly. To see what was really before her: what was fact and what was (and she cursed herself for using this word, but it fit) hypochondria. She needed to separate the real from the imagined.

Before the police captain left the small hotel, Alexis had gone upstairs to her room and retrieved the energy gels she had found on the road and given them to him inside the plastic bag. She had used her phone to show the officers the images of the spot where she had discovered them, and then airdropped the photos of the topography onto the captain's phone. She'd told him precisely how many kilometers they were from the hotel when she had lifted them from the asphalt. She'd also brought downstairs

Austin's passport, and the day manager for the little hotel made photocopies of every page for both the police and the FBI attaché. She'd turned over to the police his laptop and his tablet.

After the two officers had left, Alexis asked Toril if she could have a moment alone with her. Toril said yes, and the two women walked out into the morning heat and stood beneath the trees on the eastern edge of that enticing infinity pool.

"It's nighttime now in the Berkshires," Alexis began. "When we were inside, you said the embassy was going to call Austin's parents. He's been gone nearly twenty-four hours. I want to pick up the phone and call them myself. Pull them from whatever they're watching on TV and ask, 'What the hell? Who is your son really?' Ask the dad, 'Did you lie or did your son?'"

"Yes, you could do that, but you've never even met them. At this point, why go there?"

"Because I want to. Because I want to know the truth."

"Let's assume that Austin . . . exaggerated. If he did, he had his reasons for telling you one thing—"

"For lying," she corrected Toril.

"Okay. For lying. And there are lots of reasons why he might have lied that have nothing to do with his disappearance. I think everyone's first instinct inside was the right one. Occam's razor: the most likely explanation is probably the correct explanation. For whatever the reason, he was ashamed of his father's service record. That may be all there is to it."

"I know. It makes me a little sad that he wouldn't tell me the truth, if that's all there is to it. But . . ."

"Go ahead."

"But it's also possible that there's a link between his lying and the fact he's gone missing."

The attaché sighed and adjusted the cuffs on her blouse. "Which is precisely why you shouldn't follow up and we should. Or, to be precise, why we will support Captain Nguyen when his team follows up. The CSCD knows what they're doing. They're good, Alexis. They're really good."

"We were supposed to fly home tomorrow. Tomorrow night. Austin, me. Some of the others on the bike tour. Ride in the morning, have a farewell brunch, and start the long trip back to America."

Toril seemed to think about this. "We should know more before then. We should know more by tonight," she said finally, but her tone was utterly without conviction.

· · ·

Alexis dabbed at the beads of perspiration on her forehead and watched the black SUV drive away, wondering if she'd ever see Toril again. She knew she would hear from her. She wandered around the villa to the patio off the dining room, thinking, her mind conjuring accidents and abductions, but also conspiratorial eddies that lived in the undertow she could feel but never quite see.

Finally, she decided to get it over with and phone her mother. It was well after dinnertime in New Jersey now—or lower Manhattan if she'd had a client dinner—but her mother would still be awake. The skies had grown overcast, formless and gray, and already the air was sticky. As one, the rest of the bike tour had chosen not to check out of the hotel and ride south as planned to their final destination and their final night as a pack. They wanted to stay with her in Hoi An, and it was only at her urging that the rest of them had gone with Giang and Colleen for a short ride in the area, while Scott remained back at the hotel to assist Alexis in any way that he could. But they all seemed genuinely desirous of remaining here and waiting for news of their missing compatriot.

Her mother picked up the phone on the third ring and began, "Alexis, what's happened? You're still in Vietnam, aren't you?"

"I am," she said, "and, yes, something has happened. Are you alone? Home?"

"Yes, I'm alone and, yes, I'm home. Talk to me."

And so Alexis did. She told her mother most of what she

knew, a sort of *Reader's Digest* condensed version, fending off her mother's interruptions—her questions, her incessant need for clarifications—as if she were fencing, and eventually reached the present: that she was standing alone on the patio of a stylish boutique hotel in Hoi An and there was little she could do now but wait. She had chosen not to tell her that it seemed Austin had lied to her about his family, both because she didn't have any answers yet to explain why he would, and because she was hoping to avoid the inevitable judgment it would elicit, a condescension that Alexis knew she would feel even through the satellites and cell towers—a gossamer of thin or even non-existent air—that linked them. Perhaps if her father were still alive and on the phone, too, she would have told them. He might not have had helpful advice, but at least he would have been sympathetic.

"Will you still start home tomorrow night?" her mother asked her when she was done.

"I don't know. But I doubt it. I hope to know more later today."

"What are the people like? The people on the bike tour with you?"

"They're fine. Two single women older than me from the Midwest. A nice couple from North Carolina. A husband-and-wife pair of very athletic accountants."

"What do the others do? The ones who aren't accountants."

"As in for a living?"

"Yes."

"The couple from North Carolina are retired. Now, it seems, they travel. The other two? Talia is head of ethics and compliance for some pharmaceutical company in St. Louis. Sheri is a lawyer."

"Good, enlist her right now to—"

"No, there is nothing to enlist her to do," Alexis said. "She's about to leave on her bike with everyone else. They're going to go for a short ride."

"Well, I can make some calls at this end. The FBI, the American embassy."

"The FBI attaché was just here. I told you that. She came because I called the American consulate."

"I can call someone in Washington."

"No. You can't. Or you shouldn't. Trust me, there's no one you can call in America."

"There's always something more you can do. You know that. It's like a political campaign. There's always one more phone call you can make, always one more house you can visit, always one more door—"

"Not this time. I'm sorry, but sometimes there just isn't. Sometimes—" And she stopped herself, not because she had had an epiphany about Austin and what might have happened to him, but because she was recalling one of those moments when someone had died in her little cubicle because there was just nothing more that she or anyone else in the ER could do. People died. Rain fell. The leaves changed. "Sometimes," she continued, "you just have to accept the fact that it's either someone else's responsibility now or you've done all you can. You do nothing. You wait."

"Is that what you do when someone comes into the hospital and—"

"Yes. Sometimes you do nothing because there's nothing more you can do," she said. She watched a mosquito land on the back of her free hand and blew him away. She recalled the Hollywood codes she'd been part of over the years. When someone's mother or daughter, father or son, was dead and not coming back, but their family was in the ER, sometimes you worked and worked to try and resuscitate the body even though it was beyond repair. They called it a Hollywood code because it was little more than bad acting. It wasn't really calculated: no one ever said, *Let's pretend to do something because the stiff's husband is eight feet away.* It was only when you were done, sometimes hours later when you were having a cup of coffee or staring aimlessly at your locker, that someone would mumble, *Hollywood code.* And you'd murmur, despondent that someone had died, *Yup, he was always a doubtful.*

"Alexis," her mother said.

"Mom."

"Are you—"

"No. I'm not. Of course not. It's been years. I'm fine. Or I'm as fine as I can be, under the circumstances."

Somewhere in the trees on the property was a bird whose call sounded something like a monkey's, and she looked out toward the lush jungle and tried to spot it, but she couldn't.

"What do his parents think? What are they doing?" her mother asked.

She heard human chatter as well. It was coming through the screens in the French doors. It was Talia and the Coopers. They were talking about water bottles and energy gels because they were gearing up for their ride. She considered running upstairs and offering them Austin's unopened gels since it didn't seem like he was going to need them, even if they found him or (miraculously) he returned that very moment. But her mother was repeating her questions, her tone growing adamant.

"I haven't reached them," she answered.

"You haven't reached them?" It was one of her mother's favorite ways to prod her: to change a pronoun but essentially repeat exactly what her daughter had just said, transforming the statement into a question. *You haven't studied for the MCATS? You haven't called the landlord? You haven't asked anyone about a different schedule?*

You haven't called your therapist? You're a doctor, for God's sake!

Haven't. If she were ever to make a list of her least favorite contractions, *haven't* would win. Even on the other side of the planet, Alexis could see her mother shaking her head in disdain as she spoke.

"No," she replied simply. "I've left them messages."

"And they haven't called back? Good God, you're in Vietnam. I'm in New Jersey. Give me their number. I'll call them right now."

"You don't need to do that. The consulate here is—"

"I do need to," her mother said, cutting her off. "I want to help. It's not a big deal. It will take five minutes."

"Five minutes? Seriously? You're going to call people you've never met and tell them their son is missing in Vietnam and you think it will take five minutes? If you managed that call in five minutes, it would be . . ."

"It would be what?"

"It would be a case study in cruelty. Besides, the FBI is on it. The American consulate is on it. They're calling."

"Cruelty."

"Yes."

"I was only trying to be efficient."

She felt a raindrop on her shoulder and another on her upper arm, and so she ducked inside. She was relieved the other cyclists hadn't set off yet. If they waited fifteen minutes, the rain might be done for the morning. Perhaps for the day. And they'd be spared.

"I know," she told her mother, regretting the way she had snapped at her, but only because it wasn't worth the energy it had demanded—and would demand in remorse. Her mother was who she was. Not once had she asked her daughter how she was feeling, not once had she expressed any sympathy that the man that her child had been dating for over six months had disappeared. Her mother had started to ask if her anxiety had led her to resume cutting herself, which perhaps was as close to empathy as her mother got—at least overtly. But Alexis was done with that and reassured herself that she had been for years. "I get it." Then she said good-bye and told her mother that she would call her in the morning in New Jersey—before bed in Vietnam. She said she would know more by then.

"It's okay to wake me up," her mother said. "Call me the minute you get any news."

"Sure," she agreed, though she understood that she had kept from her mother the absolute latest news: the sad truth that the man she had been dating, that man she had texted into the black hole of his vanished cell phone the words *I love you,* was, for whatever the reasons, a liar.

9

And once more Alexis was at the infinity pool, alone with her magazines and her phone, once again anxious and unable to focus. It wasn't a revelation to her that she was most grounded in the madness of the emergency room—a world that demanded she work fast and solve problems quickly, and that her attention invariably be on someone else—but the realization had never been more clear to her than in the last twenty-four hours in Vietnam, when most of the time all she could do was sit and wonder and wait. It didn't help that Austin's parents hadn't called back, but it was clear from her conversation with the FBI attaché that it was unlikely they would now that the FBI was handling it.

She considered going to her room and getting into her bathing suit. She might as well swim. A little exercise always helped. But that seemed frivolous. And she felt the need to be dressed, just in case.

Though just in case of what, she couldn't say. The hotel was empty now of everyone but the housekeeping staff and two people in the kitchen who had little to do since there were no guests but the bicyclists, and all but one of them had gone for a ride and wouldn't return until midafternoon. She didn't expect the police would be back anytime soon.

And so she compromised. She slipped off her sandals and pulled her dress up to midthigh, and sat on the tile with her legs extended into the warm water of the swimming pool. She studied her toes and noticed that already she needed a pedicure.

Austin, she knew, had very hairy toes, which was a sign of excellent cardiac health. It meant that he had good circulation. She had teased him about it one of the first times they had been together in bed.

Earlier that week, they'd biked past a life-size wooden stand of a woman in a tight blue dress that fell to her knees and a matching cap—a uniform that looked like it belonged on a flight attendant but judging by the red cross on her cap was apparently supposed to be that of a medical professional of some sort—and Giang had explained it was the sign for a Western or American pharmacy. The stand was in front of a shack, and Austin had joked that the patients at their own hospital would be better served if the doctors and nurses there dressed like the woman in the ad stanchion instead of in scrubs.

Now she heard the patio door opening and the efficient young chef who made them their eggs—omelets and scrambled and even Benedict for the two accountants—was approaching with a tray of thin coconut cookies, a teapot, and a cup and saucer. She started to stand, but he shook his head and called out to her to relax, to stay where she was. He knelt beside her, and even in his pants and a crisp white shirt, he was so thin and bony that she thought him birdlike. Based on his skill, she guessed he was nearing thirty; but a part of her thought he looked barely twenty-five.

"I thought you should eat," he said.

She gave him a half smile. He could have sent out an assistant or bellman with the tray, but he had brought it himself. "You're right. I probably should. Thank you."

He told her the tea was steeped and ready, and asked her if there was anything else she needed. She told him no, though of course there was actually a very great deal that she needed.

He pointed at the pair of decorative ponds near the pool. "If you'd been here in June, the lotus flowers would have been in bloom. They're my favorite part of the gardens."

"I've had lotus soup and lotus tea. They were delicious."

"My grandmother won't eat them."

"Lotus flowers?"

"She thinks they're sacred. Especially the red lotus."

"I'm not surprised. I saw so many crypts in the city of the dead outside of Hue with beautiful lotus flowers carved on them."

He touched his chest. "The heart. They heal a broken heart—but not medicinally. Spiritually. Hers are so beautiful. Here at this villa, in our ponds, we have white ones and red ones. She grows only the red ones."

"Because she had a broken heart?"

"Because everyone has had a broken heart."

"I'm sorry I missed them."

"You should come back next year. It's our national flower."

"The red lotus?"

He nodded.

"I should come back," she agreed, but he was smart: he probably knew she was only being polite. He bowed ever so slightly and returned to the kitchen inside the mansion.

For two months, once she had started to settle into a schedule at the hospital in Manhattan, she'd tried yoga. There were classes at the gym. She could handle it physically, but not mentally. She'd sit in the lotus position, her legs crossed and her heels on her upper thighs, her spine straight, and she was incapable of clearing her head. She finally accepted the reality that she was not hardwired for meditation. If she was connected to the earth like a lotus—a soul climbing from silt to sky through the water—she was never going to be the sort to reach heaven or find peace through quiescence. For better or worse, she was clearly her mother's daughter in this regard.

She looked at her phone and calculated what time it was in New York City. She understood that Captain Nguyen and his team were investigating Austin's disappearance here in Vietnam, but she wondered what was occurring back in America. Someone had reached out to Austin's parents. But what else? Who else?

His supervisor at work? Yes, she thought, definitely his boss. Her name was Sally Gleason and Alexis had met her two times, both brief. The first was when Austin had introduced her when the three of them—Austin, Sally, and herself—had all been in the hospital cafeteria at the same moment. The second was at a summer fund-raiser for the hospital at a rooftop bar overlooking the East River. If it weren't so late at night on the East Coast, she'd see if she could find her number and call her. She presumed that Austin had lied to her, too.

She speculated that even the very first time she had met Austin, that Saturday night in the ER, their meeting had been built around a lie. Perhaps he hadn't been shot by a junkie in a bar.

But hadn't the police investigated the crime? Of course they had. There had been witnesses. Still, this trip was grounded on a fabrication, and his family history was a fiction, and who knew what else was smoke and mirrors. No wonder he wanted nothing to do with the social networks.

An idea came to her. Austin wasn't on Facebook, but his boss, Sally, likely was. She went to the app for the social network on her phone and found Sally right away and sent her a friend request. She did the same thing on Twitter and LinkedIn. She didn't know if she'd ever hear back from the woman and, if so, when, but Alexis wanted to know what stories, if any, he had shared about his family and their history here in Vietnam. She was curious what the people at the hospital knew about him.

She poured herself a cup of tea and sipped it as she ate the cookies. Yesterday there had been moments when she had envisioned Austin in an emergency room somewhere in Vietnam and had pictured a young doctor like her tending to him. She had seen the scrubs and the gloves and the stethoscopes that dangled like necklaces. She had seen him conscious and unconscious. She had seen nurses taking his blood pressure and physicians using trauma shears to cut off his jersey and bike shorts. But today? The tableaus were different, both because he hadn't turned up in a hospital and because he had morphed into a human cipher.

She scrolled aimlessly through news stories and apps on her phone and saw, much to her surprise, that Sally Gleason already had accepted her friend request on Facebook. The woman was awake. And so she typed her a message:

As you know, Austin and I are in Vietnam. I see you're still up. May I call you?

Within seconds, Sally said sure and provided her phone number. And so Alexis took a deep breath and rang her, despite the fact that it was nearly ten thirty at night on the East Coast. It dawned on her as she pressed in the digits that she had no idea where the woman lived. It was a Westchester area code, but in an era of cell phones, that meant nothing. Sally was in her midforties, and Alexis knew she was married. She guessed the executive had children, but she hadn't mentioned them in their brief encounters that day in the cafeteria or at the fund-raiser.

"Sally Gleason," the woman said formally.

"Wow," Alexis said, smiling slightly to herself. "Pretty formal for this time of night, especially since you knew it was going to be me."

"A reflex. It's how I answer the phone."

"Is now really an okay time to talk?"

"It is. My husband's asleep and the kids are asleep. Just me. I was on my iPad when you sent that friend request. All good."

"How old are your kids?" Alexis asked.

"Is that really why you called? Seriously?"

"No. I was just . . ."

"You were just being polite, I get it. That's sweet. Olivia is eight and Freddie is five. Look, I know Austin is missing."

Alexis watched two swallows playing along the surface of the pool and wondered if it was the same pair as yesterday. They were just so happy. She couldn't decide whether they were flirting—there was something lubricious about the pursuit—or whether it was a more innocent, avian version of tag. But it didn't matter.

They just looked like they were having so much fun. "The police called you?" she asked.

"Called me? Hell, no. They came to my office at the hospital. In person. And it wasn't the police. It was two FBI agents in dark jackets and boring neckties. 'International police cooperation,' they called it. Both were male, both straight out of central casting. They showed up around five fifteen, when I was trying to get out the door. They wanted to know what Austin does here and whether he was seeing someone for work in Vietnam. They wanted to know about you."

"Me?"

"You work here, too. At the hospital. Who knows? Maybe they spoke to people in the ER when they were done with me."

"No one I work with called me."

Even over the phone, she could hear the woman sigh. "They only left my office four and a half hours ago. So, for all I know, they only left the ER three and a half hours ago. If they even went there. And it's Thursday night—the start of the weekend for the serious partyers in our neighborhood. We both know what sort of chaos your friends might be dealing with. Maybe they were swamped at the end of the day. And maybe they're worried about you and saw no reason to add more crap to whatever you're dealing with. That would be kind of like piling on."

"I guess. But the FBI can't possibly think I had something to do with his disappearance. Certainly, the police here don't. Austin went off alone. He didn't even have one of the bike tour leaders with him."

"I have no idea what the FBI thinks, or whether they suspect you were involved with something, I don't know, unsavory. Until you told me that he went off by himself, all I knew was that he was missing. I think they were just doing the Vietnamese police a solid: helping out at the request of the FBI attaché in that corner of the world. Austin is, after all, an American citizen and he's disappeared."

Alexis closed her eyes and rubbed the bridge of her nose. She explained to Sally what had happened, filling in the blanks for her, and then got to the point of her call. "Austin claimed he was on this pilgrimage. That's why we came here. But I think he was lying," she said, and then she told the woman what he had told her about his family and what she knew now was the truth. "And so he brought me here . . . he brought me here kind of under false pretenses. He was lying. Did he ever talk to you about his family and why we went on this bike tour?" she asked when she was done.

"He told me the same fairy tale he told you. His dad and his uncle were both war heroes."

"Well, his uncle might have been. But nowhere near here."

"Right."

"And Austin definitely wasn't seeing some big donor?" she asked Sally.

"Yeah, our hospital has an extensive collection of high-roller philanthropists eleven or twelve time zones away. We depend upon big givers in communist Vietnam because they view us as an integral part of their estate planning," the woman replied, the sarcasm deep and rich.

Alexis felt a gust of wind and watched the thinner branches on an ancient tamarind, gnarled and skeletal, bow in the breeze. "So, you have no clue why he was really here," Alexis said.

"None. I mean, maybe he was up to no good. But we don't know that. Maybe he just had—excuse me, *has,* let's go with *has*—this one weird quirk: he lies about his father because he's ashamed of him, but he didn't have a nefarious reason for going to Vietnam."

"Did he ever lie about anything else? Did he ever get in trouble for anything?"

"At the hospital? No."

"Outside the hospital?"

"Not that I know of," Sally answered.

"I've been moving between devastation and confusion a lot the last few hours. I mean, I was a mess last night. A disaster. I wasn't great this morning. And then, when I learned he had lied to me—and what a strange and needless lie it was—I was baffled and hurt. I mean, why did we come here?"

"Maybe he'll tell you himself. Today. Tonight. When he turns up."

"You think there's hope?"

"Of course I do. There's nothing that would give me greater pleasure than to see him back in his office next week, having to listen to me give him grief for worrying the shit out of all of us, and for telling tall tales about his family."

Alexis nodded as if they were in the same room together. "Yeah. I like that idea. I like that image."

"Keep sending good vibes out there, Alexis. It can't hurt."

"I will," she said, and then they said good-bye and hung up. She suspected that Sally Gleason felt some of the shock she herself was experiencing—as well as the puzzlement—but none of the despair. This was, perhaps, the difference between two people whose relationship revolved around work and two people who, she realized, might once have been in love.

. . .

A few minutes later, her friend Ellie texted her, asking if there was any news. Alexis texted back that there wasn't. And so Ellie said she was still awake and asked if now was a good time to call. Instead of texting that it was fine, Alexis called her and brought her up to speed on what was occurring. After a moment Ellie observed, her tone hesitant, "Okay, let's suppose Austin does have a secret. Maybe it has something to do with his first visit to Vietnam."

"Such as?" Alexis asked.

"Maybe he met someone."

Instantly she understood what Ellie was suggesting. "I would use the word *mistress*," Alexis said, "but we're not married. Still, I hear what you're saying."

"I'm not sure you do. Maybe it was like a fling last year and he was just seeing her again for old time's sake. Maybe it's not even sexual now."

"And he wouldn't tell me? He wouldn't tell anyone?"

"Possible. Maybe he has a baby. A love child. Maybe there's some cute little infant he wants to meet."

She thought about this. "As far as explanations go, that one's better than a lot of possibilities."

"I mean, it's a reach."

"But not an absurd one. I'm going to share the idea with the police or the FBI here," she said. Then she thanked Ellie for checking in, and reminded her that she had animals to see in a couple of hours and should probably get some sleep.

. . .

The fact that she could do nothing and there was nothing to do was toxic, and so Alexis popped a Xanax and lay down on the bed in her room, hoping she might fall asleep until the other bicyclists returned. Scott had checked in on her at the pool, solicitous and kind as an uncle, but there really wasn't anything that he or the bike tour company could do, either.

And she did doze, but it was fitful, and she wasn't rested when she was pulled from a shallow sleep by the sounds of car doors slamming. By the time she went to the window, she saw a Vietnamese police car parked in the roundabout, but its occupants were already out of sight and, she presumed, entering the hotel's portico. She hoped they were bringing news that Austin had turned up in a hospital, hurt but with injuries from which he would quickly recover, but she feared they were bringing news that was far more dire. She ran her fingers through her hair and, as she started for the door, picked up her phone. She saw she had missed a call and didn't recognize the number. But she had a hunch and compared it to the direct dial number on the business card that Toril Bjornstad had given her, and sure enough it was a match. The voice mail was short and businesslike: the FBI attaché wanted Alexis to call her back.

She heard someone walking down the corridor to her room, and a moment later there was a knock on her door. As she expected, it was the day manager, a genial host, his shirt no match for a stomach that pillowed over his belt like a water balloon. "So sorry to bother you. Are you awake, Ms. Remnick?" he asked through the wood.

"Yes, thank you," she said. She didn't open the door. She was dressed but couldn't bring herself to face him. To face them. Not yet. In her head, she heard her mother's voice, judgmental and harsh: *Why didn't he call you Doctor?* And she heard her response, at once placating and exasperated. *Because he didn't know. He isn't clairvoyant.*

"The police have returned. Can you come downstairs?" he asked.

"I can," she replied. "I'll be right there."

Should she call back Toril first? Or should she let the captain tell her . . . whatever?

"Very good," he said, and she listened to him retreating down the hallway and then pounding his way down the stairs.

She decided she would ring Toril. If it was the worst news? She would rather hear it alone in this room, not downstairs with the officers from the CSCD. And so she sat down on the side of the bed on which she had been dozing and called the woman. When she got the agent's voice mail, she hung up and rang the consulate in Ho Chi Minh City. There a duty officer, a fellow with a deep, officious baritone for a voice, said Toril was unavailable.

"I'm returning her call," Alexis said. "It's important. I believe she has news about my boyfriend. An American named Austin Harper."

"I understand. The ambassador is down from Hanoi, and she's in with him. But I don't think it will be much longer."

Alexis sighed. "All right. Thank you. Just tell her I called back." And then she bent over and pulled on her sandals. She stood and considered brushing her hair, but saw no reason to bother. She could cope; she would cope. But it seemed frivolous to brush her hair. And if the news was the worst it could be? Her hair probably should be a mess. Oh, she wouldn't be a widow; far from it. She wasn't even sure what she thought this afternoon of the man who just last night she had thought that she loved. But she was definitely the girlfriend of a man who was, she feared— and another term came to her from the ER—*unfixable*. Beyond repair. One of the doubtfuls. Her hair probably should be a mess given the reality of what she was about to learn.

And so she opened her door and started down the hallway and then down the stairs. And there they were in the lobby, not even in the library. Captain Nguyen and Officer Vu of the CSCD. They were standing near the small, black marble obelisk where the guests checked in and checked out—there was a computer screen built into it at the top of one of its steep sides—chatting aimlessly with the day manager. Nguyen saw her and stood up a little straighter, his hands clasped behind his back. He bowed his chin, a nod of greeting, and when he raised his head their eyes met and an understanding flashed between them. The news was bad. That was clear.

"Captain," she said.

"Dr. Remnick."

"You've found him?"

He surprised her by shaking his head, but when he spoke she understood that really there had been no stay of execution at all. This was just a brief, flickering pause in the pain.

"We don't know," he explained, "but we may have. We are hoping you can—and I am very sorry to ask this of you—identify a body."

The news left her more weak-kneed than she expected, and she leaned her hips into the side of the obelisk. She doubted any-one had noticed. At least she hoped they hadn't. The day manager already was retreating, scurrying toward the kitchen and, Alexis presumed, the safety of hospitality: no doubt, he was going to return with afternoon fruit and tea for them.

"Yes, certainly," she said. "Where was he found?"

"We don't know for sure it is him."

"But it's a male. And I'm going to wager it's a male in bike shorts and the cycling jersey I described for you yesterday."

"I'm sorry to say that's all correct."

"Any identification?"

"More or less."

"More or less? What does that mean?"

"We haven't found his cell phone, but we have found his wallet."

"So it is him."

"It's likely him. The wallet was about fifteen meters from the body. The pockets in the bicycling jersey were empty."

"Anything in the bike bag? The touring company gives us these lunchbox-like things that sit on the backs of our bikes."

He shook his head. "There wasn't one on the bike. How are they attached?"

"Velcro straps to a bar above the wheel."

"I'm guessing it was thrown from the bike. We'll go back and see if we can find it."

The younger officer wrote this down, concentrating so intently on his pad that she had a feeling he was relieved he had an excuse not to make eye contact with her. Did she look stricken?

"You didn't say where he was found," she said. "And, while I'm asking, what's the condition of the corpse? How did he die?"

"The coroner says it was a traumatic head injury. But he had multiple injuries. He was hit by a car, it seems."

"You ran the roads," she said. "The leaders of the bike tour and I ran the roads. We saw no trace of him. Had he detoured someplace? Was he on the wrong road? Might he have been lost?"

"No. It was just . . ."

"It was just what? You can tell me."

"Just one of the hairpins south of the summit on the Hai Van Pass . . ."

"Go on."

"The cyclist was, we believe, hit by a vehicle there. He was sent over the guardrail and onto the rocks below. East side—the sea side. The bicycle was pretty badly mangled."

She recalled those switchbacks near the peak. She and Giang had looked over the side in a couple of spots and seen nothing. The drop wasn't far, maybe twenty or twenty-five feet. Still, that was plenty far if you were clipped into a bike and had just been slammed into by a truck or an SUV or one of those tour buses that took up most of the narrow road. "We were there yesterday. What time was the body found? And was the coroner able to establish a time of death?"

The captain smiled wistfully. "It's probably good you're a doctor. You can ask him if we leave now."

"The morgue is at the hospital . . . where? Here in Hoi An? Hue?"

"Da Nang. Dr. Tran speaks pretty good English, too. You should do fine together."

"Thank you," she said. Then she took the pen she found in a slot on the obelisk and scribbled a note for the day manager to give to Scott or the other bike tour leaders when they returned, telling them where she was going and what time she was leaving. "Let's go," she told the captain. "I don't want to miss the coroner."

Rat math is mind-boggling. It's not that it's complicated, even for me. It's just that everything about it feels exponential. Everything feels supersonic or—and I am choosing this word carefully—surreal.

Begin with the urban brown rat. The city slicker of rodents. The ones you glimpse when you're hailing a cab a little before midnight or you see racing into an alley as you're walking back to your apartment building or hotel.

Take their teeth, because in them you can see both Darwinian wizardry and rat analytics. Look at their incisors. They grow roughly five inches a year. Now, you don't see a rat with five- or ten-inch-long chompers, because they chip or wear down. But what may be even more remarkable than the speed with which a rat's teeth grow is how its teeth function: the two front teeth open a bit like a curtain when it eats, and a fold of skin serves as a dam between them, stopping the animal from swallowing something that it can't digest.

Better still, spend a moment with rat reproduction. One rat mom can give birth to ten to twelve litters a year, and the litters are fifteen to twenty baby rats.

Now, those figures assume there is plenty of garbage. But if there is? A rats' nest in the basement of your apartment building can quickly become a rats' nation. Oh, we work to poison them. Some people shoot them. We try and break their necks and backs in traps. But a rat isn't a mouse. A rat is a formidable enemy. A brown rat in a city stretches sixteen inches from its tail to the twitching, whiskered tip of its nose. And just as they're about sixteen inches long, they weigh about sixteen ounces. Sixteen and sixteen. That's what I mean by surreal.

10

The smell of the morgue in Da Nang instantly reminded Alexis of the smell of the morgue she had visited as a medical student. Antiseptics and bleach. It propelled her back to the biology labs those days her first year when she and the other aspiring doctors would dissect human cadavers. But those classrooms had had windows, while a morgue invariably has none. Not in America and not here in Vietnam. A morgue was a world of sharp, frigid lines and chrome that glistened, of kidney-shaped steel dishes for organs, and long, sloping autopsy tables with drains. Of body bags and walk-in coolers with body racks. She knew the odor would change when she saw the corpse. When she saw . . . Austin. The smell would become a stench, as the stink of decomposition superseded the aroma of cleanliness. It always did. Death trumped all. Always had and always would.

Toril Bjornstad had called back when they were driving here from the hotel, Alexis in the backseat of the cruiser, and they hadn't spoken long. Alexis by then had known at least as much as the FBI attaché. But they had agreed that they would speak more after Alexis had ID'd the body.

Dr. Tran, the coroner, was a tall man, slender but with broad shoulders beneath his scrubs. His hair had not yet begun to gray, and he had a trim chin curtain of a beard. She could imagine him cycling with Austin or throwing darts with Austin or simply drinking with Austin at some hipster bar in Greenwich Village or SoHo. The two CSCD officers had joined her in the first-floor corner of the hospital that housed the morgue, and so there were four of them in the sterile room. When Captain Nguyen had introduced her to him, he had told the coroner that Alexis, too, was a physician. It was clear the two men had a friendly relationship forged over crime scenes and cadavers.

"What kind of doctor?" Tran asked her.

"ER."

He nodded. "Well, then. Let me show you what we have."

He led them around a corner to a wall with refrigerator lockers and a steel table, and there, beneath a white sheet, was the corpse. Already she could smell it. Tran stood on the far side of the table, at the head, and said to her, "I know you've seen dead bodies before. That won't be a shock. But have you seen dead loved ones?"

"My father," she told him, which wasn't the truth. The casket had been closed. But she knew what was coming. She didn't bother to add that it had been years and years ago that her father had died.

"Okay, then," he murmured, and he handed the captain a jar that she understood was, despite the Vietnamese words, Vicks VapoRub. "Quang? Want some?" he asked.

The captain nodded and unscrewed the lid and put some just below both nostrils. His young assistant, Vu, did the same. Then Quang handed her the jar, but she shook her head. She felt a moral obligation of sorts—a loyalty, despite the fact that Austin had lied to her so egregiously—to smell her boyfriend now in all his putrescence.

"Ready?" Tran asked, and with two hands he pulled back the sheet to the chest and there he was. Austin. She did not recoil from the mephitic stink and the gas, breathing through her mouth as she gazed at him for a long moment and felt, despite her years around the sick and the wounded and the dead, a small rupture inside her, a flutter of shock. Then a wave of sadness. Had she been hoping for a miracle, that his wallet was nearby because of some unfathomable and inexplicable coincidence? Apparently, she had.

"Yes," she said, her voice flat. "It's him. That's Austin." This was clear despite the fact that Vietnam was a land of heat and humidity, and already the decomposition was advanced. It was October, but the air was still hot and moist.

"No doubt?" Quang asked.

"None."

The right side of his face, his cheekbone, was swollen like a pear, and there were jagged cuts and runnels filled with dried blood from his lips to his eyes. His right eye had been pressed shut by the contusions, but his left looked closed in sleep. She presumed someone—perhaps this coroner—had shut it.

"As you can see," he said to her, "the bugs have already begun to feast on him. Especially in the lacerations and abrasions. I'm sorry."

He reached for the top of the sheet to cover him once again, but she stopped him and asked, "May I look some more?"

The pathologist shrugged and said it was fine, and so she pulled the sheet all the way down, revealing the entirety of his poor, savaged, naked body. Much of it was blotched with bruises, and she could see instantly that his right tibia and fibula, the bones linking his ankle to his knee, were badly broken, and a portion of the larger bone, the tibia, was sticking through flesh like a small shark fin. It looked as if his left knee had been twisted—wrenched hard—perpendicular to the way it was meant to move. The cleat from the bottom of his cycling shoe had probably stuck like glue to the pedal as his body had careened over the guardrail, shredding the ligaments and the menisci. She noted that all along his body, the blood had settled on the right: the skin there had the reddish tint of livor.

"Had rigor mortis set in when you found him?" she asked.

"It had."

"Cause of death was blunt trauma?"

He nodded and she started to reach for Austin's head, but he stopped her. "I would advise against that," Tran said. "But if you insist, you'll need gloves."

"And you'd advise against it because . . ."

"Because a helmet can only do so much to protect against this kind of injury. Part of the back of his head is gone."

"Gone," she repeated.

"We have bits of his"—and he paused, seeming to search for the word in English, and then touched his cranium where it extended out from the back of his neck.

"Occipital bone," she said.

He snapped his fingers. "Yes. Thank you. We found pieces of his occipital bone in the brush beside him and scraped brains and scalp off a nearby rock." He went to a drawer and pulled out a pair of blue latex gloves. "You're sure?"

"I'm sure," she said, and she put them on and cradled Austin's head gently in one hand and turned it slightly so she could see the damage for herself. She took comfort in the idea that he had probably died about as close to instantly as possible. But, still, it had not been instant. There had been a moment of awareness of what was about to occur. She assumed, unless you were fortunate enough to die in your sleep or you were so doped up on morphine, there always was.

Beside them, Captain Nguyen's phone rang, and he excused himself, adjourning to the other side of the L-shaped mortuary. His assistant followed him like a dutiful puppy.

"Tell me what you believe happened," she said to Tran. "Please. The sequence. The captain has told me a bit."

"As far as I can tell, he was riding down the hill and was hit by a vehicle going up it. I suppose they were both close to the middle of the road, and they were both going fast. The vehicle, which I believe was a truck, hit him and sent him over the guardrail. If the injuries were survivable after the impact, they weren't when he hit the rocks below. But I suspect he was already dying from the collision."

So, that moment of awareness of what was happening to him?

Had it been as he had been flying over the guardrail or had it been a second or two earlier, when he saw he was about to have a head-on collision with a speeding truck or a car? She'd never know.

Tran motioned toward the right side of Austin's face. "I'm guessing that the front wheel of his bike met the bumper of the vehicle and he was thrown hard into the front edge of the vehicle's roof. That's the head wound there, and it was probably enough to kill him. It broke off a part of his helmet. Also, look at the marks around the broken bones below his right knee. That's a grill mark. His leg hit it on the way up and into the roof. The mark could be from a Range Rover, but that's speculation. Could also be from an Innova—a Toyota. It's really not clear enough to be definitive."

She held her breath and leaned in close for a look. But already he was directing her attention toward Austin's neck. "Note also the injuries below his jaw—how deeply the helmet strap dug into the skin."

"Time of death?" she asked.

"Yesterday or last night."

"Last night?" she repeated.

"Maybe early evening."

"He was riding after dark?"

"Possibly."

She pondered this and thought of the cerebral side of the ER: pattern recognition. The whiteboard of her mind. On the one hand, that would explain why neither she nor the bike tour leaders had seen Austin's body when they had peered over the side of the guardrails near the summit. But why in the world would he have been on the road when the sun had just about set or had set, and most (or all) of the light was gone? He was too smart for that. Too experienced. He'd only have been on the road at night if he had to be.

"We found him at noon today," the coroner was saying. "He'd

been dead at least twelve hours. But based on the decomposition? Could have been eighteen. Or twenty."

"Who found him?"

"Da Nang police."

"I assume you have his bike and his helmet."

"We do. They're evidence in the event the police ever find the driver."

"And his bike clothes? His gloves, his jersey? Are they evidence, too?"

"No." He pointed at a plastic bag on a spotless steel counter. "They're in there. You want them?"

She didn't, but the jersey was his blue and yellow Speed Racer cycling shirt that he had loved because he had been such a fan of the vintage cartoon as a boy. She thought maybe his parents—whoever they really were—would want it and so she nodded. "Sure. I'll take the bag," she said.

"Okay," Tran said. "It's yours."

"The wallet was found in the brush nearby. But not his phone and not his bike bag. Do I have that right?"

"You do."

"Tell me: Do you think the police will ever find the driver?"

The pathologist shook his head. "No, I don't. Sorry."

"But they'll try?"

"They will. A little. They'll get some help from the traffic police. The CGST. But we don't even know for a fact that your friend was hit by a Range Rover or an Innova. It could have been one of the oil tankers that can't use the tunnel beneath the mountain. Or some farmer with a truck full of pigs. I think it was an SUV, but I don't know that for a fact based on the injuries. I just suspect it, given the grill mark on his leg. But given how far he was thrown over the guardrail? For all I know, it was a bus that hit him."

"You'll look for those models of SUVs?" she asked.

"That's up to the police. If they do look for the vehicle, they'll also have to look for Honda CR-Vs, Fortuners, Land Cruisers, and, for all I know, just about anything else you can find in a dealership."

"What about the back of his head? Broken open on the rocks below?"

"Yes, I think so. He probably landed on his head. And by then, his helmet—whatever was left of it—was likely askew. It was pretty worthless."

"Will the corpse be sent home?"

"Absolutely. Or the ashes, if that's what the family prefers."

For a long moment, she surveyed his ruined body, knowing it was the last time she would ever see it. She said good-bye to him in her mind, and tried to forgive him for lying to her. To everyone. What sort of sad, private wound was he cradling to make up that kind of story? She had stood there so long in silence that Tran finally murmured, "Would you like me to leave you alone?"

She came back to herself. To the two of them. "No. I'm fine."

He nodded and looked up as the CSCD captain and the younger officer returned. "Don't bother to go home," the captain said to the pathologist, "I'd appreciate it if you can come with me." Then, to Alexis, he continued, "Officer Vu will drive you back to your hotel. Would you forgive me?"

"What's happened?" she asked.

He looked sheepish. "Da Nang isn't the gang capital of Vietnam. Far from it, despite what the video games might tell you. But there seems to have been an execution here today. Or last night. Two young toughs and a woman a little older. They were all shot in the head."

"The crime scene is near here?" Tran asked.

"It is. Just north of the city. Sounds like some kind of lab. Meth lab, but that's a guess. There's fire damage."

Alexis was about to pull off her gloves, but stopped herself. She noticed something on Austin's right hand. A puncture wound near the anterior capitate bones—some of the larger metacarpals. She lifted his hand and, despite everyone's desire to move on now, studied it. The bone was clearly broken based on the bruising.

"What do you think of this?" she asked Tran.

"I think it's another broken bone."

"No," she said, her tone more adamant. "The wound. It looks like it was done with a . . . a spike or something. A skewer."

"There are so many possibilities. A stick—"

"A stick wouldn't do this!"

"The tip of a pointed rock then," the coroner said. "When he landed."

The captain leaned over and looked at it. "It sure isn't what killed him."

"No," Tran agreed. "It's just one more wound among many." He started to pull the sheet over the corpse, but Alexis stopped him. The puncture wasn't the only odd wound that marked his body. She thought back on her short history with the man. There were also the scars on his fingers from the cat bite in the bakery and the scar on his upper arm from the gunshot. She took out her cell phone and snapped a series of close-up photos of the hole on the back of Austin's hand. Just in case, she took photos as well of the scars from the bite marks on his fingers and the spot where she had pulled a bullet from his biceps. And then, because she was thorough, she photographed his legs and his face and what remained of the back of his head.

.   .   .

"I wouldn't say the case is closed," Toril told Alexis on the phone. Alexis was sitting on the side of the bed in her hotel room in Hoi An and staring at her and Austin's suitcases. "But I rather doubt a whole lot of energy is going to be directed toward a possible hit-and-run. I mean, we don't even know for sure he didn't just fly off the road."

"No, we don't," Alexis said. "But the coroner certainly believes someone hit him. There is what might be a grill mark on his broken leg."

"Still, it's not a homicide. It's manslaughter. Maybe. The police in that corner of the country are always stretched a little thin, and that's going to be especially true in the coming days."

"Because of the triple murder north of Da Nang?"

"You heard about that?"

"Captain Nguyen got the call when we were at the morgue."

"God, I'm so sorry, Alexis. You will leave Vietnam with the most horrible memories of this place. But, actually, it's such a beautiful country. Please know that. It's such a beautiful world with such kind and remarkable people. This nightmare you're experiencing? It's so awful and so rare."

"It is a nightmare," she agreed. "But I won't forget how lovely the country was for most of the trip. I'll try and focus on that."

"Good."

"Will we investigate his death?"

"We, meaning Americans?"

"Uh-huh. Some FBI agents went to his boss's office at the hospital."

"No," the attaché told her. "We won't do any more. We sent someone to his office in New York as a courtesy to the police here, when we thought he might still be alive. Asked a few questions."

"Did someone go by the ER?"

"I doubt it. We were inquiring about Austin."

"So that's it . . ."

"Yes. This remains the jurisdiction of the Vietnamese police."

"Even though he's an American citizen?"

"They're really good, Alexis. Don't fret. They know what they're doing. If there's a reason to follow up on a lead or a clue, they will."

"Tell me something."

"I'll try."

"Why do you think he lied? Was he just embarrassed about his father? It was so unnecessary. It's all so . . . so sad."

"I doubt we'll ever know."

"I mean, was there more to it? Do you think he had a lover here? Maybe even a child from his last visit?"

"Okay, I have to admit: that's something that never crossed my mind."

"Is it something the police will investigate?"

There was quiet while the attaché pondered this. "Not very likely," she said finally. "I'm sorry. If they do anything, they'll try and find the driver. Why do you think he had a mistress? Or a child? Did he say something to you that you should share with the police?"

"No, nothing. It was something a friend of mine in New York suggested to me when we spoke."

"Austin said something to her about that?"

"No. She was just speculating."

"Okay, then. I wouldn't waste a lot of energy there. I'd let that one go."

On the top of Austin's open suitcase, wadded into a corner, were his other cycling jerseys, extra bike gloves, energy gels, and a bottle of sunblock. In another corner she saw his dirty clothes and his toiletries kit. She noted the sneakers he'd worn when they weren't biking. Behind their suitcases, hanging in the closet, was the suit he had bought just two days ago in Hoi An, as well as the slinky dress he'd had made for her. That seemed months ago now. She sighed. She wouldn't carry all of his possessions back to America for his parents, but she'd bring them the suit and, after she'd washed it, his favorite cycling jersey. She might—or might not—ask them why they thought their son had lied about their history. About his history. She might try and get a sense if, in fact, it was the father who had lied to the son.

"May I ask you who was killed in Da Nang? The three people?" Alexis said.

"A couple of kids: well, not exactly kids. Twentysomethings. And a woman who was some kind of food chemist. Older. In her thirties."

"A gang of some sort?"

"Maybe."

"What was it, a meth lab?"

"A meth lab? No, I don't believe so. Why would you think that?"

"Something Captain Nguyen said at the morgue—before he left."

"Ah, okay. He hadn't been there yet. Yes, it was a—for lack of a better term—rogue lab of some sort. But I don't think they were cooking meth."

"Then what?"

"I really can't say."

"Because you don't know or you can't tell me?" Alexis asked.

"Tell yourself it's the first but presume it's the second."

"Got it." She felt a pang of hunger and rose from the bed and picked up one of the energy gels from Austin's suitcase.

"Look, the truth is, I really don't know a whole lot more than you do. They weren't Americans, so it doesn't seem to be anything that will involve me or the embassy."

She heard someone approaching her door and opened it even before whoever was coming could knock. There was Talia with a tray of cubed mango pieces, sliced rambutans, cut pineapple, and meticulously triangled dragon fruit. She was smiling sadly, sympathetically, her eyebrows an arc. Alexis held up one finger for her, indicating that she would be off the phone in a moment.

"Well, I'm glad you were here for me, Toril," she said. "I'm deeply grateful."

"I did nothing."

"No, you did a lot," Alexis reassured her, and she tossed the gel packet back into Austin's suitcase and beckoned Talia into the room. "And now you return to Cambodia?"

"I do, that's right."

It suddenly seemed immodest to have the suitcases open and vulnerable, their dirty clothes exposed, and so she shut them with the toe of her sandal. She said good-bye to the FBI agent and watched as Talia set the fruit down on the dresser, and she asked her new friend to please stay and keep her company, and to share the plenty she'd brought with her.

MONDAY AND TUESDAY

11

Douglas Webber always obeyed the lizard part of his brain—it was among the reasons why he was still alive—and those dark little folds were telling him that he shouldn't toss darts ever again in the East Village dive where, invariably, he could find a game. He'd gone there three times with Austin. He wasn't a member of the New York Dart League—he knew enough not to be a joiner—but he went to their website to see which bars had events or even tournaments lined up that Monday night and which ones were quiet. He wanted a place that was empty of serious activity, but one where he still might find a competitive player. There looked to be a possibility in Chelsea.

He'd been back in New York a day and a half now, and it felt good to be here. To be home—or what had been home for the better part of this year. He presumed that he'd flown back before Austin's girlfriend, but even if the gods had conspired against him and put the two of them on the same airline and the same flight, he rather doubted they would be in the same cabin. He certainly hadn't seen her on board or at the airport in Vietnam or waiting for the connection in Seoul.

The first thing he'd done when he returned was meet with Oscar Bolton. Bolton had been Austin Harper's backup, though Harper had no idea that he had a replacement in waiting. Bolton would take a while to fully train, but already he could liaise with the university labs in the hospital complex, and pick up a couple of the pieces before they became problematic.

Douglas's apartment was the fourth and fifth floors of a five-story brownstone on Third Street, between Avenue C and Avenue D. It was more room than his body needed, but two bedrooms were the very least that his ego demanded. He grew tomatoes and peppers and basil in pots on his rooftop terrace in the summer. Now the pots were empty and stacked in a corner, along with the tomato cages. He didn't have much of a view, but he had plenty of sun.

It was eight thirty at night now and he was deciding where he might get a bite to eat before heading to the bar in Chelsea. He was seated on his couch with his dart case in his lap, inspecting the new flights that had arrived in the mail while he had been away. They were bright red and had an image of a black rat on them. The aesthetics were not important to him: if he had wanted a rat, it would have been brown. The brown rat, *Rattus norvegicus,* had displaced the black rat, *Rattus rattus. Norvegicus* was bigger than *rattus,* bulkier, and yet had smaller ears and a more slanted nose. Not nearly as attractive a silhouette. But size beat beauty in the rat-eat-rat world of the urban alley or tenement, and now *norvegicus* was top rodent. The brown rat was the city slicker, while the black rat had been reduced to—more or less—the country mouse. What mattered to Douglas was that the flights were smooth and slim. He didn't lob his darts, he threw them hard.

His phone rang and he saw it was Bao. It was seven thirty on Tuesday morning in Vietnam.

"Good morning," Douglas said.

"Good evening. Am I interrupting dinner?"

"Nope. Haven't even started."

"You alone?"

"I am."

"Good flight?"

"Excellent. What's up, Bao? You didn't ring me to ask about the amenities on the plane."

There was a brief pause, and Douglas could sense that Bao was gathering himself. "The police in Da Nang picked up one of my guys."

"One of your guys who took care of the lab?"

"Ironically, no. It was just a coincidence that they brought him in. There are plenty of witnesses to the fact that he was at the Four Seasons in Hoi An on Friday. Getting a massage and drinking and enjoying the scenery."

Two thoughts passed almost simultaneously through Douglas's mind, but he was careful enough not to give voice to either. First, the man had an alibi. That was excellent. Second, he was paying Bao's people way too much if one of them was drinking at the Four Seasons.

"By enjoying the scenery, I presume you mean the young girls in bikinis—not the beach."

"Right."

"There are witnesses?"

"Plenty."

"Good. Have I met him?" Douglas asked.

"You haven't. But he was the driver we'd used the day before. On Thursday."

"And the police didn't ask about that?"

"Nope. Seems not to have crossed their minds there was a connection."

"Where is the truck?"

"Long gone. He drove to the resort in a silver Kia."

Douglas was relieved. Still, he pressed, "And you're positive that the police asked him nothing about our American friend?"

"Nothing. That's clearly just a hit-and-run. They've made no connection between his death and the other three—"

"Got it," Douglas said, cutting him off.

"Just keeping you in the loop."

"Thank you. I appreciate that. Tell me again . . ."

"Go on."

"There was nothing on his phone?"

"Some contact with the food chemist in Da Nang. The dates and times of two phone calls—"

"Anything to suggest she was more than a business associate of his?" Douglas asked.

"No, why?"

"You said she was pretty."

"She was. I wouldn't be surprised if she and Austin were rats with benefits."

"You took care of her phone, too?"

"Absolutely."

"And there was nothing else on Austin's phone? No emails? No cellular trail?"

"Nope. No contact with Myung—the Korean in the labs," Bao said. "But the fact that Harper was meeting with a woman here with North Korean connections has to make Myung a factor in our minds."

"I'll see what we can find out. Sinclair in any emails or apps?"

"None. And there was absolutely no information on the creation of the pathogen. No data at all. After we'd gone through everything—and I mean everything—we put the SIM card back in and then wiped it clean. We wiped his laptop, his tablet, and even his desktop at work. We erased everything."

"And there was nothing in the cloud?" Douglas asked.

"Nothing we could find."

"Where's the phone now?"

"Bottom of a rice paddy."

"Okay," he murmured. So, if anyone in Vietnam ever checked with the telecom company, they would find evidence of two phone calls between Austin Harper and one of the three dead in Da Nang. But who would check? It was the sort of worrisome, dangling thread that irritated Douglas, but he knew in his heart that it was never going to unravel . . . anything. Because no one would ever pull at that string. Because no one cared and because no one would connect the dead cyclist from the other side of the planet with the massacre the day after he happened to die on his bike.

"Has there been any fallout at your end?" Bao asked.

"Not at all. Everyone presumes it was a hit-and-run."

"Good."

After Douglas said good-bye to Bao, he decided on pasta for dinner. He was friends with the owner of an Italian restaurant who, he knew, kept his kitchen impeccably clean. Not a rat to be found.

. . .

On his way home, Douglas had the cabdriver drop him off on Sixth Street and Avenue D. It had been a somewhat more dramatic evening than he had anticipated. It had begun uneventfully, with a terrific spaghetti carbonara and a robust Brunello. But then he had gone to the bar to play darts and it had fallen apart. Not cataclysmically, not by a long shot, but in a fashion that had left him unsettled and vexed. He'd met a pair of twin brothers visiting America from Dublin, and he'd played darts with them for an hour. They were younger than he was, in their midthirties, and had family in Westchester. They were good. Very good. Better than he was, and he knew he'd win most New York City–area tournaments if he was willing to sacrifice his anonymity and enter. They took him for a couple rounds of drinks and two hundred bucks, which really was nothing to him, nothing at all, but it still meant that he had lost a lot of games that night.

Now, as midnight neared, he hoped to walk off his annoyance by heading west on Sixth, away from the FDR Drive and the taller apartments with their tree-shrouded parking lots that seemed to belong in an outer borough. He made a right into an alley where he knew there were rows of dumpsters that would not be emptied until tomorrow morning. They were filled largely by a trendy diner that specialized in comfort food, things like macaroni and cheese, mashed potatoes, and homemade creamed corn. And there he stood and watched them. The rats. There was just enough light from the streetlight that once his eyes had adjusted to the dark, he could see them as they skittered on the ground against the brick wall, their eyes occasionally meeting his, gnawing at the garbage that had fallen over the side of one of the dumpsters like coconuts on the beach or apples in an orchard. There were two whole bags on the ground. Douglas estimated there were at least a half dozen places he knew where he could watch rats, but this was his favorite. Rats had the culinary tastes of a six-year-old boy. They loved food that was starchy and cheesy. They hated things like beets and celery and cauliflower. So, the refuse from this diner? It was perfect.

He counted six animals and assumed there were more he was missing. One of the black bags on the alley pavement had movement inside it, and he imagined a baby chick pecking its way from its shell. But, of course, it was a rat that had gnawed a hole in the bag or had found one. Douglas stood still, and they didn't seem to mind his presence any more than they would a Norway maple. They embraced the shadows, but they were far from dependent on the dark. He noticed a rat trap near the dumpster. So, it seemed, did they. They ignored it, either because they were smart or because it was baited badly.

A mile or so north of here were all of those university hospitals, three of them he could think of, including the one where Austin Harper had worked. It was among the locations in the city where scientists were studying the pathogens rodents carried that were proving to be spectacularly resistant to drugs. Among the worst of the pathogens was the one that looked a lot like the bacteria corkscrews called leptospirosis, spread mostly by rat urine. But this new bacteria was longer than lepto and didn't give a rat's ass about doxycycline. It ignored every antibiotic the scientists had thrown at it. Scoffed at the very notion there was a drug it should fear. And then there was the one Sinclair was cooking up at Austin's old haunt that was a variant on the plague, but also antibiotic resistant. The work should have been going on in a BSL-4 lab, and the university's was only BSL-3. But that also made it possible to fly under the radar. They'd christened that one the red lotus, because their transgenic lab rats had genes from their Vietnamese counterparts.

An idea came to Douglas and then, right behind it, an impulse. The idea was that he had lost tonight to the Irish brothers not merely because they were better than he was, but because of the brand-new flights he had been using. The ones with the cartoon profile of a rat. Maybe they weren't slim enough. Maybe they were offering more drag than he liked. The notion was curative, reassuring.

Carefully, almost in slow motion, he opened his dart case and removed one. He guessed he was no more than ten yards from the rats, which was a lot longer than most tournament tosses, but still not terribly far. The impulse was that he would spear one. Skewer it.

He took aim at a cluster of three that were eating what he presumed was some sort of bread—a stale bagel with a bit of cream cheese or a baguette with some butter—and then at one in particular that was offering him the full length of his side. He threw hard, a missile shot, and hit it solidly in the midsection. It screamed a great rat scream, a sound that was reminiscent both of a growl and of a creature hyperventilating. It was like a mammalian lawn mower that wouldn't quite start.

For a moment he was satisfied, and he wondered if the other rats would start to eat it. That would be interesting. He might stay and watch that.

But then he realized that his fingerprints were all over both the barrel and the flight. And while he couldn't imagine any sane person really caring that someone had killed a rat with a dart, for all he knew some animal rights crazy who lived nearby would discover the dead creature before the trash collectors and bring it to the nearby humane society or police station. And so he wandered over to the rats, which scattered quickly, and put the toe of his shoe on the wounded animal. It wasn't quite dead yet, but he didn't care. He grabbed the dart by the shaft and yanked it out, eliciting another one of those rat shrieks, though this one was softer and less frenzied. He tossed the dart into the dumpster and left the rat to finish dying. He rather doubted that the other rats would wait for it to stop breathing before feasting upon it.

He made a mental note that when he got home, he would be sure to spend an extra-long time washing his hands.

Why do you ask that? Isn't it obvious?

Look, delivery systems for biological weapons often revolve around bombs and (and I love this little word) bomblets. The goal is to disperse as widely as possible your anthrax or tularemia or smallpox or cholera. You need an aerosol component. Or you need to get the pathogen into the water system.

I gather it's a hell of a lot more difficult than you think.

The same is true with chemical weapons. Even the monsters who have used chemical weapons in our lifetime haven't found them a whole lot more effective than quite literally pushing bombs in barrels from hovering helicopters. Primitive, right?

Well, maybe primitive is best. Sometimes I think technology is over-rated. I really do.

Among the first people ever to use biological weapons was a British general in North America named Jeffery Amherst. He used woolen blankets infected with smallpox to kill Indians in New England in 1763. It was ingenious. Very creative.

But even Amherst had crafted a delivery system that was less efficient than nature. Let's face it, in all of human history, the most effective delivery vehicle for mass death ever to exist on earth has been—wait for it—the rat.

12

Alexis arrived in America only a day after the rest of the bike tour. The embassy was going to take care of returning Austin's remains to Boston, where, Toril told her, his parents had made arrangements to have them retrieved. Officer Vu had returned to the little hotel before she checked out and given her both Austin's laptop and his tablet. Then she had flown alone to JFK, leaving on Sunday and arriving on Monday. Much to her utter shock, her mother had volunteered to meet her at the airport and drive her either to Alexis's own East Village apartment or to the house in New Jersey where her mother lived and where Alexis could, to use her mother's own words, *veg and recover.* She passed on both of her mother's offers, much as she liked the idea of becoming an ostrich, a pile of pillows its sand. Unfortunately, she was unable to imagine either "vegging" or "recovering" under her mother's intense scrutiny in the evenings, or in the solitary confinement of that suburbia during the day. She liked the house and the neighborhood just fine, but there wasn't a damn thing for her to do there anymore, especially since her mother would need to take the car to the PATH train or the ferry into Manhattan. She'd be wandering aimlessly through the withering remains of her childhood: the stuffed animals that hadn't aged well and the books that she'd loved at ten and which still stood shoulder to shoulder on her shelves. Besides, she was, more or less, okay. At least she thought she was. And, of course, she had a job.

And so she took a cab into the city after she landed, arriving home not long after lunch. She'd been traveling nearly twenty-four hours, and though the Xanax had helped her doze on the plane, the slumber had never been deep and she wanted nothing more than to collapse into her own bed and return to eastern time in America. She was supposed to work on Tuesday, but she had already told the hospital that it was in no one's best interest for her to be in the ER that day, and so she wasn't planning to return to work until Wednesday. Her revised schedule meant that her shift would begin at noon, which seemed the perfect time to slide back into a routine.

And by then? By then, she assumed, she would have recovered. At least mostly recovered. Physically recovered. She presumed the jet lag would be behind her. But the rest? It would take more than a day and a half to treat the emotional bruising from the death of her boyfriend and the discovery that he had likely been lying to her and she had no idea why he'd really wanted to return to Vietnam. It would take even longer to parse the meaning of the body she had identified on the slab, and what that body had meant to her when he had been alive.

· · ·

She slept deeply in her own bed in her own apartment. She recalled a detail of one dream as she awoke: she was in a window seat on a plane—an Airbus—flying no more than a hundred yards above the city of the dead near An Bang, the hills an endless, undulating carpet of crypts they'd biked past last week, and it was clear the plane was trying to climb and wasn't going to make it. It was going to slam into the magnificent dragons and pillars, some ten and fifteen yards high, that marked the lavish family plots, many more colorful and ornate than the nearby pagodas. She saw the dead—curled in despair into small, round balls—cringing beneath their piles of stones as the wings decapitated serpents and basilisks and swans, and sheared off the tops of the columns. The plane was operated by an American carrier and this mattered to her, but when she tried to explain what was happening to Austin, she discovered that he wasn't in the seat beside her.

When she opened her eyes, she saw it was the middle of the morning and remembered it was Tuesday. Through a crimp in her bedroom blinds she could see the crisp, blue New York sky.

She reached for her phone on her nightstand and saw that she had a text from her neighbor Ellie, asking her if she needed anything. There was a text from Talia, her new friend from the bike tour, asking how she was doing. The lead guide, Scott, had texted her, as well—again, just checking in. There was nothing else. No other missed texts, no calls at all. There was nothing pressing in her emails. She texted Talia and Scott that she was fine, thanking them, and then she texted Ellie that she would love to have a drink that night when Ellie returned from her own job at the animal hospital.

She fell back into the pillows and scrolled through her photos from Vietnam and her photos of Austin. She decided that her favorite photo from the trip was, of all things, the image of the man mugging in the tailor's shop in Hoi An as the cuffs of his pants were chalked, his face boyish and ebullient, his smile infectious. That was how she wanted to remember him. She liked it more than the exotic birds and the pristine beach and the rice paddies and pagodas, and certainly more than any of him—of them—on bikes. She stared at a shot of the two of them resting on their bikes, one leg on the ground and one clipped into a pedal, before the city of the dead near the massive tomb of Khai Dinh, and winced, her nightmare coming back to her. Often those bike photos were in the rain or in the shade, and usually their faces were sweaty or hidden by helmets and sunglasses, or smeared with sunblock that in some cases looked like war paint. But this one, with those exquisite monuments to the deceased stretching, it seemed, to the horizon? With the sun high and their features clear? It was too much, it was too goddamn prescient.

She guessed that she liked the photo from the tailor's shop best because Austin looked like such an innocent. He didn't look like he was up to something.

And while it seemed likely that he had been up to something, she reminded herself that she didn't know this for a fact. Shame was a powerful motivator, and maybe that's all this was. Perhaps she'd get an inkling into what he was thinking when she brought his parents that new suit and his Speed Racer cycling jersey.

The most recent photos on the phone were the ones from the morgue in Da Nang. She decided to steer clear of those until she had had some coffee.

.   .   .

But, of course, there was no half-and-half in the apartment. Even the cheese in the crisper in the refrigerator had started to turn a little brown in her long absence. And so she showered and dressed and wandered to the coffee shop around the corner from her apartment, and there, over a cheese omelet and bad coffee with fresh milk from a tinny creamer, she pored over the photos on her phone from the morgue. She had a table she liked by the window. She studied especially the wound on the back of Austin's hand. At first, it reminded her a bit of a god-awful bug bite. There was a circle and swelling. But what insect had a stinger as big as that perfect point? It wasn't a mosquito, and it wasn't a mosquito with malaria, because those bites looked no different from an ordinary puncture. Besides, she had insisted they both take Atovaquone, an antimalarial, even though he hadn't taken the pills the last time he had gone to Vietnam and had returned home perfectly fine. And if he'd scratched the bite? The scabbing would have been different. No, this swelling was due entirely to a broken bone. She knew that from the pathologist, but even if she had just looked at a photo, she could have diagnosed the injury from the inflammation and the black-and-blue mark.

When she looked up, there was a young pug at the end of a leash on the other side of the window and she waved at the dog.

The animal tilted his head and put his front paws on the glass, his round eyes dark and happy. The dog's owner was a statuesque older woman in a stylish jeans jacket and red leather gloves, which were nice but not essential today, because it was probably forty-five degrees outside and the sun was beaming down on the city. But the gloves made Alexis think of something. She scrolled back to the photo of Austin's right hand. There were no other scrapes on it, no other broken bones. No broken fingers. There were no other abrasions at all. There were, however, cuts on the tips of his fingers on his left hand.

She recalled that he'd been wearing his cycling gloves. If this puncture wound on his right hand had been caused by a collision with a vehicle or by a sharp rock when he had gone careening over the guardrail, there would be blood on the inside of the glove and, very likely, a tear of some kind in the material. She could check this: the gloves were still wadded in the plastic bag with his cycling jersey that the coroner had given her. They were in her suitcase.

She swallowed the last of her coffee and stood. She didn't bother to wait for the server to return. She went straight to the cashier, paid her check, and raced home to her apartment.

13

There was no rip in the right cycling glove. No puncture, no tear. There was no blood on it, either. The fabric was yellow along the section that would have covered the hole in the back of his hand, so she would have seen a bloodstain, if there had been one. But there was none at all on the outside and so she turned it inside out, and there wasn't a drop on the inside.

She sat on her couch and tossed the glove onto the glass coffee table. Of course, there wasn't any blood; there wasn't a rip.

She recalled the three Psych energy gel packets she had found on the road in Vietnam. They had been Austin's, that seemed clear to her now, and they were a distress flare. Someone had abducted him, and he had left the Psych on the pavement as a beacon. Then someone had hurt him: she imagined a person taking a screwdriver—a Phillips head—or the tip of a knife and pounding it into the back of his hand. No, not a knife. An awl: that's how round the wound was. But that didn't matter right now. What did was that the wound had occurred well before the bike accident. She was sure of it.

But then they had let him go. They'd learned from him what they wanted or gotten from him what they needed—clearly torturing him to get it—and released him.

But they'd kept his phone, perhaps because there was something on it.

Which meant that something might be on one of his computers.

Austin's laptop and tablet were both in his suitcase, where she'd packed them after that Vietnamese police officer had brought them back to her in Hoi An. She dug them out now and placed them both on the coffee table. She had learned when she had booted them up in Vietnam that she would need a password to see the contents of either, and so she didn't bother to turn them on. She had absolutely no idea what in the world his password might be. She could try dozens and dozens of words that she thought might have meaning to him, but if he had secrets— which, it seemed, he did—he had very secret passwords.

Actually, that was the solution . . . or part of the solution. If she tried and failed enough times, the computer would ask her to reset her password.

But she would need his Apple ID to do that, which might be his email address. But then again, it might not. And, either way, she didn't have access to his email without the password.

And, of course, who knew what sort of crazy encryption he might be using.

Still, the world was filled with tech geeks and hackers for whom getting into his laptop would be child's play—or, if not child's play, a task they might be willing to take on. She just had to find one.

.   .   .

That afternoon, she went to the hospital, but she went nowhere near the ER. She'd be there tomorrow, beginning at noon, and that would be soon enough.

Instead she went to the wing on the other side of the building from admitting and emergency, and rode the elevator to the seventh floor: the hospital administrators, public relations, and advancement. It was the wing with the executives and the scientists. The offices and the labs. Hers was a university hospital with teaching and research components, and the university labs were extensive. The wing was linked by a glass walkway to the sky-scraper next door, a building that housed a couple of Big Pharma companies with their executives and their labs, too. She'd called Sally Gleason that morning once she saw that she wasn't going to be able to access either Austin's computer or tablet, and the development director said she had a brief window at three thirty. Alexis had been on the floor twice before, first when Austin was showing her his office soon after they met and then again when she had used that office to change into a dress he had bought her as a surprise. They were going to a summer fund-raiser for the hospital: not a black-tie sort of gig, but flashy, and he surprised her with the perfect white cocktail dress for the occasion.

An administrative assistant, a young guy with moussed hair the color of corn silk and an ill-fitting black-and-red-check blazer—he couldn't have been more than twenty-one or twenty-two years old, and Alexis speculated he was some hospital ad-ministrator's or physician's son interning here—ushered her back into a corridor with offices that faced the East River and the northernmost tip of Brooklyn. Sally was sitting on the side of her desk with another executive standing beside her, sharing with her pages from a notebook presentation. He was a handsome guy roughly her age, with a chiseled nose, sharp cheekbones, and a hint of a five-o'clock shadow. He had leaned into his baldness by shaving his head, and it worked for him. He was in a black suit with a gorgeous blue-and-gold paisley necktie. She thought she'd seen him before, and presumed if she had it had been at an event with Austin.

When Sally saw Alexis and the assistant in her doorway, she beckoned her in, and in a pair of short sentences and a single ges-ture managed to thank and dismiss both of her employees. She didn't introduce either to her, but the one who had shaved his head nodded at Alexis flirtatiously on his way out. Then Sally motioned for her to take a seat on the leather couch by the cre-denza and sat down beside her. The office was big and well appointed, and Alexis thought her mother would approve. Beside the couch, instead of a small end table, was the sort of eccentric touch that her mother appreciated: an art deco standing ashtray about three feet high, the rim a pair of porcelain panthers, black and menacing. The basin for ashes and cigarette butts was now a planter, and there was a succulent growing there that looked a little pink in the afternoon sun.

"I'm so sorry to see you again under these circumstances," she said to Alexis, and for a moment she thought the executive was going to take hold of her hands. "I much prefer seeing you on Austin's arm at galas."

"Me too," Alexis agreed.

"Do you want some coffee?" the administrator asked. She was a tall woman with a round, surprisingly cherubic face and dark hair that was now sprinkled with white. She was wearing a crisp, impeccably tailored navy-blue skirt and blazer. Her lipstick looked fresh and moist, as if recently reapplied. The ridiculous sports jacket the kid who had escorted her back here was wearing probably drove Sally crazy.

"No, I'm fine."

"Not jet-lagged?"

"A little."

"Do you work tonight?" Sally asked, a hint of wariness in her voice.

"No. My next shift isn't until tomorrow at noon."

"You'll get a good night's sleep?"

"I will," Alexis replied. She considered joking that she'd pop a Xanax tonight to be sure, but she doubted she would. Besides, she had a feeling a joke like that would not merely fall flat: it might raise alarm bells. Then she said, her tone light, "So, a friend of mine had an interesting theory: Austin had met someone on his first trip to Vietnam and was seeing her when he died."

"As in another woman?"

"Uh-huh. I offered it as a reason for his disappearance to an

FBI attaché in Vietnam. You know, that's where he was going the day he died. She didn't put much credence in the idea."

"I don't either."

"He never mentioned anyone? I mean, he was single then. A single guy on a bike tour. It wouldn't have been wrong."

Sally folded her arms across her chest and gazed down at the pointed tips of her shoes. When she looked up, she said, "He wasn't going to tell me about some random hookup when he came back. That wasn't the sort of thing we'd talk about when we weren't talking about work."

"Not a random hookup. More of a—"

"I think your friend was grasping at straws."

The abruptness of her answer was strangely unsettling, but it was clear that Sally gave the notion absolutely no credence. And so instead Alexis asked, "Have you heard again from the FBI?"

"Not a peep, and I doubt I will. When he was missing, there was a logic to allocating some manpower. Now that we know he died in a bike accident, there's no reason. There's no point. It's a tragedy, but not a crime."

Alexis nodded and took a breath, pausing, because she knew that what she was about to say would sound paranoid—especially after pressing Sally about the possibility that Austin had met someone on his first journey to Vietnam. "Something happened to him before the bike accident—before he was killed," she said carefully. She pulled from her purse his right bike glove and showed it to the administrator. "He was wearing this when his body was found."

Sally looked at it and waited. She could tell there was something more coming.

Alexis opened her phone and showed her the wound on the back of Austin's hand. "Note there's no tear in the glove and no blood anywhere on it. Not a drop."

"You took that photo of his hand in the morgue?" Sally asked.

"I did, yes."

"I'm sure a pathologist could explain it," she said.

"He couldn't to my satisfaction when I asked him."

"Maybe an accident reconstructionist would have a suggestion."

"Here's what's clear," Alexis said. "The wound occurred before Austin got back on his bike to return to the hotel. That's the obvious explanation."

Sally sat back deep into the couch and gazed out the window. The sun was falling fast into the west, and the room, which faced east, was losing the daylight quickly. "In other words, he had some other accident in that period when he was missing."

"I don't believe that's an accident wound."

The other woman still didn't meet her eye. She seemed transfixed by the reflection of the sun on a glass building across the river in Brooklyn. "Then what? Are you saying that someone hurt him?"

"Precisely. It looks as if someone jammed something round and solid and very sharp into the back of his hand and broke a bone."

"Or he banged it on something. You work in an ER, Alexis. Think of the ridiculous things you treat every day you're down there. The mind-numbingly stupid accidents. Good Lord, people drop weights on their feet at the gym, they slice off their fingertips cutting bagels. They—"

"Oh, I know," Alexis agreed. "Trust me, I know. But here's the pattern I see. Walk through it with me. First of all, he lied about why he wanted to be alone that day. Then he disappeared. He didn't respond to texts or phone calls. He got hurt or was hurt—that wound on the back of his hand. Then, after dark or pretty nearly after dark, he climbed back on his bike, which is insane for a serious bicyclist. It's insane for any bicyclist. He didn't call me or anyone on the bike tour and ask for the support van. He didn't even tell me or anyone from the bike tour that he was on his way back. And then he was hit by a car or truck and was killed."

Sally adjusted the framed photo of her two children on the credenza beside the couch. "Because he lost his phone. That would explain a lot of it. Also? As you said, he may have been lying. To call for help would have revealed his lie."

"Maybe. Maybe not. He could have borrowed a phone or made a call from anywhere in Hue or Hoi An or Da Nang—wherever he was. He still had his wallet. He still had cash and credit cards."

Sally turned to face her directly, and her countenance had grown so stern that Alexis was taken aback. "What are you after? I have to ask. Why are you here? I don't mean that in any way that's antagonistic. I swear I don't. But I'm serious. Why have you come to me?"

"Because you knew him, too."

"I did," she replied. "At least, I thought I did. So did his friend Oscar. So did a lot of people. I still think he was a good guy. I know he was good at his job. But maybe he was like a lot of folks you pass every single day on the street or see on the subway: he had secrets. Or a secret. I'm sorry that he lied and we'll never know why, because I liked him. I really did. I'm sure you feel that lie as more of a betrayal than I do. But for me? He lied about his family. Not the worst crime. He probably had his reasons."

"And what if those reasons were because he needed a pretext to return to Vietnam? Maybe he had a good reason for lying and maybe he didn't," she answered. "That's my point. We don't know. But what we do know—at least I believe this—is that when he was missing, he was tortured. I don't think that word is hyperbole."

"That's a pretty big leap," Sally said, and she stood and switched on the overhead fluorescent lights on the ceiling.

"I want to go through his office. May I?" Alexis asked. "I want to look at his office computer."

"I can't allow that. That belongs to the hospital."

"If I get police permission?" Alexis asked, aware of the urgency creeping into her voice.

"Sure, if you get police permission. But why in the world would they allow that? Why would they give you permission?"

"Because—"

"He's gone, Alexis. Accept that. The police aren't going to do anything. Certainly not in New York and I rather doubt in Vietnam. It's over, it's done. I know you miss him. I do, too. Maybe he lied to you. Maybe he broke your heart. If he did, I'm sorry. I really am. But you need to move on."

Alexis stood. She didn't appreciate sitting there like a scolded child while this other woman seemed to tower above her. "If I don't touch his computer, may I look around his office? Just take a peek? I wouldn't open any drawers or boot up his computer."

"Sure, fine. If his father says yes, you can do that. The man arrives tomorrow. Join him here. His father is coming to town to see what he needs to do to clear out the office and to scope out his son's apartment. See how much work it will be to clean it all out."

"Tomorrow. What time?"

"I don't know, but midafternoon, I think. Rich will know."

"Rich is your assistant?"

She nodded. "Yes, the young man who showed you in."

"I'm in the ER tomorrow afternoon, but I'll make sure I get away for at least a few minutes. I've never met Austin's father, but I got his phone number while I was in Vietnam. I'll call him again. But could you ask Rich, please, to let me know when he's here?"

"I will. You can, too."

"Is his father getting into town tonight or tomorrow?"

"I don't know. And, actually, it's Austin's mother and father. I believe his mother will be here, too."

She and Austin had never exchanged apartment keys. She had assumed that someday they would. His apartment had doormen, and she knew at least two of them by name. She wondered if one might be on duty later today or tonight whom she knew—and who would be willing to give her a spare key so she could rummage around Austin's place before his parents arrived.

"Can I make a suggestion?" Sally asked.

Alexis leaned back against the credenza. She started to fold her arms defensively across her chest but stopped herself. "Go ahead."

"Why don't you get a private detective? If you feel so strongly about Austin's disappearance, hire the sort of person who can dig deeper than you or I can. You and I know the importance of a specialist as well as anyone. Maybe, if you really want to find out what happened, that's the way to go."

Alexis was both appreciative and surprised. She'd expected Sally to tell her—once more but with different words—to move on. "That's a great idea," she said. "A really great idea."

The other woman shrugged modestly. "Sometimes I get lucky."

"Do you have any names? I guess I could Google one."

Sally went to her desk and opened a drawer. She rummaged inside it a moment and then found a business card. She handed it to Alexis, and Alexis looked briefly at the name: Ken Sarafian. It appeared that he worked alone and he covered the tri-state area. His office was on lower Broadway.

"May I ask why you have this? Is this guy good?" Alexis asked.

"Yeah, I think he's pretty good."

"You've used him?"

"I haven't."

"How do you know him?"

The other woman's eyes briefly—and it was very brief—looked unexpectedly wistful. "He's a family friend. He used to play golf with my dad growing up. Back then, Ken was NYPD."

"And now he's retired?"

"From the police force, yes. My dad passed away four years ago, and I've only seen him once since the funeral. But as far as I know, Ken's still working—on his own. I'd guess he's seventy or seventy-one now."

"Thank you," Alexis said.

"And there's a bonus to hiring a guy like Ken."

"And that is?"

"He's a Vietnam veteran. I don't know a lot of details, but my dad told me a little bit. The two of them hung out at the golf course—a public course they both liked on Long Island."

"I'll give him a call. I like the idea."

"He's a good guy. I should have done a better job of staying in touch. Say hi for me, will you?"

"Sure," Alexis said. "I will. You said you saw him once after your dad's funeral. I'm guessing that wasn't business because you said you never used him. Was it pleasure?"

"Alas, not. He had a daughter. Kathleen. She died in April— no, May. She was pretty close to your age, I'd guess. I went to the funeral out on Long Island."

"Oh, God. I'm sorry. That's horrible."

"It was. It is." And then Sally Gleason surprised her. She wrapped Alexis in her arms and held her, murmuring, "And I'm really, really sorry about Austin. This just sucks and I wish there was something more I could do than give you a business card." Alexis nodded into the other woman's shoulder, a little stunned by the embrace, and found herself blinking back tears.

14

Alexis supposed she was due: it had been months since anyone had airdropped a dick pic onto her phone on the subway. But there it was. The car was full—not shoulder to shoulder and thigh to thigh packed, not the sort of crowd in which a winter flu spreads like spilled gasoline—but there were two dozen people standing and every seat taken. She had a seat and was reading a news story she'd clicked on at a stop with Wi-Fi, and now there was Wi-Fi again, and there it was on the front of her screen: dick pic.

Usually when she was flashed this way, she just deleted the image and shut off her phone. Not today. Not this afternoon. She wasn't completely sure why, but it made her angrier than usual. Maybe it was the jet lag. Maybe it was Austin's death. Maybe it was just one too many assholes sending her dick pics. Quickly she scanned the car to see if there were any children present; there weren't. And so she rose from her seat somewhere between Fifty-First Street and Fifty-Ninth Street and held up her phone with the photo, pointing it in all directions, and said loudly but calmly, "Who's the pervert in this car who just sent me a dick pic? Who's the loser who gets off on this crap?"

Some of the people groaned and some looked away—or down at their own screens, as if they were afraid their phones had been infected, too—and some, like her, studied every male in the car: the older businessmen and the delivery guys and the young dude in the denim jacket. One man, a handsome fellow her age in a gray business suit and a duster about four feet away, let go of the metal pole and held up both of his hands as if he were being robbed, and shook his head. She glared at every man in the car, but none except for the guy in the duster would make eye contact with her. Then he asked her, "You okay?"

The car squealed to a stop at Fifty-Ninth. She had planned to ride to Sixty-Eighth Street, Austin's stop. But she just hated this shit. She hoped she had shamed the degenerate, but somehow she doubted it. She looked at the young executive who had asked if she were okay, nodded that she was, and exited the subway. She'd walk the rest of the way.

She felt at once bullied and relieved when the subway pulled away from the station.

.   .   .

Would the doorman on duty at Austin's apartment be among the few who knew her? Would he know that the resident of 13D had died?

Alexis stood for a long moment on the corner of Sixty-Ninth and Third, about forty yards from the awning, trying to decide. There'd been nothing in the newspapers, and there might never be. He'd died in a bike accident on the other side of the world. Things happened. It wasn't as if the bike tour was going to go out of its way to publicize the story. The question was whether Austin's parents or one of his friends had already said something to the superintendent of the building. But did his friends even know yet? She hadn't had time to try and track down any of them. Had his parents? Perhaps. But he wasn't on the social networks, so it wasn't as if there was going to be any centralized mourning on Facebook or Instagram or his fifteen seconds of posthumous fame there.

If the doorman knew that Austin was dead, it was likely be-cause his parents had informed the super that they were coming to town tomorrow to assess how difficult it would be to clear out his apartment.

She realized that his parents were actually the key to a lot of things. For instance, would they want to sue the bike tour company for negligence? For allowing their son to bike alone? Yes, all the guests had signed release forms, but that didn't mean that the tour company wasn't going to have to contend with parental wrath in the form of a lawsuit. And what about the way he had misrepresented his family history? The way he had lied—or been lied to? Would his parents ever hear of that and, if so, what would they make of it? How would that affect their grief and how they mourned their only son? What kind of funeral would he have once his remains had been returned to America?

For the moment, however, none of that mattered. All that mattered right now was this: she had to hope that either Diego or Sean was the doorman on duty. They were the two who had seen her most often and would be most likely to give her one of the extra keys they kept to his apartment. If it was one of them, she decided her plan would be to presume that he knew Austin was never coming back, and she would share how devastated she was that he was gone.

.   .   .

Sure enough, it was Sean who was behind the desk and opened the glass door for her. Sean was in his late fifties, and his uniform jacket buttons worked hard to keep a great barrel of a chest confined. He was cheerfully gruff, with a walrus mustache that was as white as his hair, and massive brown eyeglasses that looked like they came from a vintage clothing shop in Greenwich Village.

"Alexis," he began when she was inside the lobby with him, "I'm so sorry about Austin."

"You heard?"

"Yeah. His father called. Told us to let his friend in yesterday afternoon. I gather his parents will be here tomorrow. Both of them."

She nodded, absorbing this. Someone had already been upstairs. Someone had beaten her here—and with Austin's parents' permission. "Was it Stephen?" she asked, making up a name just to elicit a response. She hoped she sounded knowing.

"No, it was that bald fellow. Guy Austin's age who I guess works with him at the hospital. He came straight from the office. Was still in his suit."

"Of course. That's"—and she stopped and rolled her eyes in frustration, hoping it looked as if the name were on the tip of her tongue but she just couldn't quite remember it.

He reached for a notebook behind the counter and scrolled back a page. "Oscar," he said. "Oscar Bolton."

She noted the last name. It would be easy enough to confirm that this was the same Oscar who had been in Sally Gleason's office earlier that afternoon. But she was almost certain it was.

"Do you mind if I go upstairs?" she asked.

He seemed to think about this. He seemed on the verge of asking her why, pressing her for details. He seemed about to say no. And so she considered hinting there was something of hers that she didn't want Austin's parents to find—something vaguely sexual and embarrassing—and was fully prepared to go with this ruse. As she began to fabricate a story in her mind, she stammered, "I . . . I left," and then wiped at her eye, even though there was no tear there and quickly looked away. She sniffed, a gesture that was histrionic but, she suspected, helpful. For all she knew, her eyes were still red from the moment she had parted with Sally Gleason.

And it worked. She didn't have to concoct a story. She'd given him just enough. He went into the closet behind the counter where they stored the residents' dry cleaning and packages that arrived during the day and returned with the spare keys.

"Make sure you bring them back when you're done," he said.

And then, perhaps fearing he had sounded too harsh, added, "I don't know if his parents have a set. They might need them tomorrow."

. . .

For a long moment she stood at the living room window of his apartment and stared down at the street thirteen floors below. The window—the windows of the whole building—needed cleaning badly. The glass was speckled with black dirt.

Being here was hitting her hard. She knew it would, and now she had turned away to face the outside world instead. Six and a half months they had had together. Not a lot, but enough. She knew how she had felt in Hoi An before she had learned he had lied: she had thought that she loved him. Maybe she loved him still. She knew only for sure that she was still trying to navigate a maelstrom rich with both confusion and grief. And though they had spent more nights at her place than his, they had spent enough time here that she could feel the emptiness and the loss in a way that was causing her eyes once more to well with tears.

Finally, she turned around and surveyed the room. She wiped her eyes. From where she stood, she could see into the kitchen as well. Most of the things in the apartment were tasteful. The problem, she had teased him on occasion, was how badly everything fit together. The couch and the chairs around the small dining table were black leather and modern, the shapes from a futuristic sci-fi movie. Meanwhile, he had decorated the walls with five classic cartoon cels, each impeccably framed behind archival glass, four of which were Looney Tunes images of Bugs Bunny and Marvin the Martian, but one was a drawing of the Grinch from the original 1966 production that he'd insisted was worth thousands. He'd loved the Grinch. Told her once he couldn't wait to watch the original with her over Christmas. She'd observed they could watch it right now, online, and he'd replied, no, no, you had to watch it live on network television in the weeks before

Christmas, as if it were 1970. That was the ritual and that was what made it wonderful.

They'd never gotten to do that together. Now they never would.

There was also a love seat with a dark floral slipcover: Victorian, he had told her, and it had once belonged to his grandparents. There was a barnwood coffee table that matched neither the couch nor the love seat nor the prints on the walls. Twice they'd sat on the floor beside it and eaten Mexican takeout off of it. He had tile coasters with prints from the 1964 World's Fair in Queens, including one of the Unisphere amidst its fountains, and they were in their usual spots on the side tables on either side of the couch. The remotes for the television were in their usual spot on the small shelf beside the TV. On one of the side tables was a photo of his parents and him in windbreakers beside a bright-red sugar maple in the autumn. They were in the shade, and his father's face was partly hidden by the bill of a Red Sox baseball cap. When she studied the man now, he looked more like Austin's grandfather than his father, but Alexis had known that he'd married late and had children late; his wife did look eight years younger than her husband. And that made sense, since even if he had only been—and the expression Captain Nguyen had used came back to her now—a Rear Echelon Mother Fucker, he had still served in Vietnam.

She realized two things as she stood there: First, that nothing seemed different to her. Nothing looked changed. The second was that this was a fool's errand. She didn't know what she was looking for, if anything, and if there was something here that might shed some light on what had happened to Austin, Oscar had likely removed it when he had been here yesterday afternoon.

Still, she sighed and pressed on. Maybe this was a Hollywood code she was performing for herself: going through the motions to satisfy some longing for closure.

His bedroom was tiny, barely big enough for his bed—which

was, she'd always been grateful when they'd spent the night here, a queen—a dresser, and a small black lacquer desk. But, God, how lovely had it been in the summer to lie there beside him, the air conditioning a lulling hum, a hint of dampness on their bare skin, always (it seemed) her left thigh curled atop his leg, her cheek against his chest. She wouldn't move until it was clear that his arm, wrapped beneath her, had gone to sleep.

Before leaving for Vietnam, he had pulled the comforter up to the pillows and smoothed it in a half-assed, single male sort of way. She sat down on the mattress and laid her head on the side of the bed he slept on when they slept here together. On the pillow. On his pillow. Finally, she could inhale him. His scent. Yes, the apartment was musty and empty, but here he was. She had, at last, found him—at least a trace. Again, she felt her eyes growing moist. This time she didn't fight it and she didn't wipe the tears away. She let the pillowcase sponge them up.

. . .

Austin hadn't owned a desktop computer, and so the surface of the desk in his bedroom usually had nothing upon it but catalogs, junk mail, and development materials from the hospital. Brochures, presentations. That was the case right now, she saw when she had regained her composure. There was the framed photo of the two of them he liked that had been taken at a party in Montauk in July. They were in bathing suits around a fire pit at dusk; it looked to her like a still from a beer commercial, but she understood why it made him happy. In the background were a few of her friends. She picked it up and examined it closely. You could see some of the scars on one of her thighs. Usually she would have wrapped a towel around her waist to hide the scars there, but she had been so happily tipsy that evening that she hadn't bothered. Thank God, she was wearing a tank suit. No, there was no need to thank God; she hadn't worn a bikini in years and never would again. Her abdomen had often been a target of hers, some scars low—a cesarean affectation—but others circling her navel the way lions might surround a baby zebra.

Her friends, she thought. They never saw his friends. Or hardly ever. There were people he'd mention, and two or three times she had been able to put a face and a trace of a personality to a name when they would meet at a bar. But their social life was either just the two of them or the two of them and some of her pals or the two of them at an event involving the hospital and fund-raising.

On the floor, beneath the desk, was a printer, which was linked via Wi-Fi to his laptop. The printing tray empty.

She went through the desk drawers, but the most interesting thing she found was his checkbook. Like her, she saw he really wrote very few checks. He paid most bills online. There was nothing there that either puzzled or surprised her.

She rummaged through his dresser: his casual shirts and sweaters, some of which she had given him, his underwear and socks. She pulled aside the suits and dress shirts that were hung in his closet and saw his rack with his neckties, including one she had given him a month ago. She found his condoms. Even though she was on the pill, she'd insisted he use condoms their first three months together. He worked in a hospital and was fine with that. He wanted to wear them, as well.

The bathroom revealed nothing she hadn't expected: no prescription drugs at all, nothing hidden behind the stack of bath towels or under the sink.

She returned to the kitchen and scanned the cabinets and the pantry, but she really wasn't sure what she was searching for and came across nothing she hadn't expected, except for the confirmation that he really did like his olive oil. She saw three different kinds, including the basil-infused olive oil he'd used when he'd made them a delicious pesto a month ago. They'd eaten it by candlelight. He was an attentive chef and an attentive lover.

And he might have been a liar. She could not lose sight of that.

But she also could not lose sight of the possibility that he had had a good reason to lie. It was, perhaps, why she was here now in his apartment. She owed it to him to find out the truth—to find out what really had happened to him.

Most of the front hall was taken up with his bicycle and bicycle gear. She went there and gazed at the bike before leaving. Usually his helmet and shoes would have been there, too. There was a small white cabinet in which he kept his jerseys, his shorts, his gloves, and his energy gels. Sometimes he kept his keys there so he wouldn't forget them. Now the top of it was empty. She turned on the hall light and knelt down in front of the cabinet. She looked at the dust upon it—or, specifically, the section where no dust had accumulated in the nearly two weeks he had been gone. She couldn't be sure, but she thought it was possible that whatever Oscar had taken had been a rectangle perhaps seven or eight inches wide and ten or eleven inches long, and it had been sitting right here.

With her camera, she leaned over and snapped a photo of this, too.

She looked at the image to see if the dust pattern was clear and saw that it was. She used her thumb and index finger to expand the image, and when she did, she noticed there was something behind the cabinet. Some papers, maybe. She put her phone down on the floor, reached behind the wood, and with her fingertips grabbed three pieces of printer paper. Either Austin had printed something at work and brought it home, or he'd printed something in his bedroom and planned to bring it to work—and it had fallen behind the cabinet. It was possible that these papers had been atop the cabinet, and Oscar accidentally had knocked them to the floor. Or, when he'd walked past it, his breeze had blown them there.

She sat on the hardwood floor and looked at the material. It

was a three-page abstract and summary of a much longer academic research paper about Vietnamese rats and the long-term
effects of Agent Orange on the animal, and the resistance of their
descendants to certain diseases that previously had killed them. It
baffled her, and so she folded the papers into a square that fit into
her purse and was about to leave.

But then she decided that she wanted—that she needed—one
more thing. She went back to his bedroom and also took with her
the framed picture of Austin and her at the party.

. . .

She was nearing the subway, the framed picture of Austin and
her at the beach clutched under her arm and her purse slung over
that same shoulder, when her phone rang. She pulled it from her
back pants pocket and paused on Lexington Avenue. She knew
instantly that it was one of Austin's parents. She'd called that
number from Vietnam and she'd called it again while waiting for
the connection in Seoul and she'd even called it earlier today. It
seemed oddly fitting that his father or mother was phoning her
now, right after she had been in their son's apartment and smelled
him on the pillowcases and heard his voice in her head mimicking
the deep baritone of the narrator for the Grinch.

"Hello?" she began, knowing how tentative her own voice
sounded.

"Is this Alexis?" It was a man, his tone as faltering as hers.

"It is, yes. Mr. Harper?"

"Please. I know we've never met, but call me Peter."

"Okay. Peter. I'm sorry," she said, and suddenly she was
choked up. She hadn't expected this. How many times had she
stood in the hospital waiting room or a hospital corridor and told
fathers and mothers and brothers and sisters and children that they
had done all they could, they had tried everything, but someone
had died? Too often. She understood the anguish and shock he
was feeling, and now she was feeling it, too. Again. It was like

a roller coaster that seemed never to end. One moment she was functioning, dimly aware of the dread on the ascent, but thinking, and the next she was shrieking inside on the downslope.

"I know," he said simply, hearing the way her voice had broken. "I'm sorry we haven't called you back sooner. But this has been very hard on us, especially his mother."

"How is she now?"

"She's upstairs, resting. We're coming to New York tomorrow, and we had to pack. It took a lot out of her—packing."

"It does even in the best of times," Alexis said.

"And these sure as heck are not the best of times."

Other than roughly his age, she knew almost nothing for certain about the man, because Austin had lied about his service in Vietnam. The FBI attaché had said in Hoi An that the family came from old money—and lots of it—but Austin had never implied the family was anything more than comfortable. He'd also said he was an only child. Was even that true?

Still, she held the photo of Austin and her between her knees so she had a free hand to root inside her purse for a tissue and wiped her cheeks.

"Have the doctors given her anything?" she asked.

"We both have a little help, yes," he replied. "Austin told us you're an ER doctor."

"I am."

"And you ID'd the body back in Vietnam, right?"

She sighed. "That's right."

"I don't want to know the details, but . . . thank you. Thank you for doing that."

There was so much she wanted to ask him, but she wanted to be careful: she didn't want to hurt his feelings by not knowing things she would have if Austin hadn't been hiding something—or, for whatever the reason, been fabricating something. And so she moved gingerly, as if walking on ice.

"The hospital told me you were coming to town and you were going to stop by Austin's office. Clean it out, I guess."

"That's right. We're also going by his apartment. Of course."

"Can I join you when you're at the hospital? I'm working tomorrow, but unless there's a subway derailment or natural disaster, I should be able to get away for a few minutes. A weekday afternoon is relatively quiet."

"Sure. Absolutely. It will be nice to meet you. I know Austin liked you very much."

Liked you very much. She tried not to dwell on that. When people liked something very much, it meant that they didn't love it. If you liked rum raisin ice cream or cheesecake very much, it meant you'd eat it at a dinner party if it was served for dessert, but it wasn't something you'd order if you had a choice. She knew, for instance, that she loved French toast with real maple syrup and whipped butter, but she only liked pancakes very much—and only then if she was in the right mood.

"What time do you think that will be?" she asked.

"I guess it depends on the traffic. We're driving into the city. But I'm thinking around three thirty or four."

"Thank you. Why don't you text me when you arrive?"

"Sure."

"May I ask you something?" she began cautiously. Austin had said his father was a semi-retired ad man. He no longer worked for an agency in Boston, but he still did some freelance work. This might be safe ground on which to move and test for small, seismic faults.

"Certainly. Ask me anything."

"Are you still in advertising?"

"Technically, yes. But I left advertising agencies years ago. I'm a consultant now."

"What kind of consultant?"

"I worked a lot in pharmaceuticals, which is a great way to remain employed in a young man's business after fifty. Now I consult for pharmaceutical companies on their communication strategies. I travel a bit and work from home. But I also garden and ski. I couldn't do that if I had a regular nine-to-five job."

"And your wife?"

"She's a professional volunteer, if you know what I mean. She volunteers at the school and the library. She wants to be around children."

This made sense. Austin had said she'd recently retired as a school principal.

"Is it at the same school where she used to work?"

"No. She worked in a middle school. She volunteers at the elementary school. The kids are cuter. She calls them nuggets. She can read to them. Draw pictures with them. Things like that. Why?"

"Just curious," she said. Then: "This could probably wait until tomorrow, but it's a really big question, and it's been weighing on me since I first met with the FBI's legal attaché in Cambodia and Vietnam. Toril Bjornstad. You've talked to her, right?"

"Yes. Three times. Maybe four."

"Did she tell you what your son told me—about you and your brother?"

"No."

She took a breath and stood up straight, a reflex: it was her pose for delivering bad news in the ER. "Austin told me that you and your brother had both been soldiers in Vietnam. In the war. He'd said your brother had died there and you'd been wounded. Austin was alone the day he was killed, and he went riding alone because, supposedly, he was making a pilgrimage to the sites—roughly—where his uncle had died and where you were wounded."

There was silence at the other end of the phone. "Peter?" she said finally, when the quiet had gone on for seconds.

"Just digesting that," he said carefully.

"I understand."

"I mean, we talked about Vietnam before he went last year and before he went this year. But he was nowhere near where his uncle or I were stationed the day he was hit by the truck—or whatever ran into him."

"You were wounded at Long Binh—near Ho Chi Minh City. Is that right?"

"You keep saying 'wounded,' and *wounded* isn't exactly the right word. It implies that it was combat related."

"It wasn't?" she asked, with a twinge of guilt at the way she was leading him on since she knew the truth.

"God, no. I was in a—what do they call them . . ."

She waited until he found the right word.

"A go-cart," he continued finally. "I crashed the damn thing into a side wall. It was like a clown car, but without a roof. There were five of us crammed into it. We were kids screwing around. And I was injured. Broke my hip and my leg. But it wasn't exactly a Purple Heart–worthy wound," he said.

"And Austin knew that?"

"Why wouldn't he?"

"And your brother?" Alexis asked.

"Yes, he was KIA. That's true. Killed in action. But he was north of where you all were biking. Austin was nowhere near there when he was killed."

"And you're absolutely positive that Austin was aware of this—of all of this?"

"Of course he was. It's not like his uncle and I were spies. We had a real soldier and a real paper pusher. I was the paper pusher."

And a lifeguard, she thought to herself.

"I was the lucky one," he continued. "Obviously. But it's not like we were hiding anything."

"He . . ."

"Go ahead," said Peter.

"He said you were shot. An ambush. He said his bike ride that last day would bring him past the jungle where his uncle died and the rice paddies where you were hit. Why do you think he would have told me that?"

"I have no clue," Peter began, his tone a little clipped and defensive now. "That's completely absurd."

A delivery truck started to back up near Alexis, the beep to alert people it was moving backwards nearly deafening her, given where she was standing.

"No idea?" she asked, speaking loudly as she retreated from the truck.

"None," he replied. "Are you sure you understood him?"

"You couldn't misunderstand that. And that was the story he told all the other people on the bike tour, too. The guests. The guides. It wasn't just me."

"Well, I don't know what to tell you," he said. "Maybe he was ashamed of me, but I don't think so. This whole thing is just nonsense." Everything had changed in their conversation, that was clear to Alexis. They were no longer two people grieving Austin's death. He was, yes; but in his eyes, now she was defaming his son's character with some wild accusation or tall tale. "Look," he continued, "my son is dead. I don't have the emotional capital at the moment to care about the idea he may have told one of the women he was dating something . . . exaggerated."

"Exaggerated?" she repeated, stung by the idea that in his eyes she was merely one of the women her son was dating. She had just been in his apartment. There certainly weren't signs of any other women in his life. And yet the words he had used couldn't help but remind her of Ellie Thomas's suppositions. A mistress. A baby mama. Her tone more defensive than she would have liked, Alexis said, "That's not an exaggeration, that's a lie."

"Look, this is the first I'm hearing of any of this. I have no answer, and I really don't want to have to explain it or justify it," he said firmly.

"I'm sorry," she told him. "I'm sure there was a good reason."

And then they said good-bye and hung up. She was relieved that he hadn't decided to bar her from his son's office tomorrow.

. . .

It was dark now, and Sally Gleason had one last thing to do before leaving the office: she wanted to connect with Ken Sarafian, her late father's friend. She didn't view it as a warning, precisely: she hadn't sicced a madwoman on the elderly detective. Alexis Remnick was sweet and more or less grounded, but she was obsessing over Austin Harper's death, and that couldn't be good for her. It couldn't be good for anyone. And so Sally was going to ask a favor of Ken.

"I'm calling to apologize," she began when he picked up. "I've sent someone your way."

"You want to apologize for a referral? Good Lord, why?"

"It's a young ER doctor who can't let go of a boyfriend. Alexis Remnick is her name. The poor guy was killed last week while biking in Vietnam. A truck or a car hit him. She thinks there's more to it than that, when it's pretty clear there isn't."

"And you want me to walk her in off the ledge?"

"Do you mind? She's a doctor, and she needs to be focused on her patients, not on this. Be your usual kind self, but explain to her that there really isn't anything that can be done at this point—or should be done. She might listen to you as an ex-cop and a PI. She sure as heck wasn't listening to me."

"I can talk to her."

"Thank you, Ken."

"It's fine."

"How are you?"

"I'm okay."

"Really?"

"Really. One foot in front of the other."

"It was a beautiful service," she said softly, referring to Kathleen's memorial.

"Thank you."

There was quiet at the other end of the line. "I almost didn't give Alexis your name," Sally said, wondering if she had made a mistake.

"Because of Kathleen or because it was in Vietnam that this ER doc lost her boyfriend?"

"Both, I guess. Was it okay? Reassure me it was."

Over the years, Ken had told her father bits and pieces about his time in country, some nineteenth-hole beer gab in the clubhouse, and her father, in turn, had shared bits and pieces with his family. It wasn't a betrayal. Spouses talked to spouses when the marriage was solid, and fathers talked to their children. Still, Sally was reassured when Ken told her, "No need to fret. I don't go to pieces when I hear helicopters."

When she had hung up and belted herself into her Burberry, she felt better. Ken was a good man. He would explain to Alexis that hers was a fool's errand, and the ER doctor would get on with her life.

15

It was dark now, and Douglas could see the moon from his bed. He was lying on his back, and the woman was nestled against him.

"Can you see the moon?" he asked her.

"I can," she murmured.

He ran his fingernails through her hair and along her scalp the way she liked. "It's not quite full. The full moon is what, a day away? Two?" he asked.

"Something like that."

It was a little after nine in the evening. He knew she'd leave him soon. She would roll over, dig her cigarettes from her purse, and light one with those long, slender fingers. He would rub the small of her spine, tickling her, and she would bow her back. If it was even a month earlier, she would then have climbed into her blouse or one of his shirts, and the two of them would have gone to his rooftop terrace and gazed out at the moon from there while she smoked. But it was nearing the fourth week in October. That wasn't happening tonight. Instead she would sit up and smoke in his bed, her back against the mahogany headboard, and he would rest his head in her lap. On her thigh. She would place a saucer on his nightstand and use it for an ashtray. Then she would get dressed and go home.

It was interesting to him that tonight the sex had been especially satisfying—she had been uncharacteristically affectionate with him—because Austin was dead. The man's death had saddened her in a way that he hadn't expected. She'd told him about it as soon as she'd arrived at his home, and while she hadn't cried, he'd been surprised to see her have to blink back a tear when she broke the news: the poor guy had been killed on his bike in a hit-and-run accident in Vietnam, she said. He, in return, had feigned shock and then what he supposed was a masculine variant on mourning. He'd shaken his head and looked down at his feet. Austin had been the one who had introduced the two of them.

"Are you going to show me what you filed today? Can I see the story?" she asked him.

"It's not interesting. Wait until it runs and has some nice color photos."

"Not that interesting? You didn't fall in love with the place? I adore Siena."

"Remember, it wasn't my first trip there. It was fine. It was Tuscany. But it really has become Disneyland for adults."

"That feels good," she said softly, referring to the way he was massaging her scalp. She purred. "So, tell me: did you find some gorgeous little *enoteca* that happened to have a dartboard?"

"There are a lot of English and Irish expats living there now, but, alas, I did not find a dartboard."

"Any withdrawal?"

"From darts? No. I was fine."

A thought seemed to come to her as she pulled away from him, sat up, and lit a cigarette. "I assume you put them in a checked bag. Your darts. I've seen them. I can't imagine they let you bring them into the passenger cabin. You could really hurt someone with one of them."

"With a dart? Hardly. No one's going to take over a flight deck with a dart. No one's going to hijack a plane with a dart."

"Austin used to love to play darts with you."

He sighed and hoped the exhalation would be interpreted as grief, not exasperation. A little Austin had gone a long way as an aphrodisiac; but as postcoital pillow talk, it was just a buzzkill. "I'm glad," he said simply.

"It's just so sad."

"It is."

"What's next?"

"My next assignment?"

"Uh-huh. Where are you off to next?"

"*Travel and Leisure* is sending me to Singapore," he told her.

"When?"

"Unsure."

"Italy last week. Singapore . . . soon. You do lead a glamorous life."

She tapped an ash into the saucer, and he found himself smiling. "I like my life. But, as you know, I couldn't live the way I do or in a place like this if I had to depend on the income of a freelance journalist."

"No shame in being born rich," she said.

"No. I know that," he agreed, though he really didn't know that. He was born wealthy, but his family had certainly not been among the Texas super rich. Growing up, he had always been—to paraphrase F. Scott Fitzgerald—a worst-house-on-the-best-block sort of kid. He'd been on the far side of twenty-five when his father's Dallas-based engineering and construction team had started to make a killing in Iraq after Saddam Hussein was toppled. At the time, Webber had been a marine there. He'd gone to college, graduated in 2001, and enlisted three months after 9/11. His first tours had been in Afghanistan. Then, starting in 2003, in Iraq. While he was watching IEDs obliterate his friends in Fallujah, his family had started raking in serious scratch rebuilding Baghdad. Or, at least, pretending to rebuild Baghdad. He knew the reality of some of those defense contracts. His real income lately had come from selling arms to Kurdish militia and brokering a couple of deals in Myanmar. The travel writing was a cover. A hobby. An excuse to travel. He never wanted to be mistaken for an Adnan Khashoggi or a Viktor Bout. Webber really had been to Siena, but it had actually been the month before last. He'd been there on his way back from his more lucrative work in Jordan. "Nevertheless, I also know that I play for Team Entitled," he continued finally.

She chuckled. *"Team,"* she said, emphasizing the word. "That word always sounds so corporate to me."

"That's because you don't follow sports and you never played basketball or soccer in high school. Everything sounds corporate to you."

She pinched his stomach hard, and he grunted reflexively against the pain. "I think I should be insulted," she teased him.

"Not at all. I am first and foremost a realist."

"You are nothing of the sort. You go to beautiful faraway places and write about them and you grow tomatoes in terra-cotta pots in New York City. I loved your story on Australia. You're a throwback. You're a romantic."

"Someday you should come with me."

"Not happening. At least in the foreseeable future. Our world exists in these rooms and these rooms only." He watched the smoke from her exhalation waft above him before it seemed to disappear into his ceiling fan. It was off right now, and he stared for a moment at the curve of the blade. The shape was the same elegant scythe as the bacteria.

"Just an idea."

"Understood." Then, after a beat, she said, "Well . . ."

And he knew when she said that it meant that soon she would swing her legs over the side of the bed. Whenever she said, "Well . . . ," it was the beginning of the end of their evening. It always made him a little sad. It was the damnedest thing, but he was confident that he enjoyed their postcoital time together more than she did. He suspected he liked foreplay more than she did, too. She really was the most efficient person he knew when it came to time management. Maybe she was right: maybe he really was a bit of a romantic.

"You probably know this, but koalas have chlamydia," she said. "I noticed that wasn't in your story on Sydney."

"And prairie dogs have the plague. I learned that tidbit two years ago when I did a feature on southern Colorado. But they're not near people—the prairie dogs."

"Okay, I find that frightening."

"Really?" He hadn't planned on bringing up the word *plague,* but he had, and now—almost out of curiosity—he pressed ever so slightly. "Think of the things the labs in your wing are researching every single day."

"I rarely go near the labs. You know that. That's the university world."

He chuckled. "You're a university hospital."

"That whole world terrifies me. They have mice in there, you know."

He did know that and had to restrain a small smile.

"And rats," she continued, shuddering ever so slightly.

"Rats are badass little monsters," he said. "Think of that toilet beast."

"I'd rather not, thank you very much."

Occasionally, he teased her with his horror stories of rats.

"No?"

"No," she said emphatically. One time she'd chastised him, telling him that his tales were just urban legends and he should know better. He was a journalist, after all. But they weren't urban legends, and she probably understood this as well as anyone— which was why his stories must have unnerved her and she found them doubly grotesque. Austin said one of the hospital researchers really had one time come across a rat in a toilet. It was in the guy's apartment. He tried to kill it with a toilet brush, holding it under the water because he couldn't flush it away: it was just too damn strong a swimmer. But the creature had made short work of the bristles and then started eating the handle. Finally, he had to go to a hardware store and buy a plunger, and then push the rat as far into the porcelain as he could, holding it beneath the rubber dome until the damn thing finally drowned. The scientist, a young guy from Seattle, recalled how he had kept thinking of Roy Scheider in *Jaws* when he first spotted the shark: "You're gonna need a bigger boat."

They lay there quietly for another a minute, and then she snuffed out her cigarette in the saucer. She kissed the top of his head and scooted her legs out from underneath him to leave the bed and get dressed. He sat up and watched her. He liked the way she always put on her bra before her panties. He loved her hips. Her legs.

"Did you and Austin and that girlfriend of his ever go out together?" she asked. "Did you all ever do anything interesting?"

"Never."

"She came by my office today."

He grew alert, though he kept his tone offhand. "Seriously?"

"Yes."

"What did she want?"

"I don't know. Talk to someone. Then she wanted to look around Austin's office."

"Go on."

"She's clearly having trouble processing the fact that the poor guy died. Letting him go. She cared about him," she said, her hands behind her back as she clasped shut her bra.

"Did she?"

"Care about him?"

"No. I meant look around his office."

"I said she couldn't. Protocol. But I also said she could come back tomorrow, when his parents are in town."

"Well, let me know how she seems. Tomorrow."

"I will," said Sally Gleason. "But I think she'll be fine. I think she's just kind of in shock."

.   .   .

Soon after Sally had left, Douglas got a text, and it pissed him off. Once again, he would have to give his digital etiquette lecture. Still, the information was helpful:

> Sinclair brought in a bunch of Vietnamese rats yesterday. It
> took more anesthesia than usual to knock them out.

He took serious notice of this. He texted back:

> What did they use? Halothane? Isoflurane?

The response was quick and, much to Webber's disgust, actually included a laughing-face emoji.

> That question is way above my pay grade. No idea.

He put down his phone and went to the refrigerator for a beer and a couple of ice cubes, and thought of Austin. He guessed the synaptic connection was the word *Vietnam*. But it could just as well have been *rats*.

He wished he could be sure that the moron hadn't brought any of the pathogen with him to Vietnam. They'd searched him and hadn't found any. But was it possible he'd already sold whatever he'd brought? It was. Before erasing his laptop and tablet, they'd checked his email and texts. They'd checked his apps. They'd checked his bank accounts. There was no indication that he'd already made the sale—or at least been paid for it.

Bao had reassured him that they had wiped clean his devices and all they could find on the Cloud.

And, of course, if he had sold something, the likely buyers were dead. And Bao's crew had found nothing there, either, and they'd scoured the lab thoroughly before torching it.

But the girl—the ER doc—had gone to Sally's office.

He didn't like that, and he didn't know what it meant. It might mean nothing. It probably meant nothing.

But then again, it might mean everything if her idiot boyfriend had recruited her and involved her in his scheme. He hated loose ends, and the idea was now taking root: this ER doctor might be considerably worse than a mere loose end.

16

At first, Alexis had said no when her mother had offered to pick up some Indian food after work and come by her apartment with dinner. Visiting Austin's apartment had unnerved her, as had speaking with Peter Harper, and now she wanted to be alone. She was also experiencing the slow nausea of serious jet lag. The perfect evening would have been to see if she could access online the full research article on the rats of Vietnam, read it, and then collapse into bed and sleep.

But her mother was one of the world's great negotiators—which was why she usually got what she wanted—and she had already called Ellie Thomas, Alexis's friend in the building, to invite her to dinner, too, and Ellie had said she would join them.

"Do you honestly have other plans?" her mother had asked Alexis on the phone as she emerged from the subway near her apartment late that afternoon. "You just got back from Vietnam, you're due in the ER at noon tomorrow, and you just endured every traveler's worst nightmare. Your traveling companion died."

She had paused on the sidewalk and tried to understand the reasoning behind her mother's choice of words: *traveling companion*. She could only conjecture. She considered saying, *Since when is my boyfriend my traveling companion? Are we suddenly living in an E. M. Forster novel?* She supposed she would have said something like that if Austin hadn't lied to her about why they had gone to Vietnam and if she, in turn, hadn't finally told her mother that he had. In the end, Alexis had said yes simply because it was just easier than saying no, and now the three of them had finished dinner in her small apartment—smaller than Austin's, that was for sure—drinking coffee that, strong as it was, was never going to smother the aroma of the saag paneer, the matter paneer, and the samosas. Alexis knew that when she awoke tomorrow morning, the apartment would still smell like an Indian restaurant. Their plates and silverware were in the dishwasher and the leftovers were in plastic containers in the refrigerator. Her mother would have it no other way.

"A private investigator," Ellie was saying to Alexis when her mother returned from the kitchen. "I don't know whether I find that idea interesting or disturbing." The veterinarian was sitting with her long legs curled beneath her. She was a tall woman with brown eyes and a long red braid that she toyed with sometimes when she was thinking aloud—as she was now.

"I feel I owe it to him," Alexis said, her tongue feeling a little thick from the Indian beer that Ellie had picked up when Alexis's mother told her what she herself was bringing. Alexis had drunk only a bottle and a half, but she was tired and the alcohol was hitting her hard. She was a lightweight when it came to beer and wine and booze, and didn't drink much.

"You owe him nothing," her mother said, sitting beside her on the couch. She was still in the gray skirt and the blouse she had worn to the office that day, but her suit jacket was hung up in the hall closet. She dyed her hair auburn, and it was dyed perfectly. She was sixty and looked fifty. She joked to her employees—and Alexis had seen her do this in speeches and get laughs from it— that she looked so youthful because she'd been blessed to have been a young widow. "Why he would tell you—why he would tell all of you on the bike tour—such an outrageous lie is beyond me. It's appalling. Look, I know—"

"Mother, I—"

"Please, let me finish," her mother said, steamrolling forward. "I know when things should be transparent, and I know when complete transparency is a bad thing. But he was up to something really shady. That's clear. It's not that he lied about his father's military record or where his uncle died. It's that he used those lies as a pretext to go to Vietnam—twice. Two times. I know you cared about him, Alexis. I get it. For all I know, you loved him. And his death is a terrible thing. But it's not your responsibility to bring in a private investigator. If anyone should, it's his parents. You need to move on. Sure, grieve. Though, personally, I wouldn't grieve for a man who misled you so disgracefully. I would love to know what his plan was when you found out—because you would have found out."

"Unless—" Ellie began, but then stopped herself.

"Unless what?" her mother asked, but then she nodded and understood. "Unless he never planned to be with you long enough for you to find out," she said, finishing the sentence that Ellie wouldn't.

"Look, Mother," Alexis said, pausing when her voice cracked, but not stopping, "I don't pretend to know why he did what he did or what he was doing the afternoon he went missing. I only know this: he was always—always—very good to me. He was always kind and fun. If he had any flaw that I ever saw, it was this: he was . . . boyish. Maybe he hadn't completely grown up. But I'm not sure that was a flaw. That was . . ." And once more, she brought her lips together, pressing them shut, and this time she did stop speaking when she saw Austin's smiling, boisterous face in her mind.

Ellie finished the beer she was drinking, tilting her head back for the last, likely warm drops. Then she put the bottle down on the coffee table and asked her, "Did you suggest getting a PI to his dad?"

"I didn't," Alexis admitted—and it felt like a confession, a failure. "I had planned to, but I was unprepared for his animosity when I told him how Austin had lied. He was so angry."

"And he had absolutely no explanation for that lie? For those lies?" her mother asked.

"I told you: he got defensive."

"Which is when we parry," her mother scolded her. "Either you push back or you agree. But no matter what, you reiterate exactly what you want. What you need. You negotiate."

"No!" Alexis snapped at her. "The man had just lost his son. His son had just died. Listen to what you're saying. Just listen."

"I was thirty-six when my husband died. Your father. Trust me, I don't have to imagine that kind of pain. Neither do you."

"You're wrong, Mother. This time, you're wrong. Peter Harper outlived his son. He and his wife have to shoulder that. I'm sorry, but after he pointed that out to me, it was all I could do to"—and again she ceased speaking. She had a feeling if she had continued that her mother would have reminded her that the man had referred to her as merely one of the women his son was dating; it had taken a lot to react to that observation without losing her mind the first time she had heard it.

"Did he say anything about a funeral?" her mother asked, softening.

"No. I'm guessing they'll focus on that when they know more about when the remains will be back in America."

"Have you heard from any of his friends?" Ellie inquired.

"Not yet. But I will. Maybe tomorrow I'll reach out to some. Maybe the day after tomorrow. Since he wasn't on the social networks, word spreads a lot more slowly."

"Don't you find even that strange?" her mother asked.

Alexis started to respond, but instead just made what Ellie referred to as her angry monster toddler face: squinting her eyes, baring her teeth. Sometimes she'd raise her hands and curl her fingers into claws. It was comic and it was ridiculous, and usually it made its point and defused whatever conversational bomb was nearing detonation. It did so again now.

"Tell me more about the glove, Lexi," Ellie said, after a moment of silence in the room.

"What about it?" Alexis asked.

"You're sure there was no hole in it?"

"Positive. There was nothing at all that corresponded to the wound on the back of his hand."

"Did he have any other weird scars on his body?" the veterinarian asked.

"Other than the bullet wound on his biceps? Not really. Why?"

"You're a physician. Sometimes a person's body is a road map."

"Or a biography. I see where you're going."

"I mean, in the six or seven short months you knew him, you saw some weird shit."

She nodded. "He also had those little scars on his fingertips from the cat bite."

Her mother turned to her and sat forward, her elbows on her knees. "When did a cat bite him? Why did a cat bite him? You never told me that."

And so Alexis shared with her that when Austin had arrived at the ER with the bullet wound the night they had met in the spring, he still had Band-Aids on his fingers from a cat bite. She explained that a cat had snapped at him at a bakery.

"It happens. Sometimes cats get skittish," Ellie murmured, but Alexis could see the wheels turning in her mind by the way she was fiddling with her long braid. "Tell me something."

"Go ahead."

"You're sure it was a cat bite?"

"No. But he said it was."

"Have you ever seen a cat bite?"

"Yes. Where is this going, Ellie?" Alexis asked.

"Well, when a cat lashes out, it's likely to scratch—not bite."

"But cats do bite."

"Oh, I know."

"Do you think he might have been lying?"

Ellie shrugged, asked to borrow her phone, and started typing. Alexis felt her mother's gaze upon both her and her friend. After a moment, Ellie handed the phone back to Alexis and said, "Look at those—especially the top one. Those are pretty good images of cat bites. I know you saw the wounds back in the spring, but that top photo shows cat bites on a finger. Did Austin's bite look like that?"

Alexis studied the image. It was a puncture wound. It was a couple of puncture wounds. They were clean, they were clear, they were precise. The cuts on Austin's fingers really hadn't looked like that. There was a puncture—at least she recalled one—but generally the cuts had looked more like a series of gashes.

An idea came to her, and she glanced at the photo of the scars on his fingertips she'd snapped at the morgue. Then she performed another search on the phone and went to those images on the web. It may have been the power of suggestion, given the papers she had discovered behind the cabinet in Austin's front hallway, but maybe not. These photos looked a lot more like what she remembered from that night in the ER.

She held up her phone so the veterinarian could see the photos she had just found.

"It was months ago, so I'll never be sure," she told Ellie. "But I think the bites looked more like these ones."

"Those are rat bites," the animal doctor said.

"I know," Alexis said. "I think, looking back, he'd been bitten by a rat."

.   .   .

In the night, after her mother and Ellie had left, she sat alone on her bed in her underwear and her nightshirt, and pulled it up above her waist. She tilted the shade on her bedside lamp toward her lap and stared at the scars on the insides of her thighs. She recalled the first time that Austin had seen them. God, he'd been gentle. Not a lot of men had seen them, because she hadn't had a lot of men. Med school will put a crimp in anyone's libido.

On the mattress beside her was her cutting kit. It was an airline's first-class amenities bag, deep blue and white, and she had emptied it of its earplugs and toothbrush and slippers and sleep mask. She'd filled it with a five-pack of old-fashioned, rectangular razor blades, each in its cardboard case, a scalpel, a few Medi-First alcohol wipes, a five-ounce bottle of Bactine, some hydrogen peroxide she'd poured into a 3-1-1 travel container, a couple of sterile gauze pads, and six of her favorite Skin-Flex Band-Aids. She'd assembled it as a reminder of all she had transcended when she'd moved back to New York, and as a dare she would never take. She would always, she assured herself, choose truth.

At least she told herself it was but a reminder and a dare. In fact, she feared, it was a life preserver. In case of fire, break glass.

Now she held the scalpel in her right hand very much like a pen and stared at the tip.

It had been years. Years.

But she was shouldering so much, and she had lost so much. She was lost herself.

And she was a riot of emotions, some of which were cavernous and raw, and she found herself tortured by self-loathing. Again. Intellectually, she knew it was undeserved. She knew—or, at least, she believed—that she was a good doctor. She knew that she wasn't the only person whom Austin had deceived. But how had it all come to this? She glanced at the photo of the two of them at the party that she had taken from his apartment and, though she was alone, shook her head.

She'd learned about why people cut well before med school, but she was fascinated by the clinical ways they discussed it in one of her classes. They didn't spend a lot of time on it, but they'd spent enough for her to see all the professor got right and all he got wrong. She considered speaking up and talking about thumbtacks and kitchen knives and sewing needles. At one point when the professor was saying something about how a cutter may simply be a person with too few natural opioids, she considered correcting him—telling him that it had less to do with opioids or endorphins than it did with self-loathing and release. At least in her case. It helped with both: it was simultaneously punishment and agency, the scarlet fluid filling the sluices in her skin and allowing her to whisper to herself, *This is me. This is no one else. I deserve this and I did this. Fuck you. Fuck you all.*

But she hadn't said a word to the professor.

Because that sort of "look at me" narcissism was never who she was. It wasn't who most cutters were. You hid your cuts, just as you hid your scars: the ones inside as well as the ones outside.

She put the scalpel back into her cutting kit and removed one of the razor blades. The razor blades had always been her favorite. The pain was exquisite. The lines were precise. She had always been better with razor blades than she had with the X-Acto knife she had sometimes used as a teen. She'd never used a scalpel because she hadn't owned one back then, but she presumed the sensation of the scalpel would be a bit like the X-Acto. Carefully she pulled the blade from its cardboard sarcophagus and started to press it against one of the lines of scar tissue at the seam of her panties. But she stopped before she broke the skin. She closed her eyes and rolled her head, stretching her neck and breathing mindfully. This wasn't who she was; this wasn't who she would be.

At least not tonight.

She slid the blade back into its cardboard holster and put it aside. Now that she'd removed it and pressed it against her skin, she'd throw it away. Then she zipped up her cutting kit. She considered taking it right now to the garbage chute by the elevator on her floor of the apartment building, but she knew she wouldn't. She was like that ex-smoker who always kept a pack in the nightstand. Just in case. And if she did throw it away? Tomorrow she would simply go to a pharmacy and the ER and create a new one from a new cosmetics bag.

And so she put her cutting kit back in her dresser, burying it deep behind the socks she never (or rarely) wore, invisible, and then stripped off her clothes and disappeared into the hot, hot water of the shower, once again curled on the porcelain, a body that was warm and wet and sad, but also—and this was what mattered—alive.

WEDNESDAY

Somewhere in the neighborhood of twenty million Americans take Coumadin. Most are older or downright elderly. It's a blood thinner. It treats blood clots. It decreases the likelihood of strokes. Want to see someone on it? Go to any golf course in Florida or Arizona and look for the old guys with the bruises on their arms.

Coumadin is actually an anticoagulant chemical called warfarin. A scientist discovered it caused rats to bleed to death internally. That was way back in 1948, certainly not the early years of rodenticides, but a long time ago.

These days, most brown rats are resistant to it. An exterminator can spread it on grain like brie on a cracker, and rats will eat it and ask for another. The animals were largely able to scoff at the poison by the mid-1970s. Thirty years. A very short time for evolution.

But that's the thing about rats. They evolve fast. They adapt. You don't ever exterminate them. Not ever. You just control them as best you can.

17

Quang had spent the morning kicking a soccer ball with his daughter and three of her friends at their school. The CSCD captain was an old dad, but not as old as his hair, which had gone prematurely white, made some people think he was. Some people thought he was his daughter's grandfather when they first saw the two of them together. He was actually only forty-five. Ly was a ferocious competitor and always gave him—and her friends—a spectacular workout. Afterwards, he had dropped the other girls off at their houses and brought his daughter home. Then he'd showered, put on his uniform, had a quick lunch with his family, and gone to his office at the Canh Sat Co Dong in Da Nang.

He began his shift, as he did always, by looking at any new paperwork on the open cases. Often, he was surprised. On Monday, for instance, he saw there was something interesting about last week's hit-and-run on the Hai Van Pass. The one involving the American bicyclist. On Sunday, a Chinese tourist trying to take a selfie on one of the southern switchbacks near the summit had found Austin Harper's bike bag about twenty feet from the guardrail, and turned it in to the police. It was the nylon box that sat on a platform on the back of the bike. The fellow didn't know it was Harper's because there was no identification, but he'd seen something on the news about the bicyclist's death on the mountain and presumed it had been his. Inside it had the touring company's map for the day, a bag of peanuts and dried fruit, sunblock, antibacterial hand gel . . . and a dress. It was the dress that broke Quang's heart just a little bit when he saw it: it had been tailored in Hoi An to very precise measurements, from silk that was red and purple and orange. Harper had almost certainly had it made for that ER doctor, and so he'd sent the dress to Toril Bjornstad at the American embassy in Phnom Penh to forward to the woman in America. He supposed it was likely that the cyclist had picked up the dress in Hoi An before heading up the mountain, but he suspected there was another reason it was in the bag: it was a gift and he didn't want the woman to see it just yet.

Again today there was something new about the hit-and-run—though this was far more ominous than a bike bag with a dress in it. The Psych energy gel packets that the dead man's girlfriend had picked up off the road had fingerprints on them that matched the deceased. The CSCD lab technician, a nice young guy named Xuan Le, had written that he didn't recommend bothering to see if they had his DNA as well, because it was clear now that they had belonged to Harper. Apparently, however, it was possible that they had been—and these were the words the technician had used—tampered with. The two chocolate packets had what might be tiny needle holes in the bottom fold. The tech wrote that he wouldn't have noticed it if he hadn't been looking for fingerprints. The pinprick in each packet, if that's what it was, had then been plugged with some sort of heat gun. It looked a bit as if the plastic had been cauterized so it was airtight: factory sealed, so to speak. It could still be just some sort of factory defect in the packaging, Xuan had written. But, once you spotted it, it looked like some kind of tinkering.

And now the lab tech wanted to know if he should break open the packets and analyze the contents. It wouldn't be all that expensive or all that time-consuming. It was an option.

Quang sat back in his desk chair. The answer was yes, absolutely. Of course he should. It might be nothing; it might be a waste of time and money. Moreover, there was nothing in a chemical analysis of the energy gels that was likely to lead them to the driver in the hit-and-run accident that had killed the American. So why bother? Because the American had lied to his girlfriend and he had lied to the people on the bike tour about what he was doing in Vietnam. Because he had lied about why he wanted to be alone that afternoon. They never did find out where he had gone: no trace of him in any bars in Hue or Hoi An or Da Nang, or the snack shacks on the southern slope of the Hai Van Pass. No sign of him at any tourist attractions or beaches, no visit to the Linh Ung-Bai But Pagoda. It was as if he had vanished after stopping on that road and dropping the gel packs, before being hit by a vehicle on the switchback.

And so Quang leaned forward, picked up the phone on his desk, and called the lab tech. He reached him right away.

"So, how's fatherhood?" he asked the younger man. "Getting any sleep at all?" Xuan's wife had had a baby, their first, three months earlier.

"A bit. My wife says the little guy's lips are a vacuum and he eats all the time."

"So he's not sleeping through the night yet?"

"He doesn't sleep ever. At least it feels that way."

"That's a good sign, Xuan. Supposedly, babies that sleep a little bit less tend to be smarter than average."

"Then my guy is a genius. His parents, however, are delirious."

Quang kept a photo of his wife and daughter on his desk. He looked at the pair now. It reminded him how much he had enjoyed that period in his life when his wife was breastfeeding. He'd climb out of bed in the middle of the night, change Ly's diaper, and bring the little girl from her bassinet—then her crib—to his and his wife's bed, where his wife would nurse her. The world had never seemed more at peace to Quang than in those moments.

"I read what you wrote about the American's energy gel packs," he said to Xuan.

"Weird, right? I mean, it could be a factory defect. It probably is. It's probably nothing. I hope I made that clear."

"Was it on all three packets?"

"Nope. Just the two chocolate ones. My guess, if I had to guess, is that it had something to do with the crimping machine."

"Let's suppose it wasn't a defect. What do you think's going on?" Quang asked. "What else would explain it?"

"Product tampering, to begin with. Think about Tylenol in America in 1982. Or Alisea bottled water in Italy in 2003. Those are probably the most famous cases. There are others."

"You did your homework."

"I honestly don't think we're going to find poison. The expiration date suggests these packets are old. Not past expiration, but on the shelf a long, long time. There have been no other reports of people getting sick from this brand of gel—or any brand of gel. Not a one. I checked."

"Fair enough. If it isn't tampering and it isn't a packaging defect, what's another reason, in your opinion?"

"He was smuggling something. He was smuggling drugs," Xuan answered.

"Tell me more."

"He bought something here, a little souvenir, and he wanted to bring it home. Heroin. Fentanyl. And no one at airport security or baggage handling is going to think there's anything strange about a couple of energy gel packs in a checked bag—or even a carry-on."

"Seems like a lot of work."

"Maybe. Maybe not. Maybe there's a business here we don't know about."

"I've talked to addicts who've taken fen gel off the patch—the transdermal patch—but they said they never got quite the same rush," Quang said.

Xuan chuckled. "Then they weren't doing it right."

"It works?"

"For most people, it works just fine."

"But the autopsy didn't show any signs of drug use. There was nothing in Austin Harper's system but ibuprofen. Nothing illegal, no alcohol."

"Did the coroner look for signs of use?"

"You mean on the body? Not sure, but I assume he would have seen them if they were there."

"As you know as well as I do, some addicts are very clever. They shoot between their toes, they shoot in their crotch."

"I know," the captain agreed. Then: "His girlfriend is a doctor."

"Meaning?"

"Not sure what I mean. But I didn't get the vibe that she was dating an addict. Also? The American was a really, really good cyclist, I gather. And one thing was clear from the autopsy: he was in excellent shape."

"Not a junkie's body," said Xuan.

"Nope. So let's suppose he wasn't using and he wasn't planning to bring something home. Maybe he was bringing something here. Maybe the tampering occurred back in America."

"Yeah, because our junkies can't get their shit on the streets," the tech said sarcastically. "We depend on Americans on bike tours to import it."

"Well, the same goes for America. If he was using, it wouldn't be hard for him to score his drugs back in New York City."

"Maybe he wanted to use it here. Before leaving."

"Maybe," Quang said, but he didn't think this was it. "And maybe it wasn't drugs at all."

"Then what? My tampering notion?"

"No clue. Absolutely none," he said. "But the American went off radar that afternoon. We have no idea where he was or why he lied to his girlfriend. But both things happened."

"So, we open up the packets and run some tests?"

"Yup. Let's find out what's in them."

"Again, it may just be amino acids, sodium, and caffeine. Things like calcium carbonate. Green tea. Preservatives. I don't want to get your hopes up. It may really be just an energy boost."

"I know."

"You're the boss. I'll let you know what I find."

"Thank you," Quang said. After he hung up, he adjusted the photo on his desk and looked at what else was on his docket that afternoon. He presumed you couldn't buy Psych brand energy gels in Vietnam, which was why the American had brought them with him. Harper had visited Vietnam a year ago, so he would know. But just in case, Quang thought he might call a couple of sporting goods stores—maybe even some of the bigger ones in Hanoi and Ho Chi Minh City—to see if they were available here.

18

In the morning, before breakfast, Alexis went online again and searched aggressively and methodically for the full research article about the Vietnamese rats, but for some reason, she couldn't find even the abstract and brief summary—not in English and not in any other language. The article? It was as if it didn't exist. And so all she had were the pages that she had discovered in Austin's apartment, which meant that would have to do. Over black coffee and a bowl of yogurt and frozen blueberries she found in the back of her freezer, she read them again, but a lot of it was background and then biographies of the researchers in Vietnam who had conducted the study.

The work had been done by scientists at Viet Nam National University in Ho Chi Minh City. She and Austin had flown into Hanoi on this trip—the tour had spent their first day together savoring different neighborhoods with their guides—and they had gone nowhere near the country's other behemoth of a city during the excursion. Last year, however, Austin had gone to Vietnam on a different bike tour, and that one had begun in Ho Chi Minh City. Had he been to the school then—on his first trip? Until she got into his laptop or tablet, it was unlikely she would know. But the basic point of the study seemed to be this: there had been easily hundreds of generations of rats since Agent Orange had been brought to the jungles of Vietnam, and the descendants of the rats that hadn't died of cancer were a very hardy bunch. They carried inside them diseases, some of which were usually fatal to rats, but not to these rats. And some of the pathogens were transmittable to humans. And some of them made very short work of antibiotics.

She knew this was true of New York City rodents, too, and they hadn't been exposed to Agent Orange. She presumed Austin was aware of this as well. There had been news articles about it, and he—just like her—worked in a university hospital. For all she knew, their own labs were looking into rat viruses and bacteria. She didn't know anyone who worked there, but she made a mental note to ask around.

At eight thirty, she called the name of the private investigator on the business card that Sally Gleason had given her and was relieved that his answering service was taking calls and a woman at the other end of the line had the PI's calendar. She wanted to know if Alexis could come in that afternoon, but she explained that she was an ER doctor and had a shift that began at noon, and begged for a morning appointment. She was able to get one at nine forty-five, which meant that she would have to hurry. And so she did, throwing into her bag Austin's laptop and tablet, their bike tour itinerary, the research abstract on rats, and the bike glove from his right hand. She also took with her the Speed Racer cycling jersey and the suit from Hoi An, but that wasn't for the PI: she was going to bring them to the hospital with her and, when she met Austin's parents, give them to the couple.

· · ·

The investigator had the dark, weathered face of a guy who'd watched one too many sunsets and drunk one too many margaritas at the dock in Key West. But he had a buzz cut: a gray buzz cut. His name was Ken Sarafian and, like Sally said, Alexis guessed he was in his early seventies. His accent—and it was strong—was all Queens. His office, when she stole a glance at the photos on his desk before sitting down across from him, gave her more clues into his background: there was indeed a black-and-white photo of him in Vietnam, a young man with three other soldiers, all in combat fatigues, smiling beside a massive water buffalo with two puppies playfully perched on its back. The water buffalo didn't seem to mind; the puppies looked like they were in heaven. But there was also a formal portrait of him as a New York City cop. She saw him as a much younger man in both kinds of uniforms. And there were a couple of him with a woman with creosote-colored hair, then that same woman when her hair was streaked with silver, and graduation photos of two boys and a girl. The girl, Alexis presumed, was the woman Sally had mentioned who had died earlier that year. She had dark hair and eyes that were almost black, and magnificent cheekbones. She was beautiful.

The PI had the build of a guy who had always been big and once been all muscle, but had allowed himself a little more slack as he had hit late middle age. Fewer days at the gym; fewer reps when he was there. Still, his blazer was straining hard not to tear right around his rotator cuff.

"So," he began, steepling his fingers and leaning back in a leather desk chair that looked a little tired, "you're a friend of Sally Gleason's, I gather. She's the referral?" The office was in an older building on lower Broadway that could have used, inside and out, a face-lift. The window was narrow and filled with an old-fashioned air conditioner, which meant that the little after-noon light the office was likely to get was cut in half. Now, in the morning? The place needed desperately the hundred-watt bulbs in the standing lamp in the corner and on his desk. There were steam pipes running up the wall and along a part of the ceil-ing. She was sitting in one of the two chairs on his side of the desk, both of which were eerily reminiscent of the Naugahyde seats in the ER waiting room. The principal difference? The ER chairs were dark blue and this pair was orange. It was clear that he worked alone. This room was all there was.

"I wouldn't say that Sally and I are friends," Alexis replied. "I barely know her. But we work at the same hospital and she gave me your card."

He nodded. "Are you here about a lover or a spouse? I'm guessing the former because I don't see any rings on your fingers."

"Boyfriend," she said.

"Must be a very long-term relationship if you're here about infidelity."

"No, it's not about that. He's dead. He died last week in Vietnam." And so she began, telling him what had happened and all that she knew: the lies, the disappearance, the hit-and-run, the research into rats and the possible rat bites on his fingers, and the wound on his hand that didn't match the cycling glove. He didn't seem especially interested until she got to the glove. But then? He sat forward, his elbows on his desk. She could see that she had his full attention now. Occasionally he interrupted her with a question, and he took a few notes on a yellow legal pad. When she was done, he said, "Vietnam isn't exactly my neighborhood. It hasn't been for nearly fifty years."

"I know."

"What precisely do you want me to find out?"

"I want to know why he lied. I told you, his parents had no explanation. I want to know what he was doing."

"The day he disappeared? Before he was killed?"

"And here—in New York. Maybe there's a connection. Maybe not."

He put down his pen and sat back in his chair. "You talk to his friends? You talking to them will cost a lot less than me doing it."

"I know. I will."

"You love this guy?"

It was, perhaps, the most important question. She answered honestly, almost as if she were alone and speaking aloud. "I'm not sure if I did. But I always had fun with him. I know that," she said. "I thought he was a good boyfriend. And I told you: I think someone hurt him before he started back to our hotel on the bike."

He seemed to think about this: "So you don't believe it was an accident? You called it a hit-and-run when you were telling me what happened a couple minutes ago."

"I . . ." She stopped as she pondered what he was suggesting. "Go ahead."

"I assumed it was. But now . . ."

He nodded. "Someone sticks something hard enough into his hand to break a bone? Someone takes his phone? Then his body is found over a ridge with a bunch more broken bones and a traumatic head injury? Sounds a little suspicious to me."

"No," she said, recalling that awful afternoon when she had ID'd the body at the morgue. "There was a grill mark—from a truck, most likely—on his leg. And the coroner looked at the helmet and the head wound. He said it was clear that Austin was hit by a vehicle."

"Okay, he was hit by a vehicle. But maybe it wasn't an accident."

"Can you—"

"Of course you can. Run someone over on purpose? Easier than you think. Especially at night." He looked at his watch. "So, you want to know why he lied. I get it and that makes sense. That would be as good a place as any to begin, because then we might understand why he really wanted to go back to Vietnam and why someone might have wanted to hurt him."

"Yes," she said, but her mind was only partly with the detective now. She was also processing the planning—the blocking—that would have gone into running Austin over. To send him hurtling over the guardrails on the switchback. It would take two people, she concluded. One to drive the vehicle, of course, and one to alert the driver when Austin was on his way down that hill.

"Have you looked at his email?" Ken was asking. "Seen whatever was on his computer and in the history of his search engines?"

She pulled out his laptop and tablet from her bag and put them on the desk, the smaller iPad stacked on top of the MacBook. "I tried. I couldn't get in."

"He's your boyfriend and you don't know his passwords?"

"Sorry. I don't."

"But you say you two were serious?"

She toyed with one of her bracelets. "You really would get along well with my mother."

He smiled, and it was good-natured and apologetic. "My bad. Got it. You don't know his passwords."

"No."

"Can I ask you something else?"

"Sure."

"How old are you?"

"Thirty-three. Why?"

His face grew mournful: she could see it in his eyes. "Your joke about your mom. It reminded me of my daughter—but in a good way. It was the kind of joke she'd make. She was about your age. You two would have gotten along."

"Sally told me she passed away. May I ask how?"

"Ovarian cancer. We thought the odds were in our favor. I mean, I guess they were in our favor. But, still, sometimes you don't beat the odds. You don't win, even then."

"No, you don't. I'm sorry. I really am."

"Thank you."

"Was she married? Did she have any children?"

"No and no." Then, almost abruptly, he gathered himself and returned to the case. "So, you don't know your boyfriend's passwords. Not a big deal—at least not usually." He motioned for her to slide the devices across the desk to him. "Mind if I try something?"

"Not at all," she told him. "I was hoping you would."

"Let's start with his MacBook. You know about TDM? Target Disc Mode?"

She shook her head as he reached behind him onto the credenza—metal and pressed wood, straight from an office supply warehouse—for a second laptop. He turned on his own computer and then attached it with a cable to Austin's. "This isn't rocket science or a serious spy hack you're about to see. Trust me, I'm no computer geek. Any IT nerd can do what I'm about to show you."

"Which is?"

He opened Austin's MacBook and, as he started to boot it up, held down a key on the keyboard. "I'm pressing on the T. Now, wait for it . . . there we go." His eyes went to his own computer. "Your boyfriend's Mac is now appearing on mine as an external device. Imagine an external disc drive."

"So you can see what's on it? So *we* can see what's on it?"

He nodded and clicked on something, then on something more, and then turned around his own laptop so she could view the screen for herself. "Of course, there's nothing to see."

It looked to her like a brand-new computer screen with an empty desktop.

"What does that mean?" she asked, confused.

He shrugged. "It means it's been wiped clean. Everything has been erased. You're looking at the factory settings."

"He erased it before he went biking that day?"

"Or he erased it from his phone."

"Of course," she said.

"The 'Find My iPhone' feature," he went on. "It's magic. A great way to find a device and a great fail-safe for whatever's on the device if it's lost or stolen. You wash it."

She thought of the word *wash*. She'd never heard it before in this context. "Still, we don't know if Austin was the one who washed it."

"No, we don't," the PI agreed.

She held up his iPad. "And this?"

"Well, that's like his phone. I can't get into that without his password. But speaking from experience?"

"Go on."

"His iPad would have appeared on that app on his phone right above or right below this MacBook." He pointed at Austin's laptop. "If someone erased this bad boy, I promise you, they erased his tablet, too."

19

Douglas looked at the photos that were spread, very much like the pieces of a collage, on the kitchen table in his apartment. They'd been printed on regular, eight-and-one-half-by-eleven-inch copy paper, but they were still crisp. Douglas could see what he wanted. Once upon a time, he had worked on his high school yearbook—one more thing for his college application, one more way to meet cute girls—and now he was having one of those Proustian flashbacks to being sixteen and back in Ms. Simonetti's air-conditioned classroom in Dallas and looking at the photos they were going to use to create a two-page spread of students mugging around the cacti that lined the school's front walkway. The images before him now, however, weren't teenagers with backpacks and books and silly (or sheepish) grins. They were rats. Dead rats. There were nine of them, printed in vivid color.

He pointed at one, its brown fur lost to open pustules or matted with dried blood. Beside it was a ruler for perspective. "Look at the length of his tail. Look at his midsection. He was a big boy," Douglas observed to the fellow beside him. It was just the two of them, and they were munching on bagels and lox. It was raining this morning, but not an especially cold and damp autumnal rain. It had actually been rather pleasant when he had gone to the deli around the corner to retrieve their breakfast. He'd worn a yellow slicker with a hood and had another of those flashbacks to when he was younger: he'd been a boy, perhaps eight, and he'd been sitting beneath the awning in their backyard, not far from their swimming pool—it was an inground pool, but it was modest, the sort everyone in that neighborhood had—while watching the raindrops on the surface of the water and examining the new baseball cards his mother had just bought him. He had been wearing a raincoat very much like the one he owned now, and he had been so happy that afternoon. It was one of his favorite memories from his childhood. "How long did it take?" he asked, once he'd swallowed another bite of his breakfast. The lox was pinker than the claret red of the blood by the rats' pustules, but his mother was an amateur painter, and she would have grouped the paint tubes of the pink and the red in nearby slots on the rack she used to sort them.

"For the rat to show symptoms or for the rat to die?" the younger man asked Douglas.

"Both."

"Hours."

"Symptoms and death in hours?"

"Yes."

Douglas thought about this. "Tell me more. Hours is . . . vague. I'm presuming you mean less than a day. Or days. But are we talking two hours or twenty-two hours?"

"Your rat scientist—Sinclair—said they usually showed symptoms in about two hours and none lasted more than a day. None. Some died within twelve hours."

"And these were all vaccinated against the original plague strain?"

"Yes. But he says the new strain is pretty gnarly stuff. Horrible. The new virus is antibiotic resistant."

Douglas licked a small drop of cream cheese off his index finger and then waved it at him to correct him. "We're not working with a virus. This is bacteria. Now, bacteria are—or can be—antibiotic resistant. But not viruses. If you're ever working with a virus, the term is *antiviral resistant*."

"Well, this sure as hell isn't rat-bite fever."

"No. Obviously, rats don't get rat-bite fever."

"You know what I mean."

"I do," Douglas admitted. Then he continued, "The incubation period is much longer for rat-bite fever in humans. A week to a month. But, interestingly, the symptoms are not all that dissimilar to . . . this. Chills and a rash. Inflamed lymph nodes. Fever, of course—hence the name."

"And rat-bite fever isn't fatal."

"Oh, it can be. But antibiotics are very effective against it. Even that old standby, penicillin, often works."

"Did you ever consider becoming a doctor?"

Douglas sighed and thought back to 2001. He did one semester at medical school before enlisting. He assumed at the time he'd go back. He never did. He recalled the raincoat he'd owned then and wondered why in the world he was so bloody wistful—so damn sentimental—today. Raincoats, baseball cards, his mother's paints. He shook it off. "I did," he admitted. "But then I found more interesting and more lucrative pursuits."

"Like this."

"I guess."

His visitor motioned at the photos of the rats. "And they can give this to people?"

"Well, they can transport it."

"That scares the shit out of me."

"It should. But, then again, perhaps it shouldn't: You don't work in the labs. You don't touch the pathogen or breathe in the pathogen or—like these rats—have it injected into your veins with a syringe."

"In the Middle Ages . . ."

"Go on."

"In the Middle Ages, a third of Europe died. How long did it take a person to die from the plague?"

"Days. A week at most."

"And they were in pain as they died?"

"Always."

"So, this is better. Because it's faster."

"Well, it would be," Douglas said, preferring to remain speculative. "If it ever comes to that. But first Sinclair has to ensure his transgenic rats are resistant to the bacteria. Right now, it kills people and it kills rodents. As you can see. The great pandemics of the Middle Ages were stalled, at least in part, because the rats died, too."

"Of the disease," Oscar said, and Douglas rather enjoyed this oddly mentorial moment.

"Yes. But also because they didn't have enough people—well, people's garbage—left to feed them. Let's face it, Oscar, rats need us. They need our refuse. And when the rats died, they couldn't act as carriers. Initially their fleas, which had the bacteria, had no place to live and looked to the humans as hosts. But then people started quarantining themselves—because they were terrified, not because they knew a damn thing about fleas and bacteria—and that further slowed the outbreak."

"Yeah. I would have stayed inside and hidden under the damn bed."

He smiled ever so slightly. "Anyway, before someone can seriously weaponize the pathogen, we need rodents that won't wind up like these poor critters on the table. We want carriers. Not corpses."

"But no one would ever actually use it. It's all deterrence."

"Yes," Douglas said soothingly to this bureaucrat with the shaved head, "mutually assured destruction." A part of him was struck by how calming his voice always became when he lied. Of course they'd use it: there was always a renegade nation or a rogue leader willing to employ this sort of horror. Usually they used it on their own people. But someday? Someday, when the Irans or the North Koreas of the world decided that the nuclear option was just too expensive, they'd see the value in playing chicken with biological weapons—that is, if they could be assured that they worked. "That's the wonderful thing about weapons like this, Oscar. They are unbelievably lucrative regardless of whether they're ever used."

"I hope so."

"No need to hope. It's a sure thing. Just be patient. You will be G5 rich by the time we're finished."

"But that's still down the road," the administrator murmured ruefully.

"Yes. But not as far as you think."

"What's next then?"

"Your acquaintance. The one who died in Vietnam . . ."

"I won't make his mistakes, Douglas. I promise."

"You don't even know what his mistakes were."

"I know he violated your trust."

"And you know that how?"

"Because he's dead."

Douglas nodded, a little impressed. The logic was infallible. "Austin was up to something really, really nasty. As nasty as the work going on in the university labs. But the difference? I don't know this for a fact, but I believe behind my back he brought—or was going to bring—a sample of the pathogen to Vietnam."

"Shit. Really?"

"Really. We took care of the buyers. His prospective buyers. But I need to know who would have given him the sample and how in the world he brought—or would have brought—it across the globe. He sure as hell didn't slip it inside a toothpaste tube. Sinclair insists he doesn't know who would have helped Austin. He insists he didn't do it himself."

"You're not sure you believe him."

"It's obviously a very small cadre of people who are in-volved. Some are more passionate than others. On the other hand, there must be thirty young researchers in those labs. Any one of them could have been bought and harvested the pathogen for Austin. So . . ."

"Go on."

"I'm not sure I trust anyone," Douglas admitted. He dabbed at his lips with a paper napkin. Then he took the photos on the table and stacked the papers together like giant playing cards—or, he thought, like giant baseball cards—and squared the edges. He made a tidy pile.

"Get a tour of Dr. Ho-jin Myung's lab. He's Korean. Explain there's a possible donor. A big giver."

"Where does he fit in?"

"He might not fit in at all. But he has family in North Korea."

"Austin was selling this shit to North Korea? That's not mutually assured destruction. They *would* use it. That's crazy! That's—"

"Yes," Douglas agreed, cutting him off. "It is. But from their perspective? Much easier to finance and hide than a nuclear program. Now, one more thing. Give me your phone."

Oscar hesitated, but only briefly, before handing it to him.

Douglas opened the app with the photos and permanently deleted all of the ones of the rats. "Is there anything else I need to erase?" he asked.

"No."

"You're certain?"

"I'm certain."

"Okay, then," Douglas said, returning the device.

"I assumed that was why you didn't want me to just email you the photos," he said. "You didn't want a trail."

"Spycraft these days depends a lot on technology, and I respect that. I certainly have plenty of tech in my world. But technology also leaves a trail. Email servers. Guccifer two-point-oh. Phishing scams and attacks. Even flash drives trouble me. There's something to be said for the tried-and-true, old-fashioned techniques. Dead drops. Clandestine meetings. I would have done well in 1935. Even 1985. As you know, I prefer not even to text."

With that, Douglas picked up the stack of papers and angled the edges ever so slightly. Then he tore them in half. "See? These will be gone in an instant."

"You need a shredder," the other fellow suggested, laughing, and then they said their good-byes and he was gone. Douglas stared at the back of his door for a long moment. He hoped he was making a better choice with Oscar Bolton than he had with Austin Harper. He thought so. Still, he had underestimated Austin. He'd have to watch and see.

Most of the world uses the term rat king *incorrectly. I mean, I did. It isn't at all what you suppose. Most people assume that a rat king is the leader of a rat pack, the alpha rodent in a colony. That's not true.*

Oh, there might be a kingpin or top dog in the burrow.

But a rat king is something more disgusting than a single big or powerful rat—and more pathetic. A rat king is a Gordian knot of rats that is going to die as one, probably cannibalizing itself in the end.

What happens is this. A bunch of rats get their tails linked together, frozen by feces or food, or stuck by whatever gluelike substance they've skittered around in. As they try and disentangle themselves, they only pull the knots tighter. Voilà: a big ball of scared, angry, writhing rats.

Grotesque, right? Grotesque and sad.

Look, everyone cares about the rats and the mice, the clean ones and the transgenic ones. We really do. It's one thing to give an animal cancer as part of a research protocol; it's quite another to anesthetize one improperly, even by accident, so the creature is experiencing real pain during a procedure.

I mention this so you understand that we're not the beasts you think we are.

All of the work that we were doing with those animals? All of the work that so many urban university hospitals were doing with those animals? Often, we were just trying to get ahead of the next pandemic and find the antibiotics that would work.

Unfortunately, if you want to test an antibiotic, that means you have to have a pathogen.

And that's where things began to get murky.

20

Alexis was grateful that Ken Sarafian had accepted the case. When she'd first arrived at his office, he had seemed so dubious that she thought he was going to try and disabuse her of the notion that it was worth either her time or his. But the more she'd told him, the more interested he had become.

The assignment was clear and well defined: he was to nose around and see if he could find an explanation for why Austin might have lied or why he had ventured to Vietnam twice in twelve months. The investigator would not focus upon how the man might have been killed or who might have been responsible. They agreed that while the police she had met probably weren't expending a lot of energy on the hit-and-run—which was how, Alexis had said, they viewed it—it wasn't something he could (or should) take on from New York City. She gave him the names of a few of Austin's friends and the name of one person who wasn't really a friend but whose name came up whenever Austin was recounting the experience of being shot while expecting only to toss darts at a bar in the East Village. Douglas. Austin didn't like to talk about it and seldom did. But it sometimes crept into conversations. How could it not? It was how the two of them had met, how their romance had begun. Austin had never seen Douglas again as far as Alexis knew, and so neither had she. But of all the stories that Alexis had shared with the detective, it was clear that this was the one that interested him the most, and she had the sense that he might begin there.

It had been raining when she had arrived at Ken's office, but it had stopped now, and the sky was lightening to the west. It felt like the sun would be out by midafternoon. She hoped this was a good sign.

. . .

When Alexis arrived at the ER, she was thrilled to see that the other physician on duty was an older woman she liked named Callula May Artois—who went by Callie May—and among the nurses were Mike Orosco and Sarah Whitten, both of whom were spectacularly competent. But she was also relieved because none of them knew that she had been dating a hospital executive named Austin Harper who had been killed in a bike accident in Vietnam. It was a big hospital: they probably had no idea yet that a fellow employee was even dead. They certainly didn't know that the person with whom she had been on vacation had been killed. Toril had been right: the FBI hadn't come here after talking to Sally Gleason. And so Alexis didn't have to begin her workday by enduring their commiseration or sympathy, she didn't have to start by answering any questions. That would come soon enough. It might be tonight. It might be tomorrow. She would hear from his friends. Soon enough she would become the girlfriend of a charismatic guy who'd died tragically—far too young—while on a bike tour. And she dreaded that. People would want details. They would want to know what she knew. They would ask her what they could do, and just imagining the conversations caused her to shiver.

And so she was grateful when Mike started to give her the rundown on the cubicles.

"There's an old woman in four who thinks her black stools are normal. We're giving her a blood transfusion right now," he began. "There's a young woman—an artist of some kind—who has a hook in her thumb in seven."

"As in a fishing hook?" Alexis asked.

"No, some kind of knitting hook. She was using it to get cat hair out of wax she was applying on top of a photo. That's a thing, apparently. She just came back from X-ray. There's an old guy who's having chest pain in two. He seems good now, but Callie May thinks we should probably check him in when there's a room. Smoker. Ischemic pain. His wife is kind of wigging out."

She looked at the paperwork on the clipboards, taking it all in. "I see we also have a kid we're treating for an asthma attack and some poor homeless guy with pneumonia."

"Who doesn't want to be admitted."

"If Callie May is in with the chest pain—"

"Possible MI. She's ordered an EKG and the lab work."

"So, she's on it. I'll go take a look at Captain Hook."

He smiled at her small joke. "How was your vacation? It looks like you got some color."

She gazed at him. He was a tall man, a runner in his early forties, with receding mousy brown hair that was starting to gray and a face that was scarred by what must have been a Herculean battle with adolescent acne. He wasn't handsome at first glance, but he was so smart and so kind that he was the sort of person who became handsome in conversation. "It was really wonderful and then it became god-fucking-awful. I mean that: god-fucking-awful. And while you are really sweet to ask, I don't want to talk about it. At least right now. But maybe over the course of this shift, when we're not extracting hooks from hands or explaining to the elderly why stools aren't supposed to be black, I'll be able to tell you. But right this second? I just want to work."

. . .

Alexis liked this older fellow in ER cubicle five, she liked him a lot. He was seventy-nine. He didn't know it, but she feared he was dying. His name was Daniel Gotfried, he lived on Thirty-Third Street, and in the time she had spent chatting with him as she'd examined him, she'd learned that he was a retired public defender, the son of a Holocaust survivor, a grandfather, a widower, and—until recently—a pretty good tennis player. His heartburn had been getting steadily worse, however, and it had become incapacitating at lunch today. He could barely swallow. He'd lurched to the ER from the Italian restaurant where he'd been dining with a friend. (Clearly, he had lots of friends.) But he hadn't told his luncheon companion that he was going to the ER. He hadn't wanted to worry or inconvenience him. So, he'd struggled here alone, and by the time he'd arrived, he was convinced he was having a heart attack.

Most likely, he wasn't. He wasn't presenting any other heart attack symptoms, and she was able to relieve the pain of the heartburn with a histamine blocker. But she had other concerns.

"I picked Italian because I figured a cream sauce or a caprese salad wouldn't do this to me," he said, his voice still hoarse. "I mean, it's not like I picked a burger joint or a Mexican place."

"That was a wise choice," she agreed. "Let me look at your eyes."

He was no longer in serious pain—certainly not in agony—but he was still uncomfortable. Nevertheless, he smiled as he pulled off his eyeglasses. "This is the mystery of medicine. I have heartburn, and you want to look at my eyes," he murmured.

"You have nice eyes," she told him, and she meant it. His irises were hazel. She shined the ophthalmoscope into his left eye. She really didn't need the light, but it helped. The eye was showing signs of jaundice, a yellow reminiscent of the end of a bruise. His skin had the same tint.

"Any changes in bowel movements?" she asked.

"Oh, God, must we go there? It's heartburn."

"Alas, we must."

"Some constipation. I deal with it."

"By eating more high-fiber foods or with fiber supplements?"

"The latter."

"I have a feeling you ate better when your wife was alive. True?"

He shrugged good-naturedly. "Well, I ate more fiber. But it wasn't like she did all the cooking. I'm actually a pretty good chef. I just don't especially like to cook alone."

"No one does," she agreed. "I'm not exactly a culinary role model, in that regard. Now, any weight loss lately?"

"I think so. Can I ask you a question?"

"Of course."

"How old are you?"

She smiled. She was asked it all the time, and sometimes she was insulted. But not this afternoon. It was clear that Daniel had no doubts about her competence.

"I'm thirty-three."

"I think I remember being thirty-three."

"It wasn't that long ago."

"Oh, it was," he murmured. "It really was."

"Okay, lie down, mister. No more stalling. Pull up your shirt."

He was wearing a white oxford shirt and T-shirt underneath. He pulled up both and, just as she feared based on what he'd been telling her and the yellow in his eyes, she felt an abdominal mass. He flinched.

"I'm sorry," she said.

"Didn't hurt much."

"Good," she said. "I want to do a CT scan. Are you free this afternoon?"

"You mean right now?"

"No time like the present," she told him, trying to strike a tone that was at once cheerful and firm.

"You're worried," he said, and suddenly he sounded remote.

She was. He likely had stomach cancer that had metastasized

to the liver. It might also have spread to the lymph nodes and the esophagus. That was the heartburn that had first presented.

"It's an emergency room. Almost everyone I see worries me."

"Nah. I've been around the block enough to know. You felt a lump in my belly."

"You felt it, too?"

"I figured hernia."

"Maybe it is," she told him, but she didn't believe that for a second.

"You think it's cancer."

"It might be," she told him, and she looked him right in the eyes and gave him a small smile. "And if it is? We take it a step at a time. This is a very good hospital with very good doctors." She took one of his hands and squeezed it between both of hers, and called in Mike Orosco, asking him to start the paperwork to get the scan going. She told Daniel that she'd check in on him after the test, gathered herself, and went to the next cubicle. She was pretty sure all she was looking at there was a high ankle sprain.

.   .   .

Around three thirty, she hung up her stethoscope, got a cup of coffee, and checked her texts. Nothing from Austin's father. No messages from Austin's friends. But things were under control in the ER and there was no incoming—nothing from the EMTs on the radio alerting them to a stroke or car accident en route, nothing horrific involving semiautomatic rifles and schoolchildren—and she had a feeling that Austin's parents had arrived at the hospital. And so she told the team that she was going to take a fifteen-minute break. She didn't say where she was going and no one asked. They presumed she was going to stretch her legs or gaze up at the sky from the East River promenade: according to some of the patients, the horizon was lavender, and the midafternoon October sun was peeking out through the jagged edges of dramatic black clouds. But she grabbed her bag with Austin's suit and his Speed Racer cycling jersey, and instead of going outside, she went down the long empty corridors to the wing of the hospital with the elevator bank that would lead her to administration, advancement, and the labs.

And when she exited on the seventh floor, sure enough, there they were. Austin's mother and father. At least she presumed that was who it was in Austin's office: a couple that looked in his case to be early seventies and in hers to be early sixties. She saw that Sally Gleason was there, too. Austin's boss dressed a lot like her mom, Alexis thought, as she surveyed the woman in a gray pinstripe suit, the skirt just above her knees, her white blouse open at the neck. Austin's parents were dressed more casually, but she could still see the money in his chinos and soft leather loafers, and in her David Yurman bracelets and pink Arlette turtleneck. But Catherine Harper's sunglasses rested atop her head like a hairband, black plastic against an impeccably styled helmet of white, and Alexis saw instantly that her eyes were red. She'd been crying over the last half hour. Maybe it was seeing her son's office. Maybe it was something she had found here. When Alexis arrived in the doorway, Sally was perched on the radiator by the window with its view of the East River and the borough across the water, her arms folded across her chest, and Austin's parents were standing beside his desk. They had a cardboard banker's box beside his computer, its lid leaning against its side. The computer, she noted, was off.

When Sally saw her, she stood all the way up and motioned at Alexis's light-blue scrubs. "Looks like someone just came from the ER," she said. Then she introduced her to Peter and Catherine Harper.

"I'm so sorry," Alexis began, and suddenly Catherine was embracing her, hugging her, and she could hear the woman sniffling and feel her body spasm with actual sobs. And so, within seconds, Alexis was weeping, too. She felt Peter's hand on her shoulder. When they pulled apart, Alexis gave them a small, self-deprecating grin and continued, "Well, that was an awkward way to meet."

"No," Catherine said. "It's sad and awful, but it wasn't awkward. It was just human. And the only way I will survive this is when people hold me and let me hold them."

She nodded. "I brought you something," she said, and she handed them the Speed Racer cycling jersey and the suit bag. She had expected to need them as a peace offering, but that seemed less likely now. She really was just bringing Austin's parents a few more small pieces of their son.

Peter took the suit bag, and Catherine held open the jersey by the shoulders so she could see the image. She brought it close to her face to inhale it and Alexis told her, "I washed it."

The older woman smiled and rolled her eyes. "I guess that was good."

Alexis nodded. "Yeah. Kind of was."

"Peter told me that Austin had made up some strange story about us," she said to Alexis. When her husband went to lean against the credenza, Alexis saw that he moved a little gingerly: that slight limp Austin had told her about. The fact that he still skied impressed her.

"Well, yes. I mean, not about you. About Peter and about his uncle. And maybe *strange* is too strong a word. But . . . exaggerated or inaccurate, maybe."

Peter sighed. "I still don't understand it. I don't understand why he would say such a thing." He turned to Sally. "Did Austin ever tell you that I was wounded—shot—in Vietnam, and this trip was to visit the sites where I was hit and his uncle was killed?"

"Yes," said Sally. "He did. He was clear that that was exactly the purpose."

Catherine blew her nose into a tissue she pulled from a small plastic pack. Then she turned back to Alexis. "Did he ever say anything about that when the two of you were with his friends?" she asked.

"We hung around mostly with my friends. Almost entirely with my friends. And, yes, he did mention it when we told them about our bike trip. It was, he said, the reason why we were going to bike there instead of, I don't know, in Italy or Spain or Virginia."

They all heard a cell phone ring and Sally pulled hers from her blazer pocket and looked at the incoming number. "Excuse me," she said, leaving. "I have to take this. I'm so sorry."

"I just can't understand it," Catherine said.

Her husband nodded. "I don't get it. I really don't. It's so strange."

"It is," Alexis said, "and so I hired a detective."

"You what?"

Telling them had been a reflex, an impulse because, she supposed, she felt bonded to them because of their shared tears. But instantly she regretted opening her mouth. She could see the transformation in both Peter's and Catherine's faces: umbrage on his, betrayal on hers. She had exacerbated their grief and she felt terrible. Her short sentence was a bombshell that seemed to suck the air from the room.

Finally, Peter put up his hands, fingers spread. "Whoa. You met with a private investigator because—so you say—Austin told you that I was shot in Vietnam instead of injured in a go-cart accident?"

"No," Alexis said, but then she corrected herself. "I mean I did, yes, but only partly for that reason. I've retained a private investigator—and I'm paying for it, this is my thing—because I have some questions about his death." She had phrased her response as delicately as she could, but she wished that she hadn't brought it up in the first place. Catherine sat down on the edge of the desk. She brought her hand to her mouth and looked stricken.

"Go on," said Peter.

"There's not much more to say. But if you really want me to elaborate, I can," Alexis told him.

"I do."

"Please," Catherine added briefly.

And so Alexis told them about the wound on the back of Austin's hand and the fact that there was no compatible mark or rip on the glove. She told them the chronology as she saw it, stressing the length of time between when he set off on his own and when he was most likely hit by a vehicle near the top of the mountain. She presented the story the way she would when presenting the worst possible news to a patient's family in the ER of this very hospital. She was calm and honest and stressed that everyone had tried their best to find him. When she was done, for a moment no one spoke. It was Peter who finally broke the silence.

"Why are you here?" he asked.

"I wanted to see you two," she said, and she hated herself for speaking a half truth. "And I wanted to look around his office," she added, coming clean.

"Do you have issues with mental illness?" he asked.

"Excuse me?"

"You heard me."

"No!" she told him, though in her mind instantly she saw her cutting kit and the scars that marked her abdomen and thighs like constellations. "Of course not."

"Because this all sounds a little paranoid to me. A little crazy."

"Well, this is a really weird and crazy world," she said defensively. "I see it every day here in the hospital. In the ER."

"The Vietnamese police said it was a hit-and-run accident. What in the name of God do you think a private investigator in New York City might turn up?"

"I don't know. But I want to know what really happened, if there is something more to the story."

Alexis felt Catherine watching her. No mother wanted to hear this. No mother wanted to hear any of this. "You wanted to look around his office," she said.

"Yes."

"What do you expect to find?"

"I don't know."

"You don't know," Catherine repeated.

Alexis shook her head.

"But you're still going to nose around his life. You've hired a detective and you're going to dredge up high school and you're going to dredge up college. You're—"

"Catherine," Peter said. "This isn't about that. This is about Vietnam. That's all. It's okay."

"Vietnam?" Catherine asked, drawing out the last syllable and raising her voice. Suddenly she was reaching into the box and pulling out a paperback guidebook of the country and throwing it hard at Alexis's feet. "How about a travel guide, in that case?" she hissed. Peter started toward his wife to calm her, but she pushed him away, her palms open on her husband's chest, and then she lifted the banker's box off the desk and turned it upside down so everything fell to the floor. "You want his pens?" she went on, raising her voice. "This stupid bobblehead doll of a baseball player? This letter opener that someone gave him that I don't think he ever—not even once!—used? Tell me, damn it, do you want his Speed Racer shirt?" She was almost hysterical now, and Peter tried to embrace his wife. But Catherine would have none of it.

"What do you want from me?" she asked Alexis, her voice plaintive and inconsolable. "What do you want from us? Why are you doing this?"

"I—"

"Why?"

Peter wrapped his arms firmly around Catherine's whole body, and he was murmuring into her ear, "Shhhhh. It's okay, it's all—"

"No," she wailed, an almost biblical ululation, "it's not okay! Nothing's okay and nothing ever will be again! My child is gone! Our child is gone!"

Alexis went to the woman to apologize, but Peter saw the small movement and shook his head no. She shouldn't even consider that. And so instead she knelt on the floor and started to repack the box, wondering—in spite of the pain she had caused—whether she might find something of interest. Something to explain what Austin had been doing and who (or what) he really was. But there was nothing that she hadn't already seen when (and it seemed so long ago, but it really had been only months) she had changed into a white cocktail dress in this very office. There was nothing surprising or unexpected or unusual. It was a small pile of photos and trinkets and office supplies. No flash drive she could secretly pocket, no Moleskine notebooks she could discreetly commandeer. The only item that had anything at all to do with Vietnam was that guidebook. She doubted it would have any use, but just in case she asked Peter if she could please have it as a keepsake. A remembrance of her last time with his son.

He continued rubbing his wife's back, but nodded. "Sure," he said quietly. "Take it."

And so she stood and slipped it into her shoulder bag. When Alexis turned around, there in the doorway was Sally's young assistant, again in that terrible blazer, and Oscar Bolton. Oscar seemed to be studying her, as well as watching Catherine Harper in her despair. He was trying to place her, Alexis realized, to recall where he had seen her. Today she was in scrubs with her hair back; yesterday, when she'd been in Sally's office, she'd been wearing jeans and a windbreaker, and her hair was down. But then Oscar's countenance changed ever so slightly: he remembered. She could see the recognition dawning on his face.

And with that, he turned and left.

.   .   .

On her way back to the ER, before leaving the administrative offices, she peered in some of the open doors, hoping to find Oscar. She wasn't sure how aggressively she would confront him: she wondered if she had the courage right now to ask him what he had been doing at Austin's apartment on Monday. She was staring into one of those offices, empty at the moment, and trying to decide if it might be Oscar's, when she felt a hand on her shoulder and jumped.

She turned and there was Sally Gleason. "Need something?" she asked. Her lipstick was a deep red wine, the gloss distinctive and moist.

"You scared me."

"No, I didn't. I startled you. There's a difference. And I didn't mean to. I'm sorry. But do you need something more?"

"No. I was just—"

"You were just snooping."

"I wasn't."

"Of course you were!" Sally told her, her tone incredulous, though even now it seemed as if she were trying hard not to smile. "But I understand. I do. But maybe it would be best if you went back to work. Don't you think?"

Alexis knew the woman was right, but she was struck by the way Sally seemed to be suppressing her bemusement—as if she were enjoying this. "Why do you always look like you're about to laugh at something?" she asked. "And why right now?"

"Oh, trust me: I see nothing funny in any of this. Austin's death and his parents' grief? It was horrifying. I was grateful a phone call took me away."

"And yet," Alexis said, "your face. You look like you're restraining a small chuckle."

"That's just the Botox talking," the other woman said. And this time she did smile. Then she added, "Let me walk you to the elevator. You'll be much better off downstairs in the ER than you are up here amidst the suits."

21

Ken Sarafian looked at the online PDF with the campus map of the boarding school in New Hampshire where Austin Harper had graduated. He was just confirming what he had already learned from a conversation he'd had with a guy who had been in Harper's class: the science building wing—and it was a little wing, but still a wing—was named after the guy's grandfather. It was clearly a quid pro quo: the school had punished Harper for unspecified violations of the academic honor code, but hadn't expelled him.

A person could change a lot as they grew up, but in Ken's experience—as a soldier, as a cop, and now as a PI—once a cheater, always a cheater.

. . .

Ken didn't mind dive bars at all. He didn't appreciate them the way he once had, but he'd spent plenty of time in them as a young man, especially the ones in some of the more down-at-the-heels Long Island suburbs where he'd grown up. (His favorite? The pub near JFK that always had a soccer game on the TV, which pleased him because he didn't give a damn about soccer, and neither did his friends when he was a young man back from the war, and so you could drink there without people turning away from you midsentence to look up at the screen to see what the hell had just happened at some faraway stadium. The place was still there, and he still went there on occasion: now it had flags along one wall from the United States, Ireland, and Armenia. It was kind of perfect.) And so tonight he went to the East Village bar where Austin Harper had been shot in the arm and where the guy had met some dart player named Douglas—a fellow who, according to Alexis Remnick, Austin hadn't seen again. At least as far as she knew.

The bartenders early tonight were a tall guy with long red hair pulled back into a ponytail and held in place with the sort of thin blue rubber bands Ken associated with asparagus in the produce section, and a muscular woman with purple hair that fell in a bob and a small metal rod at the outer edge of each eyebrow. She was wearing a denim shirt that he saw, when she turned around to get a bottle of tequila from a shelf behind the bar, had an image of horror show hostess Elvira silkscreened onto the back. There were two dartboards against a wall and three university kids, two men and a woman, rather aimlessly tossing darts at one of them. The floor was sticky in spots from spilled beer, and the place had the smell of a fraternity-house basement: humid and dank. The music was retro: a Rolling Stones song from the early seventies he liked a lot, though he died a tiny bit inside when he realized he no longer knew the song's name. How was it possible to know the lyrics but not the title? It was not only possible, he understood, it was inevitable when you were on the far side of sixty-five.

The female bartender spotted him as soon as he found a spot at the edge of the badly scratched mahogany balustrade, and he ordered an IPA the place was promoting on a chalkboard above the impeccably lit bottles of alcohol. After she brought him his beer, he pulled his card from his blazer pocket and introduced himself.

"I'm not one hundred percent sure what that card means," she said. "Are you a cop or not?"

"Not," he said. "A private detective."

"So, this isn't a police investigation." It wasn't a question.

"Nope."

"And I don't have to talk to you."

"Again, nope. But you'll be doing a solid for a very nice couple whose son died in a bike accident and a very nice woman whose boyfriend died in a bike accident."

"Same dude, I assume?"

He nodded. "Same dude. What's your name?"

"Amber."

"Hello, Amber. I'm Ken Sarafian."

She raised an eyebrow in greeting, and the piercing moved with it. He showed her a photograph of Austin Harper and asked, "This fellow was shot in the arm here on a Saturday night back in late March. Were you working that night?"

"I was," she said, and then turned away from him to take an order from a young guy in a blue Bengal-stripe oxford shirt who had sidled up to the bar beside him.

"I'll have a Pimm's and tonic," he said.

"Not here you won't," Amber told him. She waved at the bottles on the wall behind her. "Pick your poison."

But he was properly chastened and ordered a mug of cheap keg beer.

"So, what do you remember about the shooting?" Ken asked when, once again, he had Amber's attention.

"Oh, I remember plenty. You don't forget that shit. He pointed the gun at me—when he wasn't waving it like a kid with a flag at a parade."

"I like that image."

"I was pretty fucking scared," she said, her tone firm.

"It's good to be scared around crazy people with guns," he agreed. "Or sane people with guns."

"I was about to empty the cash register for him. Everyone at the bar—you know, where you're standing—had hit the ground or was backing away. But we keep the music pretty loud here, especially on a Saturday night, and it was crowded. Lot of people didn't even know what was going on." She used her thumb to point at the other bartender. "Jason wasn't here, but the dude who was working that night was standing about where he is now. And for the first five or ten seconds, even he didn't realize what was going down. No idea the guy had a gun."

"According to the police, he never took any money."

"So, you've spoken to the police?"

"Of course. I was at the precinct this afternoon."

She seemed to take this in. "The only time I've ever been around a gun that was fired was that night. It wasn't nearly as loud as I expected. More of a pop."

"It was a pretty crappy pistol."

"Maybe. But it hurt one of the guys playing darts."

He nodded. "That was the guy who died in the bike accident. Austin Harper."

"Oh, man. He had one hell of a shitty year."

"Yeah. Kinda. Tell me: you thought the junkie shot him by accident. True?"

"That's what I told the police."

"That's not what I asked."

"Yes," she said, "I do. The two guys playing darts didn't even know what was happening at the bar. The music was so loud that they didn't hear the junkie and they didn't realize people were backing away. It happened really fast. The junkie was hissing at me like a fucking zombie and then he yelled something and then I was asking him to calm down. I was opening the register to give him whatever he wanted—whatever was in there—and then the gun went off. I think he was as surprised as anyone. And when he realized what he'd done, suddenly he didn't give a damn about the money. He was just out of here."

"Like a shot," Ken said.

Amber smiled ever so slightly. "Yeah. Like a shot."

"They never caught him."

"I figured. No one ever asked me to ID him."

"I find that amazing—that they never found him. They never found the gun, either."

She shrugged and left him again to take care of a couple that wanted another round. They were a few feet away and were having mixed drinks, and so this time she was gone a little longer. He watched the college kids playing darts. They were terrible. He didn't play darts, but the group sometimes didn't even hit the board. They hit the badly scarred corkboard hammered into the wall behind it. How more people in this place didn't get hit by wayward projectiles astonished him.

He recalled his Jarts from when he was a boy. Lawn darts. The set he'd had as a child had thick metal points and must have been a foot long. You were supposed to lob them underhand at plastic rings you placed in the lawn, and the game was reminiscent of horseshoes. Instead, he and his friends hurled them as high into the sky as they could, heaving them from elevated backyard porches and second- and third-story windows to give them ever greater velocity as they fell back to earth. How many times had one nearly missed caving in his skull? Ten? Fifteen? Dozens? The metal-tipped ones were banned now. Thank God. The Internet was littered with heartbreaking stories of lawn dart cataclysms and lawsuits.

God. He'd survived lawn darts and Vietnam. He'd survived thirty-five years as an NYPD cop. And now he was talking to a bartender about some yuppie paper pusher who got himself killed on a bike tour . . . after almost getting killed by a stray bullet about twenty feet from this balustrade. The world was unfathomable. Utterly unfathomable.

Or maybe not. Maybe Harper's number had come up this year, and when the bullet didn't take him out here in the East Village, the truck did on the other side of the world.

When Amber returned, he said, "We were talking about the junkie. I want to make sure I have this correct: The guy discharges his firearm by accident. Then he flees. Right?"

"That's right," she said. "Total mistake. It was a close call and the dude was terrified. Couldn't believe he'd nearly killed someone. I mean, maybe he thought he had killed someone."

"Anyone try to chase him?"

"Nope. I guess there's not a lot of vigilante justice here on a

Saturday night. If people were concerned, they were concerned for the man who was shot. Your Austin something."

He nodded. "Harper."

"A bunch of people went over to check on him and see how badly he was hurt," she went on. "A bunch of other people just left—some, I must admit, without even closing their tabs and paying."

He smiled. "People."

"Right?"

"I'm guessing they justified it this way: someone had just been shot in the bar and they themselves might have been killed. For that? The drinks should be on the house."

"Fair."

"The gentleman who took the bullet. I gather he came in here alone and met one of the dart players. I—"

"He didn't come in here alone."

"No?"

"No," Amber said, and she was definitive and sure. "He came in with a guy he was pretty chummy with. A guy who had his own darts. And they were serious darts."

"Go on."

"They came here to play. The two of them. But first they came to the bar and ordered. And the guy with the darts? He wanted his beer on ice, because he said that's how a lot of people drink it in Vietnam."

"Was he Vietnamese?" Ken didn't recall Alexis saying that the fellow who'd come to the ER with Austin had been.

"No. He was American. Early forties. Tall. Light hair, kind of dirty blond."

"Glasses?"

"Don't think so."

"Eyes?"

"He had two."

Ken appreciated the small joke. "You don't recall their color?"

"Sorry."

"But you're positive they came in together."

"And I'm positive they were friends. They were boys in the hood, joking, laughing. And I know this was at least the second time they'd come here. Maybe the third."

"You're sure about that?"

She rolled her eyes. "Yeah. I'm sure. Beer with ice? You don't forget that, either. At first, I thought they might already be drunk and we were their second or third bar of the night. I thought they were pub-crawling. But they weren't. They were just having fun."

"Do you remember his name?"

"David, maybe? Douglas?"

"Began with a *D*."

"I think so."

"What were they joking about?"

She rolled her eyes.

"Too long ago to recall?" he suggested.

"No, too weird. They were joking about rats."

He kept his face perfectly still. He didn't want to lead her on, but he remembered the abstract for the research study about rats that Alexis had found in Austin's apartment. "Most people don't see a lot of humor in rats."

"I believe David or Douglas or whatever his name was did something with rats or was pals with someone who did something with rats."

"Exterminator?"

"Don't think so."

"Okay, this is a long shot. Did you get the address of this David or Douglas?"

She left him to pop the tops of a couple of beers and pour a very generous amount of what he suspected, based on the label, was a terrible Riesling into a wineglass. When she returned, she surprised him and said, "I don't know the exact address, but it's near here. He'd just moved to the neighborhood this past winter and told me he liked the fact that there was a bar nearby with dartboards, and so he could pop by and find a game."

"So, he's been back?"

"No, at least not when I've been here. But if you'd nearly been shot your second or third time here and your friend was, would you come back? I mean, there are plenty of bars in this city with dartboards."

"Good point. So, you know he lives near here. Anything more specific?"

"Are you going to buy another beer?"

"Nope," he said, but he got the message and put a twenty down on the bar beside his mug. When she didn't reach for it, he placed a second one there. This time she took both.

"He lives in a brownstone. Third Street, maybe? Thirteenth Street? I overheard him and Adrian—"

"Austin," he corrected her.

"Right, Austin. He and Austin," she continued, "had some joke about giving the rats their own bedroom. The place has two floors. The top two floors. He was planning to pot some tomatoes on the roof when it got a little warmer."

"But you think it was near here."

"And I want to say there was a three in the street."

He repeated back to her the little she knew. She nodded. Then he thanked her and left. Tomorrow he'd take a flyer and walk Third Street and Thirteenth Street and see if he could find a brownstone where a fellow lived on the two highest floors whose first name was Douglas or at least began with a *D*. You never knew what you might discover on the nameplates or mailboxes or buzzers outside.

.   .   .

When Ken got home, the apartment smelled of rice pilaf and lamb. He and Taleen had sold the place in Mineola when their daughter—their youngest child—had finished college, and bought this co-op in lower Manhattan. It was a two bedroom, though they had christened that second bedroom the walk-in closet with a bed. It was small, and the window was the size and shape of a very modest welcome mat. But at least once a month, one of their two surviving kids and their significant other would be there with them, and it always thrilled Ken and his wife. They needed to see those two boys and their girlfriends this year— since Kathleen had passed—more than ever. Kathleen had stayed in that room a lot the last year of her life, and Ken and Taleen had even considered using that room for her hospice care the last month. But Kathleen had refused. She hadn't wanted that room in the city; she'd wanted a hospice with more air and bigger windows and views of trees that reminded her of her childhood on Long Island. She hadn't wanted to be a burden to her parents. And so it had been on Long Island, about five miles from where she'd grown up, that she'd died.

Taleen had been a dentist, and after she'd retired but before Kathleen's diagnosis, she'd spent a lot of her free time traveling around the tri-state area to see the things she'd never visited when she'd been working. After the diagnosis, she'd devoted herself to her daughter. Once the awfulness of Kathleen's death had receded—though the emptiness was as present as ever—she'd begun to resume those explorations of New York, New Jersey, and Connecticut. Today she'd been in Washington Heights at a haunted house that had some connection to Aaron Burr.

Now, after dinner, Taleen was in the narrow kitchen with Ken, cleaning up. He was at the sink as she brought him the dishes that needed to be scrubbed or put the leftovers away. There were always leftovers, because Taleen always cooked for a family of five, even though it was just the two of them now. It usually meant that she only cooked every other day.

"Is it uncomfortable to be researching a case with connections to Vietnam?" she asked him, as she slipped their knives and forks into the dishwasher silverware basket. He found it interesting that she hadn't asked this at dinner. He had a feeling that her inquiring now was deliberate: their conversation, and her questions, would seem less intense if they weren't looking each other in the eye.

"No."

"No?"

"I'm very shallow. You know that."

She swatted the back of his trousers with the dish towel. "No. You're just such a . . . such a guy."

He smiled to himself as he scrubbed the skillet. He knew the sorts of things she was alluding to, because over the years he'd told her bits and pieces. She'd been his own VFW support group. "That's me. Scarred and repressed."

"You're not either. *Restrained* would be a better word. Or *reticent*. But if you want to talk, you know you can. We can even open that arak from the Bekaa Valley you got."

He'd seen the booze—weaponized ouzo that had been his father's favorite alcohol—at an Armenian restaurant in the Flatiron district, tracked down the distributor, and found a liquor store that ordered him the bottle. It hadn't been his best detective work, but it was still very satisfying. "Now? Nope. We'll save that for a weekend. A special occasion. Not a Wednesday night. Not the middle of the week."

"Well, if you can't sleep, wake me up."

"Okay."

"Promise?"

He nodded obediently. "I promise."

But these days, he knew, it was more likely that Taleen would be unable to sleep. Twice he had found her in the night with the old photo albums. She wasn't crying. She was simply sad and in another place.

. . .

But that night he did seem to spend a lot of hours staring up at the oyster-colored ceiling, and the shadows cast through the window blinds. He considered waking her, but he didn't. He never did, just as she never woke him.

Still, this ER doctor and her dead boyfriend couldn't help but resurrect the memories that rested most of the year—quiescent as the perennials in Taleen's Mineola flower garden until the high sun and warm air brought them back into bloom. First there were the memories of his own little girl (and she'd always be a little girl in his mind), even though Alexis looked nothing at all like Kathleen.

But then there were the synaptic leaps across decades—generations—and hemispheres. Once more in his mind he saw the muzzle flashes from the M-16s around him the first time he was in one of the bunkers outside the base at Quang Tri and the VC were probing the defense in the small hours of the morning. He'd been in country only days, and he was still struck by one thing: the heat alone was going to kill him. He'd emerged from the plane at Cam Ranh Bay, squinted against the sun, and felt his breath sucked from him like a vacuum by a wave of air so stinking hot it was like he'd opened an oven door. Outside the bunker, they had rolls of concertina and razor wire, and it encircled the entire base, and in the midst of all that skin-peeling steel they had claymore mines. So, now he was hot and terrified, a little astonished at the way some of the young guys around him were firing aimlessly into the absolute blackness before them.

But what frightened him most, at least those first nights in the bunker, were the rockets. The VC would fire rockets toward the base, and any moment he expected the whole place to become the sort of inferno you could see from space, because not far behind him, behind the wall, was the tank farm. Not tanks with turrets and cannons. Tanks filled with jet fuel. Massive tanks that had hundreds of thousands of gallons each. And the tanks didn't just feed the choppers and planes that came and went from the airfield right there, they were linked by pipelines that went as far south as Hue and as far north as the DMZ. If the rockets hit one of those tanks, it would result in the sort of end-of-days inferno that would burn until there was nothing left, and the bodies would be part of the same ash pile as the jeeps and the helicopters and the plywood huts in which they lived.

He'd been there two weeks when he mentioned his fear of the rockets to another soldier, a guy from Maine who'd been at the base nearly nine months, who smiled and explained to him patiently that the last thing the enemy wanted was to blow up the tanks. "They siphon off the fuel from the pipelines outside the base," he told Ken. "The rockets are, I don't know, show. If they wanted to lob one inside here? Wouldn't be all that hard."

And sure enough, a week after that, he was sent out with a squad to provide cover while some of the very same Navy Seabees who'd built the base repaired a break in a pipeline where the VC had been stealing fuel. It was the first of a dozen times he'd be out there in the jungle, and two of the times he'd wound up flat on his stomach, squirming backwards with the other grunts, over tree roots or through marsh, as the bullets literally buzzed their helmets.

He thought of the sunny day when they were humping west at the edge of a wide, beautiful swath of rice paddies to repair another point where the pipeline was compromised, and a guy named Conway had heaved his M60—a machine gun—into a plant with pink flowers and lush leaves (a begonia, Taleen had suggested when he'd told her this story), and announced he was done. His feet were killing him, he had a fever, and no matter how many times they fixed the line, the VC would break in and tap another part. He said he'd been vomiting all morning and shitting his pants. They had no witnesses to the first claim, but they had more evidence than they needed to corroborate the second. And it was as the sergeant was turning to Conway and ordering him to nut up and pick his gun off the goddamn ground that the rice paddies burst into flame. The water was on fire and the sergeant was screaming because he was on fire, and so was one of the Seabees, who Ken watched dive through the blaze—into the inferno—as if he thought he might be able to save himself from immolation there. He did. But he also drowned, because there was no place to swim to.

At first, they'd all assumed this was some sort of cataclysmic friendly-fire napalm fiasco, but there hadn't been any planes, which momentarily had confused them all. But then they saw the teenage kid, the girl, and they understood. They got it. The VC had been siphoning jet fuel and it spread atop the rice paddies like a thin skin of ice, and the girl had been using it to cook outside the shack in which her family lived. And it had all gone to hell. She was twirling in circles, a great human sparkler, and shrieking as the flames melted her skin and then, after she collapsed, the tissue and muscle until all that was left were her bones.

Which was when Ken felt something punch into his helmet.

For a moment he assumed he'd been hit because suddenly the VC were shooting at them, but the projectile had been a slab of bark from some massive, ancient rain-forest tree that was growing all alone by the edge of the water. He had no idea what kind of tree it was and, after the firefight, he hadn't bothered to ask. (Years later, out of curiosity he had Googled Vietnamese trees and never found an image to match his memory.) Somehow, he wound up with Conway's machine gun, and he curled up behind the tree's equally impressive roots—some had seemed nearly knee-high—and fired the weapon in the general direction of the shooting until he was out of ammunition. He caught one poor, charging son of a bitch from his forehead to his waist, unzipping him from top to bottom. He'd never forget that. Eventually, the enemy had slipped away. They counted seven dead Vietnamese, including the fellow Ken had peeled in two, but not including the girl who'd accidentally set the rice paddies on fire, and were told to report seventeen. In the war of attrition, you always counted your KIA and said the enemy had lost at least two and a half times that many—no matter what the truth was.

And yet it wasn't the near misses that usually kept him awake, or the nights in the bunker outside the tank farm, or what he had done to that enemy soldier probably his age who'd charged him.

That made him shake his head in the dark in self-loathing, but that wasn't what really gnawed at him. It was, in hindsight, the horror of what they did to the civilians. What they all did. The whole damn system. What happened to that poor teenage girl who was cooking with jet fuel. And Ken knew that he wasn't a war criminal. He knew guys who were, in his opinion. But he had always been a gentleman to the women and kind to the men. The locals, the villagers. He tried not to frighten the children. What often kept him stewing in the small hours of the morning was the ruin they—Americans—had wrought upon a whole nation. It was a burden he'd lived with nearly half a century: yes, there were the men he had killed or presumed he had killed, but what gnawed at him was the landscape his army had helped turn into one long, bleeding carcass.

And yet somehow the country had risen from the dead.

Somehow. Thank God.

He'd never know if he had made the wrong decision going to Vietnam when his number had come up. It wasn't so much that he pondered how different his life would have been had he found a way to be deferred. He knew plenty of guys who had gamed the system and stayed home, and he even had one high school friend who went to Canada. Other than his pal who went north, he rather doubted these guys would be living lives much different from the ones they were experiencing now—assuming, of course, they lived, which was not really a small assumption at all. Oh, they didn't have his memories at three in the morning. They were spared that. They were spared the guilt of being a teeny part of the inconceivably vast machine that had ground up a nation. But maybe they had a different kind of guilt: the kind born of doing nothing when a neighbor's house is on fire and others race in to rescue the children and the cats and the dog. And so, in addition to the guilt that sometimes pricked him in the small hours of the morning, there was also the pride that he had done what was asked of him when he was nineteen. He was the grandson of two people who'd survived a genocide, their families slaughtered in an Anatolian city called Elazig—Kharpert, back then—in what was now eastern Turkey, and America had welcomed them as immigrants. At this point, did it even matter whether his decision to go had been his way of repaying a debt of gratitude or a lapse in moral judgment?

"Sweetheart?"

He turned his head on the pillow. Taleen was looking at him, her eyes worried.

"You said you'd wake me," she murmured. "You promised."

He breathed in deeply. "Yeah, I never keep that promise. I'm fine," he said softly.

"You're not," she told him. "And maybe that's why I love you so much. I'd hate to think you were fine."

He pulled her into him, and they lay like that, awake but their eyes closed, for another half an hour. He thought of the Vietnam he knew and the one this young ER doc had just seen. He loved the idea of a bunch of Americans on bikes, visiting the stone mandarins that stood guard at the tomb of Khai Dinh, or buying tourist lanterns in Hoi An. It was a fantastic country, and resilient. When Americans thought of the Hoa Lo Prison—nicknamed the Hanoi Hilton by the POWs—they thought only of the naval aviators and air force pilots who had been imprisoned there. But for the first half of the twentieth century, the French had used it to confine and torture tens of thousands of Vietnamese political prisoners in conditions that were unspeakably brutal. The damn thing had a guillotine.

No, not even French barbarism and American brutality could bring the nation to its knees. Thank God.

Eventually, he fell asleep. So did Taleen. And neither moved until his alarm went off at quarter to seven.

THURSDAY

22

Quang left the interview room, confident that this latest gang-banger they'd brought in had indeed had nothing to do with the triple murder in Da Nang and really was as clueless as his ridiculous tattoos suggested. He had a merman with a mustache inked on one forearm and a shark's mouth with a baby sitting inside it—literally, on the tongue—on the other. The interrogation had been a complete waste of everyone's time. The captain was confident that the dude hadn't shot anyone and he hadn't tried to burn down the building.

What Quang found both interesting and infuriating about the triple murder was that one of the victims had visited the North Korean embassy in Hanoi a few days before the execution, but hadn't applied for a visa and had no diplomatic reason to be there. It was the woman, a food chemist for one of the country's largest producers of yogurt and powdered milk. But she seemed to own this makeshift lab, a little place that had nothing to do with her corporate job. It seemed to have nothing to do with dairy products. It was a stand-alone building that once had sold scooters, north of Da Nang on the way to the Hai Van Pass. Across the street was a down-and-almost-out restaurant. The chemist was older than the other two victims—she was in her midthirties—and she was no relation to either. His investigative team was getting absolutely no cooperation from North Korea, which also meant something—though what that something was, he couldn't say. One of the younger dead guys had worked for a few months as a dishwasher at the restaurant across the street, which likely was a connection of some sort. But, then, why the chemist would be hanging around with a dishwasher who'd left the restaurant was beyond him.

Everyone in the CSCD assumed the massacre had something to do with drugs because of the remnants of the lab tools that hadn't burned up in the fire, but the woman had no history with any known drug dealers and no connection to any known gangs. It was baffling.

It had crossed Quang's mind that the link had something to do with pest control. There had been some empty rodent cages at the crime scene, and the uncle of the second young dead man ran a pest-control service. But who kills people because of rats? Who massacres three people? Moreover, the exterminator insisted he had never met the chemist, and there was no evidence that his little company had ever done business at the lab. Still, it was the sort of connection that dogged him, and on other cases had caused his brain to race when he was trying to fall asleep in the night.

And then there was this: the woman, who wasn't married and had no children, had traveled to the United States that summer on a tourist visa. She and her sister had flown on Korean Airlines into JFK and spent six days in New York City. The sister had told Quang about the Broadway shows they had seen and the tourist sites they had visited, and Interpol Hanoi had confirmed that the woman was telling the truth. But she had no idea why her sister might have gone to the North Korean Embassy, and neither did the dead woman's associates at work.

. . .

Quang was met in the corridor by Officer Vu, who was holding a manila folder and looked agitated.

"You have no idea how much I would love some good news,"

he told Vu, "but I can see in your eyes that you're going to disappoint me. What's happened?"

"You're going to need to call the lab," he said, handing him the folder. "Xuan analyzed the American's energy gels. They weren't energy gels."

"They were drugs?"

"Well, not recreational ones."

"But they weren't just gel packs?"

"No. At least that's not how they were being used. And poor Xuan is now in the hospital. So is the cabbie who drove him there."

He looked at the paperwork, the world around him growing quiet but for the breathing of the other officer. Apparently, the tech had photographed and X-rayed each of the gel packets, and then he'd taken a pair of scissors and cut open one of the chocolate-flavored goos—and some had splattered. It was more watery than he'd expected. He was wearing gloves and goggles, but not a respirator hood. He wasn't working in the biosafety containment cabinet. Quickly he donned a hood and moved to the cabinet, but by then it was probably too late. Nevertheless, he put some of the gel in a cell culture incubator to amplify what might be growing there for testing, and he put a small smear on glass to look closely at the substance with a simple light microscope. He did a gram stain to determine whether there was bacteria that was gram positive or gram negative. Right away, he saw something. And it wasn't mere insect filth or production contaminants. It was evident that the product had been adulterated. Or it wasn't even the product at all. Certainly, it wasn't the color of chocolate. It was clear and more of a broth than a gel made with a polysaccharide such as pectin. Still, he proceeded to analyze it methodically, to try to identify the foreign ingredient.

But the fever was coming on fast, and he saw what might have been a series of blisters forming on his hands beneath his gloves. He thought he felt something growing under his arms, though he told himself that was impossible—no bacteria or virus worked that quickly—and he was panicking. Nevertheless, instead of going home, he went straight to the hospital, where he was right now in isolation.

"And the cabbie's sick, too?" Quang asked.

"Not yet—at least not as of fifteen minutes ago. But he's been quarantined, too."

"Good." He gestured at the folder. "Do we have any idea what may have made Xuan ill? Do we know what's wrong?"

"I talked to one of the other lab techs. She's pretty shaken up. We'll know more when we see what grows in the incubator."

"What about the gram stain?"

Vu looked at his paperwork. "Gram negative," he answered. "So that's a good thing, right?"

"No. It's not like a cancer test and negative is good and positive is bad. All it does is help identify bacteria. It has something to do with the cell wall. There's a lot of nasty shit that's gram negative."

"Such as?"

"Not a clue," he shrugged. "Xuan would have noted its shape."

"Rod shaped. Anaerobic."

"Where is the other lab tech? The one who's shaken up?" Quang asked.

"Xuan only spoke to her through a hood. He never touched her or breathed on her."

"That's not what I asked. She should be quarantined, too. Right now."

"Okay."

"I want everyone Xuan saw after he opened that packet until he was put in isolation looked at."

"Will do."

"And Xuan's lab?" Quang asked. "Has that been buttoned up?"

"It has. It's under quarantine and being cleaned."

"We have two—maybe three—people who've been exposed

to this and one who is already sick. Let's stop it right there," he said. He thought of Xuan's wife and infant son at home. He thought of his own daughter. Then he added, "I looked into whether Austin Harper could have bought that brand of energy gel in Vietnam. He couldn't. It isn't sold here. I'm not sure what that means. Maybe it just means he brought a bunch because he liked that brand."

"Maybe."

"But . . . shit."

"What?"

"I'm going to call the American consulate and make sure someone calls the company that makes them. Let's not wait until we get the identity of the bacteria. Also, would you touch base with the lab? I want a list of every pathogen that's shaped like a rod and gram negative."

"Will do."

"And let's go back to whatever's left of the lab where those three people were killed. This time let's sweep the debris—anything that didn't melt or burn up—for the American's fingerprints. Let's also bring in a bio team to check for contamination."

Vu looked confused. "You think a couple of gangbangers and a food chemist might have been with Austin Harper or had something to do with the energy gels?"

"I don't know. But the chemist was in New York City this summer. And Harper was near the woman's lab last week. We don't know his whereabouts for a couple of hours. And there were rat cages in the lab—and rats carry disease."

"Like the plague?"

Quang hadn't thought about that, and he hadn't meant the plague literally. "No," he said, hoping to calm the officer, but also to reassure himself. "I don't mean the plague." But he couldn't help now but wonder: was the plague gram positive or gram negative?

That's a good question.

Yes, rats are smart—or, at least, a lot smarter than you think. It's why they're used so often in psychological research.

They're also clean animals. I've watched them groom themselves, and I've watched them groom each other—their pals. And they really can make delightful pets. It's why some people love them. They'll bond with a person, much the same way that a cat or a dog will. They're much more empathetic than most people realize. Some will sacrifice a piece of chocolate to save a drowning rat from its pack. In some ways, they're as empathetic as we are. As humans. Look at the work the University of Chicago did a few years ago, and how hard some rats will work to rescue a brother or sister from a trap.

Arguably, the biggest downside to a pet rat if you're an animal lover is that they don't live very long. Maybe you'll get two good years out of the little fellow. Maybe not. If you like the critter, that's got to be depressing.

Of course, the fact that rats (and mice) don't live especially long makes them great candidates when we're studying evolutionary and genetic changes.

Now, there's likely to be a difference in temperament between a rat you buy at a pet shop and one who is rooting around the garbage in an alley behind an Italian restaurant in Chelsea at two in the morning. The former might snuggle in the crook of your arm while you're reading a book; the latter, if he winds up there, will bite your nose off to get away.

But the ones we brought to America from Vietnam—our super rats? The CDC regulates, among other animals, cats and dogs and monkeys and African rats. But not Asian rats. At first, we went through the rigma-

role of getting permits because these were small mammals that could, conceivably, have diseases that could be transmitted to humans. But then we realized we could transport them as pets in pet carriers and no one cared. No one. You can import practically anything you want from the country we nearly destroyed.

23

Alexis was awakened at nine twenty—ten minutes before her alarm was set to go off—by someone buzzing her from the apartment lobby. She struggled out of bed, a little flummoxed at first, disoriented, and pressed on the intercom. It was a woman who said she was from FedEx and she had a package that needed her signature. Alexis said she'd be right down, pulled on a pair of sweatpants, and went to the lobby in the T-shirt in which she'd been sleeping and her slippers. She wasn't expecting anything, and couldn't imagine what in the name of God the package could be.

.   .   .

It was a Tyvek pack with a diplomatic pouch inside. It had been sent across the world to her from Toril Bjornstad, the FBI attaché in Cambodia. The note was handwritten on cardstock.

Dear Alexis,

On Sunday afternoon, a tourist found your Austin's bike bag not far from the top of the Hai Van Pass, where he had been riding that day on Highway One. There was nothing inside it that shed any more light on his accident, but we all assume it was thrown from the bike when he was hit. On Monday, Captain Nguyen was kind enough to send me this one item, a dress, and I thought you should have it. Clearly, Austin bought it for you. Given what I know about mourning and grief, I thought I would forward it on to you posthaste. (Yes, this might not have been the most efficient use of your tax dollars, but it seemed a bit of kindness you deserved in this time of loss and one I think most taxpayers would champion—or, at least, forgive.)

I am hoping you are starting to mend.

Sincerely,

Toril

Alexis stared at the material in her lap. It was as beautiful as the black-and-silver cheongsam Austin had bought her at the tailor in Hoi An, but looked like it might be the sort of outfit she might actually wear in public. She recalled the white cocktail dress he'd bought her that summer. This looked to be a similar cut, but the fabric was a silk so soft she wanted to bury her face in it, and the design a kaleidoscopic array of waves, red and purple and orange. It was gorgeous.

She sighed at the mystery of the man. He must have detoured into Hoi An and picked it up the morning he had died. Maybe he was going to give it to her that night, a surprise, and he hadn't wanted it delivered with his suit and the cheongsam. Maybe he hadn't wanted her to see it because he was going to give it to her as a present in December.

She stood up and held it against her, pinning the straps against her shoulders with her thumbs and instantly felt her stomach lurch. She recalled Ellie Thomas's conjectures about mistresses and baby mamas.

She went to the full-length mirror in her bedroom to be sure, and stared at herself and the dress against the front of her body. The dress wasn't her size. It was nowhere near her size. She was five feet, six inches tall, and this was for a woman at least five or six inches shorter. It was for a woman with far smaller breasts than she had, and almost no hips—a woman who was petite. A size zero.

She looked inside the dress to see if the tailors had sewn in a tag with the size to be sure. They hadn't. But it was clear that either accidentally they had not used her measurements from when they had fitted her for the cheongsam, or Austin had had this dress made for another woman.

And given what she had learned about the man since he had died, she was quite sure it was the latter.

. . .

Alexis guessed that she might have consumed a cup of peanut dipping sauce while she and Austin had been in Vietnam, but no peanut butter. Now, back in America, she was craving it and bought a jar at a grocery store on the way to the hospital. She ate it with a plastic spoon as she climbed into her scrubs and ate some more when she was ready for work and had her stethoscope around her neck. Then she popped a Breath Saver so she didn't greet her patients with Peter Pan breath. She knew she'd be back for more during the course of the next twelve hours.

She had another day shift—which really only meant about six hours during the day, since the shift began at noon. She almost never had two day shifts in a row, but she did now because she had swapped her Tuesday shift for a Wednesday earlier that week. Before going to work, she'd called Ken Sarafian and told him about the dress. He hadn't expressed much surprise, though he did try to reassure her that it could have been an innocent mistake at the tailor's: they'd given Austin the wrong dress or, as she had speculated, inadvertently used the wrong measurements. But she had the sense from his tone that he harbored similar suspicions. Then she had emailed the lead researcher at the university in Ho Chi Minh City who had conducted the rat study—this was the second time—because she still hadn't heard back from him. If no one had emailed her by the time she finished her shift tonight, she might see if she could reach the scientist by phone. It would be nearly lunchtime by then in Vietnam.

Her mind, she feared, was a mess. A part of her was so indignant at the idea that Austin might have bought a dress for another woman that she wanted to just let him go: release his wrists at the edge of a cliff and let his memory drop from her life. But then there was the man she had known since March, who always treated her with tenderness and kindness and, yes, love. The man who, she was convinced, had been tortured before he was killed. Tortured before, perhaps, he was murdered.

And then there was the simple doggedness of who she was. How could she let this go—let him go—without knowing the truth?

She told herself that maybe tomorrow she would feel differently. Maybe. In the meantime? She would go to work and try her best to clear her head. To solve problems and make people feel better. Literally: make people feel better. In the end, when you boiled all that sap into syrup, wasn't that what she did?

The first patient she saw was a sixty-five-year-old woman with lung cancer, which she thought was still in remission—at least the woman was telling herself it was still in remission—but she was coughing up blood, and Alexis knew she was going to order a CT scan, see it was bleak, and have her admitted. She was with her husband, who kept telling both Alexis and his wife that it was probably just pneumonia, and so Alexis smiled pleasantly at this charade and went along with it while they waited, but inside her heart was breaking just a little bit. Then she saw a heavyset guy who delivered Chinese takeout on a bike and had been hit by a cab. He seemed to have dodged broken arms or ribs or legs, but he had a gash on his right forearm that needed stitches and very likely a concussion. When she looked at the fellow's cracked helmet, she was reminded of Austin's, and wondered if she'd ever get on a bicycle again. Suddenly she hated bicycles, she hated everything about them. It was unreasonable, but she didn't care. She didn't even want to sit on a spin bike again.

.   .   .

On her break, she walked outside into the crisp autumn air, a fleece pullover the color of cherries with a high collar over her scrubs, and walked to the water, past the new buildings with their signs in the lobby for the pharmaceutical companies that had offices there and past the older ones that were still units of the hospital complex. It was all a little incestuous—there was even that glass walkway on the seventh floor linking the drug companies with the hospital—but she no longer cared. She got it. It was all part of the system, a symbiotic relationship of people and pills and drugs and machines.

When she got to the East River, she gazed at the docks and the flatlands across the water and at the cluster of skyscrapers a little to the north. She watched a plane descending beneath the clouds toward LaGuardia. Then she turned around and looked back at the wing of the building where Sally Gleason and Oscar Bolton worked, and where Austin had gone in the mornings. She didn't know Oscar, and she didn't know what to make of Sally. One minute, she seemed nurturing and kind; the next, she seemed to see all the horror and sadness in the world as a joke. Austin, however, had liked the woman well enough. He certainly hadn't ever said anything negative about her. But that probably meant nothing now. Still, it just seemed so unbelievable that seven days ago he was alive and they were in Vietnam.

But, of course, she saw daily how quickly a person's world could be upended and how a life of routine could unravel. She had seen it twice already today: there was the cancer patient who was hoping she was in remission but clearly was not. And then there had been a young mother who had been trying to wrangle her toddler son and his stroller down the stairs into the subway and fallen the last dozen steps. Her maternal instincts had kicked in and she had managed to protect her son, but she had broken an arm and broken a leg, and was going to be in the hospital at least overnight. Maybe a couple of days. She was a single mom without insurance and, it was evident, a support system that consisted mostly of her own mother. She worked at a noodle bar on Seventeenth Street, and Alexis worried that the woman's fall was the start of one of those cataclysmic event cascades that would end in a homeless shelter.

And, of course, Alexis could point to her own father's death. One morning he'd gone off to work, and he'd just never come home that night. He'd probably died in that ambulance before her mother had even gotten the call that his car had slid into a concrete bridge stanchion at easily—even after he attempted to brake—fifty-five or sixty miles an hour. But when she had been eating her cereal that day at the breakfast table before school and her father had been scarfing down an English muffin at the counter and her mother had been mainlining her coffee, it hadn't crossed any of their minds that this was the last time they would all be together.

Before and after. That was the way of the world.

Years ago, in college, she'd spent a Saturday in the campus gym taking a self-defense course for women. There'd been six of them, all sophomores and juniors, and there were two instructors—also women. She'd never needed what she'd learned, and she hoped she never would. She wasn't sure how much she could even remember. But the day came back to her now when she thought of how quickly a person's world could change.

She wondered when—if—the Harpers would sit down again and watch whatever videos they had of their son as a little boy. As a teen. She knew she herself hadn't looked at the videos that existed of her father in years. It was just too painful, even now, to make the effort to get the cassettes converted into a format they could watch. She imagined it was for her mother, too.

She rather doubted her mother would ever remarry. She hoped that was because her mother had loved her father so very much, but this was something Alexis understood that she would never, ever know.

. . .

Before heading back into the hospital and the ER, she paused before a sign taped to a lamppost on the sidewalk. It was a drawing of a rat and a rose, and underneath it was, arguably, one of the world's worst limericks:

Roses are red,
Rats are gray.
They love to eat the litter buffet.

And if you don't scoop,
They'll feast on dog poop
And continue to multiply every day.

It had been posted by the city's Department of Sanitation, and for a long moment she simply took in the utter awfulness of the poem and the utter awfulness of the image of a rat eating dog shit. Thank God, the artist had drawn a rose instead of . . . that.

As she started back inside and looked up at the building, something clicked. She knew that Columbia, much farther uptown, was studying New York City rats and the pathogens they carried, and their increasing resistance to antibiotics. She thought now of the article abstract she had found in Austin's apartment and realized that somewhere in the labs in the wing where her boyfriend used to work, it was possible that her university hospital was researching rats, too.

24

Ken Sarafian was methodical and patient. The weather was changing, slipping closer to Halloween and the real gunmetal-gray cold of autumn. He climbed into a wool peacoat that fell to his thighs, buttoned it up, and walked from Fifth Avenue to the East River on the north side of Thirteenth Street, stopping at every brownstone or building that was smaller than six stories. He went east of Avenue C to the FDR Drive. Then he walked all the way back on the south side of Thirteenth. There were three five-story buildings that seemed to have duplexes with rooftop terraces where a person might grow tomato plants, but none had a first name on the buzzer outside the front door that began with *Douglas* or *D*.

And so he started south on Broadway, planning to perform this same exercise when he reached Third Street. Sometimes his mind would wander to the dress that Alexis had described for him, but it only deepened his resolve: he didn't like this Austin Harper, and he wanted to know what he'd really been up to. If his own daughter had ever dated a man like Harper? He rather doubted he would have retained much equanimity and kept his suspicions to himself. At the end, when she'd been dying, she hadn't had a boyfriend. She'd had a few in her twenties and early thirties, but she'd broken up with a fellow just before her diagnosis. He'd never know if it would have made her death easier to bear if she'd had a boyfriend beside her as well those final months. But he felt a deep, numinous stitch within him as he recalled the deaths he had seen and the one that he'd never get over, and the sad truth that no matter how many or how few people are with you at the end, you really do die alone.

God. A dress. That shit had bought a dress for some woman other than the ER doctor. He really had begun to detest Harper with the protectiveness of an outraged father.

He'd been walking half an hour when his phone rang. It was Oscar Bolton returning his call. Bolton was one of the names that Alexis had given him, people with whom Austin worked or whom she viewed as his friends. She was clear that she knew none of them well—or at all.

Ken recalled that Alexis had told him that Bolton had gone to Austin's apartment the day before her, and so he'd been intentionally vague on the message he'd left on the guy's office voice mail at the hospital. He'd said he was an investigator, but he'd implied in his message that he had been retained—perhaps by a philanthropist—and his assignment was to look into a possibly sketchy foundation. It was clear from Bolton's tone, at once ingratiating and cautious, that he was curious who this Ken Sarafian was and whether his hospital had some sort of exposure that might be troublesome. "Is this about a group we work with?" Bolton asked.

"No, I don't think you need to worry," Ken reassured him. "That's not the focus of my investigation."

"We vet our donors and our sources carefully," the hospital executive said. "Even the smaller family trusts. Most of them have been with us for years. Generations in some cases."

"I'm sure it's a very esteemed group."

"And you might be better off talking to a hospital lawyer. I'm not a lawyer."

"Nothing like that. Nothing like any of that. I'm trying to find a person who may have known your friend who died in the bike accident, and whether he was in Vietnam because of a specific philanthropist. That's what I meant in my message."

"Austin? God, devastating. What a nightmare," Bolton said, and he sounded genuinely shaken and sad when he spoke.

"You two were friends?"

"Work friends, yes. We didn't really socialize much after work. But he was a great guy and a hell of a colleague."

Ken stopped to gaze in the window of the Strand Bookstore. Taleen had bought him beautiful editions of Franz Werfel and Mario Puzo for his birthday there that summer. "So, tell me: Was he in Vietnam as part of a fund-raising venture or meeting?"

"If he were, it would be news to me. It would be news to all of us. I mean, it was a bike trip with his new girlfriend. A bike trip. His dad and his uncle were both Vietnam veterans. His dad was wounded there. Shot."

Ken assumed he would say something like this. His question was really just the prologue to his real inquiry. "There was a guy in his life named Douglas. Maybe David. Began with a *D*. What was his last name? Do you know?"

"No idea," Bolton said quickly—too quickly, the detective thought. He almost snapped back his response.

"No?"

"No. I didn't even know he had a friend named Douglas or David."

"They played darts," Ken said.

"Doesn't ring a bell."

"He was with Austin the night he was shot. He didn't mention that name on the Monday morning when he came in to work?"

"Nope."

"Didn't say who he'd been with?"

"He didn't."

"Okay, then. It was a long shot," Ken said.

"That's it?"

"That's it."

Then they said good-bye and Ken continued his stroll south

to Third Street. It really had been a long shot. Still, he felt he had learned something: he believed Oscar Bolton was lying and knew exactly who this Douglas person was.

. . .

The townhouse was between Avenue C and Avenue D. He was sure he had found the right place. Five stories, brick, likely rooftop terrace. Remodeled. It was on the north side of the street, so there was no building blocking it from the south if you wanted sunlight for your tomatoes. There were no homeowners listed on the fifth floor, which meant that the three apartments on the fourth floor were duplexes. And the name on the buzzer for 4C? D. WEBBER.

He looked at his watch. It was not quite two thirty, and the odds were slim that D. Webber was home on a weekday afternoon. Nevertheless, he pressed the small black button and waited. He was pleasantly surprised when a moment later he heard a crackle from the speaker and then a male voice asking, "Yes?"

"Is this D. Webber?"

"It is indeed."

"Ken Sarafian. I'm a private investigator. Can we chat for a couple of minutes?"

"I'll buzz you in," the guy said, and a second later he heard the fizz of the door unlocking and he stepped inside. He wasn't quite sure what to make of how quickly Webber had agreed to see him, but one thought occurred to him: Bolton had called Douglas Webber and told him that an investigator had phoned and was looking for him. Ken had a concealed carry permit for his Glock, and he was glad it was in his shoulder holster right now—beneath a blazer and under his peacoat. He didn't flip off the safety, but he did unbutton his jacket. Now he was standing inside the small black-and-white tile lobby, a little dingy, a little black with New York soot, and staring at the elevator—which looked much newer than the lobby. A bit antiseptic, but modern and chrome. He guessed this building had been a walkup until it had been gentrified. He rang for the lift, pressed four, and found himself clenching and unclenching his fingers in the pockets of his coat. Even after all his years as a cop, even though it had been nearly half a century ago that he had been in Vietnam, at moments like these he still tensed in almost the same way he had as a kid in the jungle or when he'd been crouched inside one of those bunkers outside the base in the dark of the night.

When he emerged on the fourth floor, Webber was standing there in his entryway, the door open behind him. He looked pretty much the way the bartender had described him: early forties, ash-blond hair that was well styled for a guy who was, apparently, just hanging around his apartment on a weekday, and tall. But he was even taller than Ken had expected. He was in black jeans and a white turtleneck and he was barefoot, but he still had easily four or five inches on Ken—and the detective knew that although he had shrunk a little bit with age, he was still five eleven.

"Thanks for seeing me," he said, and he extended his hand.

"Happy to," Webber said. His grasp was firm, but not excessively so. There was no alpha male craziness to the grip.

"Ken Sarafian."

"Douglas Webber. Come on in. No point in standing out here in the hallway."

The duplex was bright and modern. The hardwood floors looked newly stained and polyurethaned, the wood the color of pumpkin pine. There were two deep blue and burgundy Oriental rugs, one of which had a pattern reminiscent of the carpet in his wife's and his living room. The kitchen was against the west wall, and a dining room table and chairs were against the southern windows. There was an L-shaped leather couch and a TV so large it looked like it belonged in a Hollywood producer's screening room. And there was a dartboard framed with a square cork pad.

"The cork behind the board is for guests," Webber said, and

Ken realized that he must have been staring at it. "If my game ever gets to the point where I actually miss the board, I'll hang it up. Do you play?"

"I don't."

In the far corner, there was a thin spiral staircase with wooden steps that matched the floor and a wrought-iron railing.

"So, you're a detective. That's pretty cool. I'm not sure I've ever met a detective. What does that mean you do? Photograph philandering husbands and wives from your car?"

"Sometimes. Not the work I'm most proud of."

"But it is, as they say, a living."

"Yup."

Webber motioned at the couch. "You want to sit down?"

"Sure," he agreed.

"Can I take your coat?"

Ken nodded and handed it to him, but he was careful not to reveal the gun hidden beneath his blazer. He assumed Webber knew he was carrying, but he saw no reason to advertise where the Glock was. Webber hung the coat on an ornate rack meant to look like an art nouveau lamppost—or that may in fact have been an art nouveau lamppost—and then the two of them sat on the L-shaped couch, Ken taking one length of the L and Webber the other.

"So, what are you investigating?" Webber asked, and he sounded bemused.

"Austin Harper's death."

He looked surprised. "He's dead? How? When?"

"Bike accident in Vietnam. Hit-and-run."

"Holy shit."

"You hadn't heard?"

"No. I mean, I barely know—excuse me, knew—the guy. I met him one night at a bar, we played some darts, and then the dude got shot by some homeless crazy. I took him to the ER and gave him my digits, and I checked in with him two or three times in the days after that. But he was fine. We texted about getting together again to have a drink, but it never happened. Can I ask you something?"

"Sure."

"You said he died in a bike accident. Are you trying to find the driver?"

Ken shrugged evasively, and so Webber continued, "I mean, isn't that something the Vietnamese police would handle? And how in the world do you expect to find the driver in America?"

"It's more complicated than that."

"Got it. I won't press," Webber said, and he draped his long arm over the back of the couch. His eyes were almost twinkling. "But can I ask who has retained you? His parents, I'm guessing."

"Nope. Girlfriend."

"Interesting. Good for her."

"So, you met Austin at a bar."

"Yup. We met that crazy night."

"The night he was shot."

"That's right."

Ken knew this was a lie. Or at least he thought it was. He believed that bartender. Amber. "The bartender who was there that night says you two came in together and were already pretty chummy."

"Well, he's mistaken."

"She."

He didn't seem fazed. "Well, she's mistaken."

"Why didn't you see him again?"

"Life. He was a guy I met in a bar and we tossed some darts and then that whole madness of the junkie with the gun went down. It's not like we really had all that much in common."

"Was he any good? At darts?"

"Nope. He hadn't played in years. Maybe ever. I can't remember what he said. Maybe he tossed them a couple times as a kid. Everyone does that."

"I know I did."

"Right?" Webber asked rhetorically.

"So why were you in that bar?"

"It's in the neighborhood. It has a dartboard."

"But you haven't been back."

"Of course I have," Webber said, and he raised an eyebrow incredulously. Again, Ken had more faith in Amber's memory than in Webber's contention.

"So . . ."

"Go ahead. Ask me anything."

"What do you do? For a living?"

"Travel writer."

"Ah, that explains why you're home in the middle of the day. You're not on an assignment right now."

"Correct. I'm between gigs."

"Married? Significant other?"

"Nope and nope. And no kids."

"Have you ever been to Vietnam?"

"Are you suggesting that I ran over Austin Harper?"

"It never crossed my mind that you might have," Ken told him, and here he was being completely honest. It really hadn't. Now? He still didn't think so, but he couldn't help but wonder, and he tried to see what was hovering behind Webber's eyes.

"I didn't."

"And Vietnam?"

"What about it?"

"Ever been there?" the detective asked again. "As a travel writer? An assignment?"

"I've been there a couple of times."

"Last week?"

"Nope."

The atmosphere in the room was shifting; there was now a hint of a storm. So, Ken decided to allow himself a hint of a threat. "I mean, it wouldn't be hard for me to find out if you were there."

"Which is why I wouldn't lie," Webber responded.

"You must be really good at what you do."

"Why? These digs?"

"Yeah. As my wife would say, pretty darn posh."

"Thank you. Just for the record, I have written about Vietnam." He motioned at a wrought-iron magazine rack beside a bookcase. "Want to see my take on Barcelona in last month's *Traveler*?"

"They pay well?"

"They do. But I'm also, as my mother used to say, a man of means."

Ken leaned toward Webber, his forearms on his knees. "Must be nice to come from that kind of money."

For a long moment, Webber said nothing. "So, is that it, Detective?" he asked finally.

"I guess," he said, taking the hint and standing. "Thank you."

"I hope I was helpful," Webber told him, standing, too, and retrieving the jacket from the coatrack. The fellow clearly knew that he hadn't been helpful at all.

"Every little bit helps," Ken said as he was putting his arms through the sleeves of the peacoat.

"I couldn't see it clearly, but I'm guessing based on the grip I just glimpsed—against your left rib cage—that's a Glock seventeen you're packing."

"It is."

"I prefer the twenty-six. Easier to conceal. Maybe not quite as accurate. But I've never had any problems in that regard."

"I'll bear that in mind," Ken said. The threat wasn't especially subtle, and it certainly hadn't scared him. But he had to applaud the deftness with which it had been delivered.

FRIDAY

25

Alexis awoke and stared at the *Breakfast at Tiffany's* poster on the wall above her dresser. At the black-and-white image of Audrey Hepburn in sunglasses, her hair in a bun, as she gazed into the window of the iconic jewelry store. Alexis had been dreaming of gloves. In the dream, she'd just bought a pair of pink leather ones that cost four hundred dollars at an elegant shop on Madison Avenue that sold nothing but gloves, and she wanted to return them now because she thought rats had been gnawing holes in the fingers—rather like moths.

God, rats. Rats repulsed people. They repulsed her. But they kept appearing before her now—no, not rats themselves, thank God, but traces of them in Austin's life going all the way back to the bite marks on his fingers the night they met—like road signs on the highway as she was driving in the dark. She presumed it was unreasonable to be more disgusted by a rat than by a mouse or a squirrel or by any of the myriad other rodents that filled the world, but the rat had a distinct place in the pantheon of the despised.

Before bed last night she had called Viet Nam National University in Ho Chi Minh City and left a message with a woman who spoke English. She'd explained who she was and that she was looking for either of the two scientists who had studied the long-term effects of herbicides on rats and the animal's evolution over the last half century. Now Alexis checked her phone to see if anyone had called her back and she had slept through the call or whether anyone had emailed her. No calls and no emails from the university.

She had the day off today, but she was going by the hospital anyway. She had a ten thirty appointment with an epidemiologist from one of the university's bio labs in the research wing of the hospital to talk about the animal. She'd scheduled the interview yesterday after seeing that poster of the drawing of the rat and the limerick. The scientist, a woman named Sara Edens, was a doctoral candidate in one of the labs, a relatively junior researcher, but Alexis didn't care. She worked with Dr. Ho-jin Myung, according to the hospital website, and was willing to see her. And so Alexis was thrilled. They were going to meet at the hospital cafeteria.

After seeing the young researcher, Alexis thought she might go to the gym and work out, and so she threw some of Austin's old energy gels into her gym bag before leaving her apartment. She packed a lemon and a chocolate-flavored goo. She wondered whether anyone in Vietnam had bothered to confirm whether the ones she had pulled off the street north of Da Nang had been Austin's. She doubted the case was closed, but the authorities there—if they were doing anything at all—were searching for the driver who'd sent Austin careening over the guardrail, not whoever it was who had plunged something sharp and pointed into the back of his hand.

· · ·

Sara Edens was not much younger than she was, Alexis thought, when she saw her sipping a cup of coffee and eating one of the cafeteria's doughy and tasteless bagels at a table near the windows facing First Avenue. There was an unopened blueberry yogurt before her as well. She had broad shoulders and a big chest, which relieved Alexis: it would be too cruel a coincidence if the dress Austin had had with him when he'd been killed had been meant for Sara. She had dark hair that was cut very short, and when she looked up from her phone on the long table, Alexis noted that her eyeglasses had a tortoiseshell pattern, but the colors were blue and yellow and green. She was wearing khaki pants and a pink button-down shirt: no lab coat, because, Alexis knew, the scientists couldn't risk contaminating the public spaces. Alexis didn't bother to get a cup of coffee; she went straight to the table and introduced herself, and for easily five minutes they made small talk about the hospital and how they had wound up doing what they did for a living. Finally, Alexis told her about Austin Harper and how he had died, and that rats suddenly seemed everywhere in her life.

"I work mostly with mice," Sara said. "We work mostly with mice."

"You mean in the labs?"

"Uh-huh. The knockout or the knock-in mice. We knock out a certain gene or add a certain gene to test diseases. My work is in arenaviruses and hantaviruses. Another team studies mouse feces. It's a bit like the Columbia University research you mentioned: see what diseases are out there."

"You all lead such glamorous lives," Alexis told her.

"Saving the world, one piece of mouse poop at a time."

"And other people work specifically with rats?"

"Sure. A couple have teams. Mice. Rats. Poop. It's all toward the same end."

"Which is?"

"Understanding what's in the basements of our buildings that someday is going to kill us."

"That's a cheery thought."

"I'm kidding. Mostly. The goal is to develop therapeutic agents or, better still, antibiotics and vaccines."

"Do we even have hantavirus in New York City?" Alexis asked. "I mean, I've never seen it in the ER. I never saw it in Houston when I was there."

"Not in the city. But we will. We're up to thirty-plus states. Thirty-four or thirty-five, I think, including two cases I'm aware of on Long Island. We have plenty of deer mice here in the city and deer mice are easily infected. But so far it isn't among the shit I've found in their shit." Sara wiped her lips with a paper napkin and then went on, "Even at the best addresses in Manhattan, the little critters carry all sorts of disease-causing bacteria and viruses. My boss, Dr. Myung, lives in a pretty swank building on Park Avenue—he had us all over last year for a holiday party—and he says his apartment basement has its share of rats. And, you can bet, they have salmonella, E. coli, shigella. You know, the usual suspects."

"And the others?"

"The other pathogens? It's a long list, especially the new species. But each could, conceivably, be transmitted to humans."

"And they're drug resistant?"

"Some are. Totally untreatable by the stuff you have in your medicine cabinets in the ER. Cipro. Amoxicillin. They laugh at them."

"The bugs do."

"Yup. The bugs."

"And the mice and the rats aren't sick?"

She giggled and it was almost girlish. "The ones in your apartment building, Dr. Myung's, or the labs?"

"I was thinking of the apartments."

"Happy as can be. They're carriers of the bacteria or the viruses, that's all."

Alexis thought about this. "How would the bacteria develop a resistance to antibiotics?"

"In the wilds of your apartment basement? Unclear. Could be natural selection. Could be from munching our food or our shit."

"That's gross."

Sara nodded vigorously in agreement.

"And the endgame of your work is treatment," Alexis said, echoing what the researcher had explained a moment ago.

"Got to be ready for the next pandemic. Got to have new antibiotics. Got to know what we're up against. I mean, it's coming, and New York City is the perfect place for a catastrophe: we have lots of people living in very close quarters. We have lots—and by lots, I mean millions—of rodents. We have people coming and going and visiting all the time. We have the subways. In 2015, a guy from Weill Cornell swabbed the subways and found anthrax and the bubonic plague. How's that for disgusting? Trust me, the plague could make hantavirus look like a nosebleed."

"I would say terrifying, not disgusting."

"I stand corrected." She looked down at her unopened yogurt and the plastic spoon on top of the container. "I'm not going to eat this," she said. "I hadn't eaten since last night and I was starving when I went to the counter. I was only going to eat half the bagel, but, well, I seem to have scarfed down all of it. You want my yogurt?"

"Sure. Thank you. I was going to have a banana and an energy gel before going to the gym. I didn't bother with breakfast."

"I love it when doctors eat right," Sara told her, and Alexis smiled. The yogurt was blueberry flavored—her favorite—and she opened the container and started to eat it ravenously.

"My world has been sort of upside down since Austin died," she said. "I probably haven't been taking the best care of myself."

"I get it," the other woman agreed.

"So, tell me: what is the next pandemic?"

"It depends on what the bug is. I mentioned the plague a minute ago. Do you know you can still get the plague? We can still get the plague. It's on the Russian steppes, it's in Madagascar. I told you it was found in the subways."

"Such a cheery thought."

"Rats are supremely capable of adapting. They have a rapid reproductive rate. And so lots of things can cause mutations in them—and it doesn't take any time at all. You have literally hundreds of generations of rats in half a century," Sara said, and she finished the last of her coffee.

"Hundreds of generations," Alexis repeated. "I came across a study from a university in Ho Chi Minh City that talked about that. It seems the ones we didn't kill with napalm and herbicides in the Vietnam War are now, well, über-rats."

"Oh, the ones we have here in New York could probably hold their own against them. And they haven't even had to endure Agent Orange. Why in the world were you reading about Vietnamese rats?"

"I wasn't. I think Austin was."

"Wow. Some people Google where to find the best spring rolls or pho before going there. And your ex was looking up rats? That's disturbing."

"It is. That's why I wanted to see you," she said. "If you were to guess—and I know it's just a guess—why do you think Austin was researching the animal? Why might he have been investigating the Vietnamese rat?" Alexis asked her.

"First of all, I'm sorry: I'm really sorry your boyfriend died. It's just so freaking horrible."

Alexis grimaced involuntarily, but nodded. "Thank you."

"I never met him: Austin. I never heard of him until I heard that a hospital employee had died in a bike accident in Vietnam," she said. "I know development and advancement are in the same wing as the labs, but no one goes into the labs without clearance. It's why we're meeting in the cafeteria. The labs are, well, labs. We have protocols. Parts are BSL-three, which is pretty secure. I mean, we're not even on the same floor as the administrative offices."

"Who might he have been seeing?"

"In the labs?"

"That's right."

She shook her head. "If he was researching rats? Let's see, there are probably thirty or so of us up there. But it wasn't me. And I really don't see why he would have been researching rats. Rats aren't big philanthropists. They don't run family trusts or foundations. They aren't grateful patients who want to buy the hospital new toys. New MRI machines or robotic arms or optical scanners."

"But who? You said there were people who are studying rats."

"Well, there would be Dr. Bhattacharya. Dr. Sinclair. And, of course, my boss, Dr. Myung, does a little bit with rats—but not as much as those two. That's off the top of my head."

"I've seen their names on the hospital's research pages on our website. I'll call them."

"Let me ask around first. Discreetly."

"That would be wonderful, thank you."

"The likely candidates are Dr. Sinclair and Dr. Bhattacharya, if Austin really was meeting someone there. They do way more with rats than my boss. I'll try to see them in the next couple of days. I'll get back to you, okay? Maybe one of them could show you around or maybe, with their permission, I could show you around."

"That would be amazing."

"Not a big deal. You work here. You might not be allowed into the BSL-three sections, but we can easily get you into the BSL-twos."

"That would be so helpful."

A short fellow with receding ginger hair sidled up to the table beside them. "Morning," he said to Sara.

"Hey, Michael." She motioned toward Alexis and said, "This is my lab partner, Michael Fodder. A little of what he does, when he's not with me, overlaps with Dr. Sinclair's research. Michael, this is Alexis Remnick. She's an ER doctor here."

"Nice to meet you," he said, nodding affably. He had a cup of coffee in his hand.

"Want to join us?" Sara asked him. She took off her eyeglasses and cleaned them on a paper napkin.

"No, I just grabbed an egg sandwich and now I'm heading back to the lab. But thank you."

"So, you work with Dr. Sinclair?" Alexis asked him before he could leave.

"Not a whole lot, actually."

"But some?"

"Some," he said. And then he volunteered, "He's a nice guy. For a dude who spends most of his workday killing rats, he's pretty damn sane. But, hey: I guess it's what we all do." He steepled his eyebrows, smiled sardonically, and left.

·   ·   ·

She hadn't had much of an appetite since Vietnam, and she wondered if this was grief or sadness or anger—or something else entirely. She was lifting weights today, and so between sets on the bench she would gaze at pictures of Austin on her phone. She studied his face and thought of a quote from Walt Whitman she'd always loved: "What is that you express in your eyes? It seems to me more than all the print I have read in my life." Those green eyes, the unmistakable glint of . . .

Of what? She would have said wonder or boyishness or exuberance.

But now? Was it irresponsibility? Deceit? Devilishness?

To sleep with a man and know him so little . . .

Was it her failing or his?

The banana and the yogurt and then the cup of coffee she had grabbed on the way to the gym had fortified her, and so the Psych gels still sat in the bottom of her gym bag as she recalled the single thing she had loved best about Austin: he was fun. He wasn't one of those high-performance athletes who was all work and no play. Somehow, he could ride fifty or sixty miles on a Saturday and still have the energy to take her to a great dinner and be adoring and enthusiastic afterwards when they would retreat to his apartment or hers. Good Lord, they'd met after he'd been playing darts— darts!—with a stranger in a bar.

She wasn't sure how to reconcile the lies he had told her with the man who, on the last day of his life, had either been tortured or gotten into some sort of fight. But she wanted to. No: she *needed* to. This was more than a semantic difference.

And maybe it was the synaptic connection of fight and fun, the alliteration, but she picked her phone up off the towel on the floor and studied the image of the wound on his hand. The roundness of the prick and the way the bruise radiated in perfect circles. She magnified it with her forefinger and thumb. She had thought the weapon had been a screwdriver or an awl. But now? Now she thought dart. Was it possible that someone had slammed a dart into the back of his hand?

Of course it was. She saw it happening all too clearly in her mind. Someone had used a dart to break the bones there.

And she was positive now that all of it—the trip, the disappearance, the torture, the murder—had something to do with rats.

She thought of what she and Sara Edens had discussed, how rats mutated rapidly.

She put down her phone and lay back on the bench. Then she pressed one hundred and fifteen pounds eight times. She could go higher, but she was working without a spotter today and decided that this was where she should max out. When the bar was racked, once more she sat up. What would she do if someone showed up in the ER with swollen lymph nodes, and when she took a fluid sample, she found present there Yersinia pestis—the plague? She'd admit the patient, and the person would be given cipro or gentamicin or some other hard-core antibiotic. The hospital would quarantine the individual and get her travel history: where had the patient been and with whom had she been in contact? And the patient would likely recover.

But what if, as Sara had speculated, the pathogen was resistant to antibiotics? What if the rats didn't die of the disease and acted merely—merely!—as carriers?

And that, she began to suspect, was where the Vietnamese rat came in. Fifty years and hundreds of generations of rats ago, the

Americans had been entrenched in Vietnam, trying to bomb or napalm parts of the country into the stone age and defoliating the rest with chemicals. She didn't know what her ex-boyfriend was up to or where he had been in the hours that were unaccounted for earlier that month, but she was going to have to tell Ken Sarafian her theory. She did another set on the bench and then sat up and called the private investigator. She got his voice mail and left a message to please call her back: she had a couple of ideas she wanted to share.

It might not be the plague—it probably wasn't the plague, she told herself—but Austin's disappearance had something to do with the confluence of Vietnamese rats and disease. Austin Harper, fun as he was, had been into shit so nasty that someone was willing to smash a dart into the back of his hand—and then kill him.

They tell me that it's actually easier to manipulate the eggs of a mouse than a rat, even though rats are bigger. The basements of most teaching and university hospitals are filled with genetically modified mice.

But an egg is an egg is an egg. Now we can manipulate the eggs of rats, too. We can manipulate the eggs of most rodents. Most mammals. Most animals. We take modified stem cells and inject them into an embryo to "knock out" a gene—hence the term knockout mice. *Or we introduce a gene by "knock in." This way we learn about the links between a particular gene and a particular disease. We create animals with specific pathologies, study them, and assess the roles of the genes in the creatures.*

We were supposed to be developing new antibiotics. It was all very well intentioned. Yes, we also knew the results would be lucrative. The pharma companies were right next door.

But we heard about what they were doing in Ho Chi Minh City, the way they were working with Vietnamese rats. The descendants of the ones that had survived Agent Orange. The idea began there. Evolution is related to pressure, and the herbicides had exerted fantastic pressure on the species. They had evolved. They were hardier creatures and seemed to survive some diseases longer than other rats.

Even the plague.

And so we were injecting their plague-resistant gene into the rats who ruled the subways here in New York City. Then we would give them the mutated version of the plague—the one that did not respond to antibiotics. Imagine a rat that could carry the pathogen—that wasn't sickened by it or felled by it? You think antibiotics are profitable? Trust me, biologic weapons are infinitely more bankable. They are, after all, rare. Most civilized nations agreed years ago not to create or store or deploy them.

But not all. If we found the right buyer for a weaponized strain of plague—one that didn't kill its carriers—the sky was the limit.

The missing link wasn't biologic or chemical. It was actually sales. We needed a middleman. A broker. We needed someone who could sell anything.

26

The lab tech was gone, his death fast and horrid. Xuan hadn't lasted even through the night, the buboes swelling beneath his arms and on his neck with astonishing speed. It seemed likely a strain of plague, but hardier and accelerated. Usually the disease incubated for days. This one? Hours. And it went to the lungs fast. The young guy was sick within hours and then dead within hours. Literally, hours. He hadn't lasted twenty of them. He had evidenced many of the signs of pneumonic plague: a cough thick with blood, a fever that spiked, vomiting. And then respiratory failure and shock and death. He also had lesions on his arms and his legs and in his mouth, and the ones in his mouth bled so copiously that before he succumbed to the disease, twice he had almost choked on the fluid. One physician suggested this was a symptom of a particular autoimmune disorder that was very rare—perhaps not the plague at all. He had been treated with massive doses of antibiotics upon arrival at the hospital, but they had done nothing, nothing at all. The pathogen was oblivious to them.

Xuan was leaving behind a young wife and an infant son. And Quang suspected—because the captain had known Xuan so well—that the man had died blaming himself for leaving the woman he loved a widow and the son he loved fatherless. He hadn't been wearing a hood, an uncharacteristic bit of sloppiness, and that was probably why he was dead. Certainly, it was a factor.

They'd scheduled the autopsy, but given the protocols necessary to protect against transmission of the pathogen, the morgue
had to be prepared. The coroner, Minh Tran, reached Quang just
before lunch. He had also autopsied Austin Harper, and admitted
now that he wasn't looking forward to this one. What unnerved
him, he said, was not that they might be dealing with a plague
strain, but that the bacteria hadn't responded to antibiotics.

"Xuan went straight to the hospital and they started treatment
right away," Minh told him over the phone. "Antibiotics are supposed to kick the plague's ass."

"Supposed to?" Quang asked.

"Well, it's not like we—as in planet Earth—see the plague all
that often. But, yes, supposed to."

"Tell me something."

"Sure."

"Was the plague spread entirely by fleas in Europe, or could
humans give it to humans?"

"First of all, stop with the past tense. I said we don't see it
often. I didn't say it was ever eradicated."

"Okay."

"Yes, humans can give it to humans. It can be transmitted
directly and indirectly. A touch. A cough, once it's gone to the
lungs and taken its pneumatic form. Pneumonic is considerably
more contagious. Aerosol transmission is possible. Think Xuan."

"And second?"

"Second, stop thinking Europe. The brown rat that carried
all those fleas? It migrated there across Asia from Vietnam."

"Has the cabbie shown any symptoms?"

"When I spoke to the hospital a few minutes ago, the cabbie
was dying."

Quang closed his eyes and rubbed at his temples. "And that
other lab tech?"

"No symptoms yet. Take some comfort in that," the coroner
told him. "I am. But . . ."

"Go on."

"But whatever was in that American's energy gel? It's a lot more fucking dangerous than good, old-fashioned plague."

.   .   .

Quang asked that the phone records of the dead food chemist be checked to see if there were any calls between her and Austin Harper. He wanted to know if they had spoken the day he'd died—but also at any point in the last six months, perhaps before or after she and her sister had visited New York City. Then he joined the bio team at the site where the woman and two others were massacred, but he wasn't allowed inside what remained of the small building. Given the dozen or so people who had already been inside there without hazmat suits, including Quang himself, he didn't expect they'd find anything deadly. Still, he watched the team climb inside their lemon-yellow gear—gas-tight—and butyl gloves and respirator hoods, and was glad they were taking these precautions. While they were searching for traces of plague, Quang also wanted to know whether there was any trace of the American, such as fingerprints, inside the building. He wanted to know if Austin Harper had been with the victims before he had ridden Highway One on his bike. The blaze hadn't obliterated the building—far from it—because the fire department had arrived quickly. The ceiling still stood and much of the structure was cinder blocks and concrete. But between the damage from first the inferno and then the water, he wasn't confident they'd find much. But you never knew and you had to try.

Meanwhile, the Ministry of Health thought they had this thing contained, but the investigators he had met with that morning couldn't be sure. The plan was to visit every place that the bike tour had gone, and they already had teams scouring every location—every hotel, every restaurant, every spa, every tourist attraction—that day. They would see if anyone else had gotten sick or even evidenced any of these symptoms. But as far as they knew, no one else had shown up at any hospitals or clinics with signs of the plague.

And so while it was devastating that Xuan was dead, it was a blessing that he had been the one to open the gel, because he had been in a lab and gone straight to the ER. Moreover, Xuan had been the cabbie's last customer that day and he lived alone. That, too, was a break. Still, he shouldn't have taken a cab. He should have called for an ambulance. He was either in denial or he had panicked.

But it seemed that the pathogen had been confined to the energy gels, so the Ministry had no plan at the moment to send out a nationwide advisory and risk rattling the general population. They didn't believe it would spread any farther than it already had.

"Is that an expectation or a hope?" he had asked one of the investigators.

The investigator, a slender bureaucrat his age with long hair she parted in the middle, shook her head and shrugged. "It's a hope," she said, adding after a beat, "maybe a prayer."

. . .

It was nearly seven o'clock at night by the time the bio team had finished north of Da Nang, the vans awash in samples and swabs, and filled with items they were taking from the building, including a couple of the small animal cages that hadn't melted, a couple of microscopes that were still intact, and some garbage from cans that had been outside. They'd removed the fire-blackened refrigerator, the remnants of a couple of particle air filters, and the cleaning products and every petri dish and container in the small building that had been spared. But, they reassured Quang, they didn't feel there was anything dangerous there. This was all precautionary.

"The flames weren't meant to cover up the murders," Quang

observed to one of the fire marshals, who, like the police captain, was reduced to a spectator as the bio team worked. "Whoever did this didn't care. We knew the minute the smoke had been cleared and the firefighters had gone in that the victims had been executed."

"That's right. My guess is that this was both justice of some sort—retribution—and a message."

"So why the fire? We know there was an accelerant and it was arson. It was deliberate."

"We do," the marshal agreed. "But what we don't know is what was lost in the fire."

"An incubator?" Quang asked.

"Like for babies born prematurely?"

"No," he said. "For cell cultures. For growing . . . shit."

"It's possible. There's a lot of debris that someone will have to examine to see what it once was."

Quang was about to ask another question, but he stepped away when he heard a text and looked at his phone. He read it and rubbed the bridge of his nose. Before going home, he was now going to go to the hospital, and he was going to visit there with a heavy heart: the cabbie had died in the afternoon. He'd died exactly the way Xuan had, though he'd hung on a bit longer. He'd managed to last a little more than a day before succumbing to whatever the American had brought to Vietnam.

27

Douglas Webber didn't know if Oscar Bolton would be an obedient and responsive animal. He had thought Austin Harper was, and clearly he had misjudged him. But he was about to find out.

Now that a PI had discovered where he lived and connected him to Harper, Douglas knew there was no way in hell they could meet anymore at his apartment. That wasn't happening.

And so early in the morning, before the sun was up, he walked past the black wrought-iron gate with the elegant filigree that was the original entrance to Bellevue Hospital, now an ornament before a green, and on a column below the *B* in *Bellevue* used a piece of white chalk to make a long swipe. Bolton was supposed to check the column daily on his way in to work. If he saw a mark, he was supposed to meet Douglas at twelve thirty at the bench near the statue of Peter Stuyvesant in the little park between Fifteenth and Seventeenth Streets. This was the first time Douglas had resorted to this sort of seriously old-school way of connecting, but until he had decided what to do about Ken Sarafian or Austin Harper's old girlfriend, he wanted no further digital trail—no texts or phone calls or emails—linking them.

. . .

He was watching two squirrels when Bolton arrived. The animals were interesting to him, but not as interesting as rats were these days. They were playing. At least it looked like they were playing by the way they chased each other around the roots of a hearty linden tree, but Douglas tried not to anthropomorphize any creature. Still, he decided today he would err on the side of optimism and view what they were doing as entertaining themselves, not grubbing for survival in an endless search for shelter or food as winter drew near. Bolton was a couple of minutes early, which pleased him.

"Well done," he said simply to him when the other man collapsed beside him on the bench, his arms folded across his chest. He was wearing a gray overcoat. Douglas was in a heavy, navy-blue hoodie.

"What if I'd had a lunch meeting I couldn't get out of? What if I had any meeting I couldn't get out of? What if I was out of town?" he asked petulantly.

Douglas shrugged. "I would have tried again tomorrow."

"Not very efficient."

He turned to him and smiled. "I pay you well. You're here. Can we move on?"

"Sure. But that stupid chalk mark scared the piss out of me."

"I doubt that."

"It meant you couldn't text me."

"I rarely text you. I hate texting you. I used to call your office phone—sometimes. You used to call my cell. Sometimes. It's unlikely that either of us will do even that now for a long, long while."

Bolton nodded, but he was still glowering as he stared straight ahead. Douglas had a dart with a plastic sheath on the tip in his kangaroo pocket, and he fingered the sheath now. Attitude annoyed him. Attitude in a newbie especially irritated him. But he took a breath and remembered to keep his eye on the prize. It was what he did.

"So," he said, hoping his tone evidenced not a trace of alarm because the last thing he wanted was for Bolton to panic on him, "I had a visitor."

"The PI who called me?"

"One and the same. Thank you for alerting me."

"That scared me, too."

"It shouldn't. Remember, he's a private detective. Not a real cop. Not the police. Remember, he was hired by Austin Harper's girlfriend."

"What does she know?"

"I assume nothing, but I don't know. So, the first reason I wanted to see you today was simply to alert you to what this development means. And that is this: absolutely no communication except in person. No more phone calls on landlines and never any texts or emails or cell calls."

"Fuck."

"That's an overreaction, Oscar."

"Is it? There's a PI involved, a guy I worked with is dead, and you tell me he might have been trying to bring a sample to Vietnam—"

Douglas put his hand on Bolton's forearm. "I am telling you to relax. That's what I'm telling you. You need to be careful—and I will help you in that regard. But you're in no danger if you listen to me. And I will deal with the PI, if it should ever become necessary."

"Deal with him? What does that mean?"

"Really, why would you want to know?"

Bolton snorted and Douglas took back his hand. "Fine," Bolton said.

"You're going to be okay? You're good?" Douglas asked.

"No."

"Good enough?" he continued, and he felt like he was talking to a toddler.

"Sure," Bolton grumbled.

They sat in silence for a moment while two mothers with small children in strollers passed them, chatting casually about a new restaurant that had opened in their neighborhood. When they were no longer in earshot, Douglas said, "As a matter of fact, yes, I am still concerned that your friend smuggled something out of the labs."

"I told you, I found nothing in his apartment. Absolutely nothing. I looked for everything you said to look for, and there was nothing like that there. No biohazard bags, no needles, no syringes. None of those crazy weird vials."

"The term is *parasitology transport system*."

"None of them. No bioboxes."

"I understand."

"I can't go back. I don't think the doorman would even let me in again."

"Well, you could. I could make that happen. But it's not necessary. His parents have been there by now."

"Then what? You just wanted to tell me there's a private investigator looking into all of . . . all of this? I mean, I knew that. I called you." Douglas heard exasperation in the other man's voice, but he knew that in fact it was fear.

"Have you scheduled a tour of Myung's lab?"

"Yes. Monday."

"Good. Thank you. Now, you asked me what Alexis Remnick knows, and I told you that I don't know. So that brings me to the other reason why we're here. Let's find out. I'm adding a little more to your plate. I want you to take the ER doctor out on a date."

"I have a girlfriend."

"I don't care."

"I can't."

Douglas ignored him and pulled the dart from the hoodie's front pocket. He held it before him and studied it as if he didn't know what it was. Then he removed the plastic sheath. He was confident that Bolton would view this gesture as threatening and would respond accordingly, but Douglas had no plans to hurt the guy. At least not right now. "I'm a reasonable man," he reassured him. "You don't want to take a hot doctor on a date. I get it. But you can suggest to her that you two grab a cup of coffee together.

Tell her you want to talk about Austin. Share some memories. Share how traumatized you are by the guy's death."

"We've never spoken."

"But you know who she is?"

"Yes, of course. I saw her nosing around the offices this week. I played dumb."

Douglas resisted the straight line he'd been given and said instead, "Good. It means you have an introduction already. A . . . connection."

"So, I see her for coffee or lunch or something. Then what?"

"You become her friend. You find out what she knows. You find out what she's doing."

"Fine," he agreed, properly defeated.

"Let's meet again on Sunday. Same bat channel, same bat time."

"I don't know what that means."

"It means this bench at twelve thirty. That should give you plenty of time to find out for me—for us, Oscar, for us—what she knows."

He put the sheath back on the tip of the dart and returned it to his pocket. Then he reached for the envelope thick with one-hundred-dollar bills—too thick for a wallet—and handed it to Bolton.

"I was surprised you don't use wire transfers. I always thought that was how these things worked," Bolton said.

Douglas stood up and stretched his lanky body. "It's how they work if you want to wind up in jail," he told him, and then he left the man alone on the bench. He passed a poster with a drawing of a rat and a rose and he found himself smiling.

The university had BSL-3 labs at the hospital, but no BSL-4s—which is the highest. The most secure. But that was fine because, believe it or not, the plague is only a BSL-3 pathogen. Not four. It responds to existing drugs. The NIH sent us a sample to begin with, because of our above-board work. (Of course, even if they hadn't, it wouldn't have been hard to get one. Vials of it, along with anthrax, sit in the storerooms. Want to be scared? Watch the TED talks on how easy it is to steal some of these pathogens.)

Still, there are plenty of safety protocols at a BSL-3 lab. Protective equipment, respirators, scrub suits, the biosafety cabinets. I can still hear the ticking of the air filters. You can imagine how difficult it was to get in and get out. The key codes. The pass cards. The cameras.

The pathogen itself was treated like uranium and monitored just as carefully: far more carefully than at the NIH. I'm serious. After all, it was a new strain of plague, and we were in the middle of Kip's Bay. Manhattan. Blocks from the subway and yards from the East River

But, again, we were only biosafety level three. If people on the outside knew what we were doing, I'm honestly not sure whether rage or fear would have been the defining characteristic of the news cycle.

But we knew the risks.

Or, at least, we thought we did.

28

Ken Sarafian had listened to Alexis's voice mail about what he was already calling in his mind—an admittedly brusque and not especially accurate shorthand—the rat research. He'd reached out to Viet Nam National University and found a young male assistant in what the website called "Media" who spoke English and was willing to FaceTime with him. He had the distinct sense early into the conversation that the research had been censored. It had been taken off the university's website, which was where, he presumed, Austin Harper had gotten the abstract. The spokesperson wasn't prepared to say it had been censored; instead, he denied it existed. Said there was no study like that. When Ken asked about the two scientists whose names were on the research, he was told they no longer worked at the school and the assistant had no forwarding addresses for them. Insisted that he had no idea where they were now.

And so Ken thanked him and did a little digging online. It was pretty clear why the lead researcher hadn't responded to his client's emails. He had a feeling if Alexis checked her spam filter, she'd find that it had caught an automated email from Vietnam and quarantined it. And *quarantine* was precisely the right word, in this case, an inadvertent pun. The word in the subject line, he was quite sure, would be *undeliverable*. The scientist was dead. Died of an undisclosed illness. Ken wouldn't have been surprised in the slightest if the other one was dead, too.

. . .

Next he called Sally Gleason.

"You actually took the case?" she asked, incredulous, when he told her.

"Yes, ma'am."

"I told you not to."

The tenor of her voice surprised him. It was sharp, accusatory. He'd never heard that tone from her, and he wasn't sure what to make of it. He didn't like the way it had caused his antennae to twitch.

"You didn't know all the facts when you encouraged me not to," he said carefully.

"I snapped at you just now, didn't I?"

"Little bit."

"I'm sorry. I guess I was just shocked. And it's been one of those days."

"How so?"

"Too boring to recount. But suffice to say that Austin's death does mean we're a man down here. Same amount of work, fewer people. More fires, fewer firefighters."

"Got it."

"So Alexis called you," she murmured. "And it's not just a fool's errand?"

"Nope. It's actually kind of interesting."

"You're kidding."

"I'm not."

"She's on to something?"

"She might be. I spoke to Oscar Bolton," he told her.

"He didn't tell me."

"He probably meant to. He probably will. I've actually spoken to a lot of folks."

"And now me," she said.

"Yup."

"And that's ethical?"

"Why wouldn't it be? Because you're the daughter of one of my friends?"

"I guess. And because I was the referral."

"It's fine," he said. "It really is." And then he told her about the rats, and even in their back-and-forth over the phone, he heard what he believed was discomfort in her voice. She was clear that rats repulsed her, which was fine. They repulsed a lot of people.

"I'm obviously not indifferent to what they do in the labs. It's important medically, and it's an important fund-raising tool. I know that. I'm fine with the briefings I get once or twice a year or the news releases that public affairs sends me. But I don't go there," she told him.

"Did Austin?"

"He certainly went at least once. When you start work in advancement, you get a tour. You get shown around and taught a bit about our research. It's part of fund-raising, so it's part of training."

"Could he have gone back?"

"Sure," she answered. "Sometimes there's something they want us to see. But it really is a separate universe."

"Same wing."

"Other than an elevator bank, we don't share much."

"He have any friends there?"

"In the labs? He might have. But none that I know of."

Ken switched gears. "What did Austin tell you about the Vietnam trip?"

"What he told everyone. It was a bike tour."

"His second one."

"Ah, but his first with Alexis."

"What else?"

"He told me that it was another attempt to visit the places where his uncle died and his father was wounded."

"Which we know now was a lie."

"Yes," Sally agreed. "Sadly, we do."

"So why do you think he was there? Did he say anything else about the place? Anything else he wanted to do? Did he just want a new suit from Hoi An that badly? Does he have a thing for dragon fruit?"

"You can get dragon fruit here. You just have to know where to shop."

"Then what?"

"I wish I had any ideas. I have none."

"And he never brought up the labs?"

"No, he did. But always in the context of fund-raising. You know, we'd get a news release that we'd had some breakthrough on hantavirus," she told him. "Or there was progress toward a new treatment for MS. Or some antibiotic showed promise. But most of their money comes from grants, not from us. We use them—the labs—to remind people that this is a university hospital: a great place that does great things." Then she asked him, "Are you going to try and talk to them next? The lab rats?"

"I'll stick to the humans," he teased her.

"I have a meeting that's about to begin. You'll give my best to Taleen and the boys?"

"I will. And you say hi to your mom."

He hadn't forgotten her pique when he'd told her he'd taken the case, but he was still smiling when he hung up. He missed her dad. One time he'd shown Ken a photo of himself in an antiwar protest in 1971. The massive bell bottoms, the love beads, the crazy long hair and a beard that made him look like a caveman. He was one of two guys holding a sign that read, CHILDREN ARE NOT FOR BURNING. He hadn't meant to make Ken feel bad. He wanted to show it to him because of the outfit and what he looked like back then. He'd wound up a lawyer at a prestigious firm on Park Avenue, but he'd continued to live on Long Island and still played golf on the public course near his house right up until the day he died. He moved seamlessly between opening-night receptions at the Met and Sunday-afternoon golf with a cop like Ken.

He shook off the memory and the protest sign and put his phone in his pocket. Then he went uptown to meet Austin Harper's parents at the dead guy's apartment.

. . .

The detective had just finished interviewing Austin Harper's parents after they had assessed what it would entail to pack up his place on the Upper East Side, and he was thinking to himself that this was the worst time of the day to grab a cab. How had he done this to himself yet again? It was a little after four p.m., the period between shifts and the start of rush hour, and he was standing on the street watching the traffic inch forward, the rare yellow cab he saw in the stream invariably with its roof light dark. He dialed down his frustration and opened the app on his phone for a taxi service, and found there was a shared car three blocks distant and a private car ten. He picked the private and saw it was at least five minutes away. Five probably meant eight. But that was fine.

Austin's parents, as he had expected, were defensive when he had finally gotten around to bringing up the peculiar lies their son had told about their family history: the idea that his father had been shot in Vietnam and precisely where his uncle had died. They only grew more receptive to his questions when he told them he had found three of Austin's acquaintances—in addition to Alexis Remnick—to whom he had told these same strange stories. They all were new friends. Two worked at the hospital, and the third was the son of philanthropists who were big donors to the pediatric wing.

Eventually, they gave Ken a list of four of their son's friends from childhood and college he could speak with, all of whom obviously knew the truth because they had known Austin for years and been to the home outside of Boston where he'd grown up. They insisted that their son had never evidenced or been treated for the sort of mental illness that might compel him to fabricate a new family history. Ken had done his homework before meeting the Harpers, and had pinpointed three psychological causes for compulsive lying. The first was antisocial personality disorder, but Austin didn't fit the profile—he was pretty damn prosocial, if that was even a thing—and that also seemed to be a behavior learned from parents. And this pair? They seemed levelheaded and straightforward. The second was interdependence, or mutual lying, but it didn't appear as if Austin Harper had a codependent relationship with the ER doc. And why would lying about his father and uncle draw Alexis closer to him? Why would she feel the need to enable the lie? The third was something called conduct disorder, and that was the one that made the most sense to Ken. Patients who had this were usually lying to cover up an addiction—gambling, shoplifting, drugs, sex—or they were involved in something seriously shady, and they just kept entrenching themselves ever deeper with their fabrications. This certainly jibed with Harper's behavior in high school and college.

In this scenario, Harper needed a pretext to go to Vietnam. He'd gone there twice: once on a bike tour alone and once on a bike tour with Alexis. As far as Ken could tell, he'd told the lie first a year ago, the first time he'd announced he was traveling there. Then, when he'd returned, he had to be consistent and so he told it again. And again. He told it some more.

But the detective didn't know exactly what Harper was up to. If he had to guess, he would conjecture that the first time he had gone to Vietnam, he'd visited the university in Ho Chi Minh City and he'd met with a scientist who was now dead. He thought it possible that there was some extreme monetary value to this rat research, but there was nothing in the guy's apartment that suggested he was living beyond his means. In the lobby, before leaving, he had researched what those cartoon cells on the walls might have cost, and most had probably set him back five or six hundred dollars. Maybe the Grinch was worth more, but not much. The bike tour wasn't cheap, but he had split the cost with Alexis and they'd flown there in coach. He didn't have oligarchic silk suits or racks of leather or ostrich jackets in his closet.

Good Lord, he'd bought that suit in Hoi An because it was so bloody cheap. His watch was a Movado that cost five hundred and change, and his furniture was nice, but about what one would expect from a single thirtysomething executive in Manhattan. The only thing he spent big money on was a damn good bike and nice biking accessories.

But maybe he had simply not yet been paid. He'd died—or been killed—before the big score.

His parents didn't believe he had any debts and showed him their son's checkbook, which, Ken had to admit, suggested a pretty modest lifestyle if you subtracted out two trips to Vietnam in one year.

"Why do you think he went there?" he had asked Peter Harper.

"You know the answer to that: it was a bike tour," his father had answered, echoing Austin's boss earlier that afternoon.

"The first time?" Ken had pressed. "Yes, it was a bike tour, too, but he went alone."

"He went to bike and I'm sure he made friends," his father said. "And single people go on bike tours all the time. I see nothing suspicious in that. Do you?"

"He didn't post any pictures," Ken observed. "I mean, he's not even on Facebook."

"And why is that a crime?"

"It isn't." He knew that Alexis Remnick still had Harper's laptop and tablet. He'd suggested she not return them when she returned the suit and the Speed Racer jersey, so he could have a tech pal see if he could use one of the devices to explore what—if anything—might be left of Harper's life in the Cloud. "Did he show you any pictures?" he asked.

"Of course."

"Was anyone in any of them?"

"People he met there, I guess. A chef with some double-edged paring knife was in one. Austin thought the knife was interesting. A guy on a motorbike was in another. Great smile. He showed us one with a beautiful woman in one of those very tight silk tunics. Practically a sheath."

"And they were Vietnamese?"

"Yes."

"He give you their names?"

"No."

He thought of the dress that Alexis had told him about. "And the woman. Was she tall? Short? Heavy? Slender?"

"I don't remember."

"But you recall she was beautiful?"

Austin's mother jumped in: "Oh, she was tiny. Petite."

"I assume you don't have a copy of the photo."

"Nope," Peter said.

"Recall the background?"

Again, it was Austin's mother who added a detail. "I know a little. There was a fountain and some flags. A nice enough building behind them."

"Fountains and flags? Like a museum?"

"Maybe," she said. "But if so, it was part of a campus. When I asked, Austin said one of the words on the building behind them was *university*."

Ken was careful to keep his face utterly impassive. But he knew he'd just connected another pair of dots. "Why was he at a university?"

"The school wasn't the destination," Austin's mother told him. "I don't think he was interested in the school at all."

"No?"

Peter shook his head. "Nope. Austin had two serious interests. Bikes and girls."

"Women," Catherine corrected her husband. "You're showing your age calling that woman a 'girl.'"

"Your son had a relationship with her?" Ken asked.

"I don't know that for a fact," Peter said. "But I knew my son. I wouldn't have been surprised at all if they had a fling when he was in Vietnam."

"That first time."

"Yes. Obviously. That second time he was there, he was with the ER doctor."

"So, he'd moved on."

"Seems so."

"In that case, why do you think he went back?" Ken pressed.

"Why is that such a mystery to everyone?" Peter snapped. "He liked the country. He had fun the first time. It's a beautiful place. Even I could see that as an idiot kid in a go-cart on a military base fifty years ago. Maybe he wanted to share the place's beauty with his new girlfriend. Why is it such a stretch to believe that's all there is to it?"

Maybe, Ken thought, *because he'd lied to so many people about why he was there.* But he kept that idea to himself.

He saw a cayenne-colored Santa Fe Sport, a small Hyundai SUV, pulling up beside him. The driver rolled down the passenger's-side window. He was a young guy with short black hair and hipster scruff on his cheeks and chin, and a button-down shirt.

"You needed a car?" he asked.

Ken checked the license plate and saw that this was his ride. He climbed into the back seat, and the vehicle started off. It reached an avenue and turned left, moving south, moving quickly because they were going against the rush-hour traffic that here was headed north. He gazed out the window, his mind lost in the crowds on the sidewalk and the shops, the streaks of yellow and red in the sky to the west when they were passing through an intersection, when his phone vibrated in his pocket and he saw that it was Alexis. He owed her a phone call. She'd actually called a couple of times, but he'd always been with someone or doing something. He took the call this time and was about to apologize for not getting back to her, but she cut him off.

"It was a dart," she said, her voice animated and excited.

"What was?" he asked.

"The injury on the back of Austin's hand. The wound."

"And you know this . . . how?"

"I don't know it for a fact," she admitted. "But I was staring at the image on my phone at the gym, and I was staring at it again just now before I called you. And in between, I found a sporting goods store on Broadway that sells darts. I lined up the tip on the back of my own hand. I'm telling you, it's about as close a match as you can imagine. It's crazy."

He almost agreed with her: it was crazy. But he had been to Douglas Webber's apartment. He had a feeling she was right and would have made a hell of a cop if she hadn't chosen medicine. "Tell me something," he said.

"Go ahead."

"You're not just thinking that because you first met Austin after he'd spent a night drinking and tossing darts? This isn't a power of suggestion sort of thing, is it?"

"Nope."

"Well, then. I think we have a match."

"Excuse me?"

"I've found the mysterious Douglas," he told her. "Last name is Webber. Lives on Third Street and is clearly one hell of a dart player. When Austin was missing last week? Before he died? Don't be surprised if we find out he was with Webber—yup, in Vietnam. I also don't think they met for the first time that night in March when Austin was shot. I have a bartender who is pretty damn sure they came into the bar together, and were downright chummy when they arrived. Now, I don't know what the two of them were doing last week in Vietnam. But I don't think they went all the way there to play darts. For all I know, they didn't even go there together. But Webber is not exactly what I would call a gentle soul. That injury to your guy's hand? Clearly an extracurricular Austin wasn't expecting."

"Third Street," she murmured, and for a moment Ken was unsure why this was the element she had focused on. But then he understood: as a physician, she had already envisioned the details of the pain someone had inflicted on Austin Harper. What she hadn't imagined was that this someone lived so very close by. So very close to her.

"Yes, Third Street," he said. "One more thing."

"Keep my head down?"

"I wasn't going to say that, but that wouldn't be a bad idea."

"Then what?"

"I don't have a name, but I think I may know who Austin bought that other dress for," he told her, and then he described for her the picture. As he spoke, he realized he actually felt worse telling her about this possible other woman than he had telling her about a creep willing to plunge a dart into another man's hand.

. . .

Ken knew that he himself couldn't find out if Webber had been in Vietnam last week. He had an acquaintance at Interpol who could, however, and he called her from the back seat of the car as soon as he got off the phone with Alexis, but she'd already gone home for the day. And so he left a message on her work voice mail in Washington asking for the favor and another one on her cell. She could see if—and when—Webber had entered the country from their passport control.

When he got home, Taleen was still out, and an idea came to him. He should get the number for that CSCD captain Alexis had met. That fellow could also determine whether Webber had been in Vietnam. For all he knew, he might even have some insight into the woman Austin might have been seeing. He looked at his watch. It was nearing six o'clock in Manhattan. The guy might be in his office in Vietnam in a couple of hours if he worked on a Saturday. But, even if he didn't, he'd be awake pretty soon.

. . .

When Alexis had come to Ken's office that week, she'd mentioned how she had listened to the voice mails of Austin Harper that she still had on her phone. They were inconsequential, she said, but she listened to them to hear his voice. She said she had read and reread his texts over and over. Because her late boyfriend had ignored the social networks, this was the extent of her digital grieving, and his lack of a presence on such places as Facebook and Instagram was, Ken decided, affecting her ability to mourn the man and move on. He told Taleen this when they were finishing dinner that night. They both had voice mails from Kathleen on their phones. Their devices were rich with pictures of the girl.

Taleen was in the mood to listen to this fatherly—grandfatherly, she had teased him—monologue because earlier that week she had spent the day at an allegedly haunted New York City mansion, and today she had been at a funeral for a friend at St. Vartan's and then the woman's burial on Long Island. It was not the same cemetery where their daughter was buried, but Taleen had gone there, too, after the graveside ceremony for her friend.

Now, as they were sitting on the couch and deciding what to watch on TV, she turned to him and said, her tone pensive, "That poor girl. Such a strange limbo she's in."

"I agree."

"You've never wanted to go back to Vietnam. Right?"

"Never wanted is too strong a feeling," he replied. "I mean, I saw it. I was there for a year."

"You've never wanted to bring me there. Bring us there."

He turned to her. "Is this armchair psychoanalysis in response to my armchair psychoanalysis of the ER doc?"

"I'd say inspired by it."

"Do you want to go to Vietnam?"

"Would it traumatize you if we did?"

"As a veteran? No. Not at all. But you and me? We're a traumatized people. It's in our DNA as Armenians," he said. He hadn't known that for sure until, after he retired from the NYPD, he and Taleen had gone with a half dozen other Armenian friends and a professor who taught genocide studies at Columbia to eastern Turkey—historic Armenia—and visited the unmarked mass graves of their ancestors in places like Chunkush.

"I meant something more specific. Something specific to you."

"I'd be fine. Unless, maybe, you made me sit for hours in a ditch in the rain or told me I had to take a hill that was defended by a whole bunch of guys with machine guns who didn't want me to set foot on it. But Vietnam for Americans today? Pretty sure it's kind of like Italy: a beautiful landscape filled with lovely people who harbor no ill will, have really good food, and like the fact we want to go there and spend money. Seriously: where is this coming from? You've never, ever expressed even the slightest desire to see Vietnam."

She shrugged. "I just wonder about the timing of this case. Maybe it's a sign that you need to add a return to your bucket list. To our bucket list."

"If you want to go, I'm happy to go. But I don't need to go for therapeutic reasons, I promise you," he told her, and reached for the remote. He put it down when his phone pinged. He had a text from Captain Nguyen that he could Skype right that moment, if Ken wanted. And so he asked Taleen if they could postpone finding a new drama to start binge-watching for a couple of minutes, grabbed his laptop, and retreated into their bedroom. He didn't have an office in their apartment, but he rarely needed one.

. . .

While Ken was Skyping with the Vietnamese police captain, Taleen went to the dresser in the guest room and opened the bottom drawer. There was a shallow jewelry box in the back where she kept Kathleen's earrings and necklaces and rings. She hadn't looked at the items in there since her daughter had died. She imagined that someday, when her two boys settled down and married, she'd give the pieces to their brides or, maybe someday, to their daughters.

None of the jewelry was especially valuable. Probably the most expensive item was a gold and silver designer bracelet, an ornate cuff with amethyst and garnet stones on the edges. Tonight she found herself staring at a particular pair of her child's earrings, silver circles with the Armenian symbol for eternity: a circular fan of overlapping blades. It appeared on ancient Armenian cross stones and even on some of the cornerstones of the Soviet-built monoliths in Yerevan. She placed one in the palm of her hand and gazed at it, her eyes half closed, trying to recall what it had looked like against her beautiful daughter's hair and against her beautiful daughter's skin.

. . .

Ken was surprised by the captain's white hair, and for a moment wondered if the police officer was nearly as old as he was. But when he focused more carefully on his face, he decided that Quang was somewhere in his mid-, or even early, forties. The fellow was speaking from what looked like the kitchen in his house.

"I see I'm disturbing you on a Saturday morning," he said to Quang. "I'm so sorry. But thank you for letting me ask you some questions."

Behind the captain, a little girl in pajamas ran past him, grabbing a drink off the kitchen counter. "I don't mind at all. I'm going to be in the office this afternoon. And I felt bad for that American doctor. She seemed very nice."

"She is," Ken agreed, and he found his mind wandering as the two of them shared pleasantries about Friday night in America and Saturday morning in Vietnam. Ken couldn't help but imagine what this kind cop's father had been doing fifty years ago. The odds that Ken and Quang's father had been in a firefight or tossing grenades at each other were incalculably slim; for all Ken knew, the guy's father had been ARVN—on the side of the South

Vietnamese with the Americans. He could ask; for some reason, he wanted to ask. Maybe Taleen was on to something about his demons, after all. But he restrained the impulse and instead told the police officer what he had learned, and listened with increasing intensity as Quang shared with him what was unfolding in Da Nang: the pathogen in the energy gels and the triple murder at a lab near there.

"Okay," Ken said, unnerved by the convergence. "Here's what I'm hoping you can find out. Two things. I want to know if an American citizen—at least I believe he's an American citizen—named Douglas Webber was in Vietnam on the day that Austin Harper died. Can you check with immigration at your end?"

Quang nodded. "I will. It will take a few hours. But when you wake up in the morning? I should be able to tell you. And the other?"

"These three people who were killed near Da Nang. The food chemist. You said she was female."

"Family name Pham, given name Binh. That's right."

Ken asked him where the woman worked and to spell her name. Then, after Quang told him, he inquired, "Did she have any university connections?"

"She didn't work for one. But she had a brother who did."

"He's dead, isn't he?"

"Died last winter."

"How?" Ken asked.

"Complications from tularemia."

"From a rat?"

"Unsure."

"Can you get me her measurements? Or at least, I guess, her height?"

"You think that might solidify a connection to your dead American?"

"I do. That dress that was found in the guy's bike bag? It doesn't fit the ER doc. Not even close. But I'd be willing to bet Austin had it tailor-made for Ms. Pham."

The researchers were concerned with plague mutations—because the next plague was coming. It was as inevitable as the next strain of Ebola or Lassa or (here's one you've never heard of, but someday you might) Crimean-Congo hemorrhagic fever. It would spread via flea bite, but also via coughs in crowded subway cars or sneezes in cabs.

Would the mutated strain kill even the knockout rats? Our New York rats with the Vietnamese genes? Or would they carry the disease but not be killed by it? Eventually the Manhattan rats would get there on their own. Again, natural selection. But the scientists wanted to accelerate the process and get there first. Artificial selection.

We saw what it did to the rats. I saw what it did. They showed me. When I saw them, I was devastated. Sure, over the years, the university labs had bred or cared for thousands of rodents, all of which existed but for one reason. To be given a disease and—eventually—to die.

But the rats with our new strain of plague died horribly. Really, really horribly.

29

Alexis watched Ellie sip her Negroni at the hotel bar just north of Union Square. They went there often because Ellie thought it was the best Negroni in Manhattan—and Alexis had a feeling that Ellie might actually know—and they went there tonight because her friend had had a terrible day at the animal hospital. She'd had to put down a French bulldog that was dying of cancer, but the animal had responded well for nearly a year and a half before the disease had returned to eat away at what was left of its body and the veterinarian had grown to love the animal during its treatment.

"You must think I am such a jerk," she said to Alexis as they sat on their barstools. "The guy you were dating gets run over and killed by some bastard in Vietnam and then you find out he was lying and might have been up to something. And I'm the one crying into my Campari over a Frenchie I didn't even own. I mean, not the first animal I've had to put down."

Alexis smiled at her. Her friend's voice was always a little husky, but tonight she sounded like a woman who'd been smoking forever. She didn't smoke; never had. But the booze and the sadness had made her voice creakier than usual. Now Alexis looked down at her phone, hoping the glance had been surreptitious, but Ellie noticed.

"Sometimes I think we should keep our phones in our pockets when we're with an actual, breathing human being," she said to Alexis.

"I'm sorry. I just keep hoping I'll hear more from the researcher I met for breakfast."

"She is allowed a life, isn't she?"

"She is," Alexis agreed. "It's just that she was going to talk to some of the scientists there about whether they knew Austin."

"You want to talk rats."

"Yes," she admitted. "I do."

"I just *think* that was a rat bite on his fingers. I don't know for a fact that it was."

"I understand."

"Look," Ellie said, trying to be sympathetic, "send her a text. You're dying to."

And so Alexis picked up her phone and wrote Sara Edens:

> So sorry to be high-maintenance and interrupt your evening.
> But I'm dying to know what you found out and whether there's a
> scientist there you think I can talk to.

Before putting her phone back on the bar, she looked quickly at the texts she had sent Austin the night she had been waiting for him alone at the hotel in Hoi An—the night she had texted him that she loved him. She'd done this dozens of times since then. She had probably done it hourly when she'd been awake on the flights home. But she had known since she'd visited the morgue that he was probably dead by the time she had sent him that text. He never saw it.

"You know," Ellie was saying, "we didn't use to fail the Bechdel test when Austin was alive. Ironic, right?"

"But now?"

"Now that he's dead, I think we fail it every time we're together. We're two women at a bar talking about a man."

Alexis stared at the beautiful swirl of the orange rind, lascivious and inviting. "We're talking about him because it means postponing the eventual, most horrible phase in mourning."

"And that is?"

"Forgetting."

"We always relish the missing."

Alexis shook her head. "Until we don't. Until we forget what they sounded like and looked like and smelled like. Until days and then weeks go by when we don't even think about them at all."

"Did you . . ."

"Go ahead?"

"Did you love him, Lexi? I saw you looking at your texts to him just now."

She sipped her wine, her second glass of Pinot Grigio she had chosen primarily because it was among the cheapest whites on the list. Most of the time she didn't think about her school loans: they weren't nearly as onerous as those of some of her peers because her mother had bankrolled a healthy chunk of the costs. But still, the Vietnam trip had maxed out one of her credit cards, and she'd have that payment on top of her med school debt for a couple of years. Austin had offered to pay her half of the trip, but she'd said no. She wanted their relationship to be equitable, a level playing field. And somehow this all came to her when she thought about how she wanted to respond to Ellie's question.

"At our age," Alexis replied carefully, "whenever you've dated a guy for six or seven months, you wonder if he's the one."

"Or if you're telling yourself he's the one, but you're really just settling."

"Yes. I mean, we didn't live together. We'd never talked about marriage."

"But you didn't think he was seeing anyone else—until you got that dress out of the blue yesterday."

"That's right. And, as you know, neither was I. I'm not sure I've even scratched the surface of the worst betrayal . . . the worst personal betrayal."

"Versus whatever nastiness he was up to with rats."

"Uh-huh. I mean, Jesus Christ, Ellie: he had a dress for another woman with him when he was killed. That's what Ken said when he called me tonight. Think about that. That means he was probably going to see her that day."

"But you said this chemist was killed in her lab. It's not like he was meeting her at a hotel or some fancy restaurant—or even her home."

"Maybe they were supposed to have lunch first. Maybe they were supposed to have sex first. Or after. I don't know. I just know that no one sees any of this picture forming but me and my detective."

"Did you and Austin ever talk about children?"

"Yeah. We did."

Ellie sat up a little straighter on her barstool. "Do tell. Here I thought you'd been born without a biological clock."

"He wanted kids. He thought it was sad we were both only children. He used to joke about kids and bikes, and what it would be like."

"Oh, God."

"No, it was sweet. He imagined buying a little girl her first bike with training wheels. It always had one of those pretend white wicker baskets with plastic flowers. It had a bell."

"And it was pink? Please tell me he didn't say it was pink."

"He didn't," Alexis lied. Yes, he'd envisioned a pink bike. "And then, when he was in his fifties or sixties and his kids were in high school or college, they'd bike all these gaps in Vermont. They'd bike the Adirondacks."

"Were you ever in these fantasies?"

"Not precisely. It was always kind of . . . generic. But he was trying to initiate me into the bike cult. The Vietnam trip, in his imagination, was the first of many bike trips like this we'd take together. Maybe next year in Croatia. The year after that in the Dordogne."

"But, of course, biking wasn't the real reason you were in Vietnam."

"No," Alexis agreed. "So it would seem."

Ellie swallowed the last of the liquid in the glass so there was only one giant cube of ice and an orange peel, and tried to get the bartender's attention. He smiled at her, his way of assuring her that he would be there in a moment. He was model handsome, with dark eyes and impeccable dreadlocks along the top of his head, but his hair was shaved short into perfect triangles above his ears. "You didn't really answer my question: did you love the man?"

Alexis stared for a long moment at the impeccably lit bottles of booze behind the bartender. "I thought I might before we went to Vietnam. I knew I did that night when he was missing. Then, when I discovered his lies, I was confused."

"And now?"

"Now? Now I don't know what I'm feeling. But there's a good amount of anger mixed in with that confusion."

"It's odd how you mourn," Ellie said. "I'm not judging. But some people hibernate when they grieve. You? You're just not built that way."

"I know. I'm my mother's daughter, I guess," Alexis told her.

"Who's made of iron."

"But there's a soul there. It's just, yes, under a lot of metal." She shrugged. "I am mourning. I am grieving. And part of that is figuring out what the hell he was doing when he disappeared and what happened to him. I told you, someone slammed a fucking dart into his hand, and my detective thinks it was the guy he was with the night we met. The night he came into the ER."

"Figuring all that stuff out, Lexi? That's not mourning. That's being an ER doctor." The bartender returned, and Ellie ordered another Negroni. Then she pointed at her empty glass. "Crying into your booze over a Frenchie that wasn't even yours? Now that's mourning, honey child."

.   .   .

Was she depressed? She wasn't sleeping more and she wasn't taking Xanax now that she was back, and she sure as hell wasn't cutting. At least not yet. But, once again, she had taken her cutting kit to bed with her, and this time she had gone so far as to take a deep-brown bath towel and place it beneath her naked thighs as she sat with her legs spread on the bed. She ran an alcohol wipe along the skin near the edge of her underwear, atop the scars there, and once more pressed the edge of a razor blade against her flesh. But she hadn't cut. In the end, yes, she had gone a little farther than last time, but then she had stopped herself and put everything away.

Had she cried since she had returned home from Vietnam? Yes. Certainly, she had. Daily, it seemed. She thought of the twenty-year-old mother orca that, a few years ago, had carried her emaciated dead calf—the baby had lived but half an hour—through the waves for weeks after the animal had died. Now that was grief, that was bereavement on a scale that was biblical. That was, quite literally, not letting go.

She stared up at the ceiling or out the window at the buildings across the street, alone in her bed, and thought this: I am investigating Austin's death as a way of not letting go. I am keeping him close by trying to learn what happened.

She wanted a good night's sleep and in fact planned to sleep late tomorrow morning, because the night shift loomed. A Saturday night at that. The mad shift in Manhattan. The witching hour when the bars were starting to close. One of the hardest shifts she had had so far had been last December, SantaCon Saturday, and the ER was nearly overwhelmed by young adults with alcohol poisoning or young adults who had done monumentally stupid things because they were so bloody drunk. The participants—and she called them young adults, but some were her age and none, even the pub-crawling college kids with fake IDs, were more than fifteen years younger than she was—had fallen off terraces, been hit by cars, and attempted to eat detergent pods and dishwasher tabs. They'd cut themselves on knives and forks, they'd cut themselves on broken beer bottles and mugs, they'd cut themselves on pool cues and (she still wasn't sure how) in one case on a hookah. She'd pumped the stomachs of scantily clad elves and a slutty Mrs. Santa Claus, and a Santa who, among other things, vomited up two beautiful glass marbles. His friend, who was almost as drunk, insisted the marbles were gonads, and thought saying so was the summit of American humor.

And because that was a Saturday night, she'd also worked to save a young guy with a pair of bullet wounds in his stomach, and, two hours later, she and the trauma surgeon had been squeezing a cop's heart who'd been shot as he approached a car that was blocking the entrance to a parking garage.

God. Saturday night in the ER. It was where and when she had met Austin. Of course.

Before setting aside her phone for the night and putting it in airplane mode so nothing would wake her—so she wouldn't be drawn to its ever-beating heart if she awoke in the small hours of the morning—she checked one last time to see if there was any response from Sara Edens she had somehow managed to miss. But there wasn't a word. No texts, no calls, no messages, no emails. It was odd. It was the damnedest thing, and she couldn't help but feel (and then feed) her gift of fear. Hadn't she seen this game before in Hoi An, a person suddenly seeming to ghost her before the awful truth becomes apparent?

But then she reminded herself that the woman was an overworked and likely underpaid young scientist in a lab, striving mightily to do her work amidst the pressure and politics of a few dozen other young doctoral candidates.

She noticed among her emails, most of which were spam and solicitations this time of the night, one from a name that surprised her. It was new. And it was, in its own weird way, an email version of the classic come-hither text, "U up?" The email was from Oscar Bolton. He had written to her using her hospital email, admitting that he had figured it out because most employees had email addresses that were simply the first and last names of the person, separated by a period. He introduced himself politely and wrote that he was awake and thinking of Austin and realizing that he needed to talk to someone, and the two of them shared a relationship with the man that few others at the hospital probably did.

She sat up in bed, her back against the headboard, and wrote back, asking him if he meant now. Then she waited. She deleted emails: the nighttime solicitations to buy ankle holsters and lingerie and printer ink, to buy products that magically melted belly fat. And then he responded. He said he was just sad and the middle of the night was hard for him, but maybe they could have brunch tomorrow, or a late breakfast. He suggested a place that had, in his opinion, crazy delicious French toast that wasn't far from the hospital.

She said yes and they confirmed a time. Nine thirty. A thought came to her and she asked him one last question: had he heard anything about a funeral yet? She hadn't discussed one with the Harpers when they had been at the hospital. He wrote back that he hadn't, and they said good night.

Then she did something she wished she had done sooner: she wrote an email to Austin's father apologizing for how their meeting had unraveled at the hospital and how she wished she could go back in time and try again. She asked him when they were planning to bury Austin, and what she could do. She would participate in the funeral as much or as little as they wanted. She considered telling him how moved her son had been as they stood at the edge of the city of the dead outside An Bang and what he had said: *I wouldn't mind a dragon watching over my soul. I could probably use one.* But she didn't. She was afraid it would sound intrusive, as if she were hinting at something his son might actually have wanted—and, looking back, she knew now what he really had meant. *I'm playing with fire, Alexis, and the afterlife might not be pretty.*

Next, she sent a text to Ken Sarafian with the news that she was having brunch with Oscar Bolton. She worried on some level that she might wake him if he still had his phone on, but she was anxious on a far deeper level that if she did wake him, he would try and talk her out of it. She didn't believe the hospital executive was any more dangerous than Austin had been, but Sarafian had made clear his feelings about Douglas Webber, her dart-playing neighbor: the man was capable of anything, the detective had said, and that included killing her boyfriend.

SATURDAY

30

It was the weekend and Quang was at home, and so he carried his cell phone outside when he saw it was Vu, the officer who'd been with him that first morning they'd gone to the hotel in Hoi An, who was calling. Quang didn't want his wife or his daughter to hear even his half of the conversation. He'd felt bad enough that he'd Skyped from the kitchen an hour ago with the American detective and called Immigration about an American named Douglas Webber. Yes, his wife would ask him about his conversation in the backyard when he went back into the house. But he would be evasive, and they had been married long enough that she would know not to press.

"Your instincts were right," Vu began.

"Go ahead."

"That food chemist. The woman. She'd received multiple phone calls from Austin Harper, some from America on WhatsApp and some on FaceTime, and a local call on the day that Harper died."

"So Harper was pretty likely planning to meet with her."

"Or, for all we know, did meet with her. With them—the three of them at that lab. For all we know, he killed them."

Quang watched a nuthatch, its eyes as yellow as its beak, on a branch of one of the rubber trees they'd planted in their backyard. "We'll know soon enough, but I doubt it."

"You doubt he killed them?"

"Oh, I'd bet my house he didn't kill them. Where would he even have gotten that kind of weaponry? Besides, an American detective just told me he'd bought the woman a dress—the one that was in that bike bag."

"It wasn't for the American doctor?"

"Apparently not. No, I don't think Harper ever even got to the lab."

"But this wasn't gang-related if it involves the American," said Vu.

"I agree. The two guys? Either they were just in the wrong place at the wrong time or they were there as muscle. Or, just maybe, they were rat wranglers. Rat catchers. One's connected to a restaurant and one to an exterminator. I think Harper was bringing Pham—that chemist—the gels. She was going to reproduce the pathogen in the packets and sell it to North Korea."

"That's . . ."

"It's a theory, that's all."

"I was going to say, that's despicable. Who sells a biological weapon to North Korea?"

"Who sells arms to a lot of countries? Not exactly the work you brag about. You do it to fill your bank accounts in places like Switzerland or the Cayman Islands. You don't do it to make the world a better place."

"I know. But that ER doctor? She seemed really sweet—not the type to be dating an arms dealer."

"Maybe she is really sweet. And a really bad judge of character."

"Do you think she's involved?"

"Not for a second. She gave us the gels, remember."

"That's right," Vu said. Then he asked, "Are you coming in to the office today?"

"I am, yes. I'll see you in an hour or so," Quang told him, and then he hung up and called Toril Bjornstad in Phnom Penh, but he didn't reach her and left a message. The last he'd heard, North Korea still wasn't talking, but he'd been reassured that his own country's diplomats were meeting with North Korea embassy staff to learn why the food chemist had been there. No one liked the idea of her and a rogue American selling biological weapons to a rogue nation.

He went back inside to shave, smiling at his wife as he passed her. There was something he was missing, and it was gnawing at him. No, that wasn't quite it. It was something he hadn't done and he should do—something no one had done and someone had to do. He hoped it would come to him soon.

. . .

The clouds were low and heavy but it wasn't raining, and Quang glanced at the world clock on his phone as he returned to his office, a cup of coffee from a little tourist place in his hand. New York City was a half day behind him. Behind them. It was the small hours of the morning there. It was just after noon here. He paused to watch a group of middle school–aged girls in traditional costumes practicing with their gongs in the park across the street. He saw a series of motorcycles and scooters pass a lumbering public bus, and noted how one of the riders was wearing a mask around his nose and mouth. It was just another Saturday, and the rider with the mask had no idea that investigators with the Ministry of Health had fanned out all across the country and spent the last two days looking for some new strain of plague, while he was weaving through the light, early-afternoon traffic.

The wind was picking up, and the low-slung telephone wire overhead moved like a taut jump rope held by two girls. He thought of his daughter when she'd been younger.

Quang didn't see irony in an American bringing poison into his country, he saw only history. He had grown up with the stories of what both the French and then the Americans had done, and seen the damage wrought by the bombing and the napalm and the herbicides. By Agent Orange. He always had classmates with birth defects. And the American was now dead, and so were five Vietnamese, counting the three who'd been executed, the

CSCD lab technician, and the cabbie. He noted the numbers. Wasn't that always the way? So very many more Vietnamese had to die for every Westerner.

Austin Harper's family hadn't wanted his remains cremated, and by now the body was back in America and no one had gotten sick because of it. He would have heard, he presumed, from Toril at the American embassy in Cambodia—or, perhaps, from a duty officer right here in Vietnam. When he and Toril spoke yesterday, she was taking comfort—just like the Ministry of Health—in the fact that none of the men who had recovered the body from the ravine by the switchback and none of the people who had been with it in the morgue, including the coroner, and none of the people who had brought the corpse to the airport in Da Nang had become ill. Quang himself, of course, was fine.

And Harper hadn't died of the plague. That was clear. So, whatever it was, Toril had reminded him, it was only in the energy gel—until they had cut the packet open.

He knew there were two other gels that hadn't been opened yet. They were now stored in a biohazard locker. He also hadn't heard yet whether the company had recalled any of the product, and he made a mental note to check his computer when he got to work to see if there was anything in the news.

. . .

He read the email from Immigration carefully and then cut and pasted the critical information into an email he wrote to Ken Sarafian: Douglas Webber had arrived in Vietnam the Wednesday before Austin Harper died and left the country Saturday night—roughly thirty-six hours after Austin's body had been found. The guy, according to the American detective, had a relationship with the deceased that went back at least seven months, but likely much longer. On his immigration form, Webber had listed as his temporary residence a nice hotel in Ho Chi Minh City. Before sending the email, however, Quang rang the hotel and asked if

Webber had been there on those nights. He hadn't. He had made a reservation, but canceled upon his arrival in Vietnam. And so, it seemed, he'd used the hotel to clear customs, and then gone elsewhere—probably right here to Da Nang or Hoi An. Quang added that information to the email to Ken, and then pressed Send. It would be waiting for the detective when he woke up.

When he sat back in his chair, it hit him—what had been nagging at him since Vu had phoned about two hours ago. He should have the FBI reach out to the American ER doctor who had been traveling on the bike tour with Harper. Alexis Remnick. Harper might have had more of those energy gels with him in Vietnam. And if she'd brought some of them home with her and ever ate one? She was likely a dead woman.

And if she opened it in a crowded space in New York City? She'd be far from alone.

Look, my justifications are irrelevant. I know that. I get it.

But Thomas Malthus understood the problem well before anyone: "The power of population is infinitely greater than the power of the earth to produce subsistence for men."

It's a fact that our species is destroying the planet, and the more of us there are, the faster the deterioration. The faster the climate change.

Did I actually want a nation ever to use the pathogen as a weapon? Of course not.

But, yes, I did tell myself that if one ever did, it wouldn't be the end of the world. It might, in a twisted sort of way, in fact save it.

31

Alexis rarely walked the streets of New York with her earbuds in, but she did this morning, wanting to lose herself in a little music as she prepared for brunch with Oscar Bolton. The buds didn't drown out the incessant traffic—the frustrated cabdrivers as they honked, the beeping of the delivery trucks as they lumbered backwards into parking spaces, the bass of the young kids (usually male) who were blasting their car stereos, just asking for a noise-induced hearing loss as they drove—but every song came with a memory, and the memories tended to calm her. Music impacted first the subcortical structures, such as the cochlear nuclei and the brain stem, and then literally (and metaphorically) shimmied up the auditory cortices of a person's gray matter. When it reached the hippocampus and the frontal lobe, it triggered flashbacks and reminiscences. This morning, it made the crowds and the cars but background buzz for the parade of ghosts—most good—that came with each song. Here she was once more curled up on the living room couch with Zelda, her naughty tortie of a cat, when she was twelve, and a heat wave had broken and thunderclouds were rolling in. Eating a peanut-butter-and-jelly sandwich at the top of New Hampshire's Mount Lafayette one afternoon when she and two friends from college had hiked to the summit on a summer Sunday in August. The small, dark bedroom in her tiny off-campus apartment when she was twenty-one—not quite twenty-two—and read the email that she had gotten into medical school.

It was about a block from the restaurant that she made the mistake of checking the *New York Post* on her phone. She just wanted to see what the headlines were, because in the time it took to walk about twenty-five or thirty steps on the sidewalk she could see the latest celebrity gossip, as well as the latest appalling misbehavior of the city's social elite. In addition, here were the stories of the schoolteachers who had sex with their students and the guys who brawled in bars and the women who went claw to claw in nail salon catfights. Here were the cops who were corrupt and the pols who were sexting pics of their junk. But this morning was a mistake because the story she saw was this: a photo of rats devouring the carcass of a long-haired honey-and-white cat, and she saw it moments after thinking of Zelda, her own childhood kitty. The image had been taken in an alley beside an apartment in the Bronx, and the point of the story wasn't that the cat had been killed by the very same rats that its owner had presumed it would make short work of; rather, it was that the city had just announced a thirty-six-million-dollar effort to exterminate rodents at a dozen of the city's most infested apartment complexes. She stopped walking and stood perfectly still as she read the story, oblivious now to the song in her earbuds, the world around her fading. She felt a wave of dizziness.

Goddamn rats, she thought.

Then: just breathe. But, still, the incipient and smoldering unease of the last week now blossomed into a scorching and incandescent bonfire. She had been vacillating for days now between the focus of a physician in a life-threatening emergency and the despair of a woman or man newly widowed.

Goddamn, fucking rats, she thought.

She pulled out her earbuds and wrapped them around her phone and shoved it into her bag. She told herself that she was being unreasonable. It was a horrible image, but animals gnawed the flesh from other animals all the time. How many times in her life had she seen turkey vultures on the road picking the meat off a squirrel or skunk that had been hit by a car? How many times had crows scattered from the pavement as the car she was driving neared the roadkill they were eating off the middle of the road?

She didn't witness death every day in the ER; far from it. But she saw it a lot. She saw it often enough. In some ways, she had been forged as a child in the hot fire of her own father's death, all her strengths and all her weakness.

Still, you couldn't unsee the picture of rats eating a cat. And now she found herself leaning against the brick facade between the open-air entrance to a bodega—there were the banded bouquets of flowers in their plastic pots of water and the carts with their paper bags of autumn apples from upstate New York and Vermont—and the thin door with the clean glass windows that led to apartments above it. She guessed that she was probably standing above or beside a rat's nest. They were beneath the feet of her sneakers, nesting, scurrying, eating.

Thirty-six million dollars for a dozen apartment complexes. How many hundreds of millions of dollars would it take to eliminate rats from the city? From all five boroughs? There wasn't enough money in the budget. There wasn't enough money in the world.

Rats hadn't killed her boyfriend; at least not directly. But he hadn't been killed in an accidental hit and run. That was absolutely clear to her. It was an execution meant to look like an accident and Douglas Webber had killed him, and he'd killed him because of something they were doing with rats. Maybe something Austin had found out. Maybe something Austin was doing. She was sure of that, and Ken Sarafian was sure of that. When you examined his death dispassionately, pure pattern recognition, it was obvious. Any moment now she'd probably get a call from the detective saying that Webber had been in Vietnam when she and Austin had been there. A travel writer? That was horseshit.

Whatever Austin or Webber or the two of them had been up to, there were stakes and they were high. High enough to kill him. There were sides.

Now she was about to have brunch with a man who had reached out to her in the middle of the night and who had worked with Austin.

"Miss, you okay?"

She looked around and there was a plump young guy wearing a white apron over a New York Giants sweatshirt. He had disposable gloves on his hands. She presumed he worked inside at the deli counter of the bodega and had seen her or, perhaps, he had come outside to tend to the flowers or the apples. His face was round and wide and worried, his mustache making him look older than she guessed he was.

She nodded. She wanted to smile for him, but she didn't have it in her just yet. "Yes, thanks. I'm okay."

She couldn't bear the idea of rats gnawing at the corpse of a cat. She vowed to steer clear of Safari and the news for the rest of the day. She simply had to, both so she could focus on the meeting before her and then do her job at the ER.

"Your eyes were closed and I thought you were going to pass out. I thought you were going to faint."

"No. I was just thinking."

"You need some water?"

"No, I'm . . ."

He waited.

She took a deep breath and gathered herself. "I really am fine. But you were so kind to check on me. I appreciate it. I'm about to have brunch and I guess I really need to refuel the tank. A sugar low."

He held up a finger and reached into the pocket of his apron and pulled out a black-and-white cookie in clear plastic wrap. "I was going to save it for later. I think you need it more than I do."

"No, I couldn't. I can't."

He unwrapped it and broke it in half, not along the seam

between the chocolate and the vanilla, but perpendicular to the divide so they each had some of the black and some of the white. He pushed one of the halves into her hands and said, "Take it." Then he patted his ample belly. "This is already too big."

"You win," she told him, and she dug deep inside herself for a smile. This kindness had to be rewarded. And he was probably right: maybe she did need some additional fortification when she went into battle—it was no longer brunch—with Oscar Bolton. She didn't know what side he was on, but she knew on which floor he worked.

. . .

Oscar was already at a table near the window when she arrived at the restaurant, a cup of coffee before him. The restaurant was smaller than she expected and a notch more upscale: dark wooden paneling, abstract paintings on the walls, the tables for two round circles the size of manhole covers and draped with white tablecloths. He stood and motioned for her to take the seat that faced out toward the street, and then, when she was sitting, pointed at the pair of bulldogs on the sidewalk that were wrapping their leashes around their owners' legs as they got to know each other.

"I love dogs," he said amiably. "Just look at those faces. Those eyes. Are you a dog person or a cat person?"

The cookie she had eaten had helped, but she still felt a little weak. She wondered what he would say if she casually brought up what it was like to identify Austin Harper's body at the morgue in Da Nang, or the likelihood that before he'd been killed, he'd been tortured. She didn't trust Oscar—she had no idea whether she could trust anyone from Austin's department in the hospital—but a small part of her wanted to gauge his reaction. Did he already know the details of Austin's death? What would he make of her sharing the niceties of the morgue with him? Would he presume she was merely unburdening herself? He claimed that he and Austin were friends, which was the whole reason why he had reached out to her. Still, she knew she needed to wade into this water carefully; she knew neither the depth nor the strength of the riptide. And so instead she arched an eyebrow and said, "If we weren't here to talk about Austin, I'd give you some good-natured grief for using such a lousy pickup line."

"I really am a dog person," he said, his tone a little sheepish. He smiled and it was abashed, almost innocent. It made his shaved head so much less threatening. "Also? Honestly, not meant as a pickup."

"I know." And instantly, it seemed, there was a waitress there at the table, a woman her age in a white shirt and black slacks and a necktie, filling her water glass and asking if she wanted coffee. She ordered a cappuccino and sat back in the chair.

"Thank you for coming," he said. "I really appreciate it."

"I guess I'm glad you emailed me."

"You guess?"

"I am, maybe a little bit like you, kind of a mess. A functional mess. But still a mess."

"It's like being a functional alcoholic: you can do your job, but your head is always in two places at once."

She nodded. He'd nailed it, and her respect for him climbed ever so slightly. This also increased her wariness. She couldn't let down her guard.

"Would you like a drink? Bloody Mary? Screwdriver? Something else?"

"Nope, no booze. I'm working tonight. But thank you. I just need caffeine."

"How weird is it to be back in New York without him?" he asked.

"Very. There are little echoes of him—of us—everywhere. In my neighborhood. At the hospital. The places we met, the things we did. How weird is it for you in development? I mean, it's not like you're such a massive staff that his disappearance could go unnoticed."

"It's true. It changes a lot. I know it's made Sally's job harder. And we were friends," he said, nodding, and then, as if he had already revealed more than he wanted—a deeper emotional ravine—he picked up the menu. "I meant it last night: the French toast here is really good. They use challah, and they bring you real maple syrup from Vermont."

"Okay, I'll order it."

"You won't regret it. I'm going to have it, too," he assured her, as the waitress returned with her cappuccino. Then she took their order and retreated.

"What mostly do you want to talk about—in regard to Austin?" she asked him.

He shook his head ever so slightly and smiled at her. "Wow. You dive right in. You make me feel like I'm one of your patients in the ER."

"It's like you are. You came to me in the middle of the night and were presenting very specific symptoms."

"And those are?"

"Sadness. Wistfulness. Curiosity."

"You know them."

"I have them."

"Yup. I'd suppose so." He sat back in the chair and looked toward her, but not at her. "I guess I wonder what he was really doing."

"In Vietnam?"

"That's right."

"Me, too," she said. "So, you believed that his father and his uncle had been there—in that corner of the country—in the war."

"I did."

"Did he talk about it? Did he talk about them?"

"Not much. Not much at all. But he said that was why he was going."

"And why he went the first time?"

"Uh-huh," he mumbled, still staring almost dreamily over her shoulder. He was wearing a long-sleeve, striped rugby shirt.

"That's what he told me, too," she said.

"Did he talk about the war much when you two were there?"

"Nope." An idea came to her—a way to confirm how little she dared trust him—and she sipped at her cappuccino while she formulated the best way to ask him the question. "When I was at his apartment," she began carefully, "he never showed me any pictures of his dad or his uncle in Vietnam. And I never thought to ask."

"Why would you?"

"I should have. I was remiss not to. I mean, I was his girl-friend. I wonder what he would have done if I'd pressed him. Shown more interest. I mean, they both went to Vietnam. They just weren't near where we were biking or where he was when he went missing."

"Somewhere in his apartment, maybe there's one of those photos we see in the documentaries of a bunch of young guys with either really short hair or wearing helmets with jungle plants on them," he said.

"Exactly! They're either hoofing it through the jungle or sit-ting around with their shirts off and dog tags dangling against their bare chests. They have big, heavy guns and bandoleers of ammo."

"He never showed me any pictures like that."

"Me, either," she agreed. And then, as casually as she could, she asked, "Tell me: did you ever go to his apartment?"

"Nope."

"Why not?"

"We were work friends. Our circle never brought us to the Upper East Side together. The closest we came was one time after work when we all took the subway to Yankee Stadium. We passed his subway stop on the way. But it was a group outing. The whole bunch of us in development."

She stared deep into the white porcelain cup before her, not wanting to reveal any sort of poker tell that she knew he was lying—that she knew now that she couldn't trust him at all. "Obviously, I went to his apartment," she said, and she realized that she was actually a little frightened. She thought of the broken bone in the back of Austin's hand. "And he didn't have any pictures like that anywhere in the place," she continued carefully. "At least they weren't out or in a frame somewhere. And he never posted that sort of thing about his father or his uncle on Veterans Day on any of the social networks—because he wasn't on any of the social networks."

"You miss him?" Oscar asked.

"Yes. I do," she said.

"Even though he lied?"

"Even though. Yup."

He finished the last of his coffee and dabbed at his lips with his napkin. "Do you have any idea why he did that? Why he concocted that doozy of a lie? I saw you talking to his parents at the hospital. Did they?"

"Nope."

She looked at one of the paintings on the wall. It was an image, she supposed, of the pied piper: a medieval piper on a gothic, European cobblestone street with a trail of children behind him. But there were no rats. So, maybe, it wasn't the pied piper after all. Maybe it was just a musician and some kids. A little parade.

No, it was what it was. He got rid of the rats, *then* he took the children. Just because there were no rats in the image didn't mean that there were no rats in the subtext. Just because you couldn't see the rats in this very restaurant didn't mean that they weren't living in the alley behind it or in the basement below it. The place had an A grade in the window. But tomorrow or the day after tomorrow, or after the next inspection from the city's health department? Who could say?

"You like that picture?" he was asking. She must have been lost in it longer than she had realized.

"No. I don't. It's just that it's actually a painting about rats, and they seem to be everywhere suddenly. I mean, I was talking to Sara Edens about them just yesterday, and how I'd love a tour of the labs," and instantly she stopped speaking. She'd said too much. She hadn't been thinking.

"Who's that?" he asked. "Someone at the hospital?"

"Yeah, but just an acquaintance," she said, and quickly she brought their conversation back to Austin's mother and father. "Anyway, his parents had no idea why Austin might have rearranged so much of the family history about Vietnam."

"Do you think there's any way you can find out?" he asked.

She turned to him and asked in response, "Why would I want to? Why, at this point, do I need to know?"

"You just want to move on?"

"Yeah. I think I do."

"That's harsh."

"No. That's being kind to myself—and, maybe, to him. Accepting that we had six and a half nice months together, but part of it had been a lie. And maybe he had a good reason for lying and maybe he didn't, but he's not a part of my life anymore and I don't need to know."

He pulled at a stray strand of fabric on the cuff of his shirt and seemed to think about this, and they both were silent. "So, his parents weren't much help."

"Not in the slightest. They got mad at me."

"What else have you done?"

"Are you asking what I've done to find out why he lied? Why he created—and, to some degree, lived—this fabrication?"

"Yeah. I'm curious," he admitted, his tone matter-of-fact. She saw the waitress was returning with their brunch. "I assume you brought back his stuff from Vietnam. Was there anything revealing in it?"

She shook her head. "Nope. Not a thing."

"What was there?"

The waitress placed the French toast before them, and for a moment Alexis took in the strawberries and blueberries atop the confectioners sugar. Red, white, and blue. How inadvertently patriotic. When the waitress was gone, Alexis replied, "All I brought back was this suit he had made in Hoi An and one cycling jersey that I thought might have sentimental value to his parents. Speed Racer."

"You didn't bring back his phone? His computer?"

"His phone was gone."

"Gone?" he asked, offering her the maple syrup in what looked like an actual Wedgwood gravy boat, but she assumed was a replica designed for restaurants.

"Yup. The police in Vietnam never found it."

"That's odd."

"I guess. I just assume it went flying when he went flying, and it's somewhere in the jungle near the top of the mountain pass."

"Wow, that's . . ."

"I know. That's horrible. I've been living with this, Oscar."

"What about his computer?"

She concentrated on pouring the syrup on the French toast, pouring it slowly so she could think. She couldn't lie and say she had returned it to Austin's parents, because that might put them in danger; likewise, she certainly couldn't tell him that she'd had a detective open Austin's laptop and discovered it had been wiped clean. But if she revealed that his computer and tablet were in her apartment right now? Wouldn't that be putting herself in jeopardy? Even greater jeopardy?

"This is embarrassing," she said.

"Doubt it."

"I forgot it at the hotel. The last hotel we were in."

"In Vietnam?"

"Yup. Stupid, I know. I forgot his tablet, too."

"Don't be embarrassed," he told her. "You kind of had a lot on your mind."

"I guess."

"Have you asked them to send the devices to you?"

"They offered, yes. And I told them there wasn't a rush, but sure." She started to eat, and so he did, too. Clearly, he had been waiting for her, a gesture that was undeniably chivalrous. "This is delicious," she told him. "You weren't kidding."

"Glad you like it," he said. Then: "So they're shipping them back?"

"Yes. The computer, the tablet."

"That's good."

She cut off a piece of the bread and skewered a strawberry slice, and asked, "Why?"

"It might be revealing. I mean, like you, I'm a little creeped out by the mystery of where he went before he died."

"Do you think I should open his computer when it arrives? I could tell you what's on it."

"Would you mind? That would be very cool. I'm interested."

"It wouldn't be too, I don't know, invasive?"

"You were his girlfriend, for God's sake. He dragged you across the planet on a false pretense. You have a right to know."

"I guess. But do you have that same right?"

"Maybe not. But I thought . . . I thought the two of us were friends. Or, at least, friendly."

"I'm sure you were," she told him, though she had absolutely no idea if this were true. She and Austin had never socialized with Oscar. "So, when I get the laptop back, I'll boot it up."

"Would you?"

"Sure," she said, and her mind was picturing once again Ken Sarafian's face when he accessed the laptop and saw that it had been wiped clean. "Do you think there was anything on his office computer? His computer at the hospital?"

"Maybe. But we'll never know. Hospital IT has already taken it and I'm sure washed it so someone else can use it. If Austin had been murdered, maybe someone would have examined its contents. I guess the police, or someone. Sally told me the FBI was at the hospital when he was just . . . just missing. But he died in an accident, so I'm pretty sure there's nothing left for us to look at."

"That makes sense."

"Anything else worth sharing?"

"In regard to the mystery of Austin Harper?"

"Uh-huh."

"I told you, I haven't done a damn thing but grieve and work and sleep and not sleep. I haven't done anything."

"Okay. Got it," he said. "And you brought nothing else back?"

She shrugged. "I brought back some of his unopened Psych energy gels."

"My mother would have approved. She hated to see food go to waste."

Alexis nodded. "Mine, too."

"So, you're finished?"

"Finished? I think it will be years before I'm finished. And you?"

"I don't know. I mean, God, I was emailing you in the middle of the night. What does that tell you?"

She nodded and looked deep into him, trying to read his face, to see what he really was thinking. But she couldn't. He was, she decided, rather like her late boyfriend, a surprisingly good actor.

32

Douglas Webber gazed up at one of the leafless trees in the park across the street from the Episcopal Church, the sky behind it flat and pearl, and then at the statue of Peter Stuyvesant. He listened carefully as Oscar Bolton told him of the brunch he'd just finished with the ER doctor, and, he had to admit, the guy's reconnaissance had been solid. At first, Douglas had been annoyed that Oscar had texted him—they were scheduled to meet on Sunday—but now that they were here, he was glad.

"I knew it couldn't wait," Oscar had apologized when Douglas arrived, the irritation apparently evident on his face. "I knew it shouldn't wait." And then he told Douglas what the woman had said. Oscar had a good memory, and he had keyed in on a name: Sara Edens.

"Alexis said she'd been talking to a lab rat named Sara Edens," he was saying. "And I asked who that was, and she said the woman was just a friend. An acquaintance. She changed the subject. But Alexis had already told me that she wanted to see the labs."

"Do you know what Sara Edens does there? In the lab? She doesn't work with Sinclair. I know the names of his assistants."

"Nope."

"The Korean, perhaps?"

"That's right. She works in a group that studies hantavirus. But even that doesn't matter. What does is this: Alexis went out of her way to see someone from the labs to talk about rats. That's what she said she was discussing with Edens: rats."

Douglas absorbed this information. It was utterly amazing the way Austin Harper and his greed were sending the project off the rails.

No, that was only half right. Austin Harper had started the possible derailment, but Alexis Remnick was likely to finish the train wreck—unless he took care of her, too, which it was clear was now inevitable. "What else?" he asked Oscar.

"She wanted to know if I'd been in Austin's apartment."

"And you said?"

"I lied. I said no. But the whole idea she was asking creeped me out."

He nodded. "It should. Trust your instincts. We are animals, and we have instincts for a reason." Then he added, "And I like your instincts, Oscar. I really do. Thank you."

"You're welcome."

"I mean that. I dispense compliments judiciously."

"Also, I asked about Austin's laptop. She doesn't have it."

"I wouldn't care if she did. Everything on it has been erased—just in case."

"Wow. I guess I should have assumed you were on that."

"You were smart to ask. Still, I'm sure she's lying. I'm sure she has it."

A couple of pigeons landed on the sidewalk near them. Douglas understood why so many New Yorkers referred to them as rats with wings, but he never saw them that way. For all the fears people had of bird flu and avian-transmitted illnesses, it would be far more difficult to weaponize a pigeon than a rat.

"So, what's next?" Oscar asked him.

"I hear concern in your voice."

"I'm trusting my instincts."

Douglas couldn't restrain a small chuckle. "You guys in advancement. You—"

"Please, don't group me with Austin. I don't like how that ended."

"Nor did he. I'm sorry, Oscar. I didn't mean anything by that remark," Douglas told him, and he meant it. "I want you to call Wilbur Sinclair. Now. Tell him it's about someone who wants to fund some of his research. He'll know what that means. Ask if you can meet at the labs today."

"Today?"

"Today. Right now. He'll join you. I promise. And then when you two are together, have him invite Alexis to the labs. He should be sure to tell her that Sara Edens had approached him and said she wanted a tour. Have him quote the things Alexis said to you at brunch today."

"She's working tonight. Alexis."

"Well, she thinks she is." He glanced at his watch. "See if she can be there at one. Sinclair will make himself available."

"Do I have to be there?"

"After you have met with Sinclair?"

"Uh-huh."

Douglas considered this. Having him present would certainly entrench the fellow further—make him infinitely more culpable and infinitely more invested. But he was already going to be an accessory to murder, whether he knew that now or not. And Douglas rather doubted he had the stomach for what was likely to be the ER doctor's final act. So he told him that he didn't need to be there, once he had made sure that Wilbur Sinclair had invited Alexis Remnick into the labs. Then he gave Oscar the number for the scientist, and watched as the hospital executive asked Sinclair to meet him there. The whole conversation took about a minute and a half, including introductions.

"He says he'll be at the labs in forty-five minutes," Oscar said.

"Excellent. I'm going to assume that you two get Dr. Remnick there by one. Maybe by two. But text me one number: the time she will actually arrive."

"May I ask you one more thing?"

"Of course."

"Won't it look suspicious if Alexis is killed a week or so after her boyfriend dies in Vietnam?"

"Her boyfriend was run over. An accident. That's what the world supposes."

"And Alexis?"

"The poor girl," he said, sharing his epiphany. "The grieving girlfriend is going to kill herself. Makes all the sense in the world. Nothing suspicious about it. It's actually downright romantic."

Then he shook Oscar's hand and thanked him. This would turn out just fine; it always had in the past. Still, it was annoying that he was going to have to work again on a Saturday—even one like today, the middle of a dusky, autumnal weekend, the world above the brownstones and skyscrapers soporific and dull and de-pressing as hell.

. . .

Toril Bjornstad had virtually nothing to do with FBI opera-tions in America. She was an embassy officer in Cambodia. Like-wise, although she presumed there were now CIA operatives in Da Nang and central Vietnam, she would have to wait until Na-tional Intelligence told her anything—if they told her anything—about who they were and what they had found. She might want to know what they were doing, but she didn't need to know. Not yet. Maybe never.

But as soon as Captain Nguyen had phoned her about the energy gels the American had brought to Vietnam, she'd sent up a flare. Austin Harper was a courier or salesperson, but he wasn't the chemist. He hadn't been working alone. And while his buyer here likely was dead, Toril was confident that the food chemist hadn't been a solo practitioner who randomly—and brazenly—had decided to visit the North Korean embassy. The only ques-tion in her mind in this regard was whether Binh Pham's group had something to do with her late brother, and whether his research with rats at the university in Ho Chi Minh City had been aboveboard or a cover for something darker.

Now Toril finished a late dinner alone in her office at the embassy and took one of the sticky rice dessert cakes the chef had prepared for her to the window. Her favorite part was the sesame seeds that coated the exterior like icing.

She stared out at the lit compound as she nibbled it, separated from the street by high walls and fences and barricades—by U.S. soldiers—and thought about the ER doctor who had accompanied Harper to Vietnam. As far as Toril knew, no one at the FBI seriously believed that she was working with him. Likewise, neither did Captain Nguyen. After all, it was Alexis herself who had turned over the energy gels with the pathogen. But no one was absolutely sure. And so the FBI had begun to track her. When Toril had checked in just now, they told her that Remnick had just had brunch with a guy who worked at the hospital with Harper. This could mean nothing: she hadn't let go of her dead boyfriend. Or it could mean everything: she had in fact been working with him, but he hadn't told her the plague was in the gels. Or she was an accomplice, but she was trying now to divert suspicion away from herself, hoping that by turning them over she was suggesting her innocence.

By now, the woman had probably seen the news of the recall—or she would soon. This afternoon in New York City. It had just hit the newspaper websites and the relentless, twenty-four-hour cable news cycle.

The other piece of information they'd given Toril? They were getting officers in place right now to raid the hospital and shut down the university labs. The raid was going to occur by the end of the day. It was only taking this long because the labs were a biohazard risk in the middle of one hell of a big city, and that meant extraordinary preparations.

She wiped her fingers, sticky from the cake, on a cloth napkin. She hadn't seen betrayal as often as some of her associates in America had, because she'd only worked in the United States for four years before beginning her picaresque career at embassies around the world. This was her third. And the nature of her job in Cambodia and Vietnam was simply different from what it had been in America. But she'd seen enough in America before leaving: the husband whose wife had been laundering money and he'd never known; the mother of the grown son who'd kidnapped young girls and brought them across state lines before raping and (in one case) decapitating them; the parents of the two brothers who—as if it were 1933—were robbing little banks in Wyoming and Montana, and had shot to death tellers in both states. It was terrible for these family members to learn what the people they loved were capable of. Maybe that was why Toril had wanted the embassy posts.

Assuming Alexis wasn't Austin Harper's partner, soon she would be living with the reality that the man had not merely lied about his family history and why they had gone to Vietnam on a bike tour. He'd carried plague with him across the planet and planned to sell it to some food chemist—now dead, like Austin—who was hoping to sell it to North Korea.

She poured herself the last of the tea in the pot. Poor woman. Toril didn't see how this could possibly end well for her.

33

What do you do with the dress of a dead woman?

No, the question was far more specific than that, Alexis thought, after she finished speaking on the phone with Ken Sarafian.

What do you do with the dress of a dead woman your dead boyfriend bought for her before she was murdered? Executed?

As Alexis walked back to her apartment after brunch, she made a list in her mind of the little that she and Ken knew about Binh Pham. The woman had been a food chemist. She had a brother, also dead, who worked with rats at a university in Ho Chi Minh City. And she had come to New York in the summer.

Alexis wondered after she had spoken to Ken whether she should have asked Oscar about the woman. Whether Austin had ever mentioned her. Whether he himself had ever met her.

No, she had made the right decision. She couldn't reveal to Oscar—at least not yet—that she knew about the Vietnamese chemist.

An idea came to her: when she got home, when she could look at the images on her laptop screen rather than on her phone, she would see if Binh Pham still had her footprints on the social networks.

.   .   .

The woman did. Alexis found her Instagram and Facebook accounts and surfed through them. They had not yet been memorialized: frozen in time by a relative.

There were no photos of her with Austin or Oscar or even Douglas Webber. Not a one. But there, back on June 25, she had posted a photo of her sister and her at the top of the Empire State Building, the sky cobalt and the island stretching south to the Freedom Tower and the Statue of Liberty in the distant harbor. And standing to the side of the two tourists from Vietnam, just barely in the frame? Sally Gleason. The woman clearly had no idea she was in the photo. She was in profile, looking at something else. But that didn't matter. For a long moment, Alexis stared at the three of them, her mind moving between how petite Binh was and the simple, disturbing, unequivocal fact that she had found the link. Here it was. The food chemist had been with Austin's boss four months ago in this very city. No doubt she had been with her boyfriend as well. Alexis doubted she'd ever know, but she wouldn't have been surprised if Austin himself had taken the photo.

And if Sally knew that she was recognizable in this image on Facebook? Probably she would have insisted that Binh delete it. If she knew it was out there right now? She'd probably be livid. Or she'd just erase it herself—as she may have erased everything on Austin's laptop and tablet.

That is, if she had been the one to erase them. It was a diagnostic leap to suppose that had been the work of Sally Gleason. It was just as likely Douglas Webber.

She couldn't help but wonder if the two of them were working together.

On any other Saturday, she would have gone to the gym and then tried to grab a catnap since she had the night shift in the ER. Sometimes the gym helped: it got her endorphins going and cleared her head, and frequently she could sleep for an hour or two afterwards. But she knew how wired she already was, and working out today might only exacerbate that. And so sleeping would then demand a Xanax. And she didn't like to begin a shift with the lingering dullness of the med.

And that meant that a nap probably wasn't in the cards.

And so instead of going to the gym, she gave in to the way her mind was racing. She taped four pieces of copy paper together, placed them on her modest dining room table, and began to map out what she knew and what she didn't. See what the missing pieces were and where she might find them. Pattern recognition. She began by writing down names: names from the bike tour and names from the hospital and the names that surrounded Austin Addison Harper. She hadn't really thought much about Scott and Giang and Colleen from Vietnam, but did they fit into this web somewhere? Was there a reason that Austin had chosen this particular excursion company rather than one of the larger ones, such as Backroads or Vermont Bicycle Touring? Did someone there work with Douglas Webber? Did Webber work for them? (No. Absolutely not. She had the sense that Webber was far too alpha to work for anyone.) She kept focusing on how she trusted no one who was involved with advancement at the hospital. She recalled the word that Captain Nguyen had used when they'd first met at the little boutique hotel in Hoi An, a word that had a different meaning for him than it had for her: *doubtfuls*. People whom you couldn't decide were on your side or against you. People who might seem like they were on your side, but probably weren't. They were all doubtfuls in Austin's department at the hospital, she realized.

And the same probably went for the labs. They worked with the rats. They worked with disease. That's how Sally and Oscar and Austin were involved. That's how Webber was involved.

But, of course, the only person she knew in the labs was Sara Edens. She'd never met the mystical Wilbur Sinclair or any of the other scientists listed on the hospital website: Anil Bhattacharya or Ho-jin Myung or Judy Murray.

She recalled that Sara had offered to give her a tour or see if Sinclair would. Alexis drew a star next to her name. She had seemed trustworthy when they'd had breakfast—she'd actually seemed rather nice and fun—but she, too, should be grouped among the doubtfuls. Trust no one in that wing.

She wondered if Austin had been working with Sinclair or Bhattacharya or Myung—the ones whose work, Sara had said, involved rodents. She wondered if either Sally or Oscar was now picking up Austin's slack.

When she stared at the names and the lines she had drawn between them, it seemed clear to her that Austin either had been bringing something to Vietnam or planning to bring something back from Vietnam. Something other than that suit and her dress from Hoi An. And he was bringing it from the labs or to the labs, and the food chemist was either the recipient or the provider.

And that something had to do with rats.

. . .

Initially Alexis was excited when she got the call and the fellow with the avuncular, gentle southern voice introduced himself as Wilbur Sinclair. She was still staring at her impromptu whiteboard on her dining room table.

"Sara Edens suggested I give you a ring," he said, and then added, "She told me about the death of your friend. I'm very sorry."

She stopped what she was doing and concentrated. She wasn't surprised that somebody was at work amidst all the pipettes and spectrometers and cell cultures on a Saturday. The only people who seemed to work as hard as residents and interns were the human lab rats, the scientists—especially the competitive young doctoral candidates slaving away to earn their keep and justify their research grants. People like Sara. But, of course, this was one of the most senior university researchers calling, one of the four scientists there with their own labs and teams. And so her reflexive enthusiasm morphed quickly into what she presumed was a far more reasonable wariness.

"Thank you," she said. "You're very kind."

"Yes and no. I have manners. But I know well that no good ever comes from mistaking manners for kindness."

She smiled, though she was alone. "I'm guessing Sara told you I was hoping to get a tour of the labs."

"I never met your friend. The poor fellow who died. You know that, correct?"

"No. I didn't know that. But I hadn't supposed that you had."

"But he was interested in mice. At least that's what Sara tells me."

"Rats. I think he was more interested in rats."

"Well, you're in luck because we have both. I'm here now, and I will be here another hour. No time like the present, right?"

She recalled how she had used that very expression with that nice old public defender just the other day in the ER. "You mean, you want me to come by right now?"

"Do you live nearby?"

"Close enough."

"Can you be here at one thirty?"

"Yes, absolutely."

"Good. Do you know the floor? I can meet you at the elevator bank."

"I do," she said.

"Now, I'm not sure how I can help you. But I'll show you around. Show you the sorts of things we do."

"That would be wonderful," she told him, and then she thanked him and hung up.

She was about to slip her phone into the back pocket of her jeans, but stopped herself. She called Ken Sarafian. When something seems too good to be true, it probably is. Whatever Austin had been up to had gotten him killed.

"And so you're going to the labs right now?" Ken asked her. "Think that's wise?"

"No. That's why I wanted to be sure that someone knew I was there."

"You're scared."

"A little."

"That's good. You should be scared. Which is why I'm going to go with you."

Had she been hoping he would offer? She suspected so, but until that second, she hadn't admitted this to herself.

"Ken—"

"Save your breath, Alexis. I'm joining you. What time are you seeing Sinclair?"

"One thirty."

"So, I'll meet you outside the hospital at one twenty."

"Not the main entrance," she said, aware of how grateful she was. She told him where the doors were for the wing with the administrative offices and the labs.

"One more thing," she added.

"Yes?"

"Sally Gleason. There's a photo of her and the Vietnamese food chemist on Facebook."

"So, she's the link." He sounded sad. Disappointed. For a moment Alexis was surprised by his reaction, but then she recalled the connection: Sally Gleason was the daughter of a friend of his who had passed away.

"Or *a* link," she added quickly. "We don't know whether she's working with Webber—"

"Or whether she's his competitor," he said, already resolute and focused, and finishing her sentence for her.

Before leaving, she went to the dresser and opened the drawer with all of her socks and pulled out her cutting kit. She unzipped the airline amenities bag and removed the scalpel. It had a plastic safety guard covering the blade. For now, she'd keep the guard on the metal. For now. She placed it into the back of her jeans, right beside her phone.

And then she grabbed two of Austin's energy gels she'd

brought back from Vietnam and tossed one into her purse. She ripped open the top of the other. It was chocolate, a flavor she loathed, but she needed a boost and figured, *what the hell,* and squirted the goo into her mouth. It tasted even worse than she remembered—nothing like chocolate at all.

34

Douglas stood beside Wilbur Sinclair, focused and resolved. He sniffed the air, which even here, the elevator bank outside the entrance to the labs, smelled of chemicals and cleansers. His gaze moved back and forth between the view of the East River from the wide windows and the doors to the two elevators.

"And there are no cameras here?" he asked Sinclair again. He had asked him this before coming, but felt the need to inquire once more. To be reassured that there was no video record of his presence. He tried not to scowl, but his patience was at an end.

The scientist had his hands clasped behind his back. He was wearing a white lab coat that seemed to have more pockets than a pair of cargo pants. He had a key card in a lanyard around his neck, and in one hand he was holding a capped syringe of propofol. He shook his head, which had small beads of sweat just above his eyebrows, and pointed at the doors behind them. Sinclair was a man with lips the color of liver and a cleft in his chin that was a chasm. His weekend stubble was white and his sideburns were going gray, but he had hair that was otherwise still mostly glossy and black.

"The first camera is on the other side of the door. The real entrance to the labs," he answered.

Douglas presumed Sinclair was sweating because he was frightened. His face was flushed. For a guy who spent his days with the plague—a new plague—he was clearly a little shaky when it came to murder.

"As long as you don't enter the labs, no one will ever know you were here," he added. Still, Sinclair had suggested just making the ER doctor disappear. Carving her up and putting the pieces into the pathological waste incinerator. "It's big enough for primates," he'd said helpfully. "Couldn't we just turn her to ash?"

Douglas had to disabuse him of the notion that this was even a remotely good idea. Here he had always presumed that scientists were orderly people. Clean freaks. Good God, they worried about how they treated their rats and mice before they gave them cancer or ALS or, in this fellow's case, the plague. They insisted on humane protocols.

But they most certainly could not just make Alexis disappear. Not after Harper's death. Not after she'd brought in a PI who clearly knew what he was doing. She had to die, but it had to pass the forensic sniff test and look like a suicide.

Douglas supposed that when Alexis saw him, she would recognize him instantly from the night he and Austin had come to the ER. And that was fine. In that moment when recognition froze her, Sinclair would uncap the syringe and plunge it into her neck. She wouldn't collapse instantly; they only did that in the movies. But propofol worked fast. Douglas would wrap her in a bear hug, his arms enfolding her like a straitjacket, ensuring that she didn't bruise herself. When she was unconscious, they would get back into the elevator and bring her to Oscar's office in advancement. There were no cameras anywhere on that floor and no one would be working—unlike the labs, where at the very least there would be an assistant stopping by later to tend to the animals, and Sinclair had said he'd be shocked if one young researcher or another didn't appear at some point in the afternoon.

Then, after dark, Alexis Remnick would quite literally cut herself to death. Austin had told him that once upon a time she'd been a cutter. (After he'd gotten over the raised, wormlike scars on her abdomen and thighs, he'd even admitted that he'd found her vulnerability rather attractive.) Cutters didn't usually kill themselves, that wasn't the point of it. But they also didn't lose their boyfriends to hit-and-run accidents in Vietnam and then discover their boyfriends were liars. After dark, Webber and Sinclair would slash her wrists and throw her into the East River as she was bleeding out. She'd probably wake up when she started to breathe in the water, but not enough that she'd be able to fight it. And if she did? Already she'd be far too weak from blood loss to swim and climb out. She'd drown. It was fail-safe.

And this really was the only solution. His intuition had always been sound. It was a hunch, after all, that had led him to follow Austin to Vietnam in the first place. And he'd been right. There had been a lot to contain.

While they waited, mostly but not entirely in silence, he swiped right on his phone to see the news. He was just killing time. When he did, however, his eyes narrowed and he turned away from Sinclair. All, for a brief second, was forgotten. Some energy gel company had announced a recall because they feared product tampering. A packet had been opened in Da Nang, Vietnam, and some lab tech was dead. Some cabdriver was dead. Douglas wasn't quite sure what the hell an energy gel was and Googled it. He stared at the images on the company's website. He saw what looked like a mayonnaise packet you were given at the sort of deli shop too lazy to spread condiments on bread. He saw photos of cyclists and runners squeezing the shit into their mouths.

And he knew. He knew precisely how that stupid fuck Austin Harper had brought the pathogen to Vietnam—and it was possible, Douglas realized, that he'd flown all the way there after him and had four people killed, including the idiot American, and still he'd contained nothing. Nothing at all.

The FBI would link Harper to the university labs at the hospital. How could they not? Even if they didn't know for a fact that the pathogen had been created on this very floor, here was where they'd begin. The proximity was obvious. For all Douglas knew, they were going to be here today. They might be gathering right now.

And someone had clearly helped Austin, because on his own he sure as hell couldn't have taken the pathogen and placed it into an energy gel.

Sinclair.

Had Wilbur Sinclair betrayed him, too?

He placed his hand inside his jacket and unclipped the safety on his Glock. He might have shot the scientist right there, left him dead on the floor, but he heard the ping of the elevator, a chime that woke him. He looked up and saw Alexis Remnick emerge and Sinclair uncapping the syringe, but then the scientist stopped and dropped his arm to his side, his hand shielding the needle from the woman's eyes. Beside her was that pain-in-the-ass detective, Ken Sarafian.

. . .

Ken saw the two of them, his mind registering that the fellow beside Douglas Webber was one of the scientists here—no doubt, Wilbur Sinclair—and he had something in his hand, and that Webber was reaching for his pistol. And so Ken drew his gun from his shoulder holster, but it was already too late. Webber fired, and the bullet hit him hard in the arm, splintering the bone just above his wrist. He dropped his gun as he grimaced, grunting against the pain, understanding that he was still alive because his forearm had been in front of his chest. In front of his heart. He fell to his knees to retrieve the weapon, but it was too late.

"Don't go there," Webber was saying, and then he was lifting the gun off the tile floor and dropping it into his coat pocket, the guy's own Glock pointing down at him. Alexis was flat against the wall between the elevators, the doors now shut, and the scientist in the lab coat looked a little sickened.

But then, so did Alexis. Hadn't she said she thought she was coming down with something as they'd gotten into the elevator just a moment ago? Something about the nearness of flu season and how she'd have to get her shot in the next week or two?

"I thought she was coming alone," Sinclair was telling Webber. He sounded panicked and desperate. "What do we do with him? With her?"

"You," Webber was saying to him, and it wasn't a question.

"Me? What, Douglas?"

"You gave Harper the pathogen. The red lotus. You put it in an energy gel."

"What are you talking about? I never gave him anything. I don't even know what that is—an energy gel."

Ken watched as Webber looked back and forth between the scientist and Alexis, and then settled his gaze upon Sinclair. On the one hand, it had all happened so fast, just the way it did in the jungle in Vietnam or one time when they were storming a crack house on Avenue A or another time when a shooter was holed up in a real estate company's office and the guy was furious about . . . about something. Some way he felt he had been deceived. Ripped off. And suddenly that fellow was shooting, too. But it was also happening slowly, in moments of incremental and quixotic quiet. The way Webber was ignoring the scientist, the way Alexis was now kneeling beside him. His arm hurt like hell, pain that deadened sound at the same time that it caused him to see klieg lights behind his eyes every time he blinked. Like a puppy with a wounded paw, he let the doctor look at his arm. Webber didn't seem prepared to fire again. The guy might kill him yet—he'd meant to kill him a moment ago, an instinct when he'd seen a man reaching for a gun—but Ken wasn't absolutely convinced that it was going to end here on the floor at the entrance to the labs.

"Can you stop the bleeding without bringing him to the ER?" Webber was asking Alexis.

Ken looked down at the blood that was spreading along the sleeve of his olive peacoat from the elbow to the cuff, and puddling in his lap. Alexis was feverish and pale. He had another of those flashbacks: his one Christmas at the base in Quang Tri. The commander had wanted a Christmas tree, and so he'd managed to have one flown in from his home state of Michigan. By the time it arrived in Vietnam, it was largely needleless and made that classic Charlie Brown tree look like the monolith at Rockefeller Center. Still, they'd put it on a stand not far from the tank farm and someone had found some tinsel. But then the monsoon came. The water was knee-high at the base, and when they weren't swatting with shovels at the rats that suddenly were swimming all around them, they were trying to retrieve the tree as it floated away. And it was then that the winds took whole rows of plywood that they had belted down and ripped them from their moorings. The sheets were flying through the air like playing cards, and two of them sliced into a soldier named Powell like table saw blades. Ken couldn't recall the guy's first name now. But he dragged him out of the water and into the nearest hut, radioed the base hospital, and found a medic, a kid with Mr. Magoo eyeglasses. There they used a pair of scissors to snip through Powell's sopping camo pants as the soldier cried over and over, "My leg, my leg, no, no, not my leg," and Ken had thought to himself, *Better your damn leg than your stomach or your head.* But he hadn't said that. He'd simply done whatever the medic had told him to do. He honestly believed the guy was going to be okay. But then he saw the gash the size of his boot above the guy's knee, an alluvium maw of tissue and muscle and bone, all of it awash in blood that was pooling—no, it was streaming, pumping, it was a garden hose that wasn't going to cease until Powell was dead—and he knew he was mistaken and reflexively turned away. When he looked back at the soldier, already the guy was fading. He had stopped speaking and the light was leaving his eyes, and the medic was tying a tourniquet at the very top of the soldier's leg, near his groin. He could hear a couple of corpsmen pounding their way through the water to them, but it was too late. Powell would be dead by the time they brought him to the hospital. He'd been killed by flying plywood while shoveling rats in a monsoon. That about said it all. His skin was the color of milkweed.

Very much, Ken realized, like this ER doctor's was right now.

"Let me take off his coat so I can look at it. I doubt I can do much if you don't let me take him to the ER," she was saying to Webber.

"No ER," the guy said. "Not happening." But Webber didn't stop her from extricating his left arm from the coat and then yanking the sleeve off his right—just ripping off the Band-Aid. He gazed down at his shirt, a black turtleneck—but much blacker where it was saturated between his elbow and his wrist. The wound didn't look so terrible, he thought, when the tsunami of pain, which had come when Alexis had pulled off the coat, had subsided. This wasn't the river of blood he was expecting. It was bleeding, yes, but it was starting to slow. He could see that. It was clean.

"I know that hurt. I'm sorry, I didn't have any scissors," she said. Then she reiterated that he needed to be downstairs in the ER. "The bone's shattered. We need an orthopedist—*he* needs an orthopedist," she was saying. She took off her jean jacket and pressed it against the wound, and he inhaled deeply against the sting.

Webber seemed to think about this, but he didn't react. He turned to the scientist and said, "Get the rats."

"Which ones?"

"Transgenic. Red lotus."

"With the plague?"

"Yes, damn it! Be fast and come back here."

Sinclair paused and Ken wondered if he might disobey him. But the moment was brief: the fellow was making some sort of calculus in his mind about, Ken assumed, how many rats he could carry. He held up a syringe. "And this?"

"No. Just go."

And then Sinclair was pulling a key card from a lanyard and

pressing it against the door that led to the labs, buzzing it open, and he was gone.

"You two, up!" Webber barked at them.

"Can you stand?" Alexis asked him.

Ken nodded. He could. She was wearing a T-shirt, and now he could see the sores on her arms. She was sweating and looked sickly. Whatever she had, he thought, it really had come on fast.

At first, I thought it really was just a hit-and-run. An accident. A horrible coincidence.

It was only a few days later, when I heard about the lab in Vietnam, that I got scared. Someone had the same idea that I did. That we did.

But I still thought we might be okay. Do nothing—nothing more— lie low, and it would all go away. It was only when Sara told me Austin's girlfriend had approached her that I realized that wasn't happening. And then Ken told me he had done exactly the opposite of what I had asked, and I knew for sure the walls were closing in. And it was all because of that ER doctor. She was like a dog with a bone.

35

Was it an urban legend? Maybe.

But every ER doc in New York City had heard the story of Noah Snow. It was a Saturday night (of course) one summer in the late 1970s, and the Bronx ER where Snow worked as a physician was a madhouse. He was treating a young thug who'd been shot in the stomach. And two guys appeared in the cubicle—preceded by the shouts and screams of the other patients and a couple of terrified orderlies—with a pair of sawed-off shotguns to finish off the kid with the bullet in his abdomen. And Snow, who always carried with him a .45 pistol as well as his stethoscope because the neighborhood was so damn dicey, pulled it out and plugged both dudes by the curtain where they stood. Two shots.

First do no harm? Alexis knew that if she wanted to live and keep this old PI alive, she had to remove the safety guard from the scalpel in her back pocket. And she was going to have to do some serious harm: swipe hard and fast against Douglas Webber's carotid artery. He'd be unconscious in seconds, literally seconds, and would be gone soon after that. But she'd have to do it without getting shot first.

And she was feeling fuzzy, light-headed, and febrile. Weak. Was it the flu?

Maybe.

But it was sudden. So damn sudden.

She rose as Douglas had demanded, wobbly, but she was on

her feet. Ken rolled his eyes, took a breath, and used his left hand to start to push himself up. She bent over and wrapped an arm around his back and helped him.

Which was when it came to her.

"Did you shoot Austin?" she asked Douglas.

"God, no," he said dismissively.

"Not that night back in March?"

"No," he repeated. "Not that night in March."

Which was what she believed: there'd been too many witnesses in the bar to blame it on a homeless junkie if that wasn't what actually had happened. No, the point wasn't Webber's answer; it was the question. It was the needed distraction. As she'd asked him and he'd answered, she'd brought her right hand casually beside the rear pocket of her jeans, maintaining eye contact. With a single finger she pushed up the scalpel through the opening there.

"Not even by accident?" she insisted.

"Not even by accident," he replied, but she was already removing the scalpel with two fingers and slipping off the guard with her thumb. Then she shoved the PI back to the ground and heaved her body into Douglas Webber before he could fire, pulling him into her—wrapping herself around him—the way she'd been taught in that self-defense class, her left arm around the man's lower back and her right hand slashing the scalpel as hard as she could into his neck. They fell together, upright against the wall by the elevators. She'd missed the carotid as well as the jugular, but still he bled and he bled mightily, pounding her in the back and then trying with his free hand to yank the scalpel away from his throat. But it was too late. She had the angle, and on her third swipe she hit the artery and she could see the blood geysering onto her fingers and his chest, and feel it warm and wet against her face. He was coughing, choking, and bucking like a rodeo animal. He fired the pistol, once, twice, wild shots that hit the ceiling and one of the elevator doors, but already his knees were buckling and the two of them were sinking to the floor.

He tried to speak, but he was gagging on his own blood, and she could see the splatter all around them and streaking the gleaming metal blade.

When she looked up, Ken was beside her, pulling his own pistol from Douglas's coat pocket. He held it in his left hand as he stood above the two of them. He'd curled his wounded right arm against his chest.

"You always carry a scalpel?" he asked, his tone ironic.

She knew he'd meant this as a joke, but she couldn't smile. Not after killing a person. Even this Douglas Webber. The blood had slowed to a small rivulet that was trickling onto the tile floor. His body was still right beside her. "No," she told him.

"You should."

"You should go to the ER. Right now."

"You should, too," he said. "I'm guessing there's another way out of here. Another set of stairs on the far side of the floor."

"Why?"

"That scientist."

She nodded. Of course. She'd forgotten. She was weak and she was tired and she was aching everywhere. Everywhere. She coughed and her chest hurt. It was unexpectedly hard to breathe. Still, how in the world could she have failed to recall that the last thing Douglas had done was tell Wilbur Sinclair to get the rats? "I'm sure there's another set of stairs," she answered, and she tried to get up, but it was proving to be an impossible task. The adrenaline that had kept her vertical—what had turned her into a human projectile and sent her hurtling into the dead man beside her—was gone.

"You stay here," he told her, and then he fired at the lock on the door to the labs. He was firing with his left hand and it took three shots, the third at almost point-blank range, before he had shattered the lock and splintered the wood. And then he was gone, and in the sudden quiet—all she could hear was the ever-softening sound of Ken Sarafian's footsteps—she noticed for the first time what was happening to her arms. The sores. She put down the scalpel and felt her throat where her neck met her jaw. She felt the swelling. The buboes. They were under her arms, too.

And that's when she understood the exchange between Douglas and the university scientist. What it meant and what it meant for her. This was the fever she was feeling.

You gave Harper the pathogen. The red lotus. You put it in an energy gel.

That was what Douglas had said.

Wilbur Sinclair had denied it, but the meaning and the ramification was clear: Austin had brought some new variant of the plague to Vietnam in those Psych packets, that's what he'd been doing. He'd been bringing it to the food chemist. And whatever it was, it was airborne, she supposed. Aerosol. Transmitted by breath, as well as by touch and blood. She could feel it in her lungs. And she had actually eaten one before coming here to the hospital. Squeezed it into her mouth. There was, she was quite sure, no antibiotic. After all, that was the point.

She herself was now one of the doubtfuls. A dead woman walking.

She certainly couldn't leave this floor, she certainly couldn't struggle into the elevator and then crawl to the ER. For all she knew, on the way here, she might already have infected others. Everyone she had breathed near . . .

Everything she had touched . . .

Ken Sarafian. Poor Ken Sarafian. Any moment now, he'd be feeling the symptoms.

And spreading the pathogen.

She had no idea whether she had minutes or hours before she blacked out.

She felt spent and utterly exhausted—feeble and shaky and sick. But she wasn't scared. She was resigned to it all. It was done. They'd quarantine her and give her massive doses of antibiotics, which she presumed would be ineffectual, and then they'd give her morphine if she hadn't already fallen into a coma.

She reached for her phone. She had to call 911 before she

passed out and alert them that this floor was a biohazard. That the corpse beside her probably had some new strain of plague and that she herself was carrying some new strain of plague. That somewhere on this floor there were transgenic rats that had it, too.

When she spoke to the dispatcher, at first her voice was cracking. She sounded like a child—an utterly terrified child. But it wasn't fright. She was simply fading. She could feel herself melting. What was the word her mother sometimes used when it was unbearably hot and humid, on those stickiest of days in July and August? Puddling. Well, now she was puddling.

But she told the dispatcher where she was, and she explained what she could about Wilbur Sinclair, and said to please, please not shoot the older man if they saw him trailing the scientist.

Then she added that when they came for her they had to be wearing the space suits. "Full-on biocontainment space suits and hoods," she said. They asked her to stay on the line, and she said fine if she didn't have to talk anymore. She pressed speaker and put the phone on the tile beside her, and stretched out her legs.

What was it Ellie had said last night? *We always relish the missing.*

Ellie had meant the dead, and *missing* had been a euphemism. But, in truth, Alexis guessed now that we yearned for the missing far more than the dead. The MIAs, the disappeared, the people who were just . . . gone. We moved on from the dead. The missing were a whole other level of longing, a great open wound. If they'd never found Austin's body, she might have taken her longing to her grave.

There was that beautiful Vietnamese word again in her head: *Nhớ.*

N-yo, but as a single, mellifluous syllable. Longing.

Who, she wondered, would miss the dead man beside her? Or Ken Sarafian?

In a week or a month, Ellie would be at a bar and missing her. She'd be Ellie's French bulldog for the night. But then she'd move on. Her mother would move on. After all, that was the only way we could live. Otherwise? Stasis. Paralysis. Death. It was . . . self-preservation to move on.

She turned away from the corpse next to her. Instead she looked at her arms. Then she closed her eyes, sickened by what she saw, and—though she was all alone—shook her head.

. . .

She thought of how her mother had told her to stay inside. To stay upstairs.

The phone had woken her up. The landline. They had cell phones then. Well, her parents did, primitive ones, but she was only in elementary school, so she didn't. This call, however, had come in on the landline—the phone in her parents' bedroom—and she had suspected even as a child that a call on the landline at this hour of the night was bad news. Terrible news. Inconvenience at best, woe at worst.

Still, she hadn't gotten out of bed. She hadn't been able to hear her mother's voice because her mother had closed the bedroom door. That fact alone was a further cause for alarm.

And so Alexis hadn't fallen back to sleep when their neighbors arrived. Not her parents' closest friends, but their nearest friends. The McKennas, who lived but five blocks away. She heard all their voices and she heard the hushed crying. A woman's hushed crying. It was almost melodious, the way it rose and fell. And so Alexis climbed from her bed and went to the top of the stairs, and her mother was already dressed. She was just starting out the front door in her winter parka.

Which was when she saw that her mother was upset and Mrs. McKenna was sobbing now—it was worse than before—and Mr. McKenna just looked sad. No, it was at once different and worse than that: he looked stunned. He had his winter coat on, too, a puffy, down-filled ski jacket the color of copper. His car keys were in his hand, his finger through the ring. Mrs. McKenna had hung her coat on the rack by the front door. It was clear what was happening: her mother and Mr. McKenna were leaving the house, and Mrs. McKenna was going to babysit her.

That was when her mother turned and spotted her, and ordered—ordered!—her to stay upstairs. To stay inside.

But then she came back to herself when Alexis's face must have fallen. Even though she already had her boots on, even though she was halfway out the door, her mother ran up the stairs to Alexis and knelt before her, and she was fighting back tears. (And she was, as always, winning. Once there had been a discussion in med school about cryobiology, the exploration of how very cold temperatures impact living things, and Alexis had volunteered that her mother, whose blood clearly ran cold for a mammal, would be an interesting part of a control group.) But Alexis nevertheless began to weep as her mother started to speak. "Oh, my little girl," she murmured, her voice as soft as Alexis ever would hear it in her entire life, "my little, little girl." Her mother told her what had happened—most of it, but not all of it. Not the most important part. She'd said only there had been an accident. A car accident. It would be years before Alexis would understand that while her mother was going to the hospital, she had known then that her husband was already dead. "I'm going to need you to be a big girl now. So big from now on. I'm going to need to be so big, too."

Yes, in hindsight, her mother was scared. She was scared of what loomed—not that night, but forever. Forever. Raising her daughter on her own. Raising her daughter in a world in which she was a single parent with a job that demanded a long commute and a lot of travel, and raising a daughter in a world that never made it easy for a woman. Raising a daughter as a woman who was many, many marvelous things—she had to know that, she had to—but maternal was not among them. She must have known that her husband had always been more nurturing than she was. Which didn't make her a bad person, not at all, but in hindsight that awareness, too, must have been tragic and almost too much to bear. She knew the mistakes she would make and she knew the failures that loomed and she knew that while it might not in fact take a village to raise a child, it took more than just her, but she herself was all that she had.

She was it.

And it really was such a big world. Big and dangerous and oblivious.

And her daughter was so little. As little as the world was big.

She was going away that night, she told Alexis, but otherwise she would always be there. Always be there—she repeated, emphasizing each and every word. She would always be there, even when she wasn't.

Which was the case.

The next night, when Alexis had finally gone upstairs to her own bedroom, when all the shell-shocked neighbors had left and inside the eerily quiet house were just a young widow and a young girl without a father, she had considered asking her mother if she could spend the night in her parents' bed in her parents' bedroom with her. She wanted to sleep beside her, she didn't want to be alone. She had almost opened her mouth to say that, to admit how afraid she was, the words forming in her mind, when her mother told her as she tucked her in, "My big girl. I am so proud of how you got through today. How together we'll get through tomorrow. And the day after that."

And so she hadn't asked. She'd nodded. She would be brave. Her mother kissed her and turned off the light, and in the dark, Alexis had pulled the sheet and the comforter over her head and folded herself into the smallest ball that she possibly could, her arms around her shins as she brought her thighs to her chest—a pose she'd know well when she finally stopped cutting, a pose that she would replicate in the stalls of showers or in the wombs of bathtubs as the water rained down upon her—and eventually cried herself to sleep.

In the end, her mother had been a parent whose most obvious attributes were drive and relentlessness, but there was more to her than that. Far more. Alexis had never doubted—despite the distance and occasional downright chilliness that were as much a part of Dina Remnick as her eyes and her hair—that her mother had loved her. Her mother had loved her and saved her and helped make her who she was. And though she was never the sort of mom who would take her little girl to her first manicure or dress up in a matching Halloween costume, she was the kind who would always have her daughter's back. Always.

And now with her last breaths, Alexis wanted the woman to know that. She wanted her to know that she loved her and was grateful for her. She reached for her phone and pressed the red dot, cutting her connection with the dispatcher, and called her. She called her to say good-bye.

No, we weren't working with Wilbur Sinclair. We had Sara Edens. We didn't need someone to design the pathogen. We just needed someone to harvest it. Wilbur introduced Douglas and me—a hospital function, a fund-raiser—but we had no idea we were both trying to work the same side of the street. None. I honestly believed he was a travel writer. He honestly believed my imagination was insufficient to see the commercial potential in the new plague.

I guess it all fell apart when I, in turn, introduced Austin to Douglas. Austin betrayed me, but it was Douglas who stole my salesman. He saw in Austin exactly what I did. And Austin? I have no idea what he saw in us. Two scores, maybe. Twice the lucre. Maybe he just had to have two of everything. I am quite sure—positive—he was sleeping with my Vietnamese food chemist at the same time he was sleeping with the ER doctor.

In hindsight, he was a man-child too boyish to recognize either the utter unscrupulousness of what he was doing or the danger.

I have no idea how many of the knockout rats Wilbur injected with the bacteria that afternoon. Eight? Nine?

No, I didn't think you could tell me. But I had to ask.

I gather he thought Douglas was going to kill him when he heard the gunshots. He figured Alexis and the PI were dead, and he must have been terrified. And so he made a run for the emergency exit in the labs. The stairs.

Reassure me one more time: this—everything I'm telling you—is all covered under attorney-client privilege, right?

36

Ken could hear the echoing footsteps of the scientist on the treads on the stairwell below him, but he couldn't yet see him. He was gaining, however, that was clear, and then he spotted the fluttering white tails of a lab coat two floors below him, but it was the most fleeting of glances, and then he heard the stairwell door opening. The guy was exiting into the lobby on the first floor. Thank God, this was an administrative wing, not the main entrance to the hospital that patients and staffers used. It was a Saturday afternoon, and so it had been empty when he and Alexis had arrived here a few minutes ago. He supposed it was now.

Still, it was probably connected somehow to that vast and crowded main lobby, and Sinclair would know the labyrinth if that's where he wanted to go. Likewise, he would know the exits, and he would know the places where he might disappear into the bowels of the building or through rabbit holes that led, eventually, out onto the street.

Ken had absolutely no idea what the guy was going to do with the rats. He didn't know what the word *transgenic* meant, but he sure as hell understood *plague*. He presumed Sinclair was taking them to another lab or a safe house, but he guessed there was also a chance that he might use them as a bargaining chip of some kind. And then, if the scientist didn't get what he wanted? Release them. Of course.

But if he released them . . . where? And just how virulent were these rats? How lethal?

When Ken emerged from the stairwell, he saw that Sinclair was just nearing the corner that led toward some other section of the hospital, and so he yelled for him to stop. He yelled that he had a gun, though he feared this was a bluff if ever there was one. Upstairs, it had taken him three shots with his left hand to shoot out a door lock. Three. Pathetic. To drop a moving son of a bitch at this distance with his left? Unlikely. His aim was going to be suspect because he was firing with the wrong hand, because his right arm was still throbbing with eye-wincing daggers of pain, and because he was coming down with whatever the hell the ER doctor had. How in the name of God had it come on so fast? Shock, maybe. Blood loss. Didn't matter. He felt weedy and decrepit, and all he wanted was this scientist down on the ground, so he could collapse, too.

Fortunately, Sinclair paused when he heard Ken's voice. Came to a complete stop. And that's when it dawned on him that the guy had absolutely no idea whether he was right- or left-handed, or even who was following him: all he knew was that a guy with a gun had told him to stop. Ken raised the pistol, planting his feet. He was about to tell Sinclair not to move, to put down the animal carrier and stay where he was, when the scientist abruptly took off again. Started to run. And so Ken fired. He dropped him on the third shot, the others banging off the corridor walls. The animal carrier bounced onto the floor beside him. Ken had hit him in the lower back, on the right side. He might live, the PI thought. This was a hospital, after all. It wasn't where he was aiming, but it had done the trick.

When he reached the scientist, he saw that the animal carrier was sealed. The rats were still inside it.

"I'd read you your rights," he said, standing over him, "but I'm not a cop anymore."

"Get away from me," Sinclair said softly, his brow furrowed against the pain. "Get away from me."

"Happy to," Ken told him, but he didn't holster his gun when he backed off. He looked down at the pistol, the barrel a little longer than the model that Webber had said he preferred. But that longer barrel, and the accuracy it offered, had sure as hell been an asset just now. With the toe of his shoe, he pushed the animal carrier a half dozen feet away from the scientist. He didn't want him to rally and roll over, and release the little bastards. Then he texted Alexis where he and Sinclair and the animal carrier were and called 911. He was on the line with the dispatcher, telling her that the rats on the floor near him might have the plague, when somewhere in the distance he heard sirens, and they were growing louder and louder as they cut through the crisp autumn air.

He sighed. He couldn't stand up another second, and so he sank against the wall and looked at the scientist. Clearly the guy was in serious pain, but when their eyes met, he said, "I told you, don't come near me. Stay where you are."

Ken considered replying that he was in no position to demand anything, but the PI really didn't care. Sinclair was down, and he was far from his bloody rats.

He looked at his right forearm. It was a mess. It was still trickling blood.

But the damnedest thing? He had a feeling that the sores that were growing with the speed of dandelions in May on his left were a far bigger problem. He coughed and shook his head. This wasn't the flu and this wasn't shock. He could kid himself and tell himself that it was one or the other or both. But this was bad. This—*this*—was why Sinclair kept telling him to keep his distance. He understood now. He got it.

Ken never wanted to worry Taleen, but for the first time since he'd fallen in love with her, he had an urgent sense that he probably did need to worry her—even after all those years as a cop—because more than anything he wanted to thank her for being her and, yes, to say farewell. And so he balanced his phone on his thigh, put it on speakerphone, and called her.

She sounded great when she said hello.

He took a deep breath. He decided that he should, too.

SUNDAY

37

Dina Remnick flipped past the photo in the tabloid, her principal thought that the pop star's new tattoo looked nothing at all like the actor she was marrying. But even if it had been a better likeness, wasn't it always a bad idea to tattoo your fiancé's face onto your biceps?

Until a few minutes ago, Dina had been standing outside the quarantined section of the ICU at the hospital, but even a mother could only stare at her daughter through the sealed glass window of a quarantine cubicle for so long. Alexis was in a medically induced coma, her beautiful face hidden mostly by the mask of a respirator, her arms and neck—stippled with sores—above the white sheet that was draped over the rest of her body.

Now Dina was alone in the waiting room on the other side of the nurses' station, reading the newspaper someone had left on a chrome and glass side table. She read the gossip stories on Page Six, because she was distracted and really couldn't focus on much else. There was a television in the room, but she silenced it because she couldn't bear to hear the Sunday-morning talking heads bicker. Finally, she put the paper down and scrolled aimlessly through the contacts on her phone, trying to make sure she hadn't forgotten to call someone to tell them what was occurring—what had happened to Alexis. She looked again at the business cards from the two FBI agents. She guessed they had both been roughly Alexis's age. Early to midthirties. It reminded her how young the world was. One was female, the taller of the pair, and one was male.

It seemed that her daughter had gotten a strain of plague from something called an energy gel. The only reason why they were cautiously optimistic that she was going to live was because most of the pathogen in the gel was dying or dead. The bacteria could live for days without oxygen, but not forever. And so, as sick as she was, this was actually a mild case by the standards of this disease. They expected to pull her from the medically induced coma within days. Tuesday, if all went well. Maybe Wednesday or Thursday, to be safe. In the meantime, her system was getting an IV drip of something called vancomycin 3.0, as they tried—to quote the attending physician—to nuke the infection.

But the doctor had told her that every moment had mattered, and if Alexis hadn't called her and she—Dina—hadn't been so ferociously demanding and gotten her daughter off the floor with the labs and into the ICU so fast, Alexis would very likely be dead now.

Somewhere in the hospital, she didn't know where, was Dr. Wilbur Sinclair. He was under arrest and being treated for a bullet wound in his lower back. He was going to live.

But the fellow who'd shot him? The detective Alexis had retained? He'd died yesterday on the phone with his wife. He'd gotten the plague from her daughter, and he hadn't made it. The physicians had suggested it was because he was older. A little more frail. Also? He'd been shot by the arms dealer, that Douglas Webber, and he'd lost some blood, which had weakened him further. He was, they had told her, a retired cop and Vietnam War veteran, but he was going to be remembered now for what he had done to stop a pandemic.

What he and her daughter and some Vietnamese police captain had done to stop a pandemic.

She looked up when she saw a slim woman a little older than her in the doorway. She was dressed in a lime-green skirt and a white blouse, a blazer draped over her arm, but otherwise looked about as tired and unkempt as Dina knew she herself did. She had shoulder-length hair that was silver and black, and dark eyes. Dina was about to return to the newspaper when the woman spoke to her.

"They said I might find you here. You're Alexis Remnick's mom?"

"I am," she said cautiously. Was this woman a reporter? Or did she work for some government agency? Dina thought she was done with both for the moment. "Dina Remnick."

"My name is Taleen Sarafian," the woman told her, and Dina nodded. The PI's wife. She braced herself and considered standing for the castigation and vitriol that loomed. She could give as good as she got, however, and was prepared to defend her daughter. Alexis had nearly died herself. Yes, Dina was sorry that Alexis had given this woman's husband the disease that killed him, but she hadn't known that she had it. Dina felt bad for this widow, but how dare she come here and attack her daughter? Grief could morph into anger; Dina knew that as well as anyone. But to come here to a waiting room while Alexis was in a coma in the ICU? That was beastly, and Dina wouldn't stand for it.

"I wanted to see you," Taleen continued.

And with that, Dina did rise. "Look—" she began, but Taleen cut her off.

"Sit," she said. "I'll take this chair."

"No. I can stand. I'm sorry about your husband. I lost my husband years ago, but—"

"I know," Taleen continued, and she rested her hand so gently on Dina's arm that she was able to restrain her natural inclination to recoil. "I know. I heard. They told me."

Warily Dina sat, and the other woman sank into the chair beside her. "I hear she's going to make it. Thank God," Taleen said.

"She's not out of the woods yet. But the prognosis is . . . okay," Dina told her. "Maybe even good. But a lot can happen, and I don't want to jinx it."

"No, of course not."

For a moment neither woman said anything, and Dina understood that Taleen hadn't come here to attack her. And so she broke the silence and said, "You must be devastated about your husband. I'm sorry."

"Me, too. He was"—and her voice broke ever so slightly—"one of the good ones. One of the real good ones. We had almost a half century together. Not quite. But almost." She reached into the pocket of the blazer in her lap for a tissue and blew her nose. "It's been a bad year."

Dina nodded. "You have children?" she asked. She supposed the woman did.

"Two. Terrific boys. Men. We had three."

Dina took this in. "When did you lose one?" She hated herself for using the word *lose*—it felt weak, as if they were discussing a cell phone or a wallet she'd forgotten somewhere—and almost clarified herself. But already Taleen was taking something from her purse: a small envelope.

"This year."

"This year?" Dina was incredulous at the horror of it: this poor woman had lost a child and her husband within months of each other.

"Yes. Kathleen. Cancer. She died in the spring. She was roughly your daughter's age."

"Oh, God."

"I know," Taleen agreed, and she was opening the envelope. But it wasn't a card or a letter or a note that was inside it. It was a pair of round silver earrings with a circular design that looked runic and medieval. "I know Ken liked your daughter. He thought she was smart and kind, and he wanted to do right by her."

"He did," Dina said.

Taleen took her hand and Dina let her. Then she watched as the woman put the earrings into her palm. "These were Kathleen's. I thought someday I'd give them to a daughter-in-law or a granddaughter. But who knows if I'll ever have either. My sons aren't showing a lot of interest in domesticity at the moment." She rolled her eyes. "But they're pretty spectacular. They're both downstairs right now. They wanted to come with me, but I told them I wanted to do this alone."

"This . . ."

"When I heard that Alexis was going to make it—or might make it, as you said, let's not jinx it—I thought she might like these. The earrings. When they wake her up."

Dina found her own eyes welling and fought it. She'd so badly mistaken why this woman was here. "They're beautiful," she said, surprised by how quiet her voice had become. "What does it mean? The symbol? Do you know?"

"Eternity," the woman answered. "It's an Armenian symbol for eternity."

Dina took this in. She asked when her husband's funeral was going to be, and Taleen said she hadn't finalized the date. She would get to that later that day or tomorrow.

"If Alexis is . . ." she started to tell Taleen, but Taleen smiled wanly and shook her head.

"It will probably be Wednesday. Maybe Thursday. You and the doctors shouldn't feel any pressure to somehow get Alexis there. Don't even think about that."

"Okay."

Then they both grew silent, and in the awkwardness looked up at the television. There again were pictures of Alexis and Ken, and then the four hospital employees who were under arrest. That woman who ran advancement and one of her associates; the young lab researcher; and the scientist with the bullet wound. So far, at least four people at the hospital were involved, in addition to the man who'd been her daughter's boyfriend. But there were going to be others, that was clear. More arrests were expected.

And then there was that travel writer. Or the guy who had pretended to be one. The guy who'd likely killed Austin in Vietnam—or had him killed.

Dina felt a confusing mix of maternal pride and relief that

her exquisite and driven ER doctor was alive, and despair that the husband of the woman beside her was dead. Taleen reached for the TV remote and clicked on the volume just as they were cutting to photos of Douglas Webber and her daughter's boyfriend, and then a lovely image of some mountain road in Vietnam linking Hue and Hoi An. The media was celebrating Alexis and the PI and a cop in Da Nang for their sheer persistence. Their doggedness. The FBI wasn't precisely sure yet how far along the plague project was, and no one had been able to piece together precisely what had occurred on the lab floor yesterday afternoon because Alexis was too weak to talk when they reached her and Sarafian had passed away moments later. But this morning, at least, the news cycle was enamored of the PI and the physician.

When the TV station cut to a commercial, Taleen murmured, "The red lotus."

"I know."

"Imagine naming a plague after that beautiful flower."

"It's just a name," Dina said.

"A lotus sinks at night. The flower. It curls up under water. Then it rises again at dawn."

"I didn't know that."

Taleen nodded. "Rather like a resurrection. Or, if you will, the resurrection."

"I'm not especially religious."

"I wasn't until Kathleen died. Then I took a lot of comfort in that idea. Your girl . . ."

"Go on."

"She's the real lotus in this nightmare. I know it. She'll rise. She'll bloom again."

Then she stood to leave, and so Dina rose, too. "Thank you," Dina said. She motioned at the earrings. "I know Alexis will love these."

Taleen wrapped Dina in her arms, and Dina—uncomfortably at first, but then succumbing gratefully to this kindness—held the other woman in return, her chin nestling in Taleen's neck, and lost herself in the citrus scent of Taleen's shampoo.

When she was gone, the news was back, and a reporter was saying something more about Austin Harper. Dina turned the set off instead of merely muting the sound. She wondered if someday, when Alexis was better, she should ask her daughter what she was thinking, dating a guy like Harper. How had she misjudged him so badly?

No. Dina shook her head, even though she was alone in the waiting room. She gazed down at the earrings and thought with wonder at the idea of eternity. Maybe this time—this one time— she could let something go.

I get it, I checked the criminal code. It's ten years versus life imprisonment. Mere possession versus attempting to sell the shit to another country. And then there is the matter of quantity. We didn't have a lot.

Look, I'm a big talker, I can tell them lots. Can we cut a deal that way?

I don't expect we can ever completely rehabilitate my name, but "Sally Gleason" also doesn't have to go down in history like, I don't know, "Benedict Arnold" or "Julius Rosenberg."

Besides, Austin never made it to the lab in Da Nang. He never turned over the pathogen. So, we dodged a bullet, didn't we? That has to count for something, right? Right?

EPILOGUE

The young woman had arrived in Hoi An from Dien Quan, a hamlet in the northwest. The province of Lao Cai. She was from a poor family in a poor village in a poor region of the country.

But through a combination of pluck and luck, she had made it first to Hanoi and then Hue and, now, Hoi An. An American-based NGO had supported many children in the small school, including her, and her individual American sponsor had done far more than simply have forty dollars automatically billed against his credit card every month. He'd been writing the child since she was ten, and had visited the village with his wife and two sons when he'd brought his family to Vietnam one year. She was sixteen then.

Now she was a housekeeper at the beautiful boutique hotel with the infinity pool and the small ponds where lotuses bloomed in June and July. Among the myriad things that the day manager knew about her was that she was diligent and resourceful, and that she had a younger brother who was equally driven. She was helping to support him and had brought him south, too. He was a bellman at another, bigger hotel on the ocean in Hoi An. And so when the American emergency room doctor was leaving that Sunday and told the day manager that he could have most of Austin Harper's possessions—she didn't even bring the suitcase with her—he gave them to the housekeeper to give to her brother. Maybe he'd have some use for them.

The housekeeper saw her brother that evening and handed him the suitcase.

He kept some of the clothing, even though it was too big for him, as well as the suitcase itself. The toiletries he tossed into the hotel dumpster behind one of the hotel's three restaurants. The energy gel, which he thought was candy, he gave to a homeless boy who was living that week in an alley behind a tailor shop in Hoi An.

The boy was dead by lunchtime the next day.

His body was found that afternoon by two American tourists, a pair of teenage girls, who were following a stray cat they thought was particularly adorable down the alley while their father was fitted for a suit. They nearly fainted when they discovered the corpse curled up behind piles of trash and eaten by rats. The rats were Vietnamese, of course, and didn't give a damn about the pathogen. And so the hold that an ER doctor and a Manhattan hospital had on the news didn't last long, because an American family landed in Washington, D.C., and all of them—as well as the passengers around them and two of the flight attendants—were near death.

In the months to come, as the CDC worked to contain the pandemic, the names of the American teens would be largely forgotten, although the older of the pair, who was also the first to evidence the symptoms, would be remembered as Patient Zero.

This was, arguably, an improvement over the moniker that the survivors would use for the American who had brought the pathogen to Vietnam in the first place. Austin Harper would be called, with the gallows humor of the beleaguered who fear that death is but a sneeze distant, the Rat King.

Acknowledgments

I had a terrific time researching this novel, and not simply because I fell in love with Vietnam. I enjoyed my homework for this book because of the people I had the privilege of meeting or, in some cases, working with once again.

Jerrold H. Bamel, a retired FBI Supervisory Special Agent and now a corporate fraud investigator, was a lifesaver when I was trying to understand how an American consulate might help an American abroad whose boyfriend has suddenly disappeared—and where the FBI might fit in. (He also appears in the acknowledgments of *The Flight Attendant*. He's the kind of guy who quite literally has made the world a safer, better place. If he ever writes a thriller, buy it.)

Dr. Kimmery Martin, an emergency room doctor and a novelist (*The Queen of Hearts* and *The Antidote for Everything*), read this novel as a rough draft, and gave me invaluable guidance as both a physician and a writer. The next time you're in a bookstore or library, pick up her books.

Inessa Manuelyan is a gifted doctoral candidate in the field of molecular virology at the University of Vermont Larner College of Medicine. She was kind enough to walk me through some of the labs, and share with me her knowledge of microbiology, knock-in and knock-out mice, and research protocols. She also read a rough draft of this manuscript and patiently corrected my mistakes—of which there were plenty.

Jerry Everett, a gunsmith in Texas, was kind enough to read some key sections in this novel and patiently explain to me the differences between the Glock 17 and the Glock 26. This is the second time he has generously shared his knowledge with me. (He corrected my egregious Beretta mistakes in *The Flight Attendant*.)

Here in Vermont, I imposed upon some of the "usual suspects" who have helped me with so many books in the past: Lauren Bowerman, assistant attorney general for the Department of Children and Families; Emmet Helrich, formerly a lieutenant with the Burlington Police Department; Dr. Mike Kiernan, an emergency room physician; Dr. Steven Shapiro, chief medical examiner for the State of Vermont; and my biking friends, Andrew Furtsch and Stephen P. Kiernan, who listened patiently to every possible twist as we rode.

I'm grateful as well to Jennifer Nachbur, public relations director at the Larner College of Medicine at the University of Vermont, who graciously told me about her job and first brought me to the university labs; to Scott I. Remick, an information and technology professional, who helped me understand how one might (or might not) be able to access someone else's computer; to Dr. Peter Daszak, president of EcoHealth Alliance, who spoke with me about pandemics (and rats) when I first began imagining this story; to my neighbor Van Thi Tran, who grew up in Saigon (Ho Chi Minh City today) and helped me name my Vietnamese characters; to Khatchig Mouradian, a gracious (and candid) reader; and to young Sarhad Melkonian, who one day in Armenia when he was ten years old gave me sound advice about storytelling.

I want to thank the Vietnam veterans I interviewed for this novel—for their service, and for telling me their stories. Some of them are my neighbors and friends: Dan Adam, Bob Bougor, and Bill Finger.

As always, I amassed a small library researching this novel, and I have to give special thanks to a pair of books that I loved—as a reader and as a researcher. First, I want to thank Robert Sullivan for his interesting, astute, and moving chronicle of his year investigating the life of the rat in New York City, *Rats: Observations on the History and Habitat of the City's Most Unwanted Inhabitants*. Second, I was inspired and touched by the candor of Dr. Paul Austin's beautiful memoir, *Something for the Pain: Compassion and Burnout in the ER*. I learned so much from these two remarkable books.

I extend my deepest thanks to my brilliant editor, Jennifer Jackson. This is our seventh book together, and I shudder when I think of what my novels might be like without her wisdom and judgment. But I am thankful as well for the hard work and creativity of the entire team at Doubleday, Vintage, and Penguin Random House Audio: Todd Doughty, Maris Dyer, Sarah Engelmann, John Fontana, Kelly Gildea, Zakiya Harris, Suzanne Herz, Judy Jacoby, Ann Kingman, Jennifer Marshall, Anne Messitte, Sarah Nisbet, Charlotte O'Donnell, the late Russell Perrault, John Pitts, Nora Reichard, Paige Smith, William Thomas, David Underwood, and Lori Zook.

I am so grateful to my agents: Deborah Schneider, Jane Gelfman, Cathy Gleason, and Penelope Burns at Gelfman/Schneider ICM; to Brian Lipson at IPG; to Kate Pines at ICM Partners; and to Miriam Feuerle and her associates at the Lyceum Agency. Thank you for always having my back and for the great gift of friendship.

Finally, I am—as always—so appreciative of the insightful, honest counsel of my lovely bride, Victoria Blewer, and our daughter, the always amazing Grace Experience. Victoria has been the first reader of every word I have written since we were eighteen years old; Grace has been diligently reading and improving my work since she was in high school—and bringing many of my characters to life as one of the best audiobook narrators in the business.

I thank you all.

WATER WITCHES

Patience Avery is a dowser—a "water witch." Her natural gifts enable her to locate lost items, missing people, and aquifers deep within the earth. This last skill is more in demand than ever, as her home state of Vermont is in the grip of the worst drought in years. Patience's brother-in-law, Scottie Winston, has spent the summer lobbying for permits to expand Powder Peak, a ski resort—and his law firm's biggest client. The resort is seeking to draw water from the Chittenden River, despite opposition from environmentalists who fear that the already weakened waterway will be damaged beyond repair. As the pressure mounts, Scottie finds himself pushed toward a life-changing moral crisis. *Water Witches* is a prescient environmental and political drama that's even more relevant today than it was a quarter of a century ago.

Fiction

THE SLEEPWALKER

Gorgeous, blond, successful, living in a beautiful Victorian home in a Vermont village, Annalee Ahlberg has another side: she sleepwalks at night, and her affliction manifests in ways both devastating and bizarre. A search party combs the woods, but there is little trace of Annalee, and her family fears the worst. Her daughter Lianna leaves college to care for her father and younger sister. She finds herself uncontrollably drawn to Gavin Rikert, the hazel-eyed detective investigating the case, and the two become involved. But Gavin seems to know more about Lianna's mother than he should. As Lianna sifts through the life Annalee has left behind, she wonders if the man sleeping next to her could hold the key to her mother's mysterious disappearance.

Fiction

Cassandra Bowden is no stranger to hungover mornings. She's a binge drinker, her job with the airline making it easy to find adventure, and the occasional blackouts seem to be inevitable. She lives with them and the accompanying self-loathing. When she awakes in a Dubai hotel room, she tries to piece the previous night back together, counting the minutes until she has to catch her crew shuttle to the airport. She quietly slides out of bed, careful not to aggravate her already pounding head, and looks at the man she spent the night with. She sees his dark hair. His utter stillness. And blood, a slick, still-wet pool on the crisp white sheets. Afraid to call the police—she's a single woman alone in a hotel room far from home—Cassie begins to lie. Soon it's too late to come clean—or face the truth about what really happened back in Dubai. Could she have killed him? If not, who did? Set amid the captivating world of those whose lives unfold at thirty-five thousand feet, *The Flight Attendant* unveils a spellbinding story of memory, the giddy pleasures of alcohol, the devastating consequences of addiction, and murder far from home.

Fiction

ALSO AVAILABLE

Before You Know Kindness
The Buffalo Soldier
Close Your Eyes, Hold Hands
The Double Bind
The Guest Room
The Law of Similars
The Light in the Ruins
Midwives
The Sandcastle Girls
Trans-Sister Radio

VINTAGE CONTEMPORARIES
Available wherever books are sold.
www.vintagebooks.com

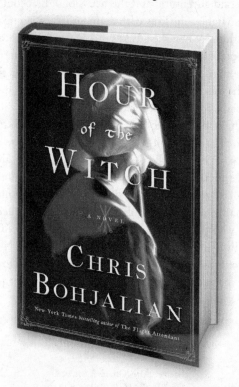